THE BARRICADED TOWER

A Sebastian Dorrell Adventure

Jocelyn Almond

At Heydn Hall, the ancestral home of the Earls of Newhaven, five people have disappeared mysteriously, including two former earls, an estate manager, and a visiting countess.

Why have weird lights been seen in the sky?

Why has the Prince's Tower been barricaded?

What is the purpose of the strange glass prism on the roof?

Has the current earl gone completely crazy? If not, then why has he engaged the services of a psychiatric doctor?

And what is really going on down in the cellars?

When the Jewish mystic and philosopher, Professor Aaronberg, disappears after writing a book about the disappearances, his friend, sceptical sleuth Sebastian Dorrell, following the dubious advice of a delusional mental patient, begins to investigate.

Jocelyn Almond is an author and tutor, and lives in Hertford-shire, England. She is married, and has a PhD in philosophy.

THE SEBASTIAN DORRELL ADVENTURES

The Barricaded Tower

The Rubber Vampires

Bogwoman!

The Mercy Killings

I Slept with a Golem

THE

BARRICADED

TOWER

A Sebastian Dorrell Adventure

by

Jocelyn Almond

with illustrations by the author

LULU

First published 2010
by Jocelyn Almond
at Lulu
www.lulu.com

Typeset in Book Antiqua 11/15pt

ISBN 978-0-9559825-0-7 (paperback)

In memory of my friend

Douglas MacEwan

CONTENTS

ILLUSTRATIONS

CHAPTER 1

The Vanishing of Miss Gladys Armstrong

There was a winding road which ran between the villages of Newhaven and Seaford, very narrow – at some places along its five-mile length diminishing to a lane – a muddy stream in winter, but in summer transformed to a green tunnel bounded by steep banks on which tall, ancient oaks grew, spreading their boughs in a vaulted, leafy roof. Nearly two miles eastward along this road from Newhaven, to the south of the road, close to the sea, was built the great grey stone mansion, Heydn Hall, the home of Lord Stephen Horsley-Mitchell, the twentieth Earl of Newhaven.

It was three days after Julian Crucefix, the Earl's estate manager, had read in the newspaper about the mysterious disappearance of Professor Joshua Aaronberg, the philosopher, mystic and well-known television personality. It was a blazing hot afternoon of late summer, and the blackberries were ripe in the hedgerows, and Julian Crucefix, as he made his tour of inspection around the Heydn Hall estate, could not have known that on this same afternoon Sebastian Dorrell, whom Julian had never met in his life, was driving down from London to Newhaven in his old green sports car. It was the same afternoon that Miss Gladys Armstrong, who was gathering blackberries in the lane outside Heydn Hall, also mysteriously disappeared.

Miss Gladys, carrying a trug on her arm, and Miss Amelia Armstrong, her sister, bearing a white-enamelled colander, scrambled along the bank by the hedge, the long skirts of their floral print frocks fluttering in the warm breeze. Both ladies were in their late seventies.

'Let me see,' said Miss Amelia, tilting Miss Gladys's trug so as to look inside at the poor handful of fruit. 'You haven't got many there,' she scolded. 'What have you been doing?'

'But you've picked them all,' Miss Gladys explained feebly. 'There were hardly any left for me.'

Her sister gestured impatiently towards the other side of the lane, in the direction of the bleak, grey mansion, Heydn Hall, just visible, from where they stood, through the dark barrier of trees. 'Go and look over there, you silly girl,' said Miss Amelia. 'You don't have to trail along behind me. There're plenty in the other hedge.'

Miss Gladys adjusted her spectacles on her nose, peering across the lane. 'I'm afraid I didn't notice. It's all a mass of stinging nettles a little way back.'

'Well, you go and have a look, dear,' Miss Amelia instructed, returning her attention to the hedge. 'But don't go too far away, will you now? And don't do anything silly.'

Meekly, Miss Gladys crossed the lane to the other side, climbing up the grassy bank into a patch of sunlight close to the hedge. She could feel the sun very hot on her back; it was almost too hot, despite the breeze, she thought, to be out without some protection against the heat. She was wearing her shady straw hat, but Miss Amelia had left their cottage bare-headed. Miss Gladys began to hum softly to herself as she picked the blackberries, dropping them one by one into her trug.

*

Julian Crucefix smiled timidly as he completed his inspection of the damaged fence. He turned encouragingly to the workman who was with him and remarked in his soft, nervous voice, 'Not as bad as I'd imagined. When you've done this, perhaps you'd take a look at the hedge over there. People have been trespassing on the estate and they've broken down the wire.'

'Where?' the man asked.

Julian gestured vaguely. 'Over by the hawthorn hedge on the east side of the paddocks. The Earl says he wants new barbed wire put all along there, both sides of the hedge.'

'There's a public footpath over at the far end,' the man objected, scratching his chin doubtfully. 'I saw someone'd put up a bit of fencing so you can't get through. Maybe that's why you've had people trampling through the hedge.'

Julian frowned, running his thin fingers through his fine, pale hair. 'The Earl closed off the footpath himself. He gave very specific instructions about all the hedges and fences along the boundaries of the estate, too. Apparently,' he explained uneasily, 'he doesn't want any holiday-makers wandering into the grounds sight-seeing while the house is closed to visitors and repairs are under way.'

'I see,' said the man doubtfully. 'Seems a bit funny to me, though – specially after what the gardener was saying.'

'What was he saying?' Julian asked.

'Blue and green lights he said he saw,' the man replied. 'Floating around the tree-tops, over the other side of the house – over by the Tower – lights flashing in the windows, about nine o'clock Thursday evening, just when it was getting dark. Said he heard noises too.'

'What has that to do with mending the fence?' Julian asked, rather shortly.

The man shrugged. 'It's just that there have been some funny goings-on around here this past month or two, by all accounts – since the Hall's been closed to the public. Lights, noises, people seeing things ... and now the Earl acting strange, making the place into a fortress with his barricades and barbed wire.'

Julian Crucefix laughed his soft, nervous laugh. 'The Earl's a very private man. Some people seem to see something suspicious in other people's privacy, but I respect it myself. There's certainly nothing mysterious or unusual about it. As for this gossip about weird lights – I don't believe a word of it.' He smiled. 'This stuff about ghosts and UFOs and what have you that I've been hearing since I moved here – I'm afraid I'm very down-to-earth when it comes to that sort of thing. I've no time for any of that.' He looked a little sheepish, as if it were an admission that embarrassed him.

'I expect you're right, sir,' the man agreed. 'Well, I'll see what I can do with this fence. All the same,' he added, as Julian began to walk away, back along the path towards the gaunt stone mansion, 'I shouldn't fancy being around here after dark. You do hear stories, and I dare say there's some truth in them.'

*

Meanwhile, Miss Amelia Armstrong, her colander half-filled with blackberries, scrambled along the bank close to the entrance to the grounds of Heydn Hall. Hearing a noise from further along the lane, she glanced back; it sounded like the engine of an approaching car, but she could not see the vehicle over the high hedge where there was a bend in the lane.

She waited at the top of the bank, supporting herself by holding onto a low-hanging branch of an oak tree. The birds were singing; the sun was warm on her back. A little anxiously, she looked along the lane for her sister, who had now disappeared from view.

At that moment, Sebastian Dorrell's old green sports car appeared around the bend.

Miss Amelia leaned back against the hedge, expecting the car to pass, but instead, it slowed to a halt alongside her. Sebastian Dorrell was at the steering-wheel; Miss Amelia looked at him, and at first sight she mistook him for a middle-aged woman. At a second glance, she realised with a shock that he was a young man, probably in his mid-thirties: he had a pale, angular face, handsome in an unconventional way, though not altogether pleasant; his eyes were dark brown, deep-set beneath very dark brows; his nose was narrow, turned up eccentrically at the tip; his lips were rather full and slightly pouting, which contributed to his feminine appearance, and curiously they were painted with black lipstick; but his most striking feature, which Miss Amelia had noticed at once, was his hair, which was dark brown, very thick and long, back-combed and lacquered and hanging over his shoulders and down his back. She stared at him a little suspiciously: he was not the kind of person that she was accustomed to seeing around these quiet parts.

Sebastian Dorrell smiled up at her, and when he smiled he revealed a number of unsightly gold fillings in his teeth. 'I say!' he called. 'Excuse me!'

Miss Amelia cautiously descended the bank. She was puzzled by his refined accent of speech, which seemed at odds with his appearance.

'Yes?' she said.

'I wonder,' said Sebastian, 'could you – ah ... tell me if this is the right road for Heydn Hall?'

'Oh, yes,' replied Miss Amelia. 'It's just over there.' She gestured towards her right. 'Behind the trees.'

Sebastian smiled again. 'Oh, I see. I thought I couldn't have passed it. Well – ah ... thank you. I know where I am now.'

Miss Amelia made as if to move away, but Sebastian said, 'Ah, by the way – ah ... you're a local person, I presume?'

'Yes,' she replied uneasily. She disliked this stranger and was suspicious of his questioning. Despite the fact that he spoke with the air of an upper-class gentleman, he certainly did not look like one, and the total effect was altogether disquieting. She looked in disapproval at his hands resting upon the steering-wheel: they were decorated with a number of ornate rings, and his finger-nails were painted black. She also noticed, when he inclined his head to one side, that he had a large ring in his left ear-lobe.

'Anything unusual happened around here lately?' Sebastian asked.

'I'm sure I don't know what you mean,' Miss Amelia said a little tartly.

Sebastian shrugged his shoulders carelessly. 'I just wondered. You know – any – ah ... any unusual occurrences around Heydn Hall?'

'I really couldn't say,' Miss Amelia replied.

Sebastian nodded thoughtfully. 'Ah ... well, it doesn't matter. I just thought you might have heard rumours – local gossip, and – ah ... and so forth.'

'I don't listen to local gossip,' said Miss Amelia primly.

'No,' said Sebastian. He grinned provocatively. 'I don't suppose you do.' He was about to drive off.

'You're not one of those UFO people, are you?' asked Miss Amelia suddenly.

Sebastian raised an eyebrow. 'Who?'

'We've had them round here all weekend,' said Miss Amelia. 'Such a nuisance. I can't think what they expect to see.'

'Interesting,' said Sebastian. 'Well, thanks anyway. Perhaps I'll see you again some time? Good-bye!'

'Good day,' answered Miss Amelia curtly. She watched after him with a frown of disapproval as the car drove away; she was almost certain that he had been wearing eye make-up, though she could not quite believe it. 'Such a disgrace!' she muttered to herself.

*

As Sebastian Dorrell drove further along the lane, passing through a thickly wooded area close to the gates of Heydn Hall, glancing to his left, he caught sight of a figure standing on the bank: an elderly lady who closely resembled the lady to whom he had just spoken. It was, of course, Miss Gladys Armstrong, and Sebastian, though he did not know it, was the last person to see her before she disappeared.

Miss Gladys, turning away from the road as Sebastian passed in his car, returned her attention to the hedge. She had gathered nearly a whole trug-full of blackberries now: Amelia would be pleased, she thought, chuckling to herself. She hummed a tune softly. After a while, she had a strange notion that the air around her was vibrating, humming also in harmony with her; the idea amused her at first, so that she began to hum more loudly.

*

Standing on the long grey terrace outside Heydn Hall, Julian Crucefix gazed towards the tower at the western end of the house: it was known as the Prince's Tower, since the Prince of Wales had stayed there during the time of the present Earl's grandfather, who had also been responsible for erecting on its roof a massive glass prism which was supposed to deflect the light of the sun into one of the inner courtyards of the building that would otherwise be always in shadow.

Since those days, however, the Tower had been in disuse, its lower windows and the entrance bricked up. It was a dark, gloomy place, and the great mysterious prism glistening upon its roof lent it a curiously surreal appearance, Julian Crucefix reflected: it was not surprising that ghost stories and tales of flying saucers had become associated with the Tower. He stared up at it, shading his eyes with his hand against the brightness of the sky. As he looked, it seemed to him that there was a faint humming sound in the air, and he could almost fancy that it emanated from the Tower. Quickly he held his hands over his ears and bowed his head as a sensation of dizziness came over him.

*

Miss Gladys Armstrong, at the same moment, had paused in her picking of blackberries. It seemed to be growing very dark. She stopped humming, but the humming in the air around her still persisted. She looked up at the dark clouds that were gathering overhead: the weather had changed very quickly, she thought; perhaps it was about to rain, and she had brought no coat with her. She shivered, for the air had grown suddenly chill, and now she found difficulty in seeing clearly: perhaps her vision was dimming and she was about to faint?

She dropped her trug of blackberries, clutching her hands to her head, overwhelmed by a sudden feeling of dizziness. 'Amelia!' she called weakly. 'Amelia! Help me!'

The strange noise was growing louder now, and a strong wind was blowing that whisked leaves and dust into her face; she shuddered as the soft forms brushed against her skin, as she experienced also a curious tingling, as if the air were charged with electricity. Blue and green lights sparkled before her: dazed, she staggered backwards, uttering a single cry of dismay before she felt herself falling.

A few minutes later, Miss Amelia Armstrong, strolling back along the sunlit lane with her colander full of fruit, discovered her sister's discarded straw hat lying in the long grass on the bank. Nearby was the trug of blackberries, overturned at the side of the road, but of Miss Gladys there was not a trace.

For an hour, Miss Amelia wandered up and down the lane, searching for her sister and calling her by name, but she did not find her.

CHAPTER 2

Professor Joshua Aaronberg
Receives a Warning

The disappearance of Professor Joshua Aaronberg, three days earlier, had been different from that of Miss Armstrong in a number of ways. One of these differences was that the Professor, unlike Miss Armstrong, had been fore-warned of the fate that was to befall him, but the Professor told no one of his strange experience, except Sebastian Dorrell; and even if anyone else had known about it, it was doubtful that anything could have been done to prevent the prophesy from being fulfilled: it simply was to be, and the Professor had to endure it.

Professor Aaronberg had become well-known in recent years, not only as the writer of a number of distinguished academic works, but also for several books of popular philosophy and some more obscure writings on time travel and studies in the paranormal that had gained him a cult following among Fortean and New Age enthusiasts. His round jovial face with its fluffy white halo of hair, his soft voice and patient, genial manner, had become familiar to millions through his two popular television series on philosophy, mysticism and parapsychology. In semi-retirement, he lived in the quaint Italianate seaside village of

Portmeirion in Wales – an eccentric yet idyllic environment that suited his quiet, romantic temperament.

Portmeirion was a small private village run as a hotel. The Professor lived on the first floor in a pale stuccoed villa called the Fountain, which stood near to the quayside. Here he had two small rooms and a private bathroom that were cleaned daily by the Portmeirion Hotel staff, and he would take most of his meals in the main hotel nearby. There was a steep, narrow flight of steps down the cliff-side behind the Fountain that gave access to the single entrance to the professor's rooms.

Two nights before he vanished, Professor Aaronberg locked his door and went to bed as usual. There were sliding double doors that partitioned off the small bedroom from the sitting-room, and he closed these before climbing into bed. He left the curtains undrawn, however, so that the moonlight would shine in through the sash window, which was left slightly raised. The night was quiet and cool, and very soon he drifted off into a deep sleep.

The next he knew, a low voice was calling his name, rousing him to a drowsy wakefulness. Blearily he peered out from under his half-closed eyelids. He was lying on his right side, facing the window, and the pale moonlight was shining in, dimly illuminating the walls, the light chintz curtains that stirred slightly in the draught from the open sash – and something else: something dark and bulky that stood between the wall and the bed, its left side silhouetted against the bright rectangle of the window. The Professor stared at the dark shape, trying to make out what it could be, and as he stared, it moved slowly, inclining a little nearer to him. At the same time, a voice came from it saying, 'Professor Aaronberg, don't be alarmed.'

When the Professor recognised the voice, he realised simultaneously that what he could see was the figure of a man seated in a large chair with a high, ornate, carved back and arms. With a sensation of eerie disbelief, the Professor realised that his visitor was his good friend, Sebastian Dorrell.

'Is that you, dear boy?' Professor Aaronberg asked sleepily, propping himself up on his elbow. With his other hand he rubbed the sleep from his eyes.

'I'm sorry to startle you, Professor,' said Sebastian. His low voice sounded strangely distant and hollow, as if he were speaking from the bottom of a well.

The Professor passed his hand over his forehead and stroked back his thin white hair. He blinked dreamily, straining to see his friend more clearly in the dim moonlight, but Sebastian's form was shadowy and seemed almost insubstantial. 'How on earth did you get in?' asked Professor Aaronberg. 'The door is locked ... and it's the first floor, so you couldn't have come in by the window ... '

'There's no time to explain,' answered Sebastian. His voice was strained and breathless, as if it were an effort for him to speak at all. 'Would you ... would you – ah ... come over here where I can see you,' he said.

Dazedly, the Professor scrambled from the bed, pulling around him his dressing-gown that he had left draped over the bed's foot. He tottered over to the window unsteadily. 'What can I do ... ' he began; then he fell silent abruptly, shocked when he looked into Sebastian's face.

The Professor gasped, his small hand leaping to cover his mouth. Sebastian's angular, unpleasantly handsome face was pale and indistinct, like a ghostly mask that seemed to hover within the shadowy masses of his wild hair; only his eyes could clearly be seen, deep and faintly

luminous in the bluish gleam of the moon. Professor Aaronberg stared down at Sebastian's body, and saw only darkness, like a hole in space: it was as if he were dressed in the blackest velvet that absorbed all light. And now the Professor realised also that the chair in which Sebastian was sitting was quite unfamiliar to him and had never been in that room before tonight: it was an elaborately carved wooden chair of ancient appearance, and though, unlike Sebastian's body, it was not shadowy and indistinct, its form, like his, nevertheless seemed insubstantial. Professor Aaronberg turned cold with a thrill of shock; he had the idea that if he were to reach out to touch what he saw, his hand would pass straight through it. He was convinced now that he was looking, not at a real man of flesh and blood, but at an apparition.

'Don't be afraid, Professor,' Sebastian said. 'I've come to warn you, and to ask for your help.'

Feebly, Professor Aaronberg began to speak, but he was lost for words, and could only mumble incoherently.

'I've – ah ... I've no wish to alarm you,' said Sebastian slowly and with effort, 'but something is going to happen to you two days from now. Exactly what it will be, I'm afraid I'm unable to tell you. All I know is that you will disappear and that no one will know where to find you. The reason I've come here is to ask you for any information that could – ah ... that could possibly be of relevance to your disappearance. Tell me, Professor, can you think of what it might possibly be that will happen to you?'

'Dear me,' replied the Professor, 'I'm taken aback. I scarcely know what to make of this. What can I say?'

'Then it's hopeless,' said Sebastian, almost in a whisper. He closed his eyes. 'Help me, Professor Aaronberg. Where should I look for you? If you were lost, where do you suppose that you might be found? I've nothing to go on – I don't know where to start.'

Professor Aaronberg sighed; he passed his hand over his face. Distractedly, he gazed from the window down to the Hotel's circular swimming-pool in the lawn below. The grass all around was in darkness, but the water was bright with moonlight, and glistening ripples glided slowly across its surface. 'I can't take this in, dear boy,' said the Professor, feeling as if he were in a dream.

'Then I must try to remember,' Sebastian said, 'something that you told me ... or you will tell me, tomorrow morning. A book – you mentioned a book! Can you think of ... can you think of which one it might be?'

The Professor frowned. 'Well ... the only thing that comes to mind at this moment is a chapter on mysterious disappearances in my own new book, *The Ghost Garden* – I sent you a copy a month ago. Perhaps you haven't had time to read it yet?'

'I'm not suggesting there's going to be anything paranormal about it,' Sebastian explained. 'I'm not sure that your book will be of much use in this matter. I was thinking more along the lines of some – ah ... some more mundane explanation, you know.'

'Ah, but bear with me for a moment, dear boy,' said the Professor. 'I have an interesting theory, you see, regarding the hereditary quality of the propensity to vanish – there is some evidence that it may run in families. Let me fetch the book – '

Sebastian winced, gripping the arms of his chair more tightly; he closed his eyes, as if with the effort of mental concentration. 'There's no time,' he said. 'This is not as ... not as fruitful as one might have – ah ... might have hoped.

Are you saying that members of your family have also disappeared?'

'No, no,' replied Professor Aaronberg. 'But there was that fascinating case of the Horsley-Mitchell family. Both the present Earl of Newhaven's father and grandfather vanished while they were at Heydn Hall, the family's ancestral home. But you must remember, I told you I had such a rude letter from the Earl when my book was published. I sent you a copy of his letter when I wrote to you, as it upset me so at the time, but you didn't reply. Wait a moment and I'll fetch the book.' He turned and pulled open the sliding doors.

'Don't go, Professor,' Sebastian said urgently. 'I must ask you – I never received ... '

'Just a minute, dear boy,' Professor Aaronberg answered as he tottered out into the moonlit sitting-room.

Quickly he picked from the shelf the book that he wanted, and returned to the bedroom. 'I have it here,' he said, flicking through the pages as he searched for the relevant passage. He glanced up; and then he saw that Sebastian Dorrell was no longer in the room: he had gone as swiftly and silently as he had arrived, and the strange carved chair in which he had been sitting had vanished also.

A little shakily, Professor Aaronberg took off his dressing-gown and climbed back into bed. Being very dazed and tired, he fell asleep again almost immediately. When the morning came and he was awakened by the sunlight streaming into the room, the events of the night before seemed more than ever like a confused dream. As he washed and dressed, he thought about what had happened and he could not decide whether it was real or not.

Eventually he decided to telephone Sebastian Dorrell to ask him about it. He picked up the receiver and spoke to the girl at the hotel switchboard, asking her to make the call to London for him.

Sebastian was a long time in answering, but at last the Professor heard his voice down the line.

'Hello, Sebastian?' said Professor Aaronberg.

'Uh ... hm ... yes,' said Sebastian wearily.

'How are you, dear boy?' the Professor inquired.

'Good grief,' said Sebastian, 'What d'you mean by calling me at this unearthly hour?'

'It's eight o'clock,' Professor Aaronberg replied in surprise. 'Did I wake you?'

'You should know by now,' said Sebastian, 'I'm never – ah ... never fully conscious before about mid-day. What's the matter?'

'Nothing's the matter, dear boy,' said the Professor. 'Merely a little mystery I would like to clear up, if that's possible. Did you know that you were with me last night? You were here in this room – you woke me up.'

'I see – so you're getting your own back now, are you?' said Sebastian. 'What d'you mean? I've been here in bed all night.'

'No, dear boy,' persisted the Professor gently. 'You were here with me. I went to get my book to show you the chapter on mysterious disappearances, because there was a special point that I wanted to check up, about people disappearing, you see – and when I came back, you'd vanished.'

'I say, that was a bit ironic, wasn't it?' said Sebastian. He laughed. 'What the devil are you on about, Professor? I think you've – ah ... think you've been dreaming.'

'Not at all,' Professor Aaronberg assured him. 'You warned me that something peculiar was going to happen to me in two days' time, but you said you didn't know what it was, and you wondered if I could help. What am I to make of it, dear boy?'

'Lord knows,' said Sebastian. 'I should – ah ... should forget it, if I were you. One thing I can assure you, Professor, I've been sound asleep in this bed all night, so if you did see me, all I can say is – it must have been an astral projection!'

'Ah, yes, of course!' the Professor exclaimed. 'There you have a point!'

'It was meant to be a joke, actually,' said Sebastian.

The Professor, however, was not in a mood for joking: he was extremely puzzled, and remained so until the time when the mysterious prediction came true.

CHAPTER 3

Sebastian Dorrell Receives a Visitor

Later the same day, Sebastian told his friend and lodger, Richard Mojave, about the Professor's telephone call.

'I'm – ah ... I'm afraid he's going a bit ga-ga in his old age,' said Sebastian.

'Professor Aaronberg – never,' said Richard.

They were in Sebastian's sombre drawing-room which he had decorated in brown and cream, and furnished with dark Victorian furniture.

The walls were covered with brown flock paper, and heavy brown velvet curtains trimmed with gold tassels hung at the tall windows. Upon the floor was a rich red and blue Persian carpet, and a black fur rug was spread before the hearth. There were two large bookcases with glass doors, which contained many books: the smell of their leather bindings, old and musty, lingered in the room, mingling with the perfume of incense that Sebastian had been burning. There were a large number of antique vases and other ornaments which stood on the black marble mantelpiece and on small occasional tables around the room. The large house, part of a gloomy Victorian terrace in Wigmore Street, belonged to Sebastian, and though

Richard Mojave lived there with him, it had been Sebastian who had decided upon all the furnishings and decorations, with the exception of those in Richard's own bedroom.

'Well, you explain it, then,' suggested Sebastian, who was lounging on the dark leather-upholstered Chesterfield sofa with his feet up on one of the arms.

Richard, sitting cross-legged on the fur rug, looked thoughtful and bemused; he traced the pattern on the carpet with a dirty finger-nail.

'I dunno ... there're some really weird things happen, you know,' he said at last. 'Maybe you were, you know, kinda astrally projected, like you said, without you knowing it had happened, right?' Shaking back his long, untidy red hair, he looked up at Sebastian hopefully. 'I mean, you gotta admit that it's more likely than Professor Aaronberg going funny in the head.'

Sebastian sighed. 'I don't like these paranormal explanations.'

'I think,' said Richard, 'maybe we oughta, you know ... do something.' He stroked his red beard pensively.

'What d'you mean? Sebastian asked.

'To stop whatever it is from happening to Professor Aaronberg,' said Richard. 'I mean, if it's a true prediction, right – if what he says you said to him last night is a true prediction – then something's going to happen to him.'

'If it's a true prediction,' said Sebastian, 'then it cannot also be true that we prevent it from happening, because if it didn't – ah ... didn't happen, then there couldn't have been a true prediction of its happening.'

'That's crazy,' said Richard in dismay. 'Are you saying we just sit back and do nothing?'

'Not necessarily,' replied Sebastian, 'but even if we – ah ... even if we did do something to try to prevent it, we may well end up actually bringing it about. You know, like – ah ... like Oedipus – he brought about the prophesy by trying to avoid it.'

'Bloody hell, that's just fatalism!' Richard declared.

'It's a problem,' Sebastian agreed.

'So what're you going to do?' said Richard. 'In a couple of days, suppose we hear that Professor Aaronberg's disappeared – how will you feel about it then?'

Sebastian shrugged. 'I don't know.'

'Think about it,' said Richard, getting to his feet. 'I gotta go now, or I'll be late for my appointment.'

'Where're you going?' Sebastian asked.

'The bloody Benefits Agency again,' said Richard. 'Gotta sort my benefit out. They think I'm on the fiddle.'

Sebastian smiled. 'Get a job,' he suggested.

'Get a job yourself,' said Richard. 'See you later.'

As Richard went out of the room, Sebastian's yellow-eyed black cat walked in softly and jumped up onto the sofa. Sebastian took it onto his lap and stroked it. After a moment, he heard Richard leave the house.

Sebastian picked up his copy of *The Financial Times* and began to look through it.

Presently there was a knock at the front door. He went out into the hall to see who was knocking. Opening the front door partially, he peered out.

At the top of the steps which led down to the street stood a tall, thin, elderly gentleman of imposing appearance. He had white hair and a white handlebar moustache; he was wearing a deerstalker, a brown tweed jacket, a yellow waistcoat, and plus fours.

Sebastian had never seen him before; he opened the door a little wider. 'Hello,' he said, looking at his visitor inquiringly. 'Ah ... what – ah ... what d'you want?'

The elderly gentleman seemed very bewildered. He did not speak at first; then he cleared his throat awkwardly. 'Hm ... good afternoon,' he said. He had a scrap of paper in his hand and he scrutinised it closely, trying to read what was written on it. 'Number seventy-one,' he said. 'That's right. This is number seventy-one, is it?' He glanced up doubtfully.

Sebastian pointed to the number on the door. 'Yes.'

'Hm ... ' said the gentleman. He stared hard at Sebastian, at his red satin trousers and leopardskin print shirt, long hair and strange make-up. 'My name is Fothergill,' he said at last. 'Sir Charles Fothergill. I was given this address by someone who told me that Captain Dorrell lived here.'

'Dorrell?' Sebastian queried with a frown. 'That's – ah ... that's my name, actually.'

'Ah, then,' said Sir Charles Fothergill with an air of relief. 'At least I've come to the right place! I suppose it would be your father that I want to see?'

'My father's dead,' said Sebastian, rather taken aback.

Sir Charles was visibly shocked. 'Captain Dorrell dead?'

Sebastian tugged nervously at the ring in his left earlobe. 'I'm afraid there's – ah ... there's some mistake,' he said. 'My father was a minister in the Church. There's no Captain Dorrell here, and never has been.'

'But the chap who gave me this address knows Captain Dorrell personally,' said Sir Charles. 'Captain Sebastian Dorrell – that's what I have down here.' He pointed to his piece of paper. 'Seventy-one, Wigmore Street.'

Sebastian rubbed his chin uneasily with his hand. 'My – ah ... my name is Sebastian Dorrell,' he said. 'Perhaps it's me you want?'

Sir Charles looked at him dubiously from beneath his

bushy grey brows. 'D'you know Captain Terrier?' he asked.

Sebastian shook his head.

'He was the chap who gave me this address,' Sir Charles explained.

'Well – ah ... look, won't you come in?' Sebastian invited, stepping aside and opening the door fully. 'This is very mysterious, and I'd like to get to the bottom of it.'

A little reluctantly, Sir Charles Fothergill stepped into the dark, musty hallway. Sebastian closed the front door and showed him into the drawing-room, where Sir Charles sat in the leather-upholstered armchair near to the black, cold fireplace with its black iron grate.

Sebastian sat down on the sofa again, next to the reclining cat.

'Well,' said Sir Charles, glancing around him at the antiques, the ornaments, the heavy mahogany furniture gleaming dimly in the shadowy room. He sniffed suspiciously at the scent of incense which still lingered in the air. 'It's hard to know quite where to begin.' He cleared his throat; he rubbed his large hands over his knees. 'To tell you the truth, I feel a bit foolish – especially if you're not the man I'm looking for.'

'Do you know anything about this Captain Dorrell, apart from his name?' Sebastian asked.

Sir Charles nodded. 'Only what Terrier told me. According to him, Dorrell was educated at Harrow and Oxford. Came from a wealthy family, apparently – father was in the Church ... ' Sir Charles glanced up. 'As you said your father was, didn't you?'

'Yes,' Sebastian agreed. 'Everything you've said so far is true of me.'

'And were you ever in the Army?' Sir Charles asked doubtfully.

Sebastian laughed, and when he laughed he revealed the gold fillings in his teeth. 'Well, that would – ah ... that would be just the life for me,' he said.

'What's that?' asked Sir Charles, a look of puzzlement in his grey eyes.

'It seems to me,' Sebastian remarked after a moment of thought, 'that I must – ah ... that I must be the person you're looking for. Obviously your – ah ... your friend – I'm sorry, I've forgotten his name – but obviously he's – ah ... he's somewhat confused.'

'Terrier,' said Sir Charles. 'John Terrier. His uncle, Colonel Jack Russell-Terrier, was a great friend of mine. An old Army family, you know – originated up North.' He nodded reminiscently. 'Yes, I knew quite a few of the Yorkshire Terriers. I've known young Johnny Terrier since he was a boy. But you say you've never heard of him?'

'No, I haven't,' Sebastian replied.

Sir Charles shook his head slowly, regretfully; he stroked his magnificent moustache. 'A good man,' he said. 'One of the best. Who'd have thought that a fellow like that would end up in a loony-bin.'

'Is that where he is?' asked Sebastian.

'Afraid so,' said Sir Charles. He leaned forward in the chair, contemplating the palms of his hands; he looked embarrassed, and spoke rather hesitantly; he stroked the tip of his long thin nose with his forefinger. He said, 'I suppose I'd better tell you what I came here to tell you, though in view of what you've said, I don't know what you'll make of it. Anyway, this is what he told me: *Tell Captain Dorrell*, he said, *for old time's sake – he won't let an old friend down.*' Sir Charles sighed heavily; he rubbed his chin. 'Poor fellow's relying on you, Dorrell. *If Captain Dorrell won't help, we're done for – he understands about this sort of thing.* That's what he told me.'

Sebastian raised an eyebrow as Sir Charles looked up at him hopefully. 'What – ah ... what sort of thing am I supposed to understand?' Sebastian asked.

'Ah, well – apparently there's some funny business going on,' explained Sir Charles. 'You see, there's a woman involved – the Countess of Warwick, Lady Caroline Giles. Apparently Terrier met her before his ... hm ... illness came on.' Sir Charles made a brief gesture at the side of his head to signify insanity. He cleared his throat uneasily. He said, 'According to Terrier, something strange happened to this woman, the Countess.'

'I say,' remarked Sebastian, 'wasn't it – ah ... wasn't it the Countess of Warwick who was killed in an accident recently? I read about it, I think. Her plane went down in the Channel – isn't that right?'

'Yes,' said Sir Charles. 'But Terrier tells a different story. According to him, the Countess isn't dead at all. He claims that she disappeared while she was staying at Heydn Hall, the Earl of Newhaven's place down in Sussex. You see, young Terrier's cousin is the Earl's secretary, and apparently Terrier was at the Hall at the time when the Countess disappeared. According to Terrier, the Earl covered it up by staging the plane crash. He got Terrier to dress up as the Countess and fly her light aircraft into the sea, where the Earl was waiting in his yacht, ready to pick Terrier up.'

Sebastian smiled dubiously. 'Tell me, Sir Charles,' he asked. 'Why do you – ah ... why do you believe all this?'

Sir Charles frowned; he looked surprised. 'Well,' he said, 'I didn't see any reason to disbelieve it.'

'But you say that Terrier's in a mental hospital?' Sebastian queried.

'Ah well, there's another point, you see!' said Sir Charles more eagerly. 'They put him away to keep him quiet! According to Terrier, the doctors at the loony-bin are in league with his cousin and the Earl, and they shut him up in that place because he knew too much!'

'Let me put it another way, Sir Charles,' said Sebastian slowly. Thoughtfully he stroked the cat as it lay beside him on the Chesterfield. 'Suppose someone suggested to you that you dress up as a woman and go – ah … go flying in a light aircraft and crash it in the Channel – would you do it?'

'Of course not!' said Sir Charles indignantly.

'Neither would I,' said Sebastian. 'So – ah … so what makes you think that your friend Terrier would? Of course, you could – ah … you could say it was because he's mentally ill, but that explanation doesn't exactly inspire one's confidence in his testimony – the very reason for doubting him in the first place, I would have thought.'

'Hm … ' said Sir Charles. 'To tell you the truth, I've never looked at it that way before. But Terrier, you know, he's an obliging sort of chap. Did it for a prank, I wouldn't be surprised – always did have a sense of humour. There's probably no more to it than that.'

'If he was telling the truth,' said Sebastian, 'and he collaborated in fabricating this woman's death, personally I wouldn't say it was a joking matter. But if you want to know frankly what I think about the whole business, I would say Terrier's story is a delusion resulting from his illness. I'm sorry, but the whole thing sounds downright absurd to me.'

Sir Charles did not reply, and for a long time they were both silent. The only sound was the slow, heavy ticking of the black wooden clock on the black marble mantelpiece. Sir Charles sat forward in the chair, his head bowed, staring at the lines on his hands. Outside, the summer afternoon was passing, yet here he stayed in this gloomy Victorian room, talking to an eccentric man whom he did not even know and who seemed to take him for a fool; still, he was reluctant to go.

'I was rather hoping ... ' he began tentatively. His voice sounded weak, quieter than he had intended; he cleared his throat. 'Terrier would like to see you, I'm sure,' he said. 'That was what I was really hoping – that you'd agree to go along there and talk to him yourself. He said you were an old friend, you see. He said you'd be willing to help.'

'I'm not an old friend,' said Sebastian quietly. 'Good grief, I've never met the fellow.'

'Apparently,' said Sir Charles, 'he knows you.'

Sebastian sighed. 'How does he think I can help?'

'He can't get out of the home, you see,' Sir Charles explained. 'They keep him locked up and drugged and Lord knows what. But he said that you'd go down to Heydn Hall for him, find out what's going on down there – find this missing woman, the Countess ... '

'Oh, no,' said Sebastian, shaking his head. He laughed. 'Oh, no, no. I'm not going off to Sussex on some wild-goose chase.'

'But you'll come and see Terrier, at least – talk to him, eh?' asked Sir Charles with a nod of encouragement. 'He's banking on your help, you know, Dorrell. He thinks the world of you. *Tell Captain Dorrell*, he said, *remember the old days together in the Air Corps ...* '

'As I've already told you,' said Sebastian, with growing impatience, 'I wasn't in the Air Corps, and I don't know your friend Captain Terrier. Now, Sir Charles, I think our conversation has come to an end.' He stopped stroking the cat; slowly he stood up and held out his hand.

Sir Charles eased himself out of the armchair; he looked helpless, disappointed. Suddenly he seemed very old, and for a moment Sebastian felt sorry for him and almost regretted parting with him so peremptorily.

'So you won't – hm ... won't be going to visit him, then?' Sir Charles asked.

'No,' said Sebastian.

They shook hands.

Sir Charles turned away sadly towards to the door. 'Well, I'll be off, I suppose,' he said.

Sebastian showed him out into the hall. As he opened the front door for his visitor, he relented a little and said, 'I'm sorry, Sir Charles – but I think it's plain, after all, that your message was not intended for me. And in any case, I don't see what I could do. I've – ah ... I've heard your story, and I'm afraid I'm not very impressed by it. I know that you're sincere, but ... ' He sighed. 'You'll just have to ... just have to face the fact that your friend is seriously disturbed.' He looked down at the green and white tiled floor where a patch of yellow sunlight shone, and he fell silent.

'Look,' said Sir Charles, 'look, in case you should change your mind – I'll write my telephone number down for you.' He fumbled in his pockets and found a notebook and a pen. He wrote his name and the telephone number in the book, tore out the page and handed it to Sebastian, who accepted it reluctantly. 'I'll be staying here in London for the next few days,' Sir Charles said. 'You'll be able to contact me at that number. Call me if you change your mind, won't you? Terrier was looking forward to seeing you. We could go together, one afternoon – it's not far.'

'Well ... I'm not promising anything,' said Sebastian, as Sir Charles walked down the steps into the street.

*

Later that day, in the evening, Sebastian told Richard about his visitor. Sebastian was cleaning the bath when Richard came up the stairs.

'I can see who used this last,' said Sebastian.

'Sorry – I was going to clean it,' Richard explained, 'but I forgot.'

Sebastian fitted the plug into the hole; he turned on the hot tap. He said. 'Something – ah ... something funny happened this afternoon, while you were out.'

'What's that?' Richard asked, following Sebastian into the bedroom.

Sebastian's room was dark and elegant, the walls black, the ceiling red, the furniture black-lacquered Chinoiserie. There was a scarlet brocade counterpane on the large double bed, and the curtains and lampshades were of scarlet satin.

Sebastian turned on the lights, as the daylight was failing, and sat down at the dressing-table. He said. 'An elderly gentleman came here. He said that his friend was a friend of mine, and he asked me if I'd ever – ah ... ever been in the Army.'

'Do what?' asked Richard, puzzled, sitting on the bed.

Sebastian, beginning to clean off his make-up, told Richard the full story of Sir Charles Fothergill and Captain Terrier. 'So – ah ... so apparently Terrier wants me to go down to this place in Sussex where this Countess woman is supposed to have disappeared, and look for her,' Sebastian explained finally.

'Aren't you worried?' asked Richard, nervously sucking his lip.

'No. Worried – why?' said Sebastian. 'I have no intention whatsoever of going.'

'I know, but I mean, it's kinda creepy, though, isn't it?' said Richard.

'It's certainly – ah ... certainly very odd,' Sebastian agreed. He grinned, and the gold in his teeth flashed. 'Actually, I find it rather amusing.'

Richard stared miserably at the floor; he rubbed his toe in the deep-pile red carpet. 'But don't you wonder,' he asked, 'how this guy Terrier knew your name and all about you?'

'He didn't know all about me,' Sebastian corrected him. 'He knew one or two things about me that it wouldn't – ah ... wouldn't be too hard for him to find out.'

'It's spooky,' commented Richard.

Sebastian turned around from the mirror. 'It's not spooky,' he said. 'Richard, when I tell you this story, you're supposed to laugh, you know. It's an amusing incident – you're supposed to – ah ... supposed to find it amusing. If I'd known you weren't going to see the joke, I wouldn't have told you.'

Richard frowned. 'What d'you mean, see the joke? D'you mean it isn't true, then?'

'Of course it's true,' Sebastian said with a sigh. 'At least, my part of it is. All the rest, about Terrier dressing up as the Countess is about as far-fetched as anything I've ever heard.' He stood up. 'Well, my bath's ready,' he said, 'so I'm going to have it.'

'I just don't understand you, Sebastian,' said Richard. He sounded resentful. 'Why don't you take anything seriously? It says something about you, you know. I mean, it's like you're scared of your real feelings. Like I keep telling you, if you came to the men's group with me, it would really do something for you, I know it would.'

'Oh Lord, we're not back to that again, are we?' exclaimed Sebastian in exasperation. 'Sounds absolutely diabolical, airing one's deepest feelings with a lot of strange men. I can't imagine anything more ghastly.'

'Well, that's just your prejudice coming out, that is,' said Richard. 'It's this whole thing about how men are supposed to be – how men are supposed to be tough and macho and not show those feelings, you know. But it doesn't have to be that way – there's another way of being, and you gotta learn by talking about these things.'

'You – ah ... you think this – ah ... this criticism of the male stereotype applies to me, do you?' asked Sebastian.

'Not specially to you, no,' said Richard. 'But it affects us all, just 'cos we are men, and what I'm saying is, if it doesn't apply to you, then why are you always making such a bloody big joke about everything? What about Professor Aaronberg this morning? You thought he must be off his head, just 'cos he tells you something you can't be bothered with and don't understand. Now this Countess has disappeared, and you don't bloody care about her either.'

'Why the hell should I?' Sebastian retorted. 'It has nothing whatsoever to do with me. She didn't disappear, anyhow – she crashed her plane in the sea.'

'But this bloke Terrier said it was him who crashed the plane,' Richard persisted desperately, 'just dressed up to look like the Countess.'

'Good grief! There's only one thing to say to that,' said Sebastian as he walked out of the room. 'Terrier's barking!'

Richard followed him back into the bathroom.

'I don't see that it matters to you, anyway,' said Sebastian.

'I'll tell you what matters to me,' said Richard bitterly, 'and that's the fact that you treat everything like one big laugh. Well, Professor Aaronberg is my friend as well as yours, and I'm gonna do something, even if you're not. I've decided to go to Portmeirion tomorrow, and if I can, I'm gonna stop whatever it is from happening to him.'

'You do that,' said Sebastian with a condescending smile, as he turned off the bath-tap.

CHAPTER 4

The Prophesy Comes True

The following morning, Richard Mojave's alarm clock failed him and he slept longer than he had intended.

'Why didn't you wake me?' he shouted to Sebastian as he rushed into the drawing-room and grabbed the telephone. It was nearly eleven o'clock, and Richard was still wearing his pyjamas and dressing-gown. Frantically he dialled the number for the Portmeirion Hotel.

'You're not really going to Portmeirion today, are you, old sport?' asked Sebastian, who was sitting on the sofa, nonchalantly eating cereals from a bowl and reading that morning's copy of *The Times*, which was spread on the cushion beside him. He was dressed rather unconventionally in black rubber trousers and a black string vest, and his hair was back-combed and decorated with small red feathers tied into it.

Richard stared at him. 'Jesus Christ,' he said, 'don't you care what might be happening to Professor Aaronberg? It could be too late – it could be too bloody late already!'

*

Meanwhile, far away in Portmeirion, Professor Aaronberg was not in his room in the Fountain, but was on the Portmeirion Peninsula, a quarter of a mile away from the village. Panting hard, his body clammy with sweat, he crashed through the rhododendron plantation. As he ran, he whirled his arms round energetically, up and down, in a futile attempt to propel himself along more swiftly, whilst his little legs trembled with increasing exhaustion. In his hot fist he tightly clasped the mysterious note that he had received, which told him to be up on the cliff-top by eleven o'clock, and he was already late. He would not have exerted himself so violently had the note not been signed with Sebastian's name; but he had been worried about Sebastian ever since his strange visitation two nights earlier, and now he was afraid that his friend was in trouble and needed his help urgently, for the note had suggested as much.

Unknown to the Professor, a short distance off the coast, out in Tremadoc Bay, the Earl of Newhaven's private yacht was anchored. The Earl's beautiful young dark-haired secretary, Karen Black, dressed only in a brief white bikini, was lying stretched out on a folding lounger on the deck.

Sleepily, Karen reached for her sunglasses, putting them on to gaze up at the placid azure blue sky, in which clear expanse the only moving thing was the dark object that she knew to be a helicopter, now receding into the distance towards the white shore-line of the tip of the wooded peninsula.

She returned her gaze to the deck of the yacht, glancing towards Dr Kotlowski, who was sitting, hot and uncomfortable under the blazing sun, in his black woollen suit, starched collar and tightly-knotted tie, hunched forwards like a monstrous black spider, she thought, on a deck-chair a few feet from her. He clasped his knees together between large, pale hands, his dazzling white shirt-cuffs exposed, his shoulders drawn up to his ears. He squinted and cringed, as his dark brooding eyes moved fearfully to regard Karen's magnificent golden body.

Karen giggled. 'I see you're admiring my suntan, Doctor.'

Kotlowski shuddered, shooting a desperate glance towards Lord Stephen Mitchell, the Earl of Newhaven, who had just reappeared on deck, carrying a heavy radio which he set down beside his other equipment.

The Earl was a tall, broad-shouldered, well-built man in early middle age. Like Karen, he was dressed today only in bathing attire, and his naked brown skin glistened with perspiration. His short blond hair was bleached almost white by the fierce sun.

'Hurry up, Steve,' said Karen impatiently. 'They'll be there and back again before you've finished.'

'Nearly ready,' the Earl assured her with enthusiasm, swiftly assembling the radio equipment on the deck.

'I feel that I must protest,' Kotlowski said in a tense, strangled voice; he spoke in faltering, Polish-accented English. 'Miss Black,' he went on, 'why do you not understand this fact – that we are, in a sense, missionaries, and our mission is a pure and holy one? I am a God-fearing man, Miss Black, and I am ashamed to see that you, whom I thought a virtuous young lady, expose your body before the lusting eyes of men.'

'What – me? Virtuous!' Karen squealed with mirth. 'Here, Steve – d'you hear what he just said?'

The Earl smiled briefly, though he had not been paying attention: he was more interested in the radio. He plugged in the aerial. 'All done now, Karen,' he said, standing back to admire the construction. 'Right, Kotlowski – I'll hand over to you now.'

Karen giggled again. 'This'll be fun!'

'It is not fun, Miss Black,' Kotlowski told her, rising primly from the chair to approach the radio. 'Sadly, I find myself disappointed in your attitude.'

'Oh, sorry, I'm sure!' said Karen. She sat up abruptly, shaking her short, bobbed hair. 'Some of us like a bit of fun.'

'It is,' said Kotlowski, snatching up the microphone, switching on the radio, 'one's moral duty, Miss Black, to attempt to conduct this operation efficiently, soberly and calmly. We must not fall short of the purity of our aims.' He frowned slightly at the sight of the Earl, who, having retreated into a shady part of the deck near to the cabin entrance, was exercising himself by doing vigorous press-ups. Kotlowski sniffed contemptuously; lifting the microphone close to his mouth, he said: 'Hello. Here is the Black Guardian, speaking to you, Eagle Enterprise. Hello, hello? Are you hearing me? Answer, if you please. Over.'

'They must be there by now,' said Karen.

*

Professor Aaronberg was trotting through the Dogs' Cemetery at that moment, under the cool shade of the trees. His head was throbbing, and in his misty vision sparks of yellow and electric blue seemed to flash across the deep green shadows beyond the bright region of grass and sunlight. He was near to collapsing beneath the oppressive heat.

Meanwhile, Captain Johnny Terrier and Dr Electra Vanderpump were flying in the helicopter from the Earl's yacht to the Portmeirion Peninsula. Johnny was at the controls, tears in his eyes as he flew the helicopter over the calm blue water of Tremadoc Bay, into the Dwryd Estuary. 'Johnny doesn't like you, he doesn't, Dr Vanderpump,' he complained over the headphones to the cool Dr Vanderpump, who sat beside him. 'Fed up, that's what! I'm fed up!' he declared with feeling. 'You know I'm only doing this 'cos Karen said I had to, and if I don't, she'll get disappeared, like Lady Caroline too. Don't think it's 'cos of you, Dr Vanderpump. It bloody isn't!'

Electra Vanderpump, a severely handsome woman with stiffly-lacquered, jet black shoulder-length hair, whose icy green eyes were set in a thin, impassive face, was dressed this morning in a black and white, sleeveless, backless, cotton shift dress and white stiletto-heeled sandals. She laughed serenely at Johnny's distress. 'You would do whatever I asked you to do, Mr Terrier,' she replied, speaking into the mouthpiece of her headset. 'You know you would.'

In Johnny's ears, her voice sounded cold and mocking. 'You lock me up. You're nasty to me, you are,' Johnny grumbled bitterly. 'You make me dress up in silly clothes.'

Electra laughed merrily, glancing side-long at Johnny from beneath her mascara-dark eyelashes. Johnny was wearing red trousers, a black satin jacket, and a long-haired, dark brown wig. 'I'm sick of dressing up,' he complained. 'You don't ever explain anything properly to Johnny.'

'It's quite simple,' replied Electra with a grim smile. 'Professor Aaronberg will believe that the cryptic message we sent to him is from his friend, Sebastian Dorrell. He'll go up onto the cliff-top to meet Mr Dorrell, as the note instructs him, and there we shall land to pick him up. When he sees you, Mr Terrier, he'll think that you're Mr Dorrell, and by the time he discovers his mistake, it will be too late.'

She handed Johnny a pair of dark glasses. 'Here,' she said, 'put these on – it will improve the disguise.'

Kotlowski's voice hailed them on the radio. 'Answer, if you please,' Kotlowski said.

Electra switched the radio over. 'Eagle Enterprise to Black Guardian,' she replied. 'We're flying close to the shore now.'

'Can you see Grey Mouse, Eagle Enterprise?' Kotlowski asked.

'Not yet – we're too high,' said Electra.

She gazed down upon the quiet waters of the estuary. The tide was in, but a wide white beach still extended along the wooded shore of the peninsula, below the cliffs. Electra fixed her gaze upon a point close to the tip of the peninsula, where the cliff-top was bare of trees but covered with a thick carpet of pink and mauve heather. 'I think I detect something down there,' she said.

'It's a gull,' said Johnny Terrier morosely.

'Is it a gull?' Electra frowned. 'Perhaps you're right. But let's go down, Mr Terrier. He must be somewhere nearby.' She reached for her handbag. 'Perhaps I could signal to him,' she mused. 'Yes. I think that may deceive him nicely. What do you think, Black Guardian? Over.'

Kotlowski's voice, uneasy in bewilderment, came to them on the radio. 'I do not understand. Over.'

'I'm going to flash him a message with my mirror,' Electra replied. She smiled in anticipation. 'Just to say good morning to him. That would be a nice touch, I think.' She glanced outside again. 'Down, Terrier! Down!' she cried sharply. 'I see him now!'

*

Richard Mojave slammed down the telephone receiver in helpless frustration. 'It just kept ringing,' he said. 'He wouldn't answer! Sebastian, he's not there!'

'Well – phone back later,' Sebastian Dorrell suggested, finishing his cereals and setting down the bowl on the floor. 'Perhaps he's – ah ... gone for a walk.'

'But don't you see – it could be happening now, this very minute – whatever it is that's gonna happen to him!' Richard cried.

'Good grief, nothing's going to happen to him,' said Sebastian with a sigh. 'He had a bad dream, that's all.'

*

Reeling beneath the oppressive heat, Professor Aaronberg emerged breathless from the trees, onto the cliff-top. There was a great whirring sound in the sky above him, and the summer air was strangely agitated. Oblivious to the cause of the commotion, eyes squinting against the bright sunlight, the Professor ran on. A dark shadow flowed across him as he ran along the cliff-top; a great tumult filled the air above, but he did not look up, running, arms spread out.

The cliffs were closer now as the helicopter descended, and Johnny Terrier, momentarily exhilarated by the prospect of Electra Vanderpump's scheme approaching its triumphant climax, forgot his troubles and giggled loudly, wildly.

Electra held up her pocket mirror to reflect the blazing sun. She flashed out a message in Morse code.

Johnny sniggered foolishly, excited and horrified at once, enthralled by the thrill of the moment: all at once he felt needed, he felt a vital part of the operation, and the feeling felt good. Looking below, he saw the running figure of a stout elderly man dressed in white, arms spread out flapping wildly as he careered through the heather, his white jacket billowing out like a kite, his fluffy white hair standing out around his head like the nimbus of a saint.

'There he is!' Johnny screamed. 'Hooray!'

Professor Aaronberg glanced up, as if attracted by Johnny's cry, halting at last, shielding his face with his arms from the blast of air generated by the helicopter's whirling rotor. He blinked in surprise as signals of light flashed to him a message that he did not understand. It must be Sebastian, he thought in growing excitement. He trotted forward happily.

Out of the blue summer sky, the Eagle Enterprise descended.

*

The next day, Julian Crucefix read a newspaper report about Professor Aaronberg's disappearance. Julian was sitting in his office at Heydn Hall when Karen Black flaunted in, humming the tune of a new pop song.

'Ooh – sorry!' she said. 'Didn't know you was in here! Steve wants a look at those accounts now. What've you done with them? Hey, what's that you're reading?' she added, peering over Julian's shoulder. She snatched the newspaper out of his hands, stabbing a finger excitedly at the article that he had just been reading. 'Professor Aaronberg missing!' She giggled. 'Cor, fancy it being in the paper and all! What a lark!'

Nervously, Julian rose from his desk, rubbing his small hands together in slight embarrassment. 'Yes, yes, I was quite ... um ... shocked,' he said, 'to read that there. I used to watch him on television. He was always very interesting. I wonder what's happened to him.'

Karen flushed self-consciously. 'I bet a lot of people are wondering that,' she said.

CHAPTER 5

The Demon Chair

'So it's happened,' said Richard Mojave. He was sitting on the Chesterfield sofa, the newspaper open across his knees. He gulped nervously; he rubbed his hand over his red beard. He said, 'I knew there was something wrong when I kept phoning yesterday and he never answered. It happened then, in the morning. Even if I'd gone to Portmeirion it would've been too late.'

Slowly, Sebastian Dorrell was pacing up and down the room. It was a wet and clammy day, and outside the windows, grey rain was pouring down in gloomy torrents; but it was not entirely due to the dull and sickly light that Sebastian looked so pale: his face seemed to be drained of blood. It must have been the shock of reading the newspaper report, Richard realised: Sebastian, who had never taken seriously the Professor's forewarning of his own disappearance, was now genuinely shocked to read in the newspaper that it had actually come about.

'Oh, sit down, for Christ's sake!' said Richard irritably.

Sebastian stopped pacing; he stood with his back to the window, silhouetted against the miserable grey daylight, and he stroked his hands up and down his bare arms. He was dressed as he had been on the previous day, in rubber trousers and a string vest, but with the change of weather he was feeling the cold: the dark hairs were standing erect on his forearms and he was shivering. He said, 'I was wrong, Richard, and you were right. I was wrong. I should've listened to you.'

Richard folded up the newspaper roughly and flung it on the floor; he rubbed both hands over his face. 'Well,' he said with a sigh, 'are you gonna phone Portmeirion, or shall I?'

'Why?' asked Sebastian.

'To find out what's going on,' said Richard. 'Maybe they've found him by now. Maybe ... '

'You do it,' said Sebastian. He walked to the door. 'There's something else I've – ah ... something I've got to do.'

He left Richard in the drawing-room and went upstairs. The air in the house was damp and chill, and everywhere the sound of beating rain could be heard; the wind boomed and blustered like thunder in the chimneys and gusted showers of rain against the rattling windows. All the rooms upstairs were draughty and cold, and in the dreary light, each room looked grim and cheerless with its dark heavy furniture and rich sombre decor.

Quickly Sebastian walked along the corridor to the room at the far end, the door that he kept always locked. The key was lodged up on the top of the door-frame. He felt with his fingers along the dusty ledge and found the key, taking it down and unlocking the door.

Softly he pushed it open and slipped into the room, locking the door behind him.

The room was bare of furniture. The wallpaper was old and discoloured, and brighter rectangular patches on it showed where pictures had once hung. There were no pictures now, no curtains and no carpet. Against the dirty window panes, the cold rain pattered, and the sash rattled in its frame.

Sebastian crossed the room to another door and opened it. Beyond, was a smaller room, darker, shadowy. A large tree which grew outside the window prevented much of the miserable daylight from entering. In the gusting wind, the leafy branches of the tree were tossed back and forth, so that patterns of shadow cast by the moving boughs flowed turbulently across the grey, bare floor-boards and over the stained walls.

On the far side of the room was a mean fireplace: a small rusty grate was framed by dark green tiling and a low iron mantelpiece from which the pale paint was peeling. In the recess to the left of the chimney-breast was a grey-painted cupboard, which might have been a wardrobe. In the recess on the other side stood a rack of old clothes, all shrouded in thick polythene wrappings upon which a film of dust had gathered, so that they hung there like a row of strangled ghosts.

The only other thing in the room was the Chair.

Sebastian Dorrell closed the door behind him and walked slowly, quietly, across the floor to where the Chair stood. It was a massive, grotesque piece of furniture, an elaborately carved throne that age and use had darkened and polished until the wood of which it was made resembled glossy black marble. The back was high, decorated with the intricate carving of a vine, among the leaves and fruit of which small goblins squatted and peered out with grinning malice. Portions of human faces and limbs with claw-like hands protruded from other parts of the Chair, as if deformed beings writhing within the wood had

partially succeeded in bursting free of their prison. Two hooded eyes stared out malevolently from the ends of the arms; the legs were in the form of the limbs of a hairy animal with clawed feet. The most impressive element of this gothic monster, however, was the large, ornate, demonic head with horns and protruding tongue, which crowned its back, sprouting from the forking branches at the top of the carved vine.

Slowly, Sebastian extended his hand and touched the Chair's arm with his finger-tips; he caressed it softly, tentatively, as if he were fondling an unfriendly beast that needed to be placated. The Chair felt slightly warm to the touch, despite the chillness of the air in the room.

Sebastian smiled; he laid both his hands on the wooden arms and stared steadily at the carved face set on its back. The tree swayed outside the window and the shadow of its leaves flicked across the carved demon's face so that its squinting eyes seemed to move, meeting Sebastian's gaze.

He seated himself cautiously upon the Chair's worn red velvet seat; with both hands he stroked the smooth dark arms that were curiously warm, almost like living flesh beneath his touch. He leaned back, feeling the demon's sharp features pressing into the back of his head. He smiled: now he knew what he must do.

He closed his eyes, shutting out the dreary scene of the bare room. He could still hear the rain beating down outside, and the branches of the tree tapping against the window-panes. He breathed deeply, slowly, rhythmically; he gripped the arms of the Chair more tightly, and he pictured in his mind Professor Aaronberg's room in the Fountain in Portmeirion. As well as he could, he imagined it, and he imagined Professor Aaronberg lying in the bed. It was night-time, and it was dark, but there was a waxing moon and the light shone in through the window, illuminating everything with an eerie pale blue radiance. Sebastian concentrated upon the scene, willing every detail of it into existence: it must be quite real for him.

He opened his eyes: there was darkness all around him and there was silence, and in the darkness and silence he could see and hear nothing, yet he knew that he was no longer in the spare bedroom of his house; the surroundings that had been real for him a moment before had faded and dissolved, as if they had been a mirage. But this was not going to be easy: on the night that the Professor had had his strange visitation, Sebastian had been at home asleep in bed, and Sebastian knew that it was not possible for him to be in two places at once; he could not be in Professor Aaronberg's room at the same time as he was at home in London, and yet somehow he must communicate with Professor Aaronberg before the Professor's disappearance.

Again he closed his eyes and imagined the room in the Fountain where he had visited the Professor so many times. Slowly he opened his eyes, and gradually, dimly, he began to see the scene that he had imagined.

'Professor!' he called softly. 'Professor Aaronberg!'

He called the name again and again, and now he seemed to see the startled, pale face of his old friend rising up out of the gloom before him.

'Professor Aaronberg, don't be alarmed,' said Sebastian gently, leaning forward in the Chair.

The Professor was staring at him with a glazed, sleepy expression in his eyes. 'Is that you, dear boy?' he asked dazedly. His face loomed a little closer; his hand rose up to rub sleepily at his eyes.

'I'm sorry to startle you, Professor,' Sebastian said with

effort. He was concentrating hard, trying to keep the Professor's face in focus.

'How on earth did you get in?' Professor Aaronberg asked. 'The door is locked ... and it's the first floor, so you couldn't have come in by the window ... '

The Professor's face was fading rapidly as Sebastian's concentration began to fail. He knew that he should not be here, but he must try to keep it up for a few minutes longer. 'There's no time to explain,' he said.

*

When Sebastian returned to the drawing-room, Richard had just finished making a telephone call. He looked up as Sebastian walked in.

'Christ, you look terrible,' said Richard. 'Are you okay?'

Sebastian walked unsteadily to the sofa and sat down. He said, 'Yes, I just feel slightly ... ah ... faint – that's all. It's always exhausting, but ... '

'What's exhausting?' Richard asked.

Sebastian did not reply, but rested his face in his hands.

'It's the shock,' said Richard. 'Listen, I rang Portmeirion and spoke to someone there who told me that the Professor was last seen at breakfast yesterday. After that, nobody knows what happened to him. They put me onto the Portmadoc police, so I phoned them too, and they said they're looking into it.'

Sebastian sighed; he ran his fingers through his tangled hair. 'Professor Aaronberg says he sent me his book, but I haven't – ah ... haven't seen it. It was called *The Ghost Garden*.'

'Oh, it's upstairs – I got it,' said Richard casually.

Sebastian looked at him in indignation. 'You? Why didn't you tell me that it came?'

'Well, you never seem to be interested in that kinda thing,' said Richard in surprise. 'It had both our names on it, so I opened it. It's jolly interesting too – I been reading it. Oh ... ' He tugged at his moustache thoughtfully. 'There was a letter with it for you. I shoulda given it you, but I forgot.'

'You forget everything!' declared Sebastian in annoyance. 'Go and get it now – go on! This is important – and the letter! Bring that too.'

Grumbling a little, Richard left the room. When he returned a few minutes later with the book and the letter, Sebastian took them from him eagerly.

'I don't understand you,' grumbled Richard, sitting beside him on the Chesterfield.

The daylight was very dim by now, for the weather had grown more stormy; the wind was blustering in the chimney and the rain beat up against the windows. Sebastian switched on the table-lamp that stood on a small table beside the sofa. He tore open the envelope and pulled out the Professor's letter; he began to read it.

'What's it say?' Richard asked gloomily.

'It says, *Dear Sebastian,*' said Sebastian, '*Here is my new book – I thought that you and Richard would like a copy. In it I deal with a number of topics in the paranormal that I feel will interest Richard in particular. Already I have received a few letters from people who have read the book, and they are quite complimentary about it, I am pleased to say. The publishers forwarded all the letters to me. Unfortunately, among them was a very unpleasant one from Lord Stephen Horsley-Mitchell, the Earl of Newhaven, which quite upset me when I read it. You see, I mentioned him and other members of his family in chapter five, and I regret to say that I did not ask his permission to do so, since it is a well-attested fact that Lord Mountjoy Horsley-*

Mitchell, his grandfather, disappeared in the very circumstances that I describe, and since there is no secret about the matter, it did not occur to me that I could possibly cause offence by mentioning it in my chapter on mysterious vanishings. I attach a copy of the Earl's letter so that you can see for yourself what he had to say about it. I should welcome your advice on how to deal with this. Perhaps best to keep silent and do nothing?'

'Let's see,' said Richard, tugging impatiently at the letter.

Sebastian brushed Richard's hand away and turned over the letter, folding back the photocopy of the Earl's letter which was stapled to it, so that he could read it. 'This is a funny coincidence,' he remarked. 'The Earl of Newhaven ... You know, I said that man – ah ... Sir Charles Fothergill came here two days ago, who thought I knew his friend in the Air Corps. He was talking about the Earl of Newhaven too. That countess who disappeared – it was at Heydn Hall, the Earl's home.'

Richard frowned. 'D'you think there could be any connection? I mean, between these disappearances and Professor Aaronberg's disappearance?'

Sebastian shook his head. 'I don't see how there can be.' He glanced over the photocopied letter. 'Look, he doesn't – ah ... doesn't even begin by saying *Dear Professor Aaronberg*, or *Dear Sir*, or anything like that. He just says, *Professor Aaronberg, I've read your damned idiotic book, and I've never been so disgusted by such bloody rubbish in my whole life. What do you mean by dragging in the Horsley-Mitchell family and Heydn Hall, as if there were some supernatural hocus-pocus going on here? What bloody impertinence. There's nothing wrong around Heydn Hall that can't be sorted out with a bit of guts and muscle and tough action. If you're suggesting that I will be the next to disappear, then I refute your ridiculous suggestion in the strongest terms. What is the matter with you people, you bloody bourgeois intellectuals? You're always going on about apparitions and flying saucers and God knows what, like a bunch of hysterical, potty old women. It's because of men like you that the whole damn country is going to wrack and ruin. It's nothing but hysteria – sheer women's hysteria and lunatic rubbish. You haven't heard the last of this – I'll have you up for libel, Aaronberg. Don't imagine you're going to get away with it.'* Sebastian handed the letter to Richard. 'What d'you – ah ... what d'you make of that?' he asked.

'It's kinda like a threat, I s'pose,' said Richard. 'I don't like it.'

'Personally,' said Sebastian, 'if someone sent me a letter like this, I'd chuck it straight in the bin, and wouldn't – ah ... wouldn't think anything more of it. But Professor Aaronberg evidently took a more serious view of it.'

'D'you think,' asked Richard, 'it's got anything to do with what's happened to him now?'

Sebastian laughed. 'You think the – ah ... think the Earl of Newhaven has abducted him, what? Well, judging by this – ah ... letter, he's a pretty funny fellow, but I doubt if he'd go in for kidnapping.'

'You don't know what he'd do,' Richard objected. 'He sounds a bit of a crank to me. All that stuff about people being hysterical – he's the one who's bloody hysterical, if you ask me.'

'Better watch what you say, old chap,' said Sebastian with a smile. 'He'll be having you up for slander next.'

CHAPTER 6

The Interview

When Julian Crucefix had first gone to Heydn Hall, three months earlier, his future there had looked uncertain.

Nervous and shy, he had shaken hands with the blond and burly Earl in the Lounge, where the Earl had introduced himself when Karen Black had shown Julian into the room.

'Hello! I'm Steve Mitchell!' Lord Stephen had roared as he had pumped Julian's arm up and down vigorously. 'You can call me Steve – everyone does! Mind if I call you Julian? We're all on first name terms here at Heydn.'

'Oh, I see,' said Julian uneasily, retrieving his hand from the Earl's fierce grip.

'Sit down – sit down and make yourself at home, Julian!' the Earl had invited jovially, gesturing at one of the luxurious red velvet couches.

It was a large, high-ceilinged, bright room, lit by windows along two of the walls facing one another. The windows looked out onto two large enclosed courtyards in the middle of the house: one of the courtyards was deep in blue shadow; but the other was brilliantly illuminated, and this was due to the sunlight being deflected down into it from the bright glass prism on the roof of the Prince's Tower, as Julian was later to learn.

Timidly, he sat down on the edge of the couch, nervously fingering the sleeves of his grey woollen jacket. 'I understand it's only a temporary post?' he said.

'Temporary?' repeated the Earl in surprise. He was standing before the ornate white marble fireplace, his hands in the pockets of his grey flannel trousers.

Julian stared at him, startled to notice that the Earl wore his braces fastened over the outside of his brown tweed jacket. Julian had not noticed this eccentricity at first, for the braces were partially concealed by the lapels of the jacket.

'What gives you that idea?' the Earl asked. 'See how things go, eh?'

'Oh ... ' said Julian, 'but your secretary told me that Mr Duffy ... '

'What's that? What's Karen been telling you?' roared the Earl, his mood changing abruptly to one of hostile suspicion.

Julian looked uncomfortably at his knees. 'Only that the position was temporary, while Mr Duffy, your estate manager, is on holiday,' he explained.

Lord Stephen scowled. 'I'll be straight with you, Julian,' he said. 'The fact of the matter is, old Duffy isn't on holiday – he's dead.'

'Oh, I'm sorry.' Julian blushed. 'It must be my mistake, sir. I'm sure your secretary told me that he was on holiday in Majorca, but I suppose she was talking about someone else. I misunderstood.'

'Hm ... ' said the Earl. 'No.' He stroked his broad jaw thoughtfully. 'The truth of the matter is, I told her that he'd gone on holiday. Didn't want to worry her, you see. She's sensitive about people dying, and all that sort of thing. You know what women are!' Briefly he laughed, as if to dismiss his apparent anxiety of a moment before. 'I'll tell you what, Julian – I'd be grateful if you didn't mention this to Karen. Let her think old Duffy's enjoying himself in Majorca – no need to trouble her with the truth, eh? That's the best way with women.'

'Was it ... was it sudden, then?' Julian asked. 'An accident?'

The Earl looked startled, disconcerted again. 'An accident? What the devil d'you mean? Who's been talking to you about accidents? There're no accidents here at Heydn Hall, I can tell you that!'

Julian was embarrassed, realising that he should not have pressed the matter. 'I only thought ... you said you didn't want to upset her, sir – so I thought perhaps Mr Duffy had died in tragic circumstances. Of course, it's really none of my business, I suppose,' he added quickly.

'Not at all,' said the Earl at once, smiling amiably again as he recovered his composure. 'Since you're taking over the man's job, it's understandable that you should want to know something about him. The fact of the matter is, he died of a heart attack, but that's between you and me. I'd be grateful if you didn't talk to anyone else about it.'

He looked at Julian knowingly with his fierce blue eyes, so that the young man felt quite afraid of him. 'We don't like to talk about death here, you see,' Lord Stephen explained. 'Not that there's anything wrong with it, you understand, but we don't like to dwell on it. A positive outlook and a healthy attitude – that's what we say here at Heydn.'

Julian nodded nervously; he stroked back his fine fair hair that had flopped limply over one eye. He tried to return the Earl's gaze, but found himself unable to, and instead looked up at the white marble bas-relief on the chimney-breast above the Earl's head: it depicted the goddess Diana with attendant maidens and a pack of hounds. Julian looked around the room at the hunting trophies that hung on the walls, at the paintings of horses and dogs. At the far end of the room hung a large portrait of a man who bore a resemblance to Lord Stephen, mounted upon a horse.

'That's my grandfather, Lord Mountjoy Horsley-Mitchell, the eighteenth Earl,' said Lord Stephen, noticing the direction of Julian's glance. 'He was a remarkable man – remarkable ideas he had. He was always inventing things, you know. I expect you saw the prism on the Tower, did you?'

'That big glass thing?' said Julian. 'Yes, I wondered what it was.'

'My grandfather put it up there,' explained the Earl. 'It's for the light, you see. He was full of ideas like that. Of course, I never knew him personally. It was before my time that he ... um ... ' Lord Stephen broke off, a troubled look returning to cloud his bright blue eyes; his brows descended in a worried frown.

'I see,' said Julian tentatively.

'No you don't,' retorted the Earl. He was glowering now. In agitation he began to pace up and down the room, over the rich red carpet. 'How much do you know about my grandfather?'

'Why ... nothing, sir,' Julian replied in surprise. 'Only what you've just told me.'

'Stop calling me *sir*!' the Earl ordered. 'My name's Steve. And what about my father – d'you know anything about him?'

'No,' Julian admitted bashfully. 'I'm afraid I don't know much about your family or Heydn Hall at all.'

The Earl looked relieved; he stopped pacing up and down, and he managed a shaky smile.

'It's a beautiful house,' said Julian at once. 'I've never been here before. It's open to the public, I understand?'

'That's right,' said the Earl. 'All the state-rooms are open to the public, and all the bedrooms. Why not?' He laughed uneasily. He slapped his thighs. 'Nothing to hide, after all – eh?'

'There're no visitors here today,' Julian observed.

The Earl looked awkward; in embarrassment he stroked his jaw. 'Ah, well ... ' he said, 'unfortunately we've had to close the Hall to the public this year. There're a few repairs that need to be done. However – ' He looked brighter. 'No doubt it'll all be sorted out in due course. Nothing wrong around here that can't be put right with a bit of gumption and plain common sense – that's what I always say! But that's enough about Heydn Hall – what about you?' He turned to Julian Crucefix with a reassuring smile. 'If you're going to be my estate manager, I'd like to know something about you.'

'You mean – I've got the job?' Julian asked in disbelief. He blushed, pushing back his limp fair hair. 'I'm afraid I've done nothing ... nothing of this sort before, sir.'

'So much the better!' exclaimed the Earl enthusiastically. 'We do things differently, here at Heydn. We're very free and easy, very informal, I think you'll find. You'll learn the ropes as you go along! If you don't understand anything, don't be afraid to ask, eh? That's what we're in this world for, after all – to help one another! We're all friends here – no secrets, nothing to hide!' He laughed awkwardly again.

'I wasn't really expecting to be accepted,' said Julian with a timid smile. 'I'm afraid I haven't made any arrangements yet – haven't even sorted out where I'm going to live.'

'Well, you'll live here of course!' exclaimed the Earl. 'Married, are you?'

'No,' said Julian.

'Oh well, then,' exclaimed the Earl with satisfaction, 'you can have Mr Duffy's old room upstairs.'

'Here at the Hall?' queried Julian; he rubbed at his knees in embarrassment. 'Well ... if you're sure it won't be any trouble ... ' he mumbled, blushing.

Then the Earl's change of mood was more sudden and alarming than ever before: he started as if he had been roused from a dream, his steel blue eyes wide with horror, his mouth gaping in inarticulate consternation as, slowly, his face turned a violent red beneath his suntan. At last he managed to gasp out, 'What's that? What did you say? My God!' He ran his hand over his sweating brow. 'Bubble?' he spluttered. 'Bubble? What Bubble? What the bloody hell are you talking about, man? Who the devil've you been talking to? It's damn bloody lies, and if I find out who told you such bloody rubbish, I'll give him the thrashing of his life!'

'But ... but I didn't say ... ' Julian stammered nervously, bewildered by the Earl's extraordinary outburst. 'I only said I didn't want to be any trouble to you – I mean, living actually at Heydn Hall as you suggested.'

'Trouble?' said the Earl. 'Trouble?' An expression of the utmost relief passed over his face; he almost laughed. 'Of course you won't be any trouble,' he said, recovering his composure as swiftly as he could. Affecting a casual air, he strolled up and down before the fireplace, smiling amiably, his violent temper of a moment before banished as swiftly as it had arisen, while the fierce colour faded more slowly from his cheeks. 'We all live up on the second floor, you know,' he explained. 'All one big happy family here at Heydn! Don't worry, old chap – you'll muck in with the rest of us.'

Julian Crucefix smiled sheepishly.

*

Later the same day, up in the Earl's office at the back of the house on the second floor, Karen Black asked Lord Stephen about the new estate manager.

'D'you think he's all right, Steve?' she said dubiously.

They were standing by the window, gazing out across the formal gardens to the deer park and the grey waters of the English Channel in the distance. At its southern edge, the Heydn estate was bordered by the cliffs and the private beach below.

The Earl gazed out, his hands in the pockets of his trousers, his broad clear brow troubled only slightly by the hint of a worried frown. Someone who knew him well might suspect that Lord Stephen's mind was not at peace, that some lingering anxiety continually plagued his thoughts and unsettled his concentration.

'I said, what about this bloke Crucefix?' Karen asked again.

Lord Stephen looked down at her with a strange sadness in his glance. She was wearing a black PVC mini skirt, a thin, red cotton blouse and black fishnet stockings, and a red scarf was tied around her head with an enormous bow on top.

'Crucefix is just the man we need,' the Earl assured her. 'He's clear-headed enough to do the job, and dull enough to keep his nose out of business that doesn't concern him. He's the kind of man who knows his place. Maybe it's against my socialist principles to say it – but for the present, that's to our advantage, and his too, if he did but know it.' He smiled grimly. 'At least he won't go the way of old Duffy. If he sticks to the job and minds his own business, we'll have no trouble with him, so don't you worry about him, Karen. Leave it all to me.'

Karen nodded reluctantly. She laid her small sun-browned hand on Lord Stephen's strong arm, gently stroking the rough tweed fabric of his sleeve. 'Oh, Steve,' she said passionately, gazing up at his fiercely resolute face, his stern blue eyes, 'I bloody love you, Steve!' She sighed. 'Sometimes I think we'll never get married, the way things are going.'

'You know that's not true,' said the Earl. 'You know that, Karen.' He stared moodily out of the window again. 'Just like a woman to bring it up at a time like this! Damn it all, Karen, how the hell can I marry you when there's no future for us, for all we know? God, I should never have brought you here! If you had any sense, you'd be out of here, back to London as fast as you could pack your bags.'

Karen pouted. 'Oh, don't say that! How can you speak as if I don't care?'

Lord Stephen took his hand from his pocket and ran his fingers distractedly through his short blond hair; his face was contorted with a sudden passion of despair and rage. 'What's the use?' he shouted. 'What's the bloody use in caring? Why should you bloody well care, when today, or tomorrow or next week – who knows when – we could all be blown to kingdom come!' He tugged at his hair; he shook his big fist and thumped it against the window-pane in frustrated anger. 'We're sitting on a bloody time bomb here, Karen!' He flung out his arms, almost bowling her over. The irony of what he had just said suddenly struck him and he laughed, coldly, mirthlessly. 'That's what it is – a bloody time bomb!'

'Yeah, but we got to look on the bright side, eh?' said Karen.

'That cousin of yours is half the problem,' Lord Stephen complained. Morosely he stared out of the other window, that faced towards the dark, disused Prince's Tower at the end of the house. In the afternoon sunlight, the curious prism on its roof glinted coldly. The Earl stared at the blank windows with their grimy glass that had not been cleaned in twenty years: behind the glass, the windows had been boarded up, but he sensed a brooding horror within, all the more terrible because it could not be seen. 'He might find out,' said Lord Stephen. 'He's a menace, Karen.'

'Oh, Johnny don't mean no harm,' Karen replied casually. 'He's almost like a little kid in lots of ways – specially since he had his breakdown.'

'I don't like him here, all the same,' the Earl grumbled.

'But he had to come,' said Karen. Playfully, softly, she ran her finger along one of the Earl's braces that were fastened over his jacket. 'Oh, Steve,' she said, 'don't be annoyed. You know I couldn't have left him on his own in London, could I? He's so useless without someone to look after him.'

'Look here,' said the Earl with a sigh; he frowned, rubbing his thumb across his jaw. 'I'll be straight with you, Karen – I've talked to Dr Vanderpump about this, and she agrees with me – '

'Oh no,' said Karen, withdrawing her hands from the Earl's braces. 'It's got nothing to do with that bloody bitch!

I say what happens to Johnny – you promised that, Steve, you promised!'

'Karen, Karen,' soothed the Earl, laying his large hands consolingly upon her shoulders. He looked down into her imploring brown eyes as if she were a child and he were her stern but kindly father. 'You know I wouldn't do anything to hurt you,' he said. 'Johnny needs help – professional help. There're drugs these days, and therapies ... '

'No!' said Karen, shaking her head so that her dark bobbed hair flicked across her cheeks. 'Not drugs,' she said. 'I don't believe in any bloody drugs and therapies! They're just an authoritarian means by which the capitalist-imperialist system forces dissidents to conform – that's what you keep telling me yourself! What about your socialist principles, Steve?'

'But Dr Vanderpump's private clinic,' the Earl persisted, 'is a place where they help people like Johnny. Look at it this way – with things as they are, how can we safely keep him here?'

Karen bowed her head. 'I'm sorry, Steve,' she said reluctantly. 'You know best, I'm sure. It's just that I've always been, like, close to him, you know. I hate to think of him in one of them awful places – a mental hospital, I mean.'

'That's why we send him to Dr Vanderpump,' the Earl explained, patting her shoulders gently.

Karen sucked her lower lip nervously. 'Oh, Steve,' she whispered, 'that's just what bothers me.'

CHAPTER 7

Johnny Terrier's Story

Late in the evening of the day when Richard Mojave read in the newspaper about the disappearance of Professor Aaronberg, Sebastian Dorrell was in bed in his red and black luxury bedroom. The room was dim in a deep sultry twilight, and Sebastian was drowsily drifting into sleep between the black satin sheets, when suddenly the ringing of the telephone on his bedside table vibrated disturbingly through the peaceful silence, and woke him.

Sebastian reached out for the receiver without sitting up, and pulled it down to his ear beneath the bedclothes. 'Hello,' he said.

Down the line into his ear the only reply was a heavy, sinister breathing.

'Who's that?' Sebastian asked. There was no answer, and after a moment there came a click, followed by silence; the caller had gone. Annoyed, Sebastian replaced the handset on the telephone. A moment later, it rang again. He put the receiver to his ear. He said, 'Ah, hello – is that – ah ... is that you again, hm?'

At first there was silence; and then, very softly, a strange voice began to whisper. 'Captain Dorrell,' it breathed. 'Captain Dorrell, is that you, Captain Dorrell?' It was not a pleasant voice: deep like a man's, yet eerie in its intonation, like the whispering of a malevolently teasing child. Sebastian sat up in bed, drawing the sheet slowly over his bare chest. 'My name's Sebastian Dorrell,' he said. 'There's no Captain Dorrell here.'

'Captain Sebastian Dorrell,' whispered the voice. 'Captain Sebastian Dorrell – remember me? It's your old mate – Johnny.'

'Who?' said Sebastian. 'I don't know you.'

'Captain Johnny Terrier,' breathed the voice. 'Remember now? Remember the Persephone?' There was a choking noise, like a stifled giggle. 'I sent Sir Charles Fothergill to see you, Captain Dorrell,' said the whispering voice in the same sing-song tone as before.

'What d'you want?' Sebastian demanded irritably.

'I want you, Captain Dorrell,' came the reply. 'For old time's sake, you won't let an old mate down.'

'Now look here, Captain Terrier,' said Sebastian in growing annoyance, 'I've been through all this damn business with your friend, Sir Charles. You seem to think that we've met in the past, but you're mistaken. I don't know you, I have never met you, I never heard your name until the day before yesterday, and frankly I am not in the least interested in anything you have to say to me. Now kindly stop pestering me. Good night, Captain Terrier.'

He was about to cut the connection, but Johnny Terrier's response was rapid and startling. 'What about Professor Joshua Aaronberg?' he hissed fiercely, before Sebastian had taken the receiver right away from his ear.

Sebastian was shocked, alerted by the sound of his friend's name. 'Professor Aaronberg?' he said. 'What – what d'you mean?'

'D'you know where he is, Captain Dorrell?' whispered Johnny.

'No,' said Sebastian.

Again there came the choking noise, like a stifled giggle. 'I know what's happened to him,' answered Johnny tauntingly. 'Wouldn't you like to know, Captain Dorrell?'

'Stop playing games,' said Sebastian, 'and tell me, if you've anything to tell – which I seriously doubt.'

'You're going to help me, Captain Dorrell,' whispered Johnny gleefully. 'Oh yes you are! How can I tell you now? I'm in her office – they'll catch me if I stay any longer. If you want to hear more, you'll have to come and see me.'

'Now, just wait a minute – ' Sebastian retorted indignantly. He broke off as there came a loud click in his ear: evidently Johnny had slammed down the receiver and had gone.

Sebastian was exasperated; he flung himself back upon the pillows and stared in puzzled anger at the red ceiling. How could it be, he thought, that this man, Captain Terrier, should know anything about the disappearance of Professor Aaronberg? It seemed highly unlikely that there was any real connection, beyond the vaguely disturbing coincidences that he had already noted. And this fellow was a madman: he certainly sounded mad, judging by the way he spoke, over and above the content of anything he said. Locked away in a lunatic asylum, he seemed highly unlikely to have any genuine knowledge of what had become of Joshua Aaronberg.

Sebastian sighed: it was infuriating. If he were to follow this up, it would mean getting in touch with Sir Charles Fothergill again and explaining that he had changed his mind. It would mean going on a tedious trip out of London to visit this pestering lunatic, Terrier, under the pretence of offering him assistance (which, in reality, Sebastian had no intention of doing, beyond what was necessary to persuade him to reveal whatever he might know about the Professor), and when all was said and done, it would probably turn out to be a waste of effort.

Nevertheless, Sebastian knew that his mind would not be at rest until he had done it and had proved to his own satisfaction that he had followed that particular line of inquiry into Professor Aaronberg's disappearance to its conclusion, profitable or not.

*

'Young Terrier will be pleased to see you, I must say,' remarked Sir Charles Fothergill conversationally. He was sitting in the passenger seat of Sebastian Dorrell's green sports car, and Sebastian was driving them through the Hertfordshire countryside, along a hedged road with fields and woodland on either side.

'Yes, I expect he will be,' Sebastian agreed wryly.

'You didn't tell me what made you change your mind,' said Sir Charles.

'No, I didn't,' said Sebastian. It was a warm, sunny afternoon: the rain of the previous day had passed, and the birds were singing.

Sebastian was dressed today in dark blue pinstripe jeans, a black tee shirt and a red linen jacket; around his neck hung many metal pendants and strings of coloured beads; there was a red feather ear-ring in his left ear, and his hair, which was parted on the left, was plaited in several long thin plaits on the left-hand side, while on the right side it hung loose over his shoulder.

'We must be nearly there by now,' he said.

Sir Charles leaned forward eagerly, pointing into the

distant, dark trees. 'It's somewhere over there,' he said. 'You should see the place in a minute.'

'There's a large house,' Sebastian observed, gazing through the trees in the direction that Sir Charles had pointed, glimpsing weathered dusky red brick amid the dappled shadow of greenery.

'That's it,' said Sir Charles. 'Look out for a turning on the left.'

A short distance further on, they came to the entrance to the home. The gates were open, and against the brick pillar on one side was erected a large blue notice which read TWILIGHT HOME FOR THE AGED AND INFIRM. Sebastian turned the car in through the entrance and drove slowly up the tarmacked drive, until the old red-brick manor house came into view, surrounded by ancient yew trees and dark thick clumps of holly. The broken stone plinth of a sundial stood in the middle of the lawn to the left of the wide forecourt; the brass sundial lay in the damp grass, sunlight reflecting from its smooth surface.

There were several cars parked on the forecourt, but no one was about. Near to the house, even the birds were silent. Overhead, the dark boughs of yew trees stirred, whispering quietly in the breeze.

Shadows of the moving leaves flickered across the long rain-flattened grass of the lawn, across the drive, the bricks of the house's walls, the mossy tiles of the roof; reflections shimmered across dark puddles, across window-panes, across the still, dark, glassy surface of an ornamental pool in the centre of the forecourt.

'Hm ... ' remarked Sebastian, as he switched off the car's engine, 'delightful place! But tell me, Sir Charles, how – ah ... how old is your friend, Terrier? You spoke as if he were young, but the – ah ... board at the gate says that this is an old people's home. You gave me the impression that it was a lunatic asylum.'

Sir Charles appeared bemused; he stared at Sebastian as if he had not quite understood him. 'Well,' he said, 'there's more to this place than meets the eye, if you ask me. And if you believe young Terrier, there's something fishy at the bottom of it.'

They climbed out of the car; all was silent, but it was a brooding silence, as if waiting for some lurking horror to emerge from the green shadows among the dark trees and engulf the whole scene. When Sebastian slammed the car door shut, Sir Charles started and looked uncomfortably embarrassed: it seemed improper to make sudden loud noises in this still and deathly place. It was like a cemetery.

Sir Charles walked behind Sebastian, up to the front door, where Sebastian pulled the bell-pull. They heard a distant bell ring, but from within the house there was no other sound.

After a moment, soft footsteps could be heard approaching, then the door was tugged open abruptly, and a face concealed in a gas mask peered out at them.

'Good Lord!' exclaimed Sir Charles, stepping back in surprise and alarm.

Sebastian, startled for only a moment, began to laugh.

The person who had opened the door was a young female nurse dressed in a plain grey uniform that buttoned down the front and reached below the knee; her short, blonde, wavy hair hung over the straps of her mask. Even when she removed the gas mask, Sebastian was still laughing. She stared at him, her blue eyes cold and unsmiling as he went on laughing, and when he raised a hand to his face, she stared at his scarlet nail varnish with mild disdain.

'Yes?' she said coolly. 'What d'you want?' She turned her gaze upon Sir Charles, as if expecting a more sensible reply from him, and then a slight smile, rather strained and unnatural, hovered about her lips. She said. 'Oh, you've been here before, haven't you?'

Sir Charles cleared his throat; he stroked his white handlebar moustache nervously. 'Ah ... yes,' he said. 'Sir Charles Fothergill. I've come to see Captain John Terrier. And this ... ' He gestured at Sebastian, who was still grinning with obvious amusement. 'This is Captain Dorrell – an old Army friend of Captain Terrier's. They were together in the Air Corps, you know.'

The nurse looked at Sebastian; she looked hard at his long hair, his jewellery, his make-up. He grinned at her, and she looked at the gold fillings in his teeth. 'I see,' she said, after a moment's hesitation. She stepped back, opening the door wider. 'You'd better come in,' she said. 'I think you'll be able to see Mr Terrier now. He's in bed, I'm afraid – he had another of his turns yesterday, so you may not find him very talkative at present. Still, he should be awake, at least.' She closed the door behind them as they stepped inside.

The interior of the house had been altered by the erection of walls which divided up some of the original large rooms into smaller units. The nurse led them along a narrow, tiled corridor, unlocked a door near the end, and ushered them in.

'Visitors for you, Mr Terrier,' she announced brightly.

It was a small, windowless room, the only daylight coming from the dim corridor outside, entering through a glass panel above the door.

The walls were painted pale grey, the floor tiled with grey composition tiles. In a shadowy corner stood a plain hospital bed in which someone was lying curled up, the grey blankets pulled up so as almost to obscure his head.

The nurse flipped a switch near to the door, and fluorescent lighting flickered on. Sebastian looked up at the low ceiling with its polystyrene tiles, then he looked down again at the bed, where the occupant was moving.

'Mr Terrier,' said the nurse again, 'here're your friends to see you.' She turned to Sir Charles and Sebastian. 'Well, I'll leave you with him for a bit, shall I? I'm afraid I'll have to lock the door, but if you need anything, you can ring that bell beside the bed, all right?'

Sebastian frowned, but Sir Charles laid a hand on his shoulder. 'Don't worry, Dorrell,' he assured him in a low voice. 'They always carry on like this, every time I've come.'

The nurse departed, and they heard her locking the door, before her footsteps retreated along the corridor.

'Well, well, this is – ah ... this is jolly, I must say,' Sebastian observed. 'If the place catches fire, I wonder if they'll remember that we're in here?'

Sir Charles sat down on the uncomfortable tubular steel chair near to the bed. 'Hello there, young Terrier,' he said, leaning towards the hostile lump in the bedclothes. 'He's here, your friend – Captain Dorrell.'

Slowly, a hand reached from beneath the blankets, clutching them back to uncover a shock of rough black hair and one wild eye that glared out between the hair and blankets with a look of miserable accusation. The eye roved around in its accusative glare, fixing first upon Sir Charles, and then upon Sebastian, who stood in uneasy curiosity between the bed and the door.

Then, very softly, the whispering voice that Sebastian had heard over the telephone the night before rose up eerily through the muffling cover of the bedclothes. 'Eyes and ears!' hissed Johnny Terrier. 'Eyes and ears!'

'What's that, old fellow, eh?' asked Sir Charles gently.

'They're listening!' breathed Johnny. 'They're watching me!'

'There's no one here but us,' Sir Charles assured him.

Johnny sat up cautiously in the bed and looked at Sebastian.

'Then who's he?' he asked darkly.

Sir Charles glanced up at Sebastian in surprise, and then back at Johnny. 'Why, this is Captain Dorrell,' he said. 'You know Captain Dorrell, don't you?'

'He's not Captain Dorrell,' said Johnny, quietly and deliberately. 'I don't know him.'

Sir Charles looked shocked, but Sebastian only smiled. 'I'm Sebastian Dorrell,' he said. 'But I think there's – ah ... there's some mistake. I don't know you either, Captain Terrier.'

'Here,' ordered Johnny. 'Here! Fiercely he glared, beckoning Sebastian closer with a frantic curling and uncurling of his finger.

When Sebastian approached, Johnny's hand darted out and clutched him hard by the wrist, dragging him down onto the bed. He scrutinised Sebastian's thin sensuous face, and as he did so he began to smile, as if in recognition. 'You have his face,' he said, 'the very shape of his nose. You're Captain Dorrell exactly – and yet ... different!' He grabbed suddenly at Sebastian's hair. 'Now I begin to see!' He giggled. 'Now I see the trick!'

Sebastian withdrew from Johnny's grasp, flicking back his hair behind his shoulders, out of Johnny's reach. He said, 'I even – ah ... even look like your friend, Captain Dorrell, then? Apparently we were at the same school –

both at Oxford, too. Odd that I never met this mysterious doppelganger of mine, unless, of course, we were in the same places but at different times.'

An eager light gleamed in Johnny's eye. 'Different times!' he exclaimed. 'But that could be it! Johnny doesn't understand so much of it, but wait, wait – I'll show you!' Excitedly he reached beneath the pillow and pulled out a dark long-haired wig, which he brandished triumphantly before putting it on his head, much to the surprise of Sir Charles and Sebastian. 'Now you see.' Johnny giggled again; he pointed to Sebastian, then to himself. He turned to Sir Charles with a gleeful grin. 'Which is which? Who would guess?' He laughed. 'That was how it was done, you see!'

'How what was done?' asked Sir Charles. 'I'm damned if I know what he means, do you, Dorrell?'

'The pretty hair?' Johnny sniggered. 'I thought that too. Not Captain Dorrell, I thought – but she said, *Dress up like Sebastian Dorrell*, she said. He thought Johnny was you!'

'Who thought you were me?' Sebastian asked.

'Professor Joshua Aaronberg,' said Johnny slyly.

'So now we come to it,' said Sebastian. 'You know something about Professor Aaronberg, do you? You said you'd – ah ... said you'd tell me something, and that's why I'm here.'

'But first,' Johnny cooed tauntingly, 'Johnny wants to make a deal with you!' He winked. 'You're going to help Johnny, or else he won't tell you where the Professor is!'

'All right,' said Sebastian. 'I'll do what I can. Now tell me.'

'Start at the beginning,' said Johnny. 'That's the place to start. But let me be Johnny first.' He pulled off the wig.

'Just tell me where the Professor is,' said Sebastian. 'There's a good chap.'

*

Dr Electra Vanderpump knocked perfunctorily on the door of Dr Kotlowski's office; without waiting for him to invite her, she opened the door and walked in.

Dr Kotlowski, pale and gaunt, dressed in black, leapt up in surprise from the chair behind his desk where he had been sitting, and from his hands his plastic lunch box tumbled, crashing open upon the desk-top among his papers and pens.

'Ah – you startle me!' Kotlowski cried. 'I apologise, Dr Vanderpump – forgive me.' He gestured limply at the lunch box. 'Such a stupid mess.'

Electra Vanderpump was cool and elegant in her white laboratory coat that she wore over her bright pink linen dress. Her silver-grey stockings had perfectly straight seams up the back of her slim long legs; her shoes were sleek black patent with stiletto heels. She wore blazing pink lipstick that matched her nail varnish, and her long black hair was tied back with a bright pink chiffon scarf. She looked at Dr Kotlowski with thinly-concealed contempt; she raised a haughty eyebrow. 'Don't let me stop you having your lunch, Dr Kotlowski,' she said coldly. 'It's late – I quite imagined that you'd finished.'

'I was busy,' Kotlowski explained, retrieving his sandwiches from the desk.

Electra noticed that they were wrapped in toilet paper; she looked upon the messy packages with disdain. 'I came to ask you about the little incident last night,' she said. 'Helen tells me that you discovered Terrier using the telephone in my office.'

'A minor problem – have no worry.' Kotlowski's unsteady eyes avoided her cool gaze. He edged into his seat behind the desk, nervously fingering his packages of sandwiches. 'I heard a strange noise in your office. I went in and there was Terrier, speaking down the telephone. That is all. Somehow he deceived the nurse on duty, and he escaped from his room.'

'Who was he telephoning?' Electra asked.

Kotlowski shrugged his shoulders helplessly. 'How should I know, Dr Vanderpump? I have not ask him. No doubt he calls a friend, I imagine.'

Electra sighed. 'It mustn't happen again. We must be particularly cautious with Terrier. He knows too much, and he can't be trusted. Lord Stephen is relying on us to keep Terrier out of harm's way until all this business is over. From now on he must be kept locked in his room at all times.'

'I entirely agree, of course,' said Kotlowski hastily. 'It is all due to my incompetence, my muddle, my bad mistake! I should be shot, Dr Vanderpump! What can I say? But I punish myself in my heart, to think that my neglect has caused this trouble to you – such a fine woman, if I may say so, Dr Vanderpump. If there is more people of your strength and your morality, how much better the world will be!'

'Dr Kotlowski,' said Electra sharply, 'what are you talking about?'

He cringed beneath her stern gaze and uneasily he fingered the toilet paper around his sandwiches. 'My foolish babbling!' he replied humbly. 'It is nothing. I was merely expressing my profound admiration ... and my ... how shall I say it? No, I fear to say it ... '

'What?' said Electra. She moved away from the desk and walked over to the window, looking out onto the forecourt at the front of the house.

'Only my ... regret, Dr Vanderpump,' Kotlowski explained, 'that in all the time I know you, I have never once seen you turn to your Bible for guidance and support. I have had doubts, Dr Vanderpump – sorry doubts, and even fears, I am ashamed to say. How can I even utter my fear – but yet I must. Oh, Dr Vanderpump – ' He gazed towards her as she stood, tall and imperious, by the window, and he braced himself to utter the terrible accusation.

'Dr Kotlowski!' she said at that moment, urgently, staring outside, as one of the cars parked on the forecourt attracted her interest.

'Can it be,' Kotlowski exclaimed in a burst of courage, 'that you are not a Christian woman? Ah – now I have said it, and I am filled with remorse! You have taken offence, Dr Vanderpump – you are angry with me!'

He trembled, for Electra had turned her back to the window and, standing with her hands on her hips, had her icy green eyes fixed upon him with a look of angry suspicion. 'Whose is that car parked outside?' she demanded. 'That green MG? Whose is it? Did you see anyone arrive?'

Kotlowski was dismayed. 'I know nothing,' he said.

Electra strode to the door and flung it open; she walked out into the tiled corridor, her stiletto heels tapping furiously on the tiles. The young blonde nurse who had invited in Sebastian Dorrell and Sir Charles Fothergill by chance appeared at that moment through a door at the other end of the corridor.

'Helen!' called Electra curtly. 'I want you! Come here.'

Apprehensively, Helen approached. Electra beckoned her into Kotlowski's office and over to the window. 'That green car,' she said. 'Whose is it?'

'Oh, I don't know,' said Helen in surprise. 'I suppose it must belong to those people who came.'

Electra scowled. 'Who were they?'

'They came to see Mr Terrier,' Helen explained. 'One was Sir Charles Fothergill who was here before. The other one he introduced as an old Army friend of Mr Terrier's – Captain ... um ... Dorrell, I think it was.'

'As I suspected!' said Electra in a low, angry voice. 'An old Army friend, indeed! Tell me, Helen, dear – did he look like an old Army friend? Was he wearing the uniform? Did he look like anyone even remotely connected to the military?' She smiled sarcastically. 'Or did he, perhaps, have long hair and painted nails?'

'Yes – yes he did,' exclaimed Helen, her startled blue eyes darting in bewilderment to meet Electra Vanderpump's cold, implacable gaze.

'Then why didn't you tell me immediately, for heaven's sake?' demanded Electra in exasperation. 'Wasn't it perfectly obvious that there was something suspicious about him?'

'I'm sorry, Dr Vanderpump,' said Helen. clasping her hands to her face in dismay. She glanced towards Kotlowski, as if she would seek his protection from Electra Vanderpump's wrath. 'Since Mr Terrier was never in the Army anyway – I mean, it's just part of his illness, his fantasy – then he wouldn't have any old Army friends, would he? So I thought, when this man didn't look as if he was in the Army ... '

'You stupid girl!' scolded Electra. She walked over to the door. 'Are they with Terrier now?'

Helen nodded. 'They've been in there about ten or fifteen minutes.'

'Let us hope,' said Electra icily, 'for your sake, my dear, that he has not already revealed too much.'

With a departing look of utter contempt for both Helen and Kotlowski, she marched out of the room.

*

'Just tell me where the Professor is,' said Sebastian. 'There's a good chap.'

Johnny reached up and caught Sebastian's right earlobe between his thumb and forefinger, pulling Sebastian's ear down close to his mouth, so that he could whisper into it. 'Heydn Hall,' he whispered. 'Professor Aaronberg is at Heydn Hall.'

Sebastian sat up again. He stared in suspicion at Johnny's excited face. 'I don't believe you,' he said quietly.

Johnny looked indignant; his small thin face twisted up into an expression of affronted dignity and distress. He opened his mouth to speak, but Sebastian spoke first.

'I know what you want, Terrier,' said Sebastian. 'You want me to go chasing off to – ah ... off to Sussex, don't you – to look for your Lady Caroline Giles? Isn't that right? You think that Lady Caroline is at Heydn Hall, and this is merely a device to get me down there looking for her, isn't it?' He smiled. 'It was a nice try, but I'm not that easily deceived.'

Johnny screwed his thin dry lips together petulantly, and he opened his brown eyes very wide. 'You think I'm lying, Captain Dorrell,' he said in a small strangled voice. 'That's a nasty thing to think. Johnny doesn't like you thinking nasty things about him!'

Sebastian eyed him cynically. 'I think you've been wasting my time, haven't you, Terrier?' he said. 'Somehow you've found out certain – ah … certain facts about me – about my background, my family, my friends – and you're using that to try to – ah … try to manipulate me for purposes best known to yourself.' He smiled grimly. 'For a man who's supposedly – ah … supposedly mentally ill, you're very clever and very devious, but not quite clever enough. I want the truth, Terrier – I want to know why you called me out here today, because I don't believe it was to tell me where my friend the Professor is. I don't believe you know where he is at all, do you?'

'Steady on there, Dorrell!' Sir Charles Fothergill interjected, a note of concern in his voice. He had been listening with some puzzlement through the course of the conversation. 'What is all this about Professor Aaronberg?' he asked. 'What makes you think young Terrier knows anything about him?'

'I do know,' declared Johnny. 'I'm not a dirty, smelly old liar, Captain Dorrell, and you mustn't say I am. I know what happened to Professor Aaronberg because I did it! They got me to dress up as you, with the silly wig and all, and they got me to fly the helicopter, and we picked him up on the cliff-top and took him back to Steve's big yacht. That's what happened to him! They've got him at Heydn Hall now, working on the Machine that vanished Lady Caroline – yes they have! That's what's going on down there – they're making people disappear! Steve's estate manager, Mr Duffy, he disappeared too, and they pretended it didn't happen. Then there was Lady Caroline … ' He paused, gazing at Sebastian imploringly. 'She's beautiful,' he said. 'You've got to save her, Captain Dorrell. She was good to Johnny.' His lip trembled slightly; he glanced away, and unhappily he fingered the bedclothes. 'She was kind to me when they were nasty, she was. We picked

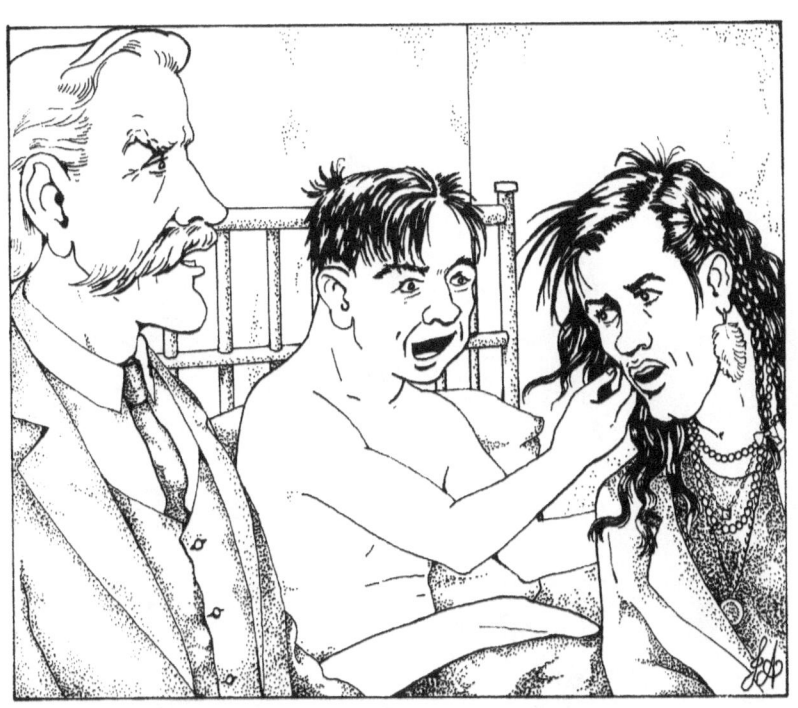

daisies on the lawn. She wore a white dress. She's got nice red hair and grey eyes. She's a pretty lady, Captain Dorrell – the prettiest lady you ever saw. She held my hand – I think she liked me.'

'Yes,' said Sebastian more gently. He sighed; seeing Johnny's distress, his attitude softened slightly. 'I'm sure she liked you, Terrier – Johnny,' he said. 'I'm sure she did. But she's not there now. You know that really don't you, Johnny?'

Johnny sniffed, and a tear rolled from his eye down his cheek.

'She's not at Heydn Hall anymore,' said Sebastian, 'so there's no point in going there to look for her.'

'I was living at the Hall with Karen,' Johnny explained, sniffing back his tears. 'She's my cousin, and she's Steve's girlfriend – he's the Earl. I was there, you see, and Lady Caroline was there ... she was visiting, in her aeroplane.'

'Yes,' said Sebastian. 'She went in her aeroplane, and flew over – '

'No!' cried Johnny fiercely. He shook his head; the tears were pouring down his cheeks. 'No, no, no!' he said miserably.

'I say, Dorrell,' cautioned Sir Charles quietly, 'that's enough – that's enough now. You don't want to upset the poor chap. I think we'd better call the nurse.'

'Wait a minute, Sir Charles,' said Sebastian.

'It wasn't Lady Caroline who went in the aeroplane,' sobbed Johnny. 'It wasn't her – it was Johnny! They made me dress up like her, you see – yes they did! They made me crash her plane and pretend that ... pretend that ... '

'Lady Caroline's dead,' said Sebastian. Softly he laid his hand on Johnny's shoulder.

'They *made* me dress up ... ' persisted Johnny.

'Who did?' Sebastian asked. 'Why should they want you to dress up?'

'Steve did,' said Johnny, wiping away his tears, 'and Karen – she's my cousin, see.'

'And they made you dress up as Lady Caroline,' said Sebastian sceptically, 'and then they made you – ah … made you dress up as me, did they?'

Johnny nodded. 'Yes,' he said. 'Steve and Karen, and Dr Vanderpump – they made me do it. I didn't want to.'

'Vanderpump?' said Sebastian. He withdrew his hand from Johnny's shoulder. He frowned. 'Who's Dr Vanderpump?'

'She's the doctor here,' Johnny explained. 'She says I'm mad. She got me put in here, because of what I know. Johnny doesn't like her,' he added bitterly. 'Lady Caroline didn't like her either.'

'That's enough now, Dorrell,' said Sir Charles. 'Listen – I can hear the nurse coming back.'

There were sharp, loud footsteps approaching along the tiled corridor.

'You don't – ah … you don't mean Dr Electra Vanderpump, do you, by any chance?' Sebastian asked Johnny quickly.

Johnny nodded his head. He said, 'That's her.'

The footsteps halted outside the door, and Sir Charles and Sebastian stood up, turning round as they expected the nurse to come in. The key rattled in the lock and the door was pushed suddenly open, but to their surprise it was not the pretty nurse who stood there: it was the cold and haughty Electra Vanderpump.

'Talk of the devil,' said Sebastian under his breath.

'Good afternoon, gentlemen,' said Electra serenely.

She and Sebastian Dorrell stared at one another, and each read recognition in the other's eyes.

'Ah, doctor,' said Sir Charles, 'this is an old friend of Captain Terrier's – Captain Sebastian Dorrell ... '

'I know who he is,' replied Electra coolly. 'But you're mistaken, I think. He's not an old friend of Mr Terrier's – he's an old friend of mine. Isn't that so, Sebastian, dear?'

CHAPTER 8

Suspicions

Electra Vanderpump's laboratory was at the back of the house, on the first floor. It was a large room, formed by knocking through the dividing wall between two of the original large bedrooms. The ceiling was high, decorated around the cornice with plaster mouldings. The walls were painted pale grey, and many pipes and wires ran over and around the walls, connected to the impressive banks of machinery that stood all around the room. The machinery was clean and white, sheathed in steel casing; there were dials and gauges and viewing screens, and panels of controls and keyboards.

Into this private domain Electra led Sebastian Dorrell, and she locked the door once they were inside. 'Now we can be alone,' she said with satisfaction. 'To talk.'

'It must look a bit – ah ... funny to Sir Charles, what?' remarked Sebastian. 'I mean, bringing him here in one's – ah ... motor car, and then sneaking off upstairs with you, leaving the poor old boy to get home by himself?'

'Dr Kotlowski, my colleague, will call a taxi,' Electra assured him. 'Really, dear! Sir Charles will understand – we're old friends, we haven't seen one another for years. In fact – ' She smiled. 'I think he suspected that we were rather more than friends, don't you? That we were lovers?' Slowly she began to unbutton her white laboratory coat.

Sebastian watched her. He said, 'Well, I was the lover, I think. But since the sentiment of love does not appear to be part of your repertoire, you, I'm afraid, my dear girl, were something else entirely.'

Electra leaned back against the door; she stroked her hands over her skirt, up her slender thighs. 'Something good, I hope?'

Sebastian raised an eyebrow. 'You – good? My dear fellow, if I didn't know you better, I would say you were joking!'

Electra laughed. 'Dr Kotlowski regrets that I am not a Christian woman!' she explained. 'He can be frightfully tedious at times.'

'A psychiatrist?' asked Sebastian. 'Like you?'

'A psychiatrist,' replied Electra, slipping off her laboratory coat and dangling it casually from one finger, 'but not like me.'

Sebastian grinned. 'Of course,' he said, 'because in that respect too, old sport, you are something else entirely.'

'No,' said Electra. 'Because Dr Kotlowski is like nothing on earth. Imagine – he wraps his sandwiches in lavatory paper! And there's no fly in his trousers – they zip up at the side.'

Sebastian frowned. 'A trifle inconvenient, I would have thought. How does he – ah ... '

'Oh, he doesn't,' Electra answered simply. 'That's the whole point.'

'Good grief,' said Sebastian. 'I suppose that explains why he uses the paper to wrap his sandwiches instead.'

'I mean,' Electra explained, stepping away from the

door and approaching Sebastian, 'that he doesn't have sexual relations. He abstains, you see – from sex, from alcohol, from entertainment and revelry, as he calls it. In fact, I've found that he abstains from most things in life.'

'Good Lord,' said Sebastian. 'Perhaps he's – ah ... perhaps he's an android, after all.'

'No, he's a Catholic,' said Electra.

'I was thinking of one of your machines, old sport,' said Sebastian. 'One of your clever electronic devices. I thought perhaps you'd constructed him out of silicon chips, what?'

Electra ran the tip of her finger down his chest; she looked straight into his eyes. She said, 'Come over here, dear, and I'll show you one of my clever devices.'

'Sounds like fun,' remarked Sebastian as he followed her across the room.

'It is,' she said. She pressed a button on one of the consoles.

Slowly, a large double bed covered by a black fur counterpane folded down out of the wall.

'Ingenious,' Sebastian commented. 'What's this in aid of, then?'

'Nothing,' replied Electra. She rested her arms upon his shoulders; she moved her mouth close to his. She said, 'That's the difference between you and Kotlowski. He does everything for charity and out of duty – you do everything for fun.'

'Now I'm serious,' said Sebastian. 'Let's get down to business.'

He unzipped her dress; she unzipped his trousers. They sat down on the bed.

'Oh, Sebastian,' said Electra with a smile, 'I've waited a long time for this. At the risk of sounding horribly sentimental – dare say I've missed you?'

Soon they were lying naked together upon the fur, their clothes discarded on the grey tiled floor. As they slowly kissed, Electra extended her slender arm over Sebastian's head and pressed another button on the console beside the bed; at once, the bed began to vibrate gently.

'I want some questions answered,' said Sebastian.

'Later, darling, later,' sighed Electra, as he kissed her neck and shoulder.

'About Johnny Terrier,' said Sebastian, as his lips moved down to her white breast.

Electra laughed. 'Oh yes,' she said, 'of course – you're a friend from his days in the Army.' She tugged at his long hair and flicked it softly against his back. 'So this is how they're wearing it in the Air Corps nowadays?' she said. 'Times have certainly changed.'

'Ah, you've noticed – the regulation haircut,' said Sebastian. 'Do you like it?' He sucked a nipple.

'Darling, I adore it,' she replied. 'But I do believe that old fool, Fothergill, really thinks you're in the Air Corps! How can he honestly believe it?'

'People believe any old rubbish if they're told it often enough,' said Sebastian.

'Oh, you think everyone's an idiot except you,' said Electra. 'You're so arrogant!'

Sebastian grinned. 'I know I am.'

'And infuriatingly handsome!' cried Electra. 'Irresistibly attractive!'

'True – too true,' Sebastian murmured.

'Oh, climb onto me – I want to feel you,' said Electra. 'Oh, Sebastian!' She sighed. 'But you're right – Sir Charles believes all that nonsense that Terrier tells him.'

'You think it's – ah ... think it's all nonsense?' asked Sebastian, gazing down into her cold green eyes.

'Of course,' replied Electra. 'Don't you?'

Sebastian stared down at her thin, handsome face: he knew that she was cunning and he knew that she had deceived him in the past. It was hard to see when she was not telling the truth, so he had learned never to trust her.

'Terrier has a psychological problem,' explained Electra. 'The medical term for it is paranoid schizophrenia. In other words, dear, he has delusions – he imagines that people are plotting against him, and that his being brought here is part of the plot.'

Sebastian pressed his mouth over hers and they snuggled into the fur in a close embrace. Electra reached out her arm again and operated another control on the console; to the soothing sound of gentle music, the bed began to move up and down, from side to side, and for a while they made love without talking. Electra pressed another button and the soothing music changed to heavy rock.

'You don't believe me!' she gasped, as their activity became more frantic.

'Why d'you say that?' asked Sebastian.

'Because you believe Terrier,' said Electra, 'and he's been telling you ridiculous tales about me.'

'Now who's paranoid?' said Sebastian with a smile.

Electra turned up the volume of the music, and they continued to make love. Presently, they collapsed exhausted on the fur.

Electra lay with her arm across Sebastian's chest, and gently he caressed her dark hair.

'You haven't changed, Sebastian,' she said.

'Neither have you,' he replied.

'No, I'm serious,' said Electra. 'I mean, you really haven't changed, have you?' She raised her hand and stroked his cheek with the tip of her finger. 'I'm talking about your Chair, Sebastian,' she said.

'What chair?' he queried.

'Don't be absurd!' Electra scolded. 'As if I didn't know! With that Chair, Sebastian, you're the master of time. You can move about in time, as you please. You need never age – you need never die.'

Sebastian chuckled softly. 'The Chair has nothing to do with it.'

Electra supported herself on her forearms; indignantly she stared down into Sebastian's mocking eyes. 'The Chair has everything to do with it!' she declared. 'The Chair is a time machine, and I know that as well as you do!'

'You're wrong there, old sport,' said Sebastian. 'It's not a machine at all.'

Electra flung herself back on the bed. 'Why do you persist in keeping it from me?' she exclaimed in exasperation. 'One of these days, dear, I'll find out your secret, whether you co-operate or not.'

Sebastian laughed. 'I'll be interested to see how you manage it.'

'Oh, I will,' Electra assured him. 'I'll find a way – it's not impossible.' She gazed up at the ceiling. 'Let's do it again,' she said.

'Again?' said Sebastian. 'Now?'

'Again and again,' said Electra. 'There isn't another man in the world like you, Sebastian, and I want you, how I want you – your power, your knowledge, everything about you. I never found a man my equal until I found you. The rest are fools and weaklings.'

'Just tell me one thing, old sport,' said Sebastian as he climbed onto her. 'How did Johnny Terrier know about me?'

Electra smiled. 'Haven't you guessed? Of course, I told him – it was part of my plan to lure you here.'

Sebastian laughed. 'Now, that I don't believe,' he said.

*

Later, when Sebastian had gone, Electra spoke to Dr Kotlowski in his office.

'I've interrogated Mr Dorrell,' she said.

'And how much has Terrier told him?' asked Kotlowski.

'Very little, I believe,' said Electra. 'Terrier is extremely incoherent, and whatever he had to say would sound fairly unconvincing. That sort of thing doesn't impress Mr Dorrell very much. However, he seemed more puzzled about how Terrier knew him in the first place, and that, unfortunately, is a mystery that even I can't explain.' She frowned. 'But I don't know ... It seems related somehow to Terrier's delusions about being in the Air Corps. I wonder ... ' She glanced at Kotlowski, and there was a gleam of excitement in her green eyes. 'May I use your telephone?' she said as she lifted the receiver to her ear. 'It's suddenly occurred to me – perhaps there's more to this than would first appear.'

'I do not understand, Dr Vanderpump,' said Kotlowski weakly. 'Your mind works so much more swiftly and astutely than my own. I am still wonder who is this man, Captain Dorrell, why does he comes here? I am still in the dark, Dr Vanderpump, when your brilliant brain sees all!'

Hastily, Electra dialled a number. She said, 'I am beginning to think, could they possibly have met before – in the Air Corps, as Terrier claims? Mr Dorrell has no recollection of it, obviously – he was never in the Air Corps. And according to Karen Black, Terrier was never in the Air Corps either, but it occurs to me ... ah, hello?' she said into the telephone. 'Is that Miss Black? No, dear, I don't want Lord Stephen, just for the moment. In fact, I was interested in asking you one or two questions about your cousin, Mr Terrier.'

*

The evening of the same day, Sebastian Dorrell telephoned Sir Charles Fothergill.

'Sorry I couldn't – ah ... drive you back, Sir Charles,' he said.

'The doctor paid for a taxi,' said Sir Charles. 'Hm ... I think they wanted to get rid of me. And that Vanderpump woman is a friend of yours? Funny coincidence, wasn't it?'

'Yes,' agreed Sebastian, 'but I'm getting used to funny coincidences lately. Actually, it's because of Electra Vanderpump that I telephoned you, Sir Charles. You see, when she's involved, there generally tends to be something – ah ... something dodgy going on, and in view of that I'm more inclined to take Terrier's story seriously.'

'So you believe him now, do you?' asked Sir Charles in surprise. 'I must say, Dorrell, I thought you were a bit hard on the poor fellow. I quite thought you didn't believe a word of what he was saying.'

'I didn't,' said Sebastian, 'until he mentioned Electra Vanderpump. That woman is the very devil, I'm telling you, Sir Charles. She'd certify a sane man, if it suited her purposes. Kidnapping, murder – I wouldn't put anything past her. On top of that, she seemed damn concerned to put me off the scent when I questioned her about Terrier, and that makes me suspicious, of course. What I wanted to – ah ... wanted to ask you is whether you're going to visit Terrier again soon, because I wondered if you'd give him a message from me.'

'Well,' said Sir Charles hesitantly, 'I would have done, but I don't know that they'll allow me back there now. As I was leaving, that Dr Kotlowski fellow – and he's a queer customer, if ever there was one – he told me that young Terrier's not up to having visitors at the moment. It's a rum show, Dorrell – a rum show. I'm not happy about Terrier's being locked up in that place – not happy at all.'

'Neither am I,' said Sebastian, 'and I'd like him to know that I'm doing something about it. If you do see him, Sir Charles, perhaps you'd tell him this – but make sure that no one else is listening. Tell him that I've gone down to Heydn Hall to see what I can find out. It should – ah ... should put his mind at rest, at least – provided Dr Vanderpump doesn't get to know about it.'

'By Jove,' commented Sir Charles, 'so you're actually going to look into it, are you?'

'Yes,' said Sebastian. 'I'll be going down to Heydn Hall tomorrow.'

CHAPTER 9

Of UFOs, PRATS,
and other Strange Phenomena

The foregoing account explains how it came about that
Sebastian Dorrell was driving along the lane to Heydn
Hall near Newhaven on the afternoon when Miss Gladys
Armstrong disappeared.

After he had been told by Miss Amelia Armstrong that
he was on the right road for the Hall, Sebastian drove back
to the small fishing village of Newhaven and found a room
at the Black Dog, an inn near to the sea front. It was seven
o'clock by the time he had unpacked his bags, washed and
eaten a meal; but Sebastian discovered that his watch had
stopped at five o'clock. He reset it to the correct time and
was pleased to find that it started again.

The evening was fine and warm, so he decided to drive
back along the lane to Heydn Hall and take a look at the
place before it grew dark. The sky was dusk as he drove
away from Newhaven, and along the lane, near to the
Hall, where the trees were old and grew densely, the
shadows were deep and cold. Sebastian switched on the
headlamps to light his way.

He drove for nearly a mile along the lane without
passing anyone. Once, he glanced at his watch, realising

that, again, it was not telling the correct time: but the light was dimming swiftly, and it appeared to be much later than when he had set out. He had brought his camera and binoculars, but it was already too dark to take photographs.

As he drew close to Heydn Hall, something pale, moving along the verge on the right-hand side of the lane, attracted his attention as it passed into the beam of the headlamps. Sebastian drove more slowly as he approached: now he could see that it was a group of three young men and three girls strolling along the side of the road, and it was the pale summer dresses of the girls that had caught the beam of the headlamps. It occurred to Sebastian, however, that there was a quality of strangeness about these people – a peculiarity in their style of dress – but before his car drew alongside them, they stepped up onto the verge and disappeared from view among the trees, so that he was unable to observe them clearly. Nevertheless, his curiosity about them had been aroused: their clothing had seemed so quaint, oddly Edwardian in style. He wondered if he should follow them, although they had perhaps entered the grounds of Heydn Hall.

He was very near to the Hall now, so he stopped the car and climbed out, taking the binoculars with him but leaving the camera on the seat. It was much darker; clouds had gathered overhead and a cold wind had begun to blow. Sebastian wondered if it were about to rain.

Quickly, he walked up the lane until he came to the place where he had seen the people before they left the road; but the hedge was thick and high, impenetrable at that point, and behind it rose a forbidding barrier of iron railings that marked the boundary of the Earl's estate, so that Sebastian was puzzled as to where the people he had

seen could have gone. He turned and walked back, peering with curiosity into the hedge, but he could see no
break in the dense, thorny growth. A gate or stile or
opening in the hedge and in the fence through which they
could have passed was not immediately apparent. It was
not until he was walking back again towards the Hall that
he noticed an iron gatepost behind a holly bush that grew
close to the fence. He mounted the bank to investigate
further, but the holly bush proved to be an obstruction,
and it was with the greatest difficulty that he managed to
press behind it.

In the darkness, he could not see the gate, but when he
touched it, he felt the iron bars, rough with flaking scales
of rust, and his hand, as he groped for the bolt that secured
the gate shut, came into contact with an ancient, rusty
chain that was wrapped around the post and the bars of
the gate, and fastened with a padlock. His fingers touched
cobwebs and soft, cold, damp growths, and the cool leaves
of climbing plants. Plainly the gate had not been opened
for many years, and it seemed impossible that the people
he had seen could have used it.

Then, a strange shriek sounded in the air above him,
startling him to stillness for a moment, so that he stood
listening in silence: it must have been the cry of a bird, he
decided, but he could hear no birds now. His eyes had
adjusted to the gloom beneath the trees and he could make
out the shadowy form of the old gate; in the wood beyond,
nothing stirred. There was no one else about and no
sounds or signs to indicate the presence of animals or men.
Sebastian laid his hands on the gate and stared between
the bars into the deep darkness beneath the trees.

He was going to turn away and walk further up the
lane to the main entrance, but just as he was about to

remove his hands from the gate, he felt a violent vibration in the iron bars, and a peculiar shuddering, whining sound set up. Sebastian tried to free his grip, but found that he was unable to do so. As the noise increased around him and he began to feel an icy tingling sensation passing through his limbs, he wondered for a moment if he had accidentally operated an alarm device or an electrical guarding system connected to the fence, but he dismissed the thought at once. Brilliant flashes of blue and green light erupted from the shadows, and a fierce wind whistled around him.

Dizzily he collapsed against the gate, but it seemed to dissolve as he fell upon it, and the ground was very far away, and he found himself floating down for several seconds through a cold, viscous substance, before he landed sprawling on the damp earth and leaves. The boughs of the trees were violently agitated, tossing and rustling overhead, and wild wailing and shrieking filled the air.

Sebastian scrambled to his feet and stumbled forward; the earth seemed to be heaving beneath him, and all around flashed blue and green lights. In the darkness also he saw other points of light that glowed, like the yellow eyes of creatures watching him. He struggled on, crashing through the dark wood and the howling storm that shook the trees, uncertain of the direction, but hoping to find his way back to the road, until at last the trees parted and he sensed the vastness of air above him filled with watching eyes and the movement of dark wings; and, high above, storm clouds were racing before the wind.

He looked ahead and saw a great building, the jagged line of its steep roof and eccentric castellations silhouetted against the livid sky: upon a high tower, gleaming whitely above the yellow glare of many lighted windows, was a

massive pyramidal prism that seemed to be the source of the cadaverous light that illuminated the trees, the bushes and the smooth lawns all around. Sebastian paused, gazing upon Heydn Hall: he realised at once that he had been running in the wrong direction, away from the road. Lit up luridly beneath the stormy sky, the great house appeared quite different from how it had looked when he had first glimpsed it through the trees, earlier that afternoon, grey and gloomy in the bright sunlight. Now it was a place of lightning and fluctuating weird shadows, eerie, forbidding, and with a strange air of unreality about it, as if it were a painted backdrop on a stage.

As though he were in a dream, Sebastian turned away and set off at a brisk pace back through the trees in search of the old gate in the iron fence, but he did not find it; instead, inexplicably, after he had been walking for a few minutes, he found himself once again in the lane.

It was raining heavily now, but above the noise of the rain, Sebastian heard another sound: persistent, strident and disconcerting. It was a car horn.

He ran along the lane to where he had left his sports car, and as it came into view, he was shocked to see that all its lights were on, the indicators flashing and the windscreen wipers moving frantically back and forth; the engine, too, was running, and the horn was blaring continuously. He stopped short in the road and stared at the car in bewilderment and consternation. He turned and gazed back along the lane: the gloom beneath the trees was still alive with blue and green sparks, but now he was not sure whether the strange lights had an objective reality or whether they emanated within his own brain. He could no longer think clearly. The sound of the horn was deafening; he felt confused, and sickness overwhelmed him. Clutching his hands to his head, he staggered away in the direction from which he had come and collapsed exhausted onto the steep bank of the verge, among the cow parsley, nettles and long grass.

When he came to himself again, the air was still and the rain had ceased; there was silence and darkness.

Cautiously, he sat up, and something behind him poked him and grabbed him by the hair. He leapt to his feet at once, turning to discover that his assailant had been nothing more dangerous than a holly bush: it was the bush which grew in front of the iron gate. Once again he reached out his hand behind the bush, feeling for the gate. He touched the rusty chain, running his hand along it, feeling the heavy padlock: the chain was still intact, fastened around the gatepost.

He could not account for it: a short time before, it had seemed to him that the gate must have opened, that he had passed through into the wood, that he had seen Heydn Hall in the storm; yet now, here he was on the outside of the locked gate, and it was as if all that he remembered had never happened.

Baffled, and with a feeling of frustration, he climbed down the bank again, onto the road. He was tired, cold and damp, and it was growing very late; he looked at his watch and found that it had stopped again. He did not feel like investigating any further that evening: he wanted only to get back to his room at the inn and take a warm bath.

The sports car was where he had left it, its engine silent now, and all the lights off. It was a mystery that he could not understand, and he did not like it.

*

When Sebastian arrived back at the Black Dog, there was a coach parked in the car park, which had brought a large party of people dressed in shabby anoraks and wellington boots, who were ambling around outside and by the entrance to the bar; Sebastian eyed them with mild amusement.

He parked his sports car, picked up his camera off the passenger seat, and went into the bar, where several of the people in anoraks had already gathered; more of them came in after him. They were talking loudly and enthusiastically among themselves, but the topic of their conversation seemed to Sebastian to be very technical and obscure. Most of them were middle-aged or elderly: the men were balding, the women had long grey hair fastened up eccentrically with rubber bands and cheap plastic slides. Many wore spectacles and hearing-aids. The women wore badly-fitting slacks or long tweed skirts.

Taking off his damp jacket, Sebastian approached the bar. Suddenly he heard a voice close to his shoulder.

'Hello – haven't seen you before,' said the man.

Sebastian turned round, looking down to see who had spoken. A small man with a wispy beard and thin greying hair combed forward to conceal baldness stood there. Like most of the other people in the room, he was wearing a shabby parka anorak with a fur-trimmed hood; his trousers were ill-fitting, slightly too long, and sagging around the ankles. He wore also wire-framed spectacles and a hearing-aid. 'I'm Cyril Luckett, the Secretary,' he said with an air of amiable self-importance. He spoke in a high-pitched nasal whine.

Sebastian smiled at him in brief acknowledgement. 'Are you – ah ... are you with this lot?' he asked, gesturing at the crowd who had just come in.

'Oh ... sorry, sorry!' said Mr Luckett. 'I thought I hadn't seen you before – you're not one of us, then? You haven't come for the PRATS convention?'

Sebastian raised an eyebrow. 'What?'

'PRATS,' said Mr Luckett again. 'We research into para-psychology, you know, and train people to develop their psi potential. Are you interested in psi at all, by any chance?'

Sebastian ordered a lemonade at the bar. He turned back to Mr Luckett. 'I say, you're not – ah ... not the UFO enthusiasts, are you?' he asked, suddenly remembering the remark made to him that afternoon by the old lady of whom he had asked directions in the lane, near to Heydn Hall.

'Ah, you've heard about the UFOs, then?' remarked Mr Luckett with a short bleating laugh. 'That's why we de-cided to hold the convention here this year, actually. Some of the members wanted to have a look at the place for themselves – Heydn Hall. D'you know it? Apparently there've been quite a few sightings around there recently.'

Sebastian sipped his lemonade. More PRATS members had gathered noisily around the bar by now, and were ordering drinks.

Mr Luckett ordered half a pint of lager. 'Of course, it's not just the UFOs,' he said. 'There's been all manner of phenomena around here, over the years. The name of this place, for instance – the Black Dog – there's a story in itself, eh?' He bleated softly. 'Know anything about Black Dogs, do you?'

'Not really,' said Sebastian.

'They're manifestations of psychic energy,' Mr Luckett explained with a knowing nod. 'My personal theory is that it can all be accounted for by the ley system. Heydn Hall, you see – its right at the junction of several ley lines. It's at these points that psi energy, passing along the leys, builds up and produces such phenomena as Black Dogs and UFOs and whatnot.'

'I see,' said Sebastian. 'And you think that's what's going on at Heydn Hall, do you?'

Mr Luckett took a gulp of his lager. 'Undoubtedly!' he said. 'A party of us went along there yesterday. We couldn't go in the house – that was something of a disappointment. There's not much to see from the outside, but some of us sensed a definite psychic atmosphere about the place. There's a coldness about it, if you get my meaning. Did you say you'd been there?'

'I went this afternoon, as a matter of fact,' said Sebastian.

'See anything interesting?' asked Mr Luckett with a bleating laugh.

Sebastian shrugged; he drank his lemonade. 'I wouldn't – ah ... wouldn't know what to look for,' he said.

'Ah, you'd know all right if you saw anything,' Mr Luckett answered with a smile. 'You know, I first heard of Heydn Hall when I was doing a talk on ley lines and UFO sightings, a few months back. Afterwards, a chap came out of the audience and told me what had happened to him. He was driving along the lane that runs from here to Seaford, past the Hall, and it was late at night, you see – dark. Then he sees these lights, hovering – blue and green lights, all around – overhead, in the trees at the side of the road, everywhere he looked. Some of them were quite big too, like glowing spheres, he said. He was terrified out of his wits, as you can imagine, but anyway, he keeps on driving. Next thing that happens, the windscreen wipers start up and he can't stop them, and the headlamps are flickering on and off, bright then dim, and the indicators are going, and the fan and the lights inside the car – the whole works. Whatever it was, these hovering lights and stuff, it'd interfered with the electrics, you see. A bit further along the road, once he got past the Hall, everything returned to normal – that was the end of it. So what d'you make of that, eh? It's one of those mysteries, isn't it? Must admit, I find these things fascinating myself.'

'Yes,' said Sebastian. He frowned.

'Anyway, cheers!' said Mr Luckett, raising his glass. 'Someone's calling me, over there.' He turned and signalled to someone across the room. 'I think he wants a word, so I'll say goodbye for the moment. Must be getting late. D'you know the time, by any chance?'

Sebastian glanced at his watch, and then he remembered that it had stopped. 'Sorry,' he said. 'My watch has been playing up this afternoon.'

'That's another thing,' remarked Mr Luckett. 'You've reminded me.' He chuckled his sheep-like laugh. 'That chap, when he was driving past Heydn Hall – his watch stopped too, and he never could get it to go properly after that! Maybe the same has happened to yours, eh?' He laughed. 'Anyway, I'll be seeing you,' he said, turning away and taking his drink with him.

Sebastian followed him with his eyes as he crossed the room. Mr Luckett's story seemed to confirm that Sebastian's own experience had not been simply an hallucination while he was unconscious.

Sebastian finished his lemonade and went upstairs to his own room. It was not until much later, when he was taking a bath, that he suddenly remembered that he had brought in only his camera from the car: the binoculars had not been with him, and he could not remember having had them with him since leaving Heydn Hall. He realised with annoyance that he had probably dropped them in the lane or on the grass bank beside the fence, where he had fallen unconscious, and that he would have to go back and search for them tomorrow.

CHAPTER 10

Lord Stephen's Fear

Standing at the window of the Morning Room, Lord Stephen Mitchell, the Earl of Newhaven, watched as two policemen climbed into the police car outside on the fore-court and drove off down the gravel drive, out of view. The Earl's brow was furrowed by a deep frown; unhap-pily, he caressed his jaw as he continued to stare outside at the deserted drive until, in great agitation, he turned his back upon the window and began to pace back and forth across the room, his hands buried moodily in the pockets of his grey flannel trousers.

The eighteenth-century furnishings and Adam decor of the room were tasteful and elegant, and the burly Earl, hot and bothered, his blond hair wildly tousled, scowling and red in the face as he strode up and down over the pale blue and gold carpet, between the delicate powder blue silk-upholstered couches, looked absurdly out of place; anyone observing him might have had good reason to suspect that his mind was greatly troubled.

Just then, the door to the left of the fireplace opened, and Karen Black came in timidly. She was dressed in a lime green mini dress and bright pink tights that made her legs look as if they had been scalded; there was a matching bow tied around her hair and it flopped down over one ear.

'Oh, Steve!' she wailed. 'Oh, Steve!'

The Earl ceased his pacing up and down; he glared at her. 'Stop whining, woman!' he said impatiently. 'Everything's under control – they don't suspect a thing.'

'But that's not the point, is it,' Karen objected, wringing her hands together awkwardly. 'It don't matter what the police think, 'cos they wouldn't understand anyhow what you're trying to do, Steve. What matters is the fact that someone else has disappeared now.'

'Good God!' roared the Earl, slapping his thighs. 'What's the matter with you? Some old woman picking blackberries in the lane disappears, the police come here making routine inquiries – and the next thing we know, you're getting bloody hysterical about it! Just like a woman – fly off the bloody handle at the least little thing! Good God, we don't even know that it's anything to do with us – she could've disappeared anyway! Probably fell down in a ditch and broke her neck. Or maybe she got absent-minded and wandered off somewhere. They do funny things sometimes, these old dears – who knows what might've happened to her. No point in jumping to conclusions and getting bloody paranoid and hysterical about it!'

'Sorry,' said Karen meekly. 'I didn't mean to. But it's just that ... it's just ... oh, Steve!' she wailed, gazing imploringly into his fierce blue eyes. 'Suppose it is our fault! First Mr Duffy, and then poor Lady Caroline – and now this!'

The Earl smiled wryly. 'Yes,' he said, 'and do you think it's any better for me? What d'you think I've been doing all this time, Karen, mm? What d'you think I've been doing down in that cellar all these years, slaving away at it day after day, night after night, until I'm bloody sick of it!' He flung up his arms in a ferocious gesture of exasperation. 'What d'you bloody well think I'm trying to do, Karen? Well, I'll tell you – I'm trying to put an end to this business, once and for all, because I care about what's happening here – I care more than anyone! And you know why, Karen – because Mr Duffy wasn't the first. What about my father – what about my grandfather? D'you think I'm doing all this just for fun? Good God, Karen – I'm trying to sort out this whole damn mess, but the way you carry on sometimes, anyone'd think I was trying to make it worse!'

Karen sighed; she walked across the room and stood with her back to him. She fingered a Meissen figurine of Venus that stood on one of the tables. 'I know what you're trying to do, Steve,' she said, 'but the fact of the matter is, it's not getting better – it is getting worse, isn't it? And what I don't like is that woman, Dr Vanderpump, and the way she's doing things here. I just don't like her way of dealing with it, and I don't like her, either.'

'Then what in God's name do you expect me to do?' protested Lord Stephen. 'I got Dr Vanderpump in on this because I knew I couldn't handle it alone, and now you blame me for the very fact that I get some expert advice when I need it!'

'Yeah,' agreed Karen, 'but she ain't really an expert on this sort of thing, is she? She's a psychiatrist or a psychoanalyst or something. I'm sorry, Steve, but I just don't see what a bleedin' psychiatrist has got to do with this business about people disappearing and that stuff what you've got down in the cellar.'

'Oh, I see, it's like that, is it?' Lord Stephen began to pace up and down again, pounding his fist into the palm of his other hand. 'You don't like me seeing a psychoanalyst, do you? That's the trouble with you working-class people – you're so proud, when it comes down to it! You think there's some stigma attached to having counselling. Well, let me tell you, some of the best people have been psychoanalysed and are all the better for it! I'm not ashamed to be under a psychoanalyst, Karen. I'll be blunt about it – I'm a blunt sort of chap – and getting myself psychoanalysed was the best decision I ever made in my life!'

Karen turned round to face him. She shook her head sadly. 'Oh, Steve, you know I'm not against psychiatrists and psychoanalysts for people what need them and everything. And it's got nothing to do with me being working-class. Anyhow, you shouldn't say such things, you with your precious socialist ideals! What's happening to you, Steve? Can't you see what that woman's doing to you? She's making it all so much worse!'

'Well, that's all you know!' declared the Earl scornfully. 'Before I had psychoanalysis, I was groping in the dark, clutching at straws. I didn't know whether I was coming or going – I was at my wit's end, I can tell you. But look at me now! I'm a new man – determined, resolute, fighting fit, and ready for action! That's what Dr Vanderpump's done for me, and I'm not ashamed to admit it!'

'Yeah, but when someone has psychoanalysis,' said Karen, 'it's to get help with their feelings, not to go down in the cellar mucking about with old machinery. That woman was never trying to help in the first place. She wants something out of you, Steve, and that's the only reason she comes here.'

'Jealousy – pure jealousy!' declared the Earl. 'That's what it is – that's your problem, Karen.'

'Me jealous of her?' cried Karen. 'Don't make me laugh! She's old, she's ugly and she's a bitch – but it ain't that I mind about so much – it's the way she made it look as if Lady Caroline was killed in her aeroplane, and the way she made Johnny go along with the cover-up by making him think I was in danger.'

'Well, you are in danger, for God's sake!' yelled the Earl, gesticulating wildly. 'We're all bloody well in danger, living here – we're sitting on a bloody powder keg, I keep telling you! What would you have done, then? Tell the whole world what really happened to Lady Caroline? Is that what you'd do, eh? Then we'd all be locked up in the bloody madhouse – not just your cousin Johnny! No, Karen, no, no – we've got to keep it secret, we've got to play it down, cover it up, until the whole damn mess is sorted out.'

'I don't care,' said Karen obstinately. 'I still don't like it. You couldn't trust Johnny to keep quiet about it, so you had him put away. Lady Caroline disappeared, so you covered it up. How long before your friend Dr Vanderpump decides to get me put away too?'

Lord Stephen sighed. 'Now, Karen, that's nonsense,' he said, stepping towards her and laying his hands comfortingly upon her shoulders.

'It ain't nonsense!' She shrugged him off fiercely. 'With Dr Vanderpump you wouldn't stop at anything – I can see it happening, Steve! What about Professor Aaronberg? That was Dr Vanderpump's idea, too. There was a time when you'd never've thought of kidnapping anybody – but you do it now, just 'cos Dr Vanderpump says so!'

'That's rubbish!' retorted the Earl. 'I don't know what

you're complaining about, anyway – you seemed to think it was a good idea yourself, not so long ago. What does it matter – he won't be missed. A silly old intellectual bull-shitter – no one'd notice if a few of his sort went missing.'

Karen tossed her short dark hair petulantly. 'If he's such a silly old bullshitter, I don't see what you wanted him for in the first place. Anyhow,' she said, 'I think he's a nice old bloke, and it's not fair to keep him shut up in the cellar. It's a rotten shame.'

'Just like a woman!' exclaimed the Earl, slapping his thigh in impatience. 'Have to make a bloody fuss, getting sentimental and emotional about everything!'

'Oh, stop it!' wailed Karen, turning her back on him and flouncing towards the door. 'You always say it's just be-cause I'm a woman, every time I say I don't like some-thing.' Defiantly, she turned to face him again, her hand on the doorknob. 'Well, Dr Vanderpump's a woman too,' she said, 'and she's not sentimental or emotional – she doesn't bloody care about anything! Why don't you stop listening to her and listen to me for a change, eh?' She flung open the door and strode out of the room.

'Come back here!' yelled the Earl. 'Come back and don't be so damn stupid!'

He heard her angry footsteps retreating, through the visitors' souvenir shop, through the entrance hall beyond.

He slammed his fist against the chimney-breast in silent, futile rage. His mind was in a turmoil, filled with disconcerting memories and his fears for what the future might hold; disturbing images from his past came welling up, and he tried to dispel them.

He remembered a night long ago, when he had been a child, when he had stood, fascinated, at his bedroom win-dow, watching the glass prism on the Prince's Tower blazing with eerie light in the darkness. He had watched in terror and awe, until his mother had come into the room and had ordered him back into bed. That night, as on many previous occasions, his father, the nineteenth Earl, had gone down into the cellars to work on a secret project; the difference on that particular occasion was that he was never seen again, and in the morning, Lord Stephen's mother had told him that his father was dead.

Lord Stephen shut the memory from his mind; he walked out of the Morning Room, through the souvenir shop (where the displays had been taken down for the period that the house was not open to the public), through the entrance hall and up the stairs. He intended to go up to his office, but before he reached the first floor landing, he changed his mind: something was urging him to go down to the cellars, and it was an urge that he could not resist.

*

The eighteenth Earl, Lord Mountjoy Horsley-Mitchell, Lord Stephen's grandfather, had mysteriously disappeared over sixty years earlier. After the death of the nineteenth Earl, Lord Geoffrey Horsley-Mitchell, rumours had begun to spread that he was not actually dead but that, like his father, he too had mysteriously disappeared. Lord Stephen, throughout his youth, had also had his suspicions about the fate of his father.

There had been a funeral, but Lord Stephen never saw his father's body. He had been told by his mother that the death was sudden, caused by a heart attack, yet he knew that his father had always been a fit man. After the funeral, the coffin was carried to the family mausoleum in the grounds of the Hall.

Since that time, Lord Stephen had always been uneasy

in his mind, and nothing said by his mother or his uncle (who had come to the Hall to help manage the running of the house and the estate after Lord Geoffrey's death) would comfort him. The thought that his father was not really dead had obsessed Lord Stephen. He wanted to know about his father's work, down in the cellars that were always kept locked now; and the sinister Prince's Tower, the single entrance and ground floor windows of which had been bricked up since the time of his grandfather, also aroused his curiosity. From the earliest age, Lord Stephen had suspected that all was not as it should be at Heydn Hall.

When he was fifteen, there had been a serious problem with the drains: the smell of putrefaction had filled the house; but for Lord Stephen's troubled mind, it had a deeper significance. One night, he had had a disturbing dream that it was his father's body, unburied and rotting down in the cellar, that had caused the terrible smell. It was this morbid thought that had finally prompted him to find out the truth about his father: to find out whether he was dead or not.

He had a simple plan: he would break into the family mausoleum at the dead of night, prise up the lid of his father's coffin, and take a look inside. It was clear to him what he must do.

The mausoleum was hidden in the woods on the estate, about three hundred yards from the house. There were high iron railings around it, with a locked gate, and the door of the building was kept locked too.

In his mother's desk, Lord Stephen had found the keys. As he passed through the woods, he felt afraid: he was scared by the moonlight on the rustling leaves, and he was scared of the whispering wind and of the sound of his own footsteps as he crept through the black shadows. More than this, however, his own guilt spread a dreadful pall of horror over everything; but he tried not to think of that, not to think that what scared him most was not the darkness and the creaking trees and the cold tombs where the bones of his ancestors lay, but the terrible thing that he had set about doing. If his suspicions should turn out to have been unfounded, he would have done what a son should never do, disturbing his father's body in its last resting place.

But thoughts of that he shut out of his mind, as, many years later, he would learn to shut out other doubts and fears and feelings that he did not like to own.

He pulled himself up easily over the railings, though he ripped his shirt as he leapt down on the other side. The blood was pounding in his head with fear. In a couple of strides, he had reached the door, and he pulled out the big iron key from his pocket, fumbling in the gloom to fit it into the lock. The heavy oak door grated on its hinges as he heaved it open and stepped in boldly, though his hand trembled when he took out his electric torch.

He hesitated then, for the idea of shining a light into that grim, windowless hall made his heart sink. He was filled with dread, but he flicked on his torch, all the same, and then he opened his eyes slowly, and looked.

It was a plain room where stone tombs stood, where carved effigies of Lord Stephen's noble ancestors lay in state. Coffins were set in niches in the walls, and his father's was one of these – the furthest from the entrance. He walked as softly as he could, trying not to let his footsteps ring on the flagstones. Cobwebs brushing up against his face startled him, and the sound of the door creaking on its rusty hinges scared him terribly. Something scuttled across the floor, and wildly he cast the torch beam about, trying to see what had made the noise. Turning round, he stepped backwards, and something cold pressed up against him, so that he staggered away in horror before he realised that what he had felt was only the side of a stone tomb as he had backed into it.

He wanted nothing more than to run away, but he gathered all his courage and went on with what he had come to do. He had brought a screwdriver and an old chisel with him, and when he found his father's coffin, he set about unscrewing the lid.

His hands shook so much that he could hardly hold the screwdriver in the head of the screws, but at last he managed to get them out. He tucked the torch under his arm so that he could see to lift up the lid. As he struggled with it, the lid came loose suddenly and slid off, clattering down behind the coffin, against the wall: the noise resounded chillingly around the stone chamber. Lord Stephen leapt back, gripping his torch in his hand, and then, gathering his courage, he stepped forward again, very carefully, steeling himself to take a look inside. He moved closer and shone the light in; and there inside the coffin he saw the face of his father, dead for seven years, yet unchanged.

Lord Stephen's first thought was that he could not be dead, but had been sleeping there all the time: and then it occurred to him that the body must be preserved in some way.

He tentatively reached out his hand to touch the face, but when he did so, it did not feel as he had expected dead flesh to feel. The shock made him drop the torch and he was plunged in sudden darkness.

For a minute, he scrambled madly on the dusty, cold floor, feeling for his torch that had rolled away, before he remembered that he had brought a candle too. He took it out and managed to light it. He shone the trembling light of the candle into the coffin, onto his father's face again. In seven years, that face had not altered: it looked as it had always looked in life, but Lord Stephen did not want to touch it again. He held the candle closer, and the wax dripped down, running in a glistening film over his father's cheek, and as Lord Stephen watched, it seemed to merge with the skin, so that the colour ran down in streaks. He held the candle flame close to the dead face, and the skin began to gleam wetly with an oily sheen, and the drips from the candle trickled down and were lost in the melting features of the nineteenth Earl. Lord Stephen knew then that his father's face, like the candle, was made of wax.

He had seen enough: more than he had courage to take in for one night. Hastily, he dragged the coffin lid back into place, screwed it down, searched around on the floor until he found his torch, and went out quietly, locking the door and leaving everything as he had found it.

He never spoke to anyone about what he had discovered; but he knew now that his mother and his uncle, together with the doctor who had signed the death certificate, had conspired to hide the truth about his father's disappearance. He guessed that his mother, a proud and secretive woman who feared the kind of publicity and sensationalism that had surrounded the disappearance of the eighteenth Earl, almost forty years earlier, had used her charm and social influence to conceal the equally mysterious disappearance of her own husband in order to avoid a scandal.

But for Lord Stephen, the discovery of the wax corpse in his father's coffin was only the beginning of the mystery and the horrors that were to plague him for the next thirty years; and as the years passed and he learned more about the true fate of his father and grandfather, he himself grew more and more desperate to conceal that truth – secrecy became an obsession, and furtiveness became a way of life.

The abduction of Professor Joshua Aaronberg was, nevertheless, a turn in a new direction: it was an extreme measure, taken in a sense of desperation, to the like of which the Earl had never before had to resort. On his way up to his office, he paused on the stairs and thought, with a twinge of remorse, of the little old white-haired man imprisoned in the cellar. Karen was right, of course: if it had not been for the encouragement of Dr Vanderpump to take whatever steps were most expedient, he would probably never even have considered doing such a thing. As it was, this drastic solution to his immediate problems had proved to be less helpful than he had hoped; and time was running out, in more ways than one, Lord Stephen reflected ironically as he turned back and set off in the direction of the entrance to the cellars.

CHAPTER 11

A Guided Tour

After breakfast, Sebastian Dorrell, who was dressed this sunny morning in black leather trousers, a leopardskin print jacket and a bright pink shirt that matched his eye shadow and nail varnish and the ribbons that he had tied in his wild hair, left the Black Dog in his green sports car and drove towards Heydn Hall. He had two purposes in mind: to try to find his lost binoculars, and to take another look at the Hall, this time in daylight. He was wondering whether it might be possible to persuade someone to show him around inside, if not today, then on some future occasion for which he could make an appointment; for he was hoping to discover whether it was true what Johnny Terrier had told him – that Professor Aaronberg had been taken to Heydn Hall.

It was a pleasant drive along the lane, the road dappled by warm sunlight that shone through the leafy boughs overhead, the birds singing in the hedgerows. Near to the Hall, the banks rose steeply on either side of the lane, and the woodland grew dense and shadowy. Through the trees on the right-hand side, Sebastian caught sight of the grey stone bulk of Heydn Hall with its castellated walls and strange gothic architectural embellishments, the glass of its mullioned windows glinting coldly, and, blazing above its grey roof-tops as it caught the morning sun, the massive glass pyramidal prism that was erected high on the tower at the back of the house. Sebastian glimpsed it only for a moment, before the dark barrier of trees obscured his view.

He drove slowly a short distance further along the lane until he came to the main gates. They were high and ornate, made of wrought iron painted black and gold, and they were hung between gaunt grey stone gateposts; the arms of the Horsley-Mitchell family were incorporated in the decoration of the ironwork. On the top of the gateposts were mounted stone figures of a dragon and a gryphon, which bore shields also emblazoned with the family's arms. To the left of the gate, crumbling amid the lush summer growth of long grass, nettles, cow parsley, greater willow-herb and dandelions, were the ruins of an old gatehouse, its roof broken and its windows shattered and roughly boarded up. Insects were humming in the sunlit grass and there were a few butterflies; the birds were twittering in the tall trees that swayed their heavy branches gently in the warm breeze. All was tranquil and bright.

Through the bushes to the right of the gate, covered slightly by the summer's growth of leaves, a large green board was visible. Upon the board, in white lettering, was the name HEYDN HALL, and below, in smaller lettering, the opening times for the general public. This lower section had been partially obscured by another board nailed across it, on which, in red letters against a white background, had been stencilled the notice: CLOSED TO THE PUBLIC – RESTORATION IN PROGRESS.

Leaving the engine running, Sebastian climbed out of the car and walked up to the gates. They were not locked, and he easily unbolted them and pushed them open. He got back into the car and drove through.

The long gravel drive extended in the green shimmering shadows beneath the trees, and turned a bend to the right. Sebastian drove slowly along it, the car bouncing over bumps and pot-holes, until he saw a sign indicating a car park on the left. He turned into the car park and parked his sports car in a corner.

There was no one about. When he turned off the car's engine, apart from the occasional twittering of sparrows and a slight rustling of leaves stirring in the tall trees that grew all around, there was an enveloping stillness. Sebastian left the car and walked out of the car park, along the drive towards the house.

He made no attempt to conceal his presence; his shoes crunched softly on the gravel as he walked. As he approached the Hall, he met no one. The facade of the house was imposing, with its columned portico, and the rows of tall mullioned windows whose leaded lights reflected back the bland sky and the dark woods, offering no glimpse of the great gloomy rooms within. Sebastian wondered whether Professor Aaronberg might be in there, locked in one of the rooms; and if he was there, Sebastian wondered how he would be able to find him.

He strolled across the forecourt, gazing up at the forbidding windows and cold grey walls: it was an unwelcoming facade, like a face without an expression, and yet there was an atmosphere of sadness about it, Sebastian fancied, more like despair than plain hostility.

He looked around him, trying to work out the position from which he had seen the Hall on the previous evening, when it had seemed to him that he had run through the woods and come upon the house quite unexpectedly, the strange prism on its tower blazing eerily beneath the stormy sky. He wanted to satisfy himself that he had really been there, that he had not hallucinated the whole bizarre experience. He gazed up at the roof, at the glass prism protruding above it: the mysterious structure fascinated him, and he realised that it was highly unlikely that he should see such a peculiarly distinctive feature in a hallucination, never having seen it before in real life. He must actually have been here in the grounds last night, he thought, though he was still puzzled by the unexplained mystery of how he could have passed through the locked gate in the iron fence.

Last night, he realised, the Tower, which was now on the opposite side of the house to where he stood, had been just visible to him, so he must have been standing much further to the right of where he now was. He walked on a little further, until he came to the garages – a converted mews on the edge of the gravel forecourt.

He left the gravel and strolled onto the grass under the trees. The land rose here in a slight incline and was thickly wooded. Sebastian saw that, if he continued to climb, he would shortly reach the fence that bounded the lane. He walked a few yards further, bearing to the left. Ahead of him now, through the trees, he could see an ornate building of Classical design, resembling a temple, but with no windows or openings in its grim stone walls. It was the mausoleum where, many years before, Lord Stephen had secretly looked inside his father's coffin and had discovered a wax effigy in place of a corpse; but Sebastian could only guess as to what purpose the building was put, and he imagined that it must be some ornamental summer-house. He had not noticed it there last night in the stormy darkness.

He turned round, gazing back towards Heydn Hall; and now he recognised that he must be standing very close to the spot from where he had seen the house on the previous evening. At the far corner he could see the Tower, its ancient walls partially covered in a cloak of ivy, and he could see now that its lower windows were bricked up, and the upper windows had also been covered by boards secured across them on the inside.

As he was wondering about this, he was suddenly startled by the sound of a voice quite near to him. He turned his head quickly and looked to the left, to see a young man striding with determination towards him, between the trees.

'Hey, you! What d'you think you're doing?' called the man. He came close to Sebastian and stopped, glaring up at him angrily. 'The Hall and grounds are not open to the public. Didn't you see the notice? You're trespassing.'

'Oh, I'm frightfully sorry,' said Sebastian with a smirk. He had regained his composure in a moment. 'I was merely – ah ... merely visiting, what? I was going to knock at the front door – nothing secret or underhand, you know.'

'Then what're you doing round here at the side?' asked the man, staring in disapproval at Sebastian's flamboyant attire. 'That's your car in the car park too, I suppose? D'you realise you left the gate open? The Earl's very particular about that sort of thing – he doesn't like it.'

'Ah ... ' said Sebastian, looking down at the young man, who was short and thin, with fine fair hair that flopped over one of his pale grey eyes, and he was dressed in a grey woollen jacket and grey trousers. 'Well, I hope the

Earl won't – ah ... won't hold it against me,' Sebastian said. 'because I was rather hoping he would – ah ... let me take a look around inside the house.'

'Out of the question, I'm afraid.' The man shook his head.

'All the same,' persisted Sebastian, 'I'd – ah ... like to ask him myself, if I may. When I say that, of course – ' he smiled, exposing the gold fillings in his teeth: 'I'm assuming that you yourself are a person with some authority here. I mean, you haven't actually told me who you are, have you? For all I know, you have no more right to be here than I have. My name's Sebastian Dorrell, by the way. You see, I've nothing to hide.'

'I'm Julian Crucefix, the estate manager,' said the man primly. 'I think I can speak on Lord Stephen's behalf when I say you're not welcome here. And I'm afraid you still haven't given me a satisfactory explanation of why you were prowling around under the trees. If you're not up to anything suspicious, you're certainly behaving as if you are, that's all I can say. I think you'd better leave.'

'Oh, there's quite a reasonable explanation, actually.' Sebastian frowned, glancing on the ground about him uneasily. 'I lost my way in the dark last night,' he said. 'I came here quite by accident, and I think I dropped something here – a pair of binoculars. I came back to look for them.' As he spoke, he cast about him, examining the ground for any sign of the lost binoculars.

'The gates are locked at night,' said Julian Crucefix. 'How did you get in?'

'I don't know – I think I must've inadvertently got through a gap or hole in the fence,' Sebastian suggested vaguely.

Julian Crucefix scoffed. 'There're no gaps or holes. All

the fences were repaired recently – precisely to keep people like you out. Now would you kindly leave.'

Sebastian was still staring at the ground, at the damp
earth and leaf mould beneath the trees.

'There's nothing here,' said Julian impatiently.

'Wait a moment!' said Sebastian, as something interesting caught his eye. He crouched down and scrabbled in
the leaf mould with his fingers, uncovering something that
was half-buried close to the root of one of the trees. He
pulled the object out and held it up for Julian Crucefix to
see: it was a pair of binoculars, but they were in a very
badly deteriorated condition.

'My God,' said Julian with a short laugh of scorn,
'you're not going to tell me that those are yours – the pair
you lost yesterday!'

Sebastian examined the binoculars in some bewilderment. They certainly resembled the pair that he had had,
but they were damaged to an extent far exceeding what
was possible during one night in the open: the fine leather
covering had peeled away and rotted, the lenses were
grimy, scratched and cracked, and all the metal casing was
badly rusted. Sebastian raised an eyebrow in mild amusement. 'You're right, of course,' he agreed. 'They can't be
mine. Mine had my name and address on – here ... ' He
turned the binoculars over, rubbing the tip of his finger
over one of the flat steel plates on the back. 'So if you – ah
... if you happen to find a pair, you'll know they're
mine ... ' He broke off; as he had wiped his finger over the
metal, cleaning off the mud, a name beneath had become
visible, close to the manufacturer's stamp. Upon the binoculars was engraved S. V. DORRELL (Capt.), and beneath
that was an Army serial number.

Sebastian was shocked: it gave him an uneasy feeling, as if he were haunted by his own ghost, or as if, mysteriously, he had someone else's memories – as if it had not been he who had run through the wood, who had seen Heydn Hall in the storm, who had dropped his binoculars, but a man who shared his name and whose life shadowed his own, while Sebastian was left with only the memories of things that he had never done.

'Come on,' said Julian with a gesture of impatience. 'Stop wasting time. You don't want me to have to call the police, do you?'

'I would very much like to speak to the Earl,' said Sebastian; but he could see that merely asking was not going to have the desired result and that he would have to say something more impressive. He could not be sure that Electra Vanderpump was known at Heydn Hall or whether her name carried any weight there, but since Johnny Terrier had spoken as if Electra was working with the Earl, he decided to try it. Quickly he said, 'I'm – ah ... not just an ordinary sightseer, you know. I'm a close friend of Dr Electra Vanderpump, an acquaintance of the Earl's. If you mention my name to Lord Stephen, I think you'll find he may even have heard of me.'

Julian frowned. 'You know Dr Vanderpump? Why didn't you say so before?'

Sebastian shrugged vaguely. 'All the rest was true too – I really was looking for my binoculars. Oh, come on!' He grinned. 'Let me see the Earl.'

'Well, I don't know ... ' said Julian doubtfully. 'Lord Stephen may be busy at the moment, but I suppose I could ask him.'

Reluctantly he took Sebastian into the house by a side

door into the Chinese Room, through the Drawing-Room and into the Marble Hall, where he left him while he went to fetch the Earl.

Ten minutes later, Julian returned with Lord Stephen, who came in scowling and red in the face. He had abandoned his jacket, and his shirt sleeves were rolled up; his hands were black with oil, his clothing grimy and smudged with cobwebs, and his short blond hair was rumpled into a startled tuft. He glared at Sebastian with an expression of disgust and suspicion. 'Good God!' he said to Julian. 'What the hell does he think he looks like!'

Sebastian grinned, and his gold fillings glinted brightly in the morning light. 'Ah, hello!' he said. 'You must be the Earl of Newhaven?'

'I'm Steve Mitchell,' retorted Lord Stephen sourly. 'I don't like fancy titles. I'm no better than the next man, and I don't pretend to be. Who're you? I've forgotten what Julian said your name was.' As he spoke, he wiped his hands over his already grimy trousers, making oily black smears above the knees.

Sebastian repeated his name.

'And you're a friend of Dr Vanderpump's?' questioned the Earl dubiously. 'She's never mentioned you. What is it you want here, anyway?'

'I was – ah ... I was wondering if someone could show me around?' Sebastian asked.

'What d'you mean?' said the Earl with a dark look. 'You want a guided tour, is that it? I suppose Julian's told you, the Hall's closed for repairs? We're not giving guided tours at present.'

'I don't see any workmen,' Sebastian remarked with a smile, 'unless, of course, you're – ah ... carrying out the

repairs single-handed.' He eyed Lord Stephen's dirty clothes significantly.

'Well,' said the Earl awkwardly, 'the work isn't ... it isn't under way yet – they haven't actually started on it.'

'I see,' said Sebastian. 'In that case, it wouldn't put you out, surely, if you were to make an exception in my case? I really am – ah ... really am most eager to take a look around. Electra's told me so much about this place, you know – I was quite looking forward to seeing it.'

The Earl trembled, and his face grew a little redder; nervously he ran his hand across it, leaving an oily smudge above his nose. 'What's she told you?' he demanded curtly. There was a desperate look in his eye.

Sebastian shrugged. 'Oh – about the – ah ... furniture, the works of art – you know, that sort of thing.'

Lord Stephen was visibly relieved. He drew Julian Crucefix to one side and spoke quietly into his ear. 'What d'you make of the fellow?' he asked. 'D'you think he's genuine?'

'I don't know what to think,' said Julian.

'Hm ... ' remarked the Earl quietly. 'He looks like a bloody poof to me, but he says he's a friend of Dr Vanderpump, so I suppose we'll have to give him the benefit of the doubt. If that woman finds out we've turned away one of her friends, there'll be all hell to pay.' He turned back to Sebastian. 'Well, Mr Dorrell,' he announced brightly, 'I'm sure we can sort something out, eh, Julian? I don't see why you shouldn't have a private viewing, so long as you don't advertise the fact – otherwise we'll have all and sundry round here before we know it. D'you think you could show the gentleman around, Julian? And try and hurry it up,' he added in an undertone, close to Julian's ear.

'Oh, gosh – thanks! I'm ever so grateful!' said Sebastian with a grin.

Lord Stephen smiled wryly and looked as if he were about to leave. Then he turned to Sebastian again with a mild frown of puzzlement and said, 'By the way, what the devil's that filthy-looking object you've got there?' He pointed to the rusty binoculars that Sebastian still held.

Sebastian lifted them up. 'These? Oh, they're just my binoculars,' he explained. 'I – ah ... I lost them in the wood last night, which is one of the reasons I came back today – to look for them, you see.'

'Good God,' said the Earl, 'if I lost something looking like that, I'd say good riddance – I wouldn't go back to find the bloody thing! Still – I must be getting on – I've got work to do.' He strode to the door with a purposeful stride. 'Enjoy yourself!' he called gruffly as he walked out of the room without looking back. They heard his heavy footsteps crossing the entrance hall outside.

'Mending – ah ... mending the car, is he?' asked Sebastian casually when the Earl had gone.

Julian looked at him uncomprehendingly. 'Why d'you say that?'

'Well, you know,' said Sebastian, 'he was – ah ... covered in oil, what?'

'Oh,' said Julian. 'He's a very private man. I don't inquire into his hobbies – that's his affair. I'm only the estate manager. I imagine he was mending the boiler, as he was down in the cellar. Now ... ' He glanced at his watch. 'I'm afraid I can't spend more than about ... Bother – my watch seems to have stopped.'

'So has mine,' said Sebastian. He smiled. 'A coincidence.'

'Well, I can't spend more than about half an hour,' continued Julian, 'so we'd better get started. This room we're in now is called the Marble Hall. It was designed and constructed in 1752 upon the request of Lord Geoffrey Horsley-Mitchell, the fifteenth Earl of Newhaven, who was the present Earl's great great great great grandfather.'

'How interesting,' said Sebastian, feigning enthusiasm.

*

During the next half hour, Julian took Sebastian on a tour of Heydn Hall, into the rooms on the ground floor and the first floor: they saw the Drawing-Room, the Chinese Room, the Tapestry Room, the Clock Court, the Dining-Room, the Saloon, the Morning Room, the Lounge, the Library, the Chapel, the Picture Gallery, the Weapons Gallery, the Music Room and all the main bedrooms. In the Clock Court, Julian explained the function of the glass prism on the tower.

'Interesting,' said Sebastian, 'but rather – ah ... rather a lot of trouble to go to, I would've thought, merely to – ah ... merely to light a somewhat uninspiring courtyard. Not exactly one of the Hall's greatest amenities, what? And personally I would say that that prism is a positive eyesore.'

Julian frowned. 'It's a question of personal taste. The Earl likes it, I believe.'

'Extraordinary,' said Sebastian.

In the Library, on the first floor, Julian apologised for his lack of knowledge about the history of the Hall. 'I'm afraid I haven't been here long,' he explained.

'How long?' asked Sebastian, his interest aroused as Julian's remark reminded him of something that Johnny Terrier had told him.

'Oh, about three months,' said Julian. 'You'll notice, the painted ceiling bosses are in the form of heraldic devices from the arms of the Horsley-Mitchell family.' He pointed at the ceiling.

'What became of – ah ... what became of the previous estate manager?' Sebastian inquired.

'You ask questions about matters which are, frankly, no business of yours, Mr Dorrell,' answered Julian.

'Do you know what happened to him?' Sebastian persisted.

'He died of a heart attack, if you must know,' Julian replied, a note of uneasiness in his voice: for suddenly he remembered the Earl's strange reaction when the matter had been raised on the occasion of his first visit to Heydn Hall, and that Karen Black had informed him that Mr Duffy was on holiday in Majorca.

'Somebody – ah ... somebody told me,' said Sebastian, eyeing Julian steadily, 'that the estate manager had disappeared and that the Earl covered up the incident.'

'Who told you that?' asked Julian.

'Johnny Terrier,' said Sebastian. 'He's the cousin of the Earl's secretary, I understand. I suppose you already know that?'

Julian smiled awkwardly; he rubbed his small hand nervously over his lips. 'Yes ... Mr Terrier had a breakdown ... '

Sebastian raised an eyebrow. 'You're sure of that?'

'It's not for me to say,' said Julian, 'and in any case, I have no intention of discussing these matters with you. It's private and personal.'

'Apparently, quite a few people have – ah ... disappeared,' remarked Sebastian, 'while they were here at Heydn Hall.'

'I wouldn't know,' said Julian with disinterest. 'The set of twelve matching drawing-room chairs are Chippendale.' He laid his hand on the back of one of the chairs as he spoke. 'I'm not an authority on furniture, though.'

'Aren't you curious as to what might be going on here?' asked Sebastian, fixing his dark quizzical gaze upon Julian's evasive eyes.

'It's the Earl's private business,' said Julian. 'It's not for me to ask questions. I'm the estate manager – I do my job, that's all.'

'You know there's something funny going on here,' said Sebastian pointedly, 'don't you, Mr Crucefix?'

Julian looked at him indignantly; there was an expression of angry bewilderment in his mild grey eyes, as if he were quite taken aback by what he saw as an unjustified interrogation about matters that he genuinely considered to be none of his business. 'Mr Dorrell,' he said in a hurt tone, 'have you come here to see the Hall, or to ask impertinent questions? Because if it's the latter, I think you'd better leave now. You may be a friend of Dr Vanderpump's, but I hardly think that gives you a licence to pry into Lord Stephen's private affairs.'

Sebastian shrugged. 'Well,' he said, 'you've recognised my reason for coming here. But it's true that I'm a friend of Dr Vanderpump's, and I'm also a friend of Johnny Terrier's, and it's because of him that I came here. You see, I'm – ah ... I'm interested in what happened to Lady Caroline Giles, the Countess of Warwick. Were you at the Hall at the time when the Countess was visiting?'

'Yes,' said Julian, the expression of wary unease still lingering in his face. 'I'd been here about three or four weeks. It was terrible, of course – a terrible accident. Lord Stephen was very upset about it, obviously – so was Miss Black. The Countess was ... she was a very, very charming lady. Everyone loved her – you couldn't help admiring her

– she was that sort of person. I don't think I've ever met anyone kinder ... ' He hesitated, and his voice trembled slightly; he fiddled unhappily with the cuffs of his shirt. 'She was considerate and very patient,' he said. 'Mr Terrier was very fond of her. I think it was because of ... because of the accident ... well it contributed to his breakdown, I think.'

'What did happen?' asked Sebastian with interest.

Julian glanced up, surprised. 'I assumed you knew? She crashed her plane in the sea. It was in all the newspapers.'

'And you believe that?' Sebastian asked.

'Of course,' said Julian.

Sebastian tugged thoughtfully at the ear-ring in his left ear-lobe. He gazed out of the window at the disused Tower with its glass prism.

He said, 'Did you – ah ... did you happen to see the Countess immediately before the accident?'

'What d'you mean?' asked Julian.

'Did you, for instance,' said Sebastian, 'see her on the day when the accident occurred – before she left the Hall?'

Julian frowned in irritation. 'I don't understand why you're asking these questions,' he said. 'I did see her – yes. I didn't speak to her, though – I just saw her from the Music Room window when she was getting into the taxi.'

Sebastian nodded. 'Can you be sure that it was her?'

'Of course it was her,' said Julian. 'She was very distinctive – she had long, reddish-blonde hair.'

'And where – ah ... where was Johnny Terrier at the time?' Sebastian asked.

'Well, I don't know,' said Julian.

'Wasn't he outside, saying goodbye to the Countess?' Sebastian suggested. 'He was very fond of her. Surely – ah ... surely he said goodbye to her?'

'I really can't remember,' said Julian. 'I think perhaps, if you've quite finished asking questions, we ought to be getting on. I'm afraid I can't spend any more time.'

'Let me put it another way, Mr Crucefix,' said Sebastian. 'When you – ah ... when you looked out of the window and saw someone whom you took to be the Countess of Warwick, are you sure it really was the Countess? Or was it, perhaps ... ' he said slowly, carefully fixing Julian with his eye, 'was it, perhaps, Johnny Terrier dressed up and wearing a strawberry blonde wig?'

Julian stared at him incredulously. 'Are you trying to be funny?' he said with a brief, awkward laugh. 'I don't think I've ever heard a more ridiculous suggestion.'

'I know it's absurd,' Sebastian agreed, 'but I want you to think about it, Mr Crucefix, and consider whether it could possibly be what really happened.'

'Mr Dorrell,' said Julian impatiently, 'what're you saying? All this is simply rubbish to me and doesn't interest me in the least.'

'Then I think it ought to interest you,' said Sebastian, 'because I think there's something in it. I don't believe that Lady Caroline Giles was killed in an aircraft accident. I think that she disappeared while she was staying here, and that the Earl concealed it, just as he concealed the disappearance of his estate manager. And before that, there were other mysterious disappearances – the present Earl's father, for instance. And – ah ... his grandfather too, I believe.'

'I don't know what you're talking about,' retorted Julian, but his voice faltered; he had suddenly remembered Lord Stephen's air of unease whenever the name of Lord Mountjoy, the eighteenth Earl, was mentioned.

'Ah,' said Sebastian, 'so there is something, isn't there?

Something about the Earl's grandfather?' He pointed out of the window at the Tower. 'The eighteenth Earl, who was responsible for erecting that glass monstrosity – ostensibly to – ah ... ostensibly to shine daylight into a dismal courtyard on the other side of the house.'

'I really know nothing about it,' said Julian.

Sebastian looked into his face for any sign of deception, but he found none: when Julian Crucefix said that he knew nothing, that he was not interested, that it was none of his business anyway, he appeared to mean precisely what he said. 'You showed me round the house,' said Sebastian, 'but so far we haven't gone into the Tower.'

'No, it's closed,' Julian replied shortly.

Sebastian raised an eyebrow. 'Closed to the public?'

'No,' said Julian. 'The entrance is bricked up – it's permanently closed. No one's been in there for years.'

'So there's – ah ... there's no way of getting in?' Sebastian asked.

'Not unless you climb through the window,' said Julian sarcastically. He turned away and walked towards the door. 'I have to get back to work,' he said. 'I'm asking you to leave now, Mr Dorrell.'

'And is that how the Earl gets in?' asked Sebastian. 'Through the window?'

In the doorway, Julian turned: he looked angry and resentful, and he was plainly losing his patience. 'I told you,' he said. 'No one goes in there. It's been bricked up since Lord Mountjoy's time. It's supposed to be haunted, or something of the sort. If you want to read about it, it's all in the guidebook. I'll let you have one when we go downstairs. Now, please, Mr Dorrell – I really can't spare any more time.'

'One more thing,' said Sebastian as they walked back to the landing. 'What does the name *Professor Joshua Aaronberg* mean to you?' He watched Julian's face carefully for a response.

'I saw his television series,' replied Julian casually. 'Oh – I read something about him in the paper a couple of days ago. He's disappeared, apparently. I don't know whether they've found him yet.'

'He's still missing,' Sebastian said.

Julian smiled. 'You seem to be very interested in the idea of people going missing.'

'I am,' Sebastian agreed.

They began to descend the grand staircase.

'You should've arrived a bit earlier,' said Julian, 'when the police were here inquiring about an old lady who disappeared. They said that she was last seen yesterday afternoon, out in the lane, picking blackberries.'

'Really?' said Sebastian in surprise, recalling at once the two old ladies that he had seen outside Heydn Hall on the previous day. 'It rather – ah ... rather substantiates what I've been saying, doesn't it?' he remarked. 'So what's the – ah ... score now? I make it five – five people who have disappeared in or near to Heydn Hall.'

Julian laughed. 'You really want to make a mystery out of it, don't you?'

They had reached the bottom of the stairs, and Julian led Sebastian through a door on the right of the entrance hall, into the souvenir shop. He found a guidebook in one of the cupboards and handed it to Sebastian. 'Maybe that'll answer any more questions you have,' he said.

'Thank you for your time,' said Sebastian. 'I wonder if it would – ah ... be possible to see you again?'

Julian looked uneasy, but before he was able to reply, the sound of heavy footsteps in the hall was heard, and a moment later, the Earl came bounding in.

He was covered in oil, as he had been earlier, but now there was a rip in his shirt and he had a wild and desperate look. 'Ah, Julian – there you are at last!' he cried. 'There's an emergency on! The bloody lights have fused! Come and help me sort this out, will you. We're in the dark down there. I'm not sure what the problem is, but we might have to switch the electricity off, so you'd better tell the staff.'

'Still mending the boiler, I see,' remarked Sebastian with an amiable smirk.

Lord Stephen glared at him in alarm, as if becoming aware of his presence for the first time. His brilliant steel blue eyes were very wide and fierce. 'You still here?' he said curtly.

'Just leaving, actually,' replied Sebastian, 'but might I say before I go, Lord Stephen – '

'Steve – my name's Steve Mitchell!' interjected the Earl with impatience. 'I told you, I don't hold with fancy titles.'

'Oh, sorry!' Sebastian grinned again, and the gold fillings in his teeth glinted. 'Then might I say, Lord Steve, how very much I've enjoyed looking around your beautiful home. And Mr Crucefix has been extremely helpful and informative. It's all – ah ... all been most charming and agreeable.'

The Earl continued to glare at him, and his disapproving gaze moved over Sebastian slowly, taking in each item of his appearance with mingled scorn and disbelief. 'Good God!' he muttered under his breath, and then without another word he turned on his heel and disappeared out of the door.

'I don't – ah ... don't think he likes me,' observed Sebastian, self-consciously fingering the ribbons in his hair.

Julian looked embarrassed. 'Oh, he's like that with everybody,' he said. 'He doesn't mean anything by it, you know. He's really very liberal-minded – he's a socialist. But he's a very private man.'

'He's a very rude man,' said Sebastian. 'I don't know about anything else. Extraordinary that one should – ah ... should require so much engine oil to mend the boiler. But I suppose you have your own generator, do you? How often does it break down?'

Julian looked irritated. 'Now you're going to make a mystery out of that too, I suppose,' he said.

'I merely wondered,' Sebastian replied, 'whether Lord Stephen makes a hobby of – ah ... of repairing it, you know.' He laughed. 'I think something that you – ah ... said earlier gave me that impression.'

Julian did not answer, but he looked thoughtful as he let Sebastian out of the front door.

CHAPTER 12

Electra Vanderpump Comes to the Hall

In the afternoon, Dr Electra Vanderpump arrived at Heydn Hall in her pink sports car. The weather was hot; Electra was wearing a red, black and white cotton print shift dress and high-heeled sandals. She had brought a small travelling-bag with her.

'I'll be staying for a few days,' she announced to Karen Black upon her arrival.

Karen showed her into the Lounge, where Electra lit a cigarette in a long onyx holder, and asked, 'And how is Professor Aaronberg? Co-operating yet?'

'No, he ain't,' said Karen miserably. 'Steve's been down in the cellars all day, trying to get the bloody thing working. If you ask me, I don't think the Professor knows anything about that sort of thing at all – that's not in his line, like – machines. He's one of them intellectual sort of blokes, isn't he?'

'Perhaps you'll tell Lord Stephen I'm here, would you, dear?' said Electra coldly. 'And would you get the bath running for me? I feel absolutely filthy. It's been hell driving down here today. All those awful holiday-makers on the roads! Thank goodness you had the sense, at least, to close the Hall for the season. I really could never have worked with them around.'

Karen's eyes narrowed in a look of resentment, but she left the room to fetch the Earl.

Ten minutes later, when Lord Stephen blustered in, Electra gave him a glance of disdain. 'For heaven's sake, you might have bothered to put your shirt on,' she said.

'It got torn,' the Earl explained carelessly. 'I tell you, Dr Vanderpump, it's been bloody chaos down there today! I blew the circuits, trying to fix the bloody ISB unit!'

'If you couldn't do it properly, you should've waited for me,' replied Electra tartly.

The Earl spread his arms helplessly; he paced up and down the room; he flung himself down onto the red velvet couch.

'Oh, for heaven's sake, pull yourself together!' scolded Electra. She walked over to the fireplace and gazed up at the bas-relief of Diana. 'You don't know the worst of it yet.' She turned to face him. 'Two days ago, a man came to the home to see Johnny Terrier. Of course, he should never been allowed in, but Helen, the stupid girl, didn't think, as usual. And I'm afraid that this man may be suspicious of us. I don't know how much Terrier told him.'

'Who's going to listen to Terrier's babbling, anyway?' said Lord Stephen. 'What does it matter about this chap – he's not likely to interfere.'

'That's where you're wrong,' said Electra. 'It does matter, because interfere is precisely what he will do. I'll tell you who he is, Lord Stephen – his name's Sebastian Dorrell, and he's – '

'Dorrell?' cried the Earl, as an expression of shock and confusion came over his face. He sat up abruptly. 'Sebastian Dorrell?'

'Yes,' said Electra. 'You remember – Professor Aaron-berg's friend.'

'Remember?' echoed the Earl. 'But this chap, Dorrell – he was here this morning.'

Electra stared at him in horror. 'Sebastian came here?' With a menacing step she approached Lord Stephen. 'What did you do? What did you say to him?'

'He said he was a friend of yours,' Lord Stephen explained in bewilderment. 'He wanted to be shown round the house.'

'And you sent him away?' inquired Electra sharply.

The Earl frowned. 'But he claimed to know you ... '

'In heaven's name!' cried Electra, her green eyes blazing. 'You don't mean to tell me you let him wander around here, just because he asked? Don't you remember who he is? He's the man we got Terrier to impersonate when we picked up the Professor in the helicopter! For heaven's sake, you couldn't forget – it was only four days ago!'

The Earl clapped his hand to his forehead in dismay. 'What a fool I am!' he cried. 'What an idiot! I should've known! You mentioned his name, of course, but it slipped my mind.' Furiously, he beat his fist against his brow. 'It should've rung a bell, but I wasn't thinking. I was trying to fix the bloody machine when he arrived. But I should've known, I should've known! The fancy clothes, the hair – it should've made me think of Terrier at once, the way you dressed him up to look like this fellow.'

'And you let him go round the house,' said Electra. 'You should have let no one in – no one! Least of all Sebastian Dorrell.'

'He didn't wander about on his own,' explained the Earl. 'Crucefix took him round.'

'Then I must have a word with Mr Crucefix.' Electra

extinguished her cigarette on the marble mantelpiece. She walked to the door. 'Is he in his office?'

'I suppose so,' answered the Earl.

*

As they climbed up the stairs, Lord Stephen was still in obvious confusion.

'But why all this fuss and bother?' he asked. 'Why should we be afraid of this fellow Dorrell? He's not the kind of fellow who frightens me, dressed up like a nancy boy – I'll soon sort him out if he comes round here again.'

'Well, you won't!' snapped Electra, her high heels tapping angrily on the stone staircase. 'He's a trouble-maker and you won't get rid of him as easily as you imagine. He could ruin everything!'

They reached the top floor and she strode along to Julian Crucefix's office, the Earl following sheepishly behind. Electra knocked on the door, opened it, and stepped inside.

Seated behind the old oak desk, Julian looked up in surprise. He got to his feet when he saw that his visitor was Electra Vanderpump in one of her worst moods.

'Mr Crucefix,' said Electra, 'you showed a gentleman around the Hall this morning.'

'Yes, I did,' replied Julian in surprise, glancing nervously towards the half-naked Earl who had just appeared in the doorway.

'And what did you talk to him about?' asked Electra.

'Well, this and that,' said Julian uneasily.

'What, precisely?' inquired Electra. 'Did he ask questions? Did you tell him what he wanted to know?'

'Well, he did ask questions, yes ... ' said Julian.

'Did he ask you about the Tower?' demanded Electra. 'Did he say anything about the cellars?'

'He wanted to know why we didn't go into the Tower,' said Julian, biting his lip tentatively.

'And what did you tell him?' asked Electra.

Julian looked from Electra to Lord Stephen and back again, and the expression of concern on their faces puzzled him: it made him wonder for a moment whether he should have taken more seriously what Sebastian Dorrell had been saying. 'I told him ... I told him the truth, of course,' Julian faltered.

'My God!' exclaimed the Earl in horror. 'Oh my God!'

Electra silenced him with a stern glance. 'What precisely did you tell him, Mr Crucefix?' she demanded.

'Only that the Tower was supposed to be haunted,' Julian said in dismay, 'and that no one had been in there for years. But I don't understand – why is it so important what we talked about? I thought he was a friend of yours, Dr Vanderpump? If he hadn't have said that, I suppose I might not have answered his questions so readily.'

'He always introduces himself as a friend, yes,' replied Electra, 'but, you see, he was actually a patient at the Twilight Home, and I treated him for a number of years. He suffers from a form of psychosis and he often believes he's a private detective investigating a murder case or a kidnapping. Sometimes he follows people with whom he's slightly acquainted – and he's done this to me on a number of occasions – and later, he visits the place himself and says he's a close friend, in order to gain access into circles from which he would otherwise be excluded.'

Julian frowned. 'You mean he's mad?'

'Oh, I wouldn't like to use that term,' replied Electra with a smile. 'He's quite harmless really. It's merely aggravating and socially embarrassing for me, that's all. I'm sure you can imagine, but that's one of the occupational hazards of being a therapist, I suppose. I like to keep an eye on his progress, however, so if he comes here again, would you be so good as to inform me, Mr Crucefix?'

'Of course, Dr Vanderpump,' said Julian.

'Good,' said Electra. She ushered the Earl out of the room.

As they went down the stairs, Lord Stephen said, 'I say, is that true about Dorrell having a psychosis?'

'Of course not!' retorted Electra impatiently. 'But I had to tell Mr Crucefix that, or he may have suspected that we had another reason for being interested in what Mr Dorrell said to him. We don't want to make him suspicious, do we? So for heaven's sake, why did you panic when he said that he told Mr Dorrell about the Tower?'

'I thought for a moment there,' admitted the Earl, 'that he knew the real truth. It was stupid, of course – he doesn't know anything. That's what I like about Crucefix – he minds his own business.'

'Let's go into the Library,' suggested Electra, leading the way through the Billiard Room. 'I spoke to Miss Black on the telephone two days ago, as she probably told you. It was about Terrier and what we supposed up until now was his delusion about being in the Air Corps. I'm beginning to wonder whether there may be more to it than we first supposed. Miss Black assured me that Terrier never received flying lessons, although from an early age it was his ambition to go into the Air Corps, like his uncle, Colonel Russell-Terrier. It wasn't until he came to Heydn Hall, however, that he began to have these delusions and to call himself Captain Terrier.'

'That's rubbish!' declared the Earl. 'How could he pilot

Lady Caroline's plane and the helicopter unless he knew how to fly?'

In the library, Electra sat down elegantly on the sunny window seat; she lit a cigarette. 'Quite,' she said. 'Terrier was always prone to depression and to periods of odd behaviour, Miss Black tells me, but she says that, until he came here, he had never had a real breakdown. And here's another interesting point – Terrier somehow knew Sebastian Dorrell, whom he calls Captain Dorrell, and he claims that they were in the Air Corps together.'

'Good God, what a load of bloody rubbish!' exclaimed the Earl, pacing up and down across the sunlit carpet. Motes of dust that his frantic movement disturbed floated in the air around him, visible in the golden light, and Electra's blue skeins of cigarette smoke silently drifted out to engulf them.

'Anyone can see that that fellow Dorrell was never in the Army!' declared the Earl. 'What does it matter what Terrier says? He's a lunatic, anyway, and I couldn't give a damn what he's thinking. What bothers me is that other people are onto us. The police were here this morning, making inquiries about some old woman who disappeared yesterday. It's upset Karen, I can tell you. She thinks this old woman's gone the same way as Duffy and Lady Caroline.'

Electra sneered. 'She's probably right, Lord Stephen. And that's why I'm concerned about Terrier. You see, it occurred to me that the man we have locked up in Twilight Home may not be Karen's cousin, Johnny Terrier, at all.'

'What the hell d'you mean?' The Earl stopped pacing and stood still, facing her with a look of angry accusation. In the sombre surroundings of the old library, its walls lined with shelves of leather-bound books, with portraits of his aristocratic ancestors whose proud eyes gazed down impassively upon the antique furnishings and the neo-Classical statues that stood on plinths at either end of the room, the burly Earl was almost ludicrously incongruous in Electra's eyes: stripped to the waist, the golden light shining upon his suntanned hairless chest and arms, his hands and face smeared with sweat and engine oil, he appeared like some uncouth labourer and not in the least like a descendent of the noble Horsley-Mitchells.

'Let us say,' answered Electra quietly, 'that the man we have at Twilight Home is not Johnny Terrier, but Captain Terrier who bears a certain resemblance in appearance and character, but who is in fact a changeling.'

'It's preposterous bloody rubbish!' The Earl slammed his fist into the palm of his other hand. 'Terrier's the least of our worries! The police are onto us! Dorrell's onto us! Crucefix smells a rat! How long can we cover this thing up, Dr Vanderpump? I've been thinking about it, and I've come to the conclusion we'll have to get rid of the staff – we can't keep them here with all this going on.'

'Oh, for heaven's sake!' retorted Electra, drawing on her cigarette in her long onyx holder. 'That's going to attract attention to our operations, if anything will! What on earth can you say to explain it? A house like this simply can't run without the staff.'

'Who cares what we say!' blustered the Earl, beginning to pace up and down again. 'People are disappearing left right and centre ... '

'Oh, really, don't exaggerate!' scolded Electra.

'It's too bloody dangerous!' declared the Earl. 'Already there're rumours going around about UFOs and God knows what. We had some cranks come here at the weekend, looking for paranormal phenomena. How do these stories start? I tell you, it's the staff beginning to notice things and spreading rumours. Sooner or later someone else will go missing. We can't take that risk – we'll have to sack the lot before it happens!'

Electra sighed. 'Very well – perhaps you're right. If we don't take precautions of this sort, we may regret it later. But it's absurd to dismiss all the staff. We're so close to success now, and when this is all over, you'll want them back again. I think the best plan is to suspend them temporarily on some pretext. How many are living in? Is it just Mr Crucefix and the housekeeper?'

'There are the two girls as well,' said the Earl, 'and the head gardener is in the cottage.'

'I suppose we may be able to manage without them for a while,' said Electra. 'I'll send for my man, Kotlowski, and he can help with some of the work about the house.'

'Oh no, we're not having him here!' declared Lord Stephen. 'Besides, he's a psychiatrist, and you need him at the home.'

'There're other doctors at the home,' replied Electra. 'Kotlowski's served his purpose as a psychiatrist, yes – or rather, he's served my purposes. At the moment, I think he would be more useful here. I'll send for him straight away, and I think I'll get Terrier down here for observation while I'm about it.'

The Earl groaned, but Electra did not argue with him; she stood up and walked to the door. 'Now I must go and see if my bath's ready,' she said, smiling slightly at the Earl's scowls. 'It's your choice, Lord Stephen,' she told him calmly. 'Either you keep the staff you've got, with whatever risk that involves, or I replace them with Kotlowski. Because I'm certainly not going to do all the cooking and cleaning myself, I can assure you. Don't worry, though – Kotlowski's frightfully good in the domestic role – so meticulous about the housework!'

The Earl continued to scowl, but he did not reply.

CHAPTER 13

The Smugglers' Tunnel

After lunch in the lounge of the Black Dog, Sebastian went up to his room and read the Heydn Hall guidebook, and chapter five of Professor Aaronberg's book, *The Ghost Garden*. From these he was able to discover that the Prince's Tower was sealed off in 1937, that the glass prism was mounted upon the roof later the same year, that Lord Mountjoy, the eighteenth Earl, disappeared in 1939, and that Lord Geoffrey, the nineteenth Earl, disappeared in 1978. All this information did not seem very helpful in his quest to find Professor Aaronberg, but he thought about it for a while.

As he was looking through the guidebook, however, he found a passage which mentioned the existence of an old tunnel, once used by smugglers, which ran from the cellars of Heydn Hall, under the cliffs, to the private beach that was part of the Heydn estate. This interested him, for he wondered whether it would be possible for him to gain entry into the house that way. Furthermore, since he had returned from the Hall, he had been thinking about the behaviour of the Earl and Julian Crucefix that afternoon, and he felt uneasy about the idea that the Earl had been down in the cellar mending the boiler. It was possible, of course, but it did not seem quite likely. Even if Heydn Hall did have its own generator, which would account for the oil on the Earl's hands and the problems with the electricity that he had mentioned while Sebastian was there, it still seemed odd that Lord Stephen himself should be attempting the repairs. Sebastian wondered whether, if he found a way into the cellar, he might discover there something altogether more interesting.

He decided to take a stroll along the beach that afternoon to see if he could find the entrance to the tunnel. He changed into some old clothes, took a battery torch with him, and went downstairs.

Before he left the inn, he remembered that he had promised to telephone Richard Mojave to let him know what had been happening, so he rang home at once.

'Hello,' said Richard's voice down the line.

'Hello, old sport – it's me,' said Sebastian.

'Christ, I've been worried! What's been going on down there?' cried Richard. 'I thought you would've phoned yesterday.'

Then Sebastian told Richard his experiences of the previous evening, about the strange blue and green lights, about how his car was affected, the story that Mr Luckett had told him later, and how this morning he had found the binoculars engraved with Captain Dorrell's name.

'It's really weird – it's creepy,' said Richard in awe. 'I've read about this sort of thing, Sebastian. When there're UFOs around, people's cars start playing up, just like yours did.'

'It could've – ah ... could've been caused by an intense electro-magnetic field that interfered with the electrics,' Sebastian agreed, 'but that wouldn't necessarily point to –

ah ... UFOs, if, by UFOs, you're implying that beings from outer space have caused it. No, it's got nothing to do with aliens – it's something that the Earl is up to, I'm damn sure of it. But it's odd, you know ... I've examined these – ah ... these binoculars, and they're the same as mine – the same make, the same design, and that's not all. I once spilled some red enamel paint over the left-hand lens, and I didn't manage to get it all off. Well, round the rim of the left-hand lens on this pair there are some traces of red paint. Then there's another thing – the strap of mine broke near the end, so I cut the end off and stapled the strap back on again. It was a bit of a botched job, but it was functional, you know. Anyway, the strap on this pair is exactly the same – mended at the same end in exactly the same way as I did mine. That's even before considering the fact that my name's inscribed on the back.'

'That's the weirdest thing of all. It doesn't make sense,' said Richard. 'What're you gonna do now, then? Are you going back to the Hall?'

Sebastian told him what he had read in the guidebook about the smugglers' tunnel. 'It's probably – ah ... probably closed after all this time,' he said, 'but it's worth a try. Then, somehow, I want to get into the Tower. The guidebook calls it the Prince's Tower, because, apparently, the Prince of Wales stayed there once. It's part of the house where, I'm told, no one ever goes, but I don't – ah ... don't actually believe that.'

'Where you said there was this thing on the roof?' asked Richard. 'I didn't understand all that, what you were saying. D'you think it's got something to do with those strange lights you saw?'

'Well, last night,' said Sebastian, 'the prism on the roof was illuminated in some way. I saw it this morning in the daylight, and it appears to be made of glass. The estate manager told me that it was erected by the eighteenth Earl for the purpose of – ah ... shining sunlight into a gloomy courtyard on the other side of the house, and that's what the guidebook says too. Well, that's patently absurd. If you saw this courtyard, you'd realise that no one would go to all that trouble, not to mention the expense – a great thing like that, solid glass, hauling it up onto the roof. No, no, the eighteenth Earl had something altogether more ambitious in mind, if you ask me.'

'You think there's something in the Tower?' asked Richard. 'Something that's causing all this UFO stuff and making people disappear?'

'It's the only thing I've got to go on,' said Sebastian, and it seems to me there's something significant in the fact that Lord Mountjoy bricked up the Tower and put this damn great contraption on the roof just over a year before he disappeared. After that, of course, all was ah ... all was quiet until 1978 when Lord Geoffrey disappeared too. Professor Aaronberg says in his book that there was a good deal of mystery surrounding the supposed death of the nineteenth Earl, and even at the time, there was speculation that he had disappeared like his father. Then nothing happened until about last year, I think, when it all started up again. Only now it's worse than ever before, because it looks as if – ah ... looks as if three people have disappeared inside – ah ... what? The last six months or so. Apparently some old woman disappeared yesterday.' He told Richard about Miss Armstrong.

'Sebastian ... ' said Richard. He sounded concerned, anxious. 'You will take care, won't you?'

'Of course,' Sebastian replied with a laugh.

'Call me again,' said Richard, 'when you get back this

evening, okay? I mean, otherwise I'm gonna be worried you've disappeared as well.'

'Listen, old sport, I'm not promising anything,' said Sebastian, 'because you'll – ah ... you'll only worry more if something comes up, or I simply forget. If you don't hear from me, you'd better just assume that the phone's packed in.'

*

Lying dejectedly on his bed in the Twilight Home, Johnny Terrier remembered Lady Caroline Giles, the Countess of Warwick. He remembered the sunny afternoon when he and the Countess had strolled together across the bright lawns of Heydn Hall, below the long grey terrace, beyond the formal Tudor garden with its low yew hedges.

In the blue sky, the clouds were white and high. The birds were singing and insects glided in the warm air. Across the lawn the Countess walked, dazzling in her thin white dress that fluttered softly around her slender body, and her thick, wavy waist-length hair was radiant copper blonde in the sunlight. Johnny ran skipping after her to give her the gift of a daisy chain that he had made.

'How sweet of you,' she said with a beautiful smile, as he helped her to hang the white flowers around her neck. He fumbled with clumsy fingers, and once he broke the chain, but she waited patiently until he had mended it again. On the grass she sat, among the daisies, her soft voile dress spread around her like a cloud, while Johnny played among the flowers, making garlands with which to adorn her.

'Johnny, dear, are you happy?' she asked him presently.

'I'm happy now,' Johnny said. 'But I didn't like it before

you came.' He placed a circlet of daisies upon her bright hair.

She reached up and gently took his hand, drawing him down on the grass beside her. 'I thought you were so sad when I first arrived. I wanted to make you happy, Johnny.'

'They don't like me,' Johnny explained awkwardly. 'They're nasty to me – Steve and Dr Vanderpump.'

'Oh, I'm sure they don't mean to be,' Lady Caroline comforted him. Her voice was soft; she smiled at him kindly as she held his hand in her lap. 'Perhaps they're busy when you want to play with them. Don't you think it's that? I know Lord Stephen is a very busy man.'

'He don't like me,' said Johnny. 'Old Steve don't like Johnny. He's angry, always shouting and grumbling, he is. Like a big bear.' Johnny shook his head, growling fiercely and clawing at the air with his fingers.

Lady Caroline laughed. 'Oh, he is a little like that, I'm afraid! Poor man – I fear he has much on his mind.'

'He won't believe I'm Captain Terrier,' said Johnny suddenly. 'He said I was never in the Air Corps, but I was.' Timidly, he looked at the Countess's serene and lovely face. 'I was in the Airs Corps,' he said, 'until my accident. They wouldn't have me after.'

The Countess nodded sympathetically. 'Do you like flying?' she asked.

'Yeah,' said Johnny. 'I love flying.'

'Then I'll take you up in my aeroplane,' said the Countess. 'Would you like that? We can go tomorrow, if the weather's fine.'

Johnny grinned sheepishly; he did not know what to say.

After a while, Lady Caroline rose, and they walked

back towards the house, close under the dark, ivy-clad walls of the Prince's Tower.

'Even when I'm happy,' said Johnny, 'I'm sad too, thinking about when you have to go away.'

'I'll come back soon,' Lady Caroline assured him gently. 'You won't be lonely, will you. You've still got Karen. She's very fond of you.'

'I'm fond of her,' said Johnny, 'but maybe she don't care no more. Now she's got Steve, she don't love Johnny. But I loved her more than anyone, and Steve don't love her at all.'

'Oh, he does, he does,' replied the Countess earnestly.

'He doesn't love nobody, Big Steve,' retorted Johnny.

'Oh, well,' said the Countess with a sigh, 'it's different for a man, of course. Sometimes I think it must be so hard for you men – so strange. How does it feel, scarcely to feel at all?'

She lifted her calm grey eyes and gazed up at the stone walls of the Tower.

'What is it like to be a man?' she said. 'So strong, mysterious, impenetrable ... almost like this tower ... ' With her white hand, softly she caressed the rough stone. 'So hard, so masculine, thrusting upwards ... '

Johnny sniggered.

The Countess blushed, withdrawing her hand at once. 'Oh, what must you think of me! I didn't mean ... what perhaps it sounded like.' She walked away a few steps. 'Johnny,' she asked more quietly, 'why is there no way into the Tower? I looked for a door, but there isn't one.'

'Ask Big Steve,' said Johnny darkly. 'He knows all the answers.'

'You don't like him at all, do you?' said the Countess. 'He frightens me a little, too.' She walked around the

corner of the Tower, into the shadow of the tall beech trees, and Johnny followed her with slow shambling steps. 'Oh, how I wish I could see inside!' said Lady Caroline.

'There's nothing there,' said Johnny. 'It's empty.'

'I suppose you're right – of course you are,' admitted the Countess. 'It's just that I fancy to myself, there must be – there ought to be something inside, you see. It seems so sad and lonely, and I want to make it a happy place. I can't bear to think of the darkness inside that will never see the sunlight again, and the lonely silence where there were once voices, and living people breathed, and I want to say, *oh, be alive and be with us again, you old, sad, pitiful thing!'* She leaned against the wall and gazed up at the moving green boughs of the trees that whispered slightly as they stirred. 'Oh, what was I saying?' she asked. 'I've forgotten. Oh yes ... about men, of course.' She laughed. 'Do you know, when I was very small, I used to have a terrible fear that I might change into a boy. I imagined it would be quite the worst thing that could happen to me. I thought perhaps a wicked witch would put a spell on me, you know! Or perhaps it would be some kind of awful punishment. I used to think, how terrible – how could I bear it? – never to be able to wear a pretty dress, or ribbons in my hair. But I was wrong, you see, wasn't I, because I was imagining my own mind in a boy's body. If I really had been changed for a boy, just think, it wouldn't just be that I wouldn't be allowed to look pretty – I wouldn't even want to, and that's the most terrible thought of all. I think that's what I find hardest to understand.'

She paused, smiling at Johnny who was staring at her hard, trying to follow what she had been saying: it made little sense to him.

'I mean,' said Lady Caroline, 'if I really were changed in

that respect, I shouldn't be me at all anymore. That's what I'm trying to say. Oh, you think I'm being frightfully silly!' She took him by the hand and they walked out into the sunlight again. 'You would think the difference was only in our bodies,' said the Countess pensively. 'Such a slight difference. But instead, it's a whole world – a whole way of being.'

Now, as he lay on his bed, Johnny remembered these things, and tears rolled down his face and soaked into his pillow. It had been the last time that he had seen the Countess, for the following day she was not to be found anywhere about Heydn Hall, and Johnny came to understand that she had disappeared. He had realised that he would never be able to fly with her in her aeroplane now: but when Dr Vanderpump had told him to dress up in Lady Caroline's clothes and to pilot her aircraft himself, it had been a curious consolation to him, almost as if, for a short time, he had been able to assume the Countess's identity.

Johnny wept as he remembered; he clutched at his pillow, and he wondered miserably whether he would see the gentle and beautiful Countess of Warwick ever again.

*

It was a hot afternoon, and the beach close to Newhaven was occupied by sunbathers and children building sandcastles. As Sebastian Dorrell strolled along the smooth yellow sands between the frolicking children and the groups of semi-naked holiday-makers, his enjoyment of the fine weather was marred by his concern for his friend, Professor Aaronberg, and by his anxiety about what might be happening at Heydn Hall.

He also experienced another feeling, of which he felt

vaguely ashamed in the circumstances, as he walked along the beach and people watched him from behind their dark glasses as he passed: it was a feeling of self-consciousness about his personal appearance, which he realised was less impressive than usual. Since he expected, or at least hoped, to find the secret tunnel under the cliff, it had seemed to him a good idea not to wear his best clothes, which could become spoiled. He was dressed instead in old jeans, a white tee shirt and plimsolls, and he carried his leather jacket over his shoulder; only his bright pink wrap-around mirror sun-glasses, and the length of pink wool with which he had tied back his hair, made his appearance at all distinctive.

Consequently, he experienced a certain sense of relief when the sunbathers were behind him and he walked along alone as the wide expanse of empty beach and calm sea spread out before him. The sand gave way to pebbles and shingle here, and the white cliffs rose on his left-hand side. He continued walking for a further mile, passing only one or two holiday-makers on the way, until at last he came to a high breakwater that ran right across the beach and was surmounted by coils of rusting barbed wire. There was a battered notice painted in red on a white board which was mounted on the breakwater. The notice read: HEYDN HALL PRIVATE BEACH. KEEP OUT.

Sebastian walked along the breakwater towards the sea. At this end, the barbed wire had been badly rusted by the salt water at high tide, and at one point it was corroded through, so that he was able to bend the wire back and climb over.

He could see at once that there were a number of cave openings in the cliff, but when he explored them, to his disappointment, he found that the caves were shallow and none of them appeared to be the entrance to a smugglers' tunnel. One cave ran further back into the cliff and, at first, his hopes were raised. He shone his torch around inside, but the light illuminated only pale limestone walls smoothed over centuries by the pounding of waves: it was a chamber formed entirely by the work of Nature, and there was no smugglers' tunnel to be found here.

Emerging again into the bright sunlight, he walked a little further along the stony beach. Then he noticed another opening, smaller than the others and about twelve feet up the cliff. Leading down from it there was the remains of a crumbling pathway which appeared to have been cut into the face of the cliff long ago.

He put on his jacket to avoid carrying it, and began to climb up, slowly and with difficulty at first, for the lower part of the cliff had been eroded away by the sea; higher up, however, there were more footholds formed by ledges on the rock face, upon which tussocks of grass and pink scabious grew, and it was not long before he reached the small cave entrance.

It was only about three feet high, and he found that, a short way inside, it was blocked by iron bars which had been set into the floor and roof of the cave. The bars were very old and corroded, however, and the chalk in which they were embedded had worn away, so that after working at them for a few minutes, Sebastian found that he could loosen them, and he succeeded in pulling out three to make an opening sufficiently wide for him to squeeze through.

He took out his torch and shone the light into the shadowy interior. The cave was much larger than he had at first supposed, and he could see that it went back far into the cliff. After only a few steps, he was able to stand upright.

He cast the torch beam around the pale walls that had been smoothed by the action of seawater long ago. At the back of the cave were the rotting remains of old wooden casks and crates, and some coils of rope, and close to these was a dark opening that looked like the entrance to a man-made tunnel. Sebastian shone the light inside: as far as his beam of light would go, the passage extended into the chalk cliff. He was sure now that he had found the old tunnel that led into the cellars of Heydn Hall.

He stepped into the tunnel and began to walk along it, shining the light ahead of him. Only once did he find his progress hindered by a fall of material from the roof, but he was able to crawl through.

He had been walking for about five minutes when he came to a door: it was very old, made of dark oak, studded with iron and set in a wall of grey stone that had been built across the end of the tunnel. There was an iron ring in the door which lifted a latch on the other side. It was hard to move the iron ring at first, but eventually Sebastian managed to turn it. He feared for a moment that the door would be bolted on the inside, after all his success in coming so far, for it resisted his efforts as he tried to push it open; however, it was only slightly jammed against the floor, and in the end he shifted it, and the rusting hinges creaked ominously as the old door swung inwards.

Cautiously, he stepped inside and shone the torch around. He was in a large vaulted stone chamber: all about stood crates and boxes, old furniture covered in dust, and things shrouded in torn and grimy sheets that were once intended to protect them; and there were several racks of vintage wine, the bottles grey with a film of dust and cob-webs.

Sebastian's torch beam picked out each item of mould-

ering junk, the cobwebs, the spiders and insects, the debris
of packing straw and old newspapers and splintered wood
littered across the stone floor. There was nothing of espe-
cial interest at all to be seen there.

Then he noticed an arched opening in the corner which
led into an adjoining cellar. He stepped through and found
himself in a much larger vaulted chamber that was so ex-
tensive that the beam of his torch would not illuminate the
far side, and everywhere that he shone the torch, its light
revealed banks of electronic machinery and technical in-
struments. Sebastian looked around in astonishment: the
place was filled with a vast array of sophisticated equipment, much of which resembled what he had seen in Dr
Vanderpump's laboratory in the Twilight Home. Around
the edge of the cellar, brick walls had been built between
some of the ancient stone pillars that supported the roof, in
order to form smaller storage areas, some of which were
completely enclosed rooms with doors.

In awe, Sebastian walked slowly along the aisles, in
between rows of machines, shining his torch on control
panels, keyboards, switches, levers, dials and visual display screens: all was bright and shiny and new, constructed of steel and aluminium and glass, perspex and
coloured plastic. Amid the dust and decay, the clutter of
old rotting crates and boxes and mouldering newspapers,
secret within the concealing darkness of the ancient crypt-
like cellar of Heydn Hall, this imposing collection of hun-
dreds of thousands of pounds-worth of modern technol-
ogy, such as would be found only in the laboratories of the
world's leading multi-national companies, was a curiously
eerie sight, almost surreal, glinting coldly by torchlight in
all its clean elegant splendour that contrasted so oddly

with the crude rough stone and brick walls of its gloomy surroundings.

As Sebastian swung his torch around, suddenly, out of the darkness at the far end of the cellar, there loomed another machine – the largest yet. It was so tall that the top of it almost touched the vaulted roof. Despite its impressive size, however, unlike the rest of the equipment, it was plainly not new: battered and rusty in places, it looked as if it had stood there untouched for decades. It was comprised of a circular platform twelve feet across, in the centre of which rose a stout metal column of about four feet in diameter that supported a circular canopy of the same diameter as the base, so that the whole structure resembled a giant spool or reel. All around the central column, in which was set a large viewing screen, control panels were fixed. Fastened across the canopy overhead, radiating from the centre like the spokes of a great wheel, were many fluorescent lighting tubes that would illuminate the working area when the machine was in operation. The floor platform was covered with flaking and faded old linoleum, and on the control panels were bulky dials and switches, and knobs made of bakelite.

Sebastian stepped up onto the platform, curious to take a look, for he had never before seen a machine like it, and he wondered for what purpose it could have been made. Plainly, it was much too large to have been moved down into the cellar, so he assumed that it must have been constructed there where it stood. Of one thing he was certain, and he smiled at the thought: it was not a domestic boiler or a generator, but it might well be the machine upon which the Earl had been working that morning when Sebastian had arrived to find him with his hands and clothing stained with engine oil. Some of the grilles in the central column had been unscrewed, Sebastian noticed, and there were a few tools lying around.

As he moved to examine the controls, all at once he was startled by a voice that echoed across the cellar, calling to him.

'Who is that?' the voice called. 'Who are you – over there with the light?'

Sebastian swung round in alarm, fearful that he had been discovered. He switched off his torch and stood still in the darkness, waiting apprehensively for whatever might happen next.

CHAPTER 14

The Rescue

Meanwhile, Electra Vanderpump was relaxing in a warm bubble-bath in the guest bathroom on the second floor. Her mind was filled with thoughts of Sebastian Dorrell, some of them pleasant, some of them uneasy, as she imagined him finding his way back into the Hall to investigate the secret places that had not been part of the guided tour that Julian Crucefix had given Sebastian that morning. If Sebastian had suspicions, how long, she wondered, could he be kept out of Heydn Hall? And if he became involved, she thought, his primary aim would almost certainly be to find a solution to the problems that were so concerning the Earl at the moment. Electra herself, on the other hand, had other desires over and above the solution that Lord Stephen sought. While her purposes ran parallel to the Earl's, she was prepared to go along with him for the time being, but she recognised that there may come a point when she would have to pursue her own ends, regardless of any objections Lord Stephen might have; but she knew that someone like Sebastian Dorrell, if he found out what was going on, was unlikely to approve of such a course.

Electra frowned: she had set her mind to it and she was going to see it through. The power that she so passionately desired was almost within her grasp, and nothing and no one was going to stand in her way now, not even Sebastian Dorrell.

Suddenly, a shrill shriek of terror pierced Electra's quiet reverie; it seemed to come from very close by, from one of the bedrooms, possibly from Electra's own room.

She climbed from the bath and dried herself quickly, slipping on her white towelling robe. Already there were sounds of commotion outside in the passage, of hurrying footsteps and voices raised in surprise and excitement. Electra flung open the door and strode out. 'For heaven's sake!' she cried. 'What's going on? Can't I even have my bath in peace and quiet?'

One of the housemaids, the housekeeper, Karen Black and Julian Crucefix were there. The maid was in tears, and Karen was trying to comfort her.

'Now look what you've done!' scolded the housekeeper with a stern glance at the maid. 'Disturbing Dr Vanderpump – what a to-do! You ought to be ashamed of yourself, Tiffany.'

'But I saw it, I tell you!' wailed Tiffany. 'It was a ghost, in Dr Vanderpump's bedroom!'

'Perhaps it was a trick of the light,' suggested Julian Crucefix vaguely.

'No, it wasn't,' declared Tiffany, wiping her eyes. 'I saw him, clear as anything. It was Mr Duffy, the old manager.'

Julian frowned, taken aback, but Karen seemed only slightly perturbed. 'How could it be Mr Duffy?' she said gently, putting her arm around the maid's shoulders. 'You know he's on holiday in Majorca.'

'It was his ghost!' sobbed Tiffany.

'What nonsense is this?' said Electra Vanderpump sharply. 'You stupid girl, there're no such things as ghosts, and even if there were, it certainly couldn't have been Mr Duffy's ghost you saw. Didn't you hear Miss Black? He's gone on holiday.'

'Wait a minute,' said Julian in puzzlement. 'I thought ... I mean, Lord Stephen told me Mr Duffy died of a heart attack.'

Karen stared at him, annoyed. 'No – that's wrong ... '

'He was all white and ghostly, and he walked right through the wall!' wailed Tiffany. 'I was making the bed, and he came right in.'

'Oh, do be quiet, for heaven's sake!' snapped Electra. She glared at Julian. 'Mr Duffy's on holiday,' she said, 'and that's the end of the matter. Now, I don't want to hear any more talk of ghosts. I've never heard such rubbish in my life.'

Tiffany began to protest, but the housekeeper drew her aside. 'That's enough of that. You'd better come and lie down, my girl.' She turned to Karen and Electra. 'A touch of the sun, if you ask me,' she said. 'All that sunbathing and sunbeds – I knew it wouldn't do her any good. Never mind, Dr Vanderpump, I'll take care of her. Sorry you were disturbed. It won't happen again.'

Electra's cold green eyes followed with a troubled gaze as the housekeeper led the maid away. Julian and Karen were leaving too, but Electra stopped them. 'One moment,' she said curtly. 'Has Lord Stephen spoken to you yet about the new arrangements?'

'What?' asked Karen sullenly.

'This is precisely the kind of incident that we feared would arise,' said Electra. 'The staff are overworked and suffering from stress, and Lord Stephen and I have decided that you all need a holiday. Fortunately it's coincided with the renovations, so this is an ideal opportunity.' She smiled. 'Karen, dear, perhaps you'd be so good as to inform everyone that they have one month's paid leave from the day after tomorrow.'

'Is that what Steve said?' Karen sounded almost accusative.

'It was the Earl's idea,' replied Electra. 'Ask him if you wish.'

Julian scratched his ear nervously. 'Everyone ... You mean ...?'

'Yes, Mr Crucefix,' said Electra impatiently. 'That includes you too, so you'd better start packing your bags.'

'But I say,' objected Julian hesitantly, 'there's a lot of work to be done, Dr Vanderpump. Mr Duffy left a backlog of stuff, you see. And I can assure you that I'm not suffering from stress.'

Electra glowered. 'Are you arguing with me, Mr Crucefix? For heaven's sake, I would've thought you'd be glad of a holiday – take advantage of the good weather for once!'

'Well, it just seems rather short notice, that's all,' said Julian weakly. 'I mean, I haven't got anywhere to go.'

'Oh, for goodness' sake, use your initiative!' retorted Electra. 'I'm sure you'll come up with something. However, bear in mind that the restorations will commence on Friday morning, and everyone must be out of the house by then, since the cleaning materials and the processes involved in polishing the marble staircase may constitute a health hazard. So if you're here after tomorrow, Mr Crucefix, consider it to be at your own risk.'

'But, Dr Vanderpump ... ' Julian began uneasily.

Electra turned away haughtily and strode into the bedroom. 'If you have any more questions, Mr Crucefix,' she said, 'kindly address them to the Earl himself. I have no time for such domestic matters.' She slammed the door shut behind her, leaving Julian and Karen standing in the darkness of the windowless passage.

'God!' said Julian with a nervous laugh. 'She's in a bit of a mood today.'

'Yeah,' agreed Karen casually. 'She always is. You'd better do as she says, though. If that's what Steve wants, there's no point in arguing.'

They walked back along the passage to Julian's office.

'Miss Black,' remarked Julian tentatively. 'I don't want to sound as if I'm being awkward, or anything. It's not that I'm questioning the Earl's authority, or his judgement, you understand, but doesn't it strike you as ... well a bit odd, you know?'

'No, I don't know, actually,' said Karen, with a toss of her head that made her big pink bow bounce up and down.

'Well, not exactly odd, then,' added Julian quickly, 'but it's almost ... ' He laughed in a feeble attempt to make his remark sound more casual than he really meant it. 'Almost as if he wants to get rid of us!' he said.

Outside the open door of the office, Karen stopped and turned to face him. In the shaft of sunlight that entered onto the shadowy oak-panelled landing, Julian could see that her lip was trembling, perhaps in anger, perhaps in distress, or both.

'What exactly d'you bloody mean by that?' she demanded.

Julian was embarrassed; he fumbled for his words.

'Well, I don't suppose I mean anything really,' he said lamely.

'Yeah, it bleedin' sounds like it!' retorted Karen. 'Steve happens to be a socialist, actually. That's why he cares about the people who work for him. Don't you want a holiday, or something?'

'I'm sorry,' Julian apologised bashfully. 'I just wasn't expecting it, I suppose, and it did seem a bit funny, coming from Dr Vanderpump like that.'

Karen's gaze dropped to avoid his eyes; she bit her lip uncertainly.

In a moment, Julian recovered his courage. He said, 'By the way, what did happen to Mr Duffy?'

Karen shrugged. 'He's on holiday. How many more times've I gotta tell you?'

'Lord Stephen told me that he was dead,' said Julian.

Karen heaved an exasperated sigh. She tossed her head; she gazed at the ceiling. 'Does it matter?' she said.

'Maybe it doesn't matter to you,' said Julian, 'but it matters to me. I've got his job, and I don't exactly relish the idea of him coming back from Majorca expecting to take over where he left off. I've given up my flat in London to come down here, because the Earl led me to believe that it was a permanent position. Quite honestly, I don't believe Mr Duffy's on holiday. Lord Stephen may be a socialist, but I can't believe he'd let his estate manager go gadding off to Majorca for three months. He told me that he didn't want you to be upset by the truth about Mr Duffy's death, Miss Black, but I can't accept that either, because Dr Vanderpump said the same thing about him being on holiday, and I can't believe the Earl told her the same story to protect her feelings too.'

'You bloody shut up! Shut up!' Karen clenched her fists fiercely; there were angry tears in her eyes. 'If you say another word, I'll – I'll ... I'll tell Steve!'

Julian almost apologised again, but he stopped himself: there was something so odd about Karen's attitude that, despite his sense of guilt at having upset her, he felt that he could not let the issue rest, now that he had gathered sufficient courage to raise his doubts.

'I don't want to upset you, Miss Black,' he explained, 'but I think there are some things that need to be said. I've been here for three months, and all this time I've tried to turn a blind eye to what I thought shouldn't concern me. But I'm sorry, I just can't do that anymore. People are talking about what's going on here. At first, I thought it was just wild tales and superstition, but I can't accept that now. Even the workman who was mending the fences has heard stories.'

'And that's all it is,' declared Karen. 'Just stories! I'm surprised at you, Julian Crucefix, listening to tittle-tattle! Like an old woman, Steve would say. He'd laugh at you, he would, if he heard you talking now. Old women's gossip, old wives' tales – that's what he'd say! When're you going to take up knitting too, eh?'

'The police were here this morning,' said Julian. 'I take that rather more seriously. Then there was that man Dorrell.'

'Oh God!' cried Karen scornfully. 'Steve told me he was a bloody poofter, dressed up in women's clothes and wearing make-up and bows in his hair. You must be daft if you believe anything a weirdo like that tells you.'

'It's a matter of who's telling the truth – nothing to do with masculinity ... ' Julian began, but then he broke off and held back his words. He felt humiliated, but he did not want to argue.

Later in his office as he tried to work, he found that he could not concentrate. For too long, he realised, he had

kept in his place, trying to explain away what he had taken
to be the Earl's eccentricities; but now he was not so sure.

In restless indecision, he gazed from his window that
looked down into the grey courtyard where the sun never
shone. He thought about Lady Caroline Giles and he tried
to remember her as he had last seen her. He remembered
Sebastian Dorrell's strange question: *Was it, perhaps, Johnny
Terrier dressed up and wearing a strawberry blonde wig?* It was
an absurd suggestion, as Sebastian had admitted, but the
more that Julian thought about it, the more uncertain he
became that he really had seen the Countess on that occasion. He remembered looking out of the Music Room window and noticing the taxi cab parked on the drive. He remembered the small figure with the mass of flaming gold
hair emerging from the portico of the house and hastening
across the forecourt, closely followed by Dr Vanderpump
and the Earl carrying the Countess's suitcase. But had that
figure really been the Countess herself? Viewed from behind, it was hard to be sure, but now that Julian tried to
recall what he had seen, he realised that he could have
been mistaken. Could it really have been the beautiful and
graceful Countess of Warwick, he wondered, walking with
that odd suggestion of a limp that he had noticed but had
not reflected on at the time? She had seemed to walk with
an almost shambling gait, he remembered now, and how
roughly Dr Vanderpump had bundled her into the waiting
taxi!

Julian turned away from the window, troubled about
what he should do. It looked as if Sebastian Dorrell had
been right: it had been Johnny Terrier, not Lady Caroline,
who had left in the taxi that day. But even if this were so, it
did not necessarily mean that the Earl and Dr Vander-

pump were engaged in any morally reprehensible or illegal activity.

Even as he considered these matters, Julian experienced a tremendous sense of guilt. As an employee at Heydn Hall, he believed that it was his duty to serve and to obey in silence, never questioning the activities of his employer; but as an individual, he did not know how to decide where his responsibilities lay.

*

In the darkness of the cellar, Sebastian Dorrell stood motionless in silence, waiting.

After a while, the voice called again: 'Can you hear me over there? It's no use turning out the light – I know you're there.'

It was man's voice, rather high-pitched and shaky, and now that Sebastian heard it again, he realised that it was familiar to him, though it took him a moment to recognise whose it was.

'Professor Aaronberg?' he called softly, hopefully. 'Is that you?'

'Who's that?' called back the Professor. 'Lord Stephen?'

'No, it's me – Sebastian,' said Sebastian. He switched on his torch and shone the pale beam around again, over the cold gleaming ranks of machinery; black shadows reared up and flickered across the walls as he moved the light around. 'Where are you?' he said. 'Professor, I can't see you.'

'I'm over here,' called Professor Aaronberg weakly. 'I'm locked in. My dear boy, I can hardly believe it. I thought no one would ever find me.'

Sebastian followed the sound of the Professor's voice across the cellar until he came to one of the brick-walled storage rooms. Professor Aaronberg's voice issued from behind the door: 'How did you find me?' he asked.

'It was your own book, Professor,' said Sebastian. 'You remember, you – ah ... told me about the chapter on mysterious disappearances in which you mentioned – ah ... mentioned the Horsley-Mitchell family. At first it was the only clue I had – that dreadful letter the Earl sent you ... But never mind about that now – I'll tell you everything later, and hopefully you'll – ah ... you'll be able to fill me in on what's going on here. Or are you as much in the dark as I am?'

'Who knows what they're about, dear boy,' said Professor Aaronberg. 'I'll tell you all I know, but first – '

'Yes, how to get you out of there,' said Sebastian, laying his hand on the panelled door. 'There's no – ah ... no key on this side.'

'I know – I can see through the keyhole,' the Professor explained. 'Lord Stephen must have taken the key away with him. They've kept me in here for days – I'm not even sure how long it's been. At first, they promised to let me out in return for my agreement to co-operate and help them with their project, but of course it was only a matter of hours before they found out that I really know very little that could be of any use to them.' He sighed.

'It's outrageous,' said Sebastian in anger and frustration that he was unable to free the Professor. 'It's a damn disgrace. They've no right to keep you here in the cold and dark. Where is the key to this door? D'you think I could find it?'

'I'm afraid it's probably in the Earl's pocket, dear boy,' said Professor Aaronberg.

'Then there has to be another way ... ' mused Sebastian.

'You must fetch the police at once,' cried the Professor. 'At once! I cannot spend another day in this terrible place!'

'You won't have to,' Sebastian assured him. 'I'll get you out of there somehow, even if I have to break down the damn door. But I don't – ah ... don't think this is quite the sort of business that the police ought to be mixed up in.'

'My dear boy, I couldn't disagree more!' protested the Professor, his voice rising to a higher pitch in his agitation.

'Just wait a minute,' said Sebastian, 'and I'll go and find something to break through this door.'

He hurried into the adjoining cellar, where he thought he remembered seeing an axe standing in a corner with some old gardening implements, but before he had a chance to look, he was startled by the sudden illumination of the large cellar that he had just left: all the electric lighting had been switched on, and now he could hear heavy footsteps ringing on stone, and the echoing of voices. Someone was coming down the stairs into the cellars.

Sebastian switched off his torch at once and crept back to the entrance of the large cellar, where he pressed himself against the wall, out of sight. Now he could recognise the voices as those of Lord Stephen Mitchell and Electra Vanderpump.

'I've dealt with it all perfectly adequately,' Electra was saying. Her cold shrill voice rang icily across the stone chamber.

'I wish to God you'd let me handle it,' grumbled the Earl loudly. 'Things look bad enough already, without giving the staff the idea that I'm not even boss in my own bloody house!'

Very cautiously, Sebastian peered around the corner of the wall into the brightly-lit cellar: now the strange scene looked even more like a highly advanced and sophisticated laboratory, under the blaze of the overhead lamps.

Electra Vanderpump, impeccable in her white laboratory coat and stiletto-heeled sandals, her long black hair tied up with a red scarf, was walking up and down the aisles, checking the equipment, while the big blond Earl, his braces fastened over the outside of his tweed jacket, was at the far end of the cellar surveying the large old machine which stood there with its bakelite control knobs and linoleum-covered floor.

'Right, I think we should run through the new programme now,' announced Electra brightly. 'I'm certain the computer will come up with a feasible solution to our power supply problem.'

'I was damn sure we'd have to build a bloody great nuclear reactor!' said the Earl with a desperate laugh as he pulled down his braces and struggled out of his jacket. 'If we can find a way round that, we're practically home and dry!' His arms flailed wildly in the air for a moment before he succeeded in getting his jacket off; he screwed it into a tight ball and hurled it aside. Enthusiastically, he rolled up the sleeves of his shirt and pulled his braces back on.

'There's rather more to it than that, I'm afraid,' said Electra, approaching the computer.

Sebastian watched her slender legs as she walked away from him; the movement of her hips excited him: he could not help but find her attractive, and even now he desired her.

'It's far from ready for a trial run yet,' she said. 'I certainly wouldn't trust my life to it. We don't know what forces may come into play as we attempt to penetrate the Bubble. Even if the Machine isn't torn apart, anyone standing on that platform could be flung off. I still think we need some kind of safety harness.'

Sebastian licked his lips; he stared at her legs.

'We'll bust in there somehow!' declared the Earl, as he got down on his hands and knees on the base of the big machine, close to the grilles that had been unscrewed in its central column earlier. 'You're too cautious, you know. You women always are. Now a man's not afraid to take a few risks, once in a while. As far as I'm concerned, I'm ready to smash through, just as soon as we've got enough power to make a go of it.'

Electra pulled up a chair to sit at the computer keyboard. As she sat down, her white coat fell open and her tight skirt rode up her thighs. Sebastian's admiring gaze was upon her legs; he wondered if she was wearing anything underneath her dress.

'Really, Lord Stephen!' scolded Electra sharply. 'It's precisely that kind of approach that could ruin everything at the very climax of our operations. You really must try to control your enthusiasm. For heaven's sake, the situation has remained the same for sixty years. I'm sure you can wait another week or two while we take a few final precautions.'

'I'm sick and tired of waiting!' grunted the Earl as he prodded with his screwdriver inside the base of the machine. 'More lubricant needed here ... I've been bloody waiting all my life. The only positive action I ever took was when I busted in.'

'Oh, for heaven's sake!' Electra interjected scornfully. 'Do you have to be so crude?' Angrily she began to type the new programme into the computer. 'Brute force is of no use whatsoever in this operation. Careful planning, patience and thoroughly reliable equipment is what's needed, and you know that as well as I do, Lord Stephen. Your equipment is not reliable – it needs a proper over-haul!'

'Bloody hell!' the Earl ejaculated. 'What d'you think I'm doing now?'

'You've blown more circuits than you've repaired,' remarked Electra. 'You're as clumsy as your father, and we know what happened to him. You seem to forget, it's not just a simple matter of penetration. Once in, one has to be able to get out again, and that, I shouldn't have to remind you, is where your grandfather made his big mistake. Of course,' she added bitterly, 'if you ever do get out, that could be when your problems really begin. Once the Bubble's been disturbed, we don't know how unstable it may become. We have to be prepared for the worst contingency. It's possible that the whole of Heydn Hall may become engulfed.'

Sebastian frowned. He could not understand their conversation, and now that his interest in what they were saying had flagged, he began to wonder what he could do about Professor Aaronberg. Plainly it would not be possible to break down the door whilst Electra and the Earl were in the cellar, and they did not look as if they would be leaving yet. Sebastian was considering whether he ought to go now and come back later, perhaps at night, when his rescue attempt would be less likely to be discovered; then he noticed the Earl's jacket that lay where he had flung it on the floor some distance away from where he was working. It suddenly occurred to Sebastian that the key to the storeroom may be in one of the pockets of the jacket.

Electra was sitting with her back to him now, busy at

the computer, and the Earl, lying on his stomach at the base of the big machine, seemed to be engrossed in his work. Very quietly and cautiously, keeping close to the wall, Sebastian began to creep towards the Earl's discarded jacket.

'Do you know, when it really comes down to it,' remarked Lord Stephen, 'I think I'd be prepared to take that risk. Damn it all, I really think I would. Just for peace of mind, Dr Vanderpump, just for peace of mind. Do you know what that means? I've been living with this damned thing since I was fifteen, and even before then – since I first had my suspicions about my father's death.'

Electra did not reply; her concentration was fixed upon the computer.

Sebastian began to crawl across the floor towards the jacket.

'I kept it to myself, shut up inside all those years,' said the Earl. 'Until I met Karen, I didn't tell a living soul. Now, what the hell have I done with my other screwdriver? Have you seen it lying about anywhere? I think it's in my jacket pocket.'

Sebastian, who was at that moment reaching for the jacket, withdrew in alarm and managed to conceal himself behind one of the large pieces of machinery, only a moment before the Earl sat up and looked around.

Crouching beside the machine, Sebastian waited in trepidation as Lord Stephen approached, stooped down and picked up the jacket. He searched the pockets until he found what he wanted, then tossed the jacket aside: it fell only a few inches from where Sebastian was hiding. Waiting a minute for the Earl to settle at his task again, Sebastian carefully drew the jacket towards him and felt inside the pockets. As he had hoped, he found a key-ring with several keys on it. He took it out gingerly, trying not to make a sound, and then he crept back along the wall, the way he had come.

'It was a stroke of luck that you knew something about matters of this sort, Dr Vanderpump,' the Earl said. 'If I hadn't decided to see you for therapy at that time, I could've been struggling on down here on my own for years, building bloody nuclear reactors and God knows what.'

Softly and silently, Sebastian crept over to the opposite side of the cellar, ducking behind the machinery and piles of old crates to avoid being seen by Electra, moving right up to the door of the storeroom where Professor Aaronberg was held prisoner. He selected one of the keys that looked suitable and fitted it into the lock, but it would not turn.

'Who's that?' said Professor Aaronberg's nervous voice from behind the door. 'Is that you, dear boy?'

'Shh!' said Sebastian. 'Yes, it's me,' he whispered. 'I think I have the key.'

He tried two more in the lock, and on the second attempt succeeded in opening the door. Hastily he beckoned the startled Professor out of the storeroom and made him hide behind the banks of machinery. The door swung back, creaking a little as it closed.

Electra Vanderpump stopped typing. She glanced up. 'What was that noise?' she asked. 'Did you hear something, Lord Stephen?'

The Earl, who had been talking, had heard nothing.

Uneasily, Sebastian and Professor Aaronberg crouched, hidden, behind the machinery.

'There was an odd noise,' said Electra. 'A kind of scuffling and rustling. I'm sure I heard something squeaking.'

'Rats, probably,' remarked the Earl with disinterest.

'Oh, how disgusting!' Electra exclaimed. 'Surely there can't be rats down here? I never noticed before. You should at least have warned me.'

The Earl laughed. 'Don't tell me you're scared of rats, are you? Just like a woman!' he scoffed.

'It's all very well for you to make a joke of it,' retorted Electra icily, 'but if there really are rats, they could gnaw through our electrical wiring and damage the circuits.' She began to type into the computer again, apparently satisfied that no investigation into the source of the noises was necessary.

Sebastian pointed out to the Professor the dark entrance into the adjoining cellar, and they crept towards it as quickly as they could, without making a sound.

The Earl, lying on his back now, continued to work at his machine, and Electra, her face set in a scowl of determination, continued to type the programme into the computer. Neither of them noticed, as Sebastian Dorrell and Professor Aaronberg left the cellars, escaping into the secret smugglers' tunnel that led out onto the beach.

CHAPTER 15

Speculations

Much later, in the quiet and quaintly rustic lounge of the Black Dog, over tea, Sebastian and Professor Aaronberg discussed what they should do about the happenings at Heydn Hall. They had both washed, and Sebastian had changed into his black rubber trousers, black string vest and leopardskin jacket. The Professor, having no change of clothing, was still dressed in his crumpled, grubby white cotton suit.

'These little cakes are quite delicious,' said Professor Aaronberg.

'I like the ones with the pink icing best,' said Sebastian, taking another from the plate.

'My dear boy,' said the Professor, 'I'm afraid I must insist upon going to the police. Those people abducted me. I was taken by surprise and didn't know what to do. I thought it was you, you see ... '

Sebastian nodded. 'And it was Johnny Terrier. Yes, I know.'

'You know Johnny Terrier?' said the Professor in surprise. 'A decidedly odd young man – mentally impaired, I would say.'

Then Sebastian told Professor Aaronberg about his visit to the Twilight Home and how he had first met Johnny Terrier there and had come to learn that Electra Vanderpump was involved in the activities at Heydn Hall.

'So you know that terrible woman too?' the Professor said in dismay. 'And do you know her colleague, Dr Kotlowski?'

'She told me about him.' Sebastian smiled. 'But I have yet to – ah ... yet to enjoy the dubious pleasure of meeting him.'

'Let us hope you never do,' replied the Professor. 'I encountered him on the Earl's yacht when they first abducted me. He is a highly disturbed and sado-masochistic man, and I would not like to think of my dear boy keeping such company. Most certainly not.' Carefully he cut his little cake into four smaller portions; he nibbled at one thoughtfully.

The Professor's small brown hand rested in a patch of sunlight upon the table-cloth, and Sebastian, reassuringly, laid his larger hand over it. 'You worry about me too much,' he said. 'I came here to find you, but now that I know you're safe, I still want to get to the bottom of this affair. I have the Earl's keys now, so I'll be able to get in.'

'My dear boy, you must never go back there!' said Professor Aaronberg in agitation. 'You must never go to that terrible place again! We're lucky to come out alive. They're all mad – quite mad, I tell you! You saw all that electrical equipment for yourself. You must have seen the machine they're building down there?'

'The circular one, like a big spool,' said Sebastian. 'Yes. What's it for? Do you know?'

Professor Aaronberg sipped his tea from the porcelain cup. He gazed out of the small leaded window, down the sunny road towards the sea front. 'It was once something I believed in myself,' he said quietly, 'but over the years I have come to change my mind. I now no longer believe it's possible, or even desirable. I'm talking about time travel, dear boy. You'll remember, I wrote a book about it. Lord Stephen Mitchell read my book and believed that I could assist him in constructing a time machine. I could not, of course. I'm not a scientist – I'm a philosopher.' He sighed and rested his teacup on the saucer. 'The arguments for the possibility of time travel are inconsistent and illogical,' he said. 'I thought for a while that I had found a way around the conceptual problems, but I was mistaken.'

'Time travel isn't impossible, Professor,' Sebastian told him quietly. 'I know, because I've done it.'

'Done it, dear boy? Whatever do you mean?' The Professor looked at him in alarm.

'You saw it happen,' Sebastian reminded him, 'last Thursday night, when I came to warn you that you would disappear. The next day when you telephoned me about it, of course I didn't remember, as – ah … as it hadn't happened yet, from my point of view. It wasn't until after your disappearance that I travelled back in time to ask you about it.'

'That night when you appeared in my bedroom?' asked the Professor incredulously. 'But you weren't really there – not there in the flesh, so to speak. Afterwards I thought I'd dreamed it.'

'I wasn't able to materialise,' Sebastian explained. 'Normally I would've been able to make my physical presence more apparent, but there appears to be some psychological block against travelling back to a time when one already existed, because one might meet an earlier stage of oneself in doing so. Bizarre – but not – ah … not logically impossible, as far as I can see. However, I suspect that the psyche resists such an encounter. It's just my guess, though.'

'It is precisely one of the reasons why I would want to reject the hypothesis of time travel,' answered the Professor. 'Dear me, it raises tremendous problems concerning personal identity. Are you saying that you already have a time machine, such as the Earl is attempting to build? I believed his aims to be futile, but if you have achieved such a thing, I must think again.'

Sebastian smiled, and told him about the Chair. 'I don't altogether understand it,' he admitted. Thoughtfully he traced a pattern with the handle of his teaspoon across the table-cloth. 'I know only that it works for me – I have to get into a certain frame of mind, and then it happens. I bought the Chair in a junk shop, years ago, and I found that if I – ah ... went into a sort of reverie about the past, while sitting in the Chair, then I would find myself somehow in that period of the past. Sometimes the impressions were vivid, particularly if it were a period before I was born, which perhaps seems counterintuitive. Yet the visions seemed absolutely real – and I can only say that, as far as I can judge, I had really time-travelled. But I have no proof, no scientific evidence – only my own subjective experience. Electra Vanderpump tried to persuade me to tell her how to do it. Psychology is her forte, but time travel is outside the area of her expertise, which infuriates her. I suspect that this is why she cannot accept that my technique is purely psychological, because she knows about psychology but she doesn't know about this. So she assumes that there must be some physical mechanism behind time travel, and she wants to possess something tangible – a weapon of physical power. She believes that if

I – ah … if I divulge my knowledge to her, she could become immortal and travel through time at will, or some
such nonsense. It's absurd! Anyway, even if I could explain to her all she needed to know, I don't think that I
would. No doubt she imagines that she can get from Lord
Steve what she can't get from me.'

'If that's really what she expects,' said the Professor,
'she's going to be disappointed, I think. The Earl seems to
understand very little of the technical side himself. He re-
fers to it as his father's time machine. From what I could
gather, it was his grandfather who first became interested
in the possibility of travelling in time, and his father continued the work and managed to build a time machine,
although it has never functioned properly. Now Lord
Stephen is following in his father's footsteps, modifying
the old machine under the guidance of Dr Vanderpump.'

Sebastian rested his elbows on the table; he rested his
chin in his hands. He frowned. 'Now it's beginning to
make more sense – his father and his grandfather … Professor, I think perhaps you were wrong in your – ah …
hereditary theory of strange disappearances. Perhaps their
disappearance wasn't so strange after all.'

'You're not suggesting they travelled in time?' exclaimed the Professor in disbelief.

Sebastian sighed. He ran his fingers through his long
dark hair. 'But it's not the whole story,' he said. Then he
began to tell the Professor about his experience on the previous evening and about the binoculars that he had found
which were not the same as the pair that he had lost. 'My
personal experiments with the Chair have led me to
speculate that time has more than one dimension,' he said.
'I discovered quite early on that one can – ah … travel lat-
erally, as it were, through time into what I assume to be

other dimensions, some of which resemble this that we occupy at present. I suppose it's similar to the philosophical concept of possible worlds, but these other worlds are actual, in a sense parallel to ours, but differing in subtle respects. A temporal disturbance at the Hall, such as might be caused by a malfunctioning time machine, could bring about a weakening of the interface between this dimension and – ah ... those adjacent to it. The effect, one supposes, might be to produce phenomena of the kind that's been seen recently. The only problem with that theory is that the Time Machine didn't appear to be malfunctioning, since it wasn't functioning at all, and from what I overheard them saying, it sounds as if they haven't even tested it yet. But even now that I know they were talking about this Time Machine, the rest of their conversation still doesn't make any sense to me. Lord Steve kept talking about things being shut up, and his having to break in, and Electra was talking about the penetration of something or other, and the problems of – ah ... of getting out again once they'd got in wherever they were trying to get. Lord Steve, I remember, said something about – ah ... taking action, and Electra said something about the situation having been as it is for the past sixty years.' He stroked his thumb across his chin and down his neck thoughtfully. 'You know, I'm sure it has something to do with that tower – the Prince's Tower – or perhaps not? I mean, the Tower was bricked up about sixty years ago – more than that – seventy. Could she – ah ... could she have been talking about the Tower? But if they wanted to go inside the Tower, why should they need a time machine for that?'

'Personally, I cannot see why one should want a time machine at all,' commented the Professor, finishing his little cake and pushing aside his plate. 'They may as well use it for that purpose as for any other, so far as I am concerned.'

'But Lord Steve sounded so bothered about it,' Sebastian remarked. 'What was it he said – that he'd had to keep the secret to himself for practically the whole of his life. Now to look at Lord Steve, you'd think a man like that couldn't keep a secret for five minutes, let alone for thirty years – he'd blurt it out sooner or later. But he hasn't. It must be something damned important – not just an old time machine that's never worked.'

'Don't trouble yourself to wonder about it,' said the Professor with a mild laugh. 'Lord Stephen is a man full of words but with very little to say of any sense or interest. He is fond of action, but whether it is appropriate or inappropriate, useful or obstructive, he does not care, so long as it is vigorous and works up a good sweat. He would rather talk nonsense than remain silent and risk appearing passive. He would rather make a bad decision than appear indecisive, do wrong rather than do nothing. My dear boy, he is the kind of man who would strive towards his own destruction in order to avoid seeming weak-willed. Whatever you heard him say, it was in all probability of very little consequence.'

Sebastian grinned. 'Come on now, Professor – don't you think you're being a bit unfair? I mean, he's not such a bad chap. From what I've seen of him, I quite like him, actually. I must admit, when I first read that letter he sent you, I was imagining some – ah ... some elderly sort of Colonel Blimp character, but he's not, is he? Well, he might be rude and aggressive and rather eccentric, but he's hardly an old reactionary. According to his estate manager he's a liberal-minded socialist.'

'In my opinion,' replied the Professor, 'the Earl is a highly disturbed man – practically deranged, I would say.'

'Well, he's obviously disturbed,' Sebastian agreed. 'But he's disturbed about something in particular, and I wish I knew what it was.' He finished drinking his cup of tea and rested his head back against the window-frame, gazing out into the street. The blue shadows were lengthening, spreading out from the nearby cottages, across the road; a few holiday-makers in beach-wear were strolling by. 'He told Electra that he'd be prepared to risk anything for peace of mind,' Sebastian remarked. 'And what – ah ... what did Electra say? I'm trying to remember. Yes, she said the whole of Heydn Hall could become *engulfed*. That was the word she used. But engulfed in what, by what, I ask myself. And whatever the risks are, why does he take them? Not just because he fancies himself as a time-tripper. The Time Machine is part of it, but he wants that machine for a specific purpose. He needs it to go somewhere, or to get something – something very important to him.'

Sebastian gazed out of the window again, and as he did so, he caught sight of someone whom he recognised.

Walking along the road in the mellow evening light, deep in thought, his head bowed dejectedly, his hands buried in the pockets of his grey woollen jacket, was Julian Crucefix.

'I say, there's Crucefix,' Sebastian observed.

'Who?' said the Professor.

'The Earl's estate manager,' said Sebastian. He stood up, pushing back his chair. 'I think I'll go and have a word with him. See you later, in the bar. I won't – ah ... won't be long.'

'I'll buy you a lemonade, dear boy!' the Professor called after him, as Sebastian hurried out of the door.

CHAPTER 16

The Doubts of Julian Crucefix:
The Memories of the Earl

In his office on the second floor of Heydn Hall, Lord Stephen Mitchell stood at the mullioned casement window, his arms resting on the ledge, as he gazed out over the formal Tudor gardens and the rolling lawns beyond. On the edge of the garden was a pergola of mellowed brick pillars, overhung by the massed blooms of pink and white climbing roses. The Earl watched the butterflies flitting among the flowers. He gazed at the tall trees on the edge of the lawns, their branches swayed by the breeze. From his window, he was able to see almost the whole extent of the grounds on the southern side of the house – from the eastern hedge, the mossy stone walls of the ruins of an old chapel, the ornamental obelisk, the giant sundial that was formed of square-clipped yew hedges – right across the wild extent of the deer park to the artificial lake and the rock garden, the shadowy woodland and the ruins of the Victorian conservatory. Among the trees he could just see the gilded ball on top of the pale green domed roof of the ornamental pavilion on the edge of the rock garden, and beyond that, beyond the dark mantle of trees, was the western hedge that marked the boundary of the estate.

Lord Stephen stared out over his inheritance, and a deep frown troubled his brow as he tried to remember a time when he had been able to enjoy it purely and simply, without the fear of losing it all. He realised that there had never been such a time, except far back in his distant childhood: too far back even for him to remember now. It seemed to him that merely to live had always been to live with fear and the terrible knowledge that gave rise to it; and so, over the years, he had learned to play a game of hide-and-seek with himself, shouting ever louder, laughing and joking more desperately, fighting ever harder, as he struggled with himself to cover up the emptiness that he felt inside, and the fear of terrible destruction, the terror of irretrievable loss.

With heavy footsteps, he turned and walked over to the other window – the window that looked out of the western wall of the east wing, facing the dark, ivy-shrouded, mysterious Prince's Tower. The evening sun was sinking low, and the edge of the glass prism on the roof glinted with a harsh red gleam, like the embers of a fire. Lord Stephen gazed upon the Tower with a dark brooding gaze, and he remembered a night long ago, after the death of his mother, when he had taken upon himself to uncover the secret that had been sealed in there since the time of his grandfather.

It had been late in the evening, and he had made sure that no household staff were about. He had gone into the room on the ground floor where the entrance to the Tower had once been. It was the room that in later years was to become the cafeteria, when the Hall was opened to the public, but in those days it was used as a storeroom. The bricked-up doorway could still be seen: it was arched, with stone carvings around it, and directly over it was the stone head of an old god – some rustic, grinning spirit of fertility or lust. Lord Stephen had locked the door of the adjoining room and kept only one hurricane lamp alight, as he set about his labour of breaking through the old doorway. He had been careful also to leave the light shining in his office upstairs, and had given instructions that he was not to be disturbed, so that anyone might think that he was working late at his desk.

Though it had still been pale dusk outside, in the Tower it was pitch black, and Lord Stephen had entered boldly with his lamp. He had not imagined that he was going to find anything so very terrible in the place. It had seemed more likely to him that there would be something there of historical interest, possibly some family heirloom or work of art: that, at least, was what his hope had been. 'And maybe I wasn't so damn far from the truth after all,' muttered the Earl to himself now, as he stared at the derelict Tower. He could not restrain a cold shudder, as he recalled his feelings of horror at his discovery – his sense of helpless frustration at his realisation that he could do nothing about it but shut it all up, brick up the entrance once more, and leave it all in darkness behind him, just as he had found it.

He remembered how he had worked frantically as the night had come down, and all the while the thought had been in his mind that this must have been just what his father had done, just as he had felt when he saw it, as he must have seen it; and there was nothing that Lord Stephen could do, nothing that anyone could do about it. At the same time, he had not even comprehended quite what he had seen, but he felt sick to think of it, even so: he had seen enough to know that it was something uncanny, something that seemed like a nightmare, all the more terrible because he could not understand it.

Lord Stephen turned away from the window and stepped over to his big mahogany desk. He opened a bottom drawer and took out a notebook bound in red leather that was flaking and cracked along the spine: it was the book that his grandfather had used as a diary, and which his father had kept for many years down in the cellar, where it had deteriorated.

Carefully, Lord Stephen opened the book on the desk and drew up a chair, sitting down to read again the words that his grandfather, Lord Mountjoy the eighteenth Earl, had written more than sixty years earlier.

I am upon the very brink, he read. *Nothing can hold me back now.*

Tonight I take that plunge into the blackness of the unknown that I have so long awaited with joy and fear! At midnight I shall plunge into oblivion, propelled by the power of the sun, and beyond the darkness – who knows? Liberty, boundless freedom – free from this life, even from this world! That freedom shall be mine, now that my will is charged, and all doubts I have cast to the wind! I cannot be restrained – I shall be a prisoner no more!

As Lord Stephen read the diary, he beat his fist in anger upon the desk; he ran his fingers in anguish through his short blond hair. It was terrible, it was pathetic; and yes, ironic too, bitterly ironic.

He swore loudly, and then he looked up, staring at the window, for a noise had come from outside: it was the sound of an approaching helicopter. He leapt to his feet and bounded over to the window. The helicopter was directly overhead now, and as he watched, it flew across the grounds of Heydn Hall, then hovered lower as it prepared to land in the private park. The Earl knew that the pilot was Johnny Terrier and that he had brought Dr Kotlowski with him.

'Bloody hell!' said Lord Stephen aloud, and he laughed wryly. 'Kotlowski and Terrier – what a joke! What a bloody farce!' Then he gazed again towards the Prince's Tower, now a dark and threatening silhouette against the reddening sky, and as he looked at it, his expression grew grave and troubled once more. 'But I wish to God I could get it over now,' he muttered to himself. 'Whatever the cost, whatever the outcome, I wish to God it was all over and done.'

*

'Mr Crucefix!' called Sebastian Dorrell. Out of the door of the Black Dog he ran, across the car park, into the road. He called again.

Julian Crucefix, further along the road, hesitated in his walking and glanced hack over his shoulder; then he began to walk more quickly, but whether or not this was because he had recognised Sebastian, it was not clear.

Sebastian ran after him, down towards the beach. Upon the pale sand that was pink in the evening sunlight, he apprehended Julian, who looked awkward and uncomfortable to see him, but who could not very well evade him now.

'Hello,' said Sebastian, as he strolled up beside Julian on the sands. 'A pleasant – ah … pleasant evening, what.'

'Hello,' said Julian, trying to sound careless and light-hearted. He gazed out over the calm sea.

'I thought you may be interested to know, Mr Crucefix,' said Sebastian with a smile, 'that I found my friend, Professor Aaronberg.'

'Oh, did you?' remarked Julian with feigned disinterest. 'That's good. Perhaps now that you've realised what I told you in the first place – that his disappearance had nothing whatsoever to do with anyone at the Hall – you'll leave us in peace.'

'On the contrary,' said Sebastian, 'since it was, in fact, at Heydn Hall that I did indeed find him – locked in the cellar, to be precise.'

Julian glanced at Sebastian in startled disbelief; he stopped walking and stood still on the sand, his back towards the sea, sweeping his fair hair away from his eyes with one nervous hand. 'In the cellar?' he asked in a shaky voice. 'What ... what d'you mean?'

Sebastian raised an eyebrow. He grinned, and the sunlight glinted like fire on the gold fillings in his white teeth. 'And you, Mr Crucefix, knew nothing at all about it until now? He's been there for four days – four days, since his – ah ... since his disappearance from Portmeirion that you read about in the newspaper, you remember? Apparently – and this may come as a surprise to you, if you really are as innocent of what's been going on at Heydn Hall as you claim to be – but apparently he was abducted by your employer, Lord Steve, aided and abetted, as one might have guessed, by Dr Electra Vanderpump, her sidekick, Dr Kotlowski, and Miss Black's cousin, Johnny Terrier, who piloted the helicopter for them.'

'Do you know what you're saying?' asked Julian, shocked. 'You can't be serious!'

'One is tempted to look for the funny side,' Sebastian agreed, 'but unfortunately, in this case, there isn't – ah ... there isn't one. Professor Aaronberg, a quiet and frail gentleman of advanced years and a nervous disposition, has, I'm sorry to say, been abducted and kept prisoner in a dark, damp and dirty cellar for four days, by the Earl and Dr Vanderpump.'

Julian looked pale and shaken as he avoided Sebastian's eyes, and he tried to conceal his face with his hand, smoothing back his soft hair that drifted in the breeze. 'I'm afraid I really can't ... ' he began tentatively. 'It really isn't up to me, you see ... I mean, there's nothing I can say, really.' Quickly he turned and began to walk away along the edge of the surf.

Sebastian watched him for a moment, and then followed after him, and they walked some distance in silence.

Presently, Julian paused, stooping down to pick up some pebbles from the sand. He said, 'I have nothing to say.' He tossed a pebble out into the sea. 'It's really none of my business,' he said. 'I knew nothing about this, and I'm not sure that I want to know. If it bothers you, Mr Dorrell, then it's up to you to do whatever you think fit. I just do my job, that's all.'

'Good grief,' said Sebastian, 'you're not still going to give me that, are you? Is that what you're going to say to the police when they come to interview you?'

'The police?' Julian looked alarmed. 'I mean, I didn't know about this! I didn't do anything wrong, and the Professor's been found now, and he's all right. I'm sure it was just ... I mean the Earl, he's the Earl of Newhaven ... I mean, surely this must be just some misunderstanding?' Quickly, to cover his anxiety and confusion, Julian tossed another pebble into the sea. The water was as red as blood now in the light of the dying sun. 'Anyway,' he suddenly blurted out defensively, 'you're a friend of Dr Vanderpump's and you say that your friend, Dr Vanderpump, is also responsible for kidnapping Professor Aaronberg. So where do you stand in all this, I'd like to know? For all I know, it's part of some personal affair you have going with Dr Vanderpump, and I don't want to get mixed up in it.' With an angry flick of the wrist, he flung the final pebble out to sea and walked off in disgust.

Sebastian followed after him. 'All right,' he said. 'I'm prepared to accept that you knew nothing about the kidnapping, but a crime has been committed, and it's a serious crime. It's up to Professor Aaronberg whether he informs the police, though he might, I suppose, take my advice on the matter.'

Julian stopped, and looked Sebastian in the face. 'Is that a threat?' he asked suspiciously.

Sebastian shrugged.

'You can't threaten me,' said Julian. 'I've done nothing wrong. Neither has Lord ... I mean, anyway, it makes no difference to what I say to you because, however you question me, I'm not going to break any confidences about private business at Heydn Hall.'

'Very noble,' said Sebastian sarcastically, 'but in terms of moral comparison, disclosing so-called private business comes a good deal lower down the scale than kidnapping a frail old man and imprisoning him in squalor. As for my relationship with Electra Vanderpump – when I said I was a friend of hers, that wasn't strictly – ah ... true, you know. It was just something I said to persuade you to let me take a look around. I know her, of course, but I don't suppose anyone could really be described as a friend of hers. She's not exactly a friendly sort of woman, as I'm sure you're aware.'

'She said you were one of her patients at the mental home,' Julian remarked experimentally.

Sebastian laughed. 'I'm not, and I never have been, I'm glad to say! My relationship with her, quite a few years ago, was sexual and intellectual. I admire certain qualities about her, but her moral character is not one of them. She's highly intelligent, which I find – ah ... stimulating, but I'm not in love with her. I've never been in love with her, though I nearly married her once, actually.' He smiled reminiscently.

Julian gave him a suspicious look. 'Perhaps you shouldn't have told me that,' he remarked. 'I'm afraid that what you just said doesn't really make much sense to me. You keep talking about morals, when now you freely admit to nearly marrying a woman you don't love. If that isn't immoral, then what is? As for me, I just do my job, which has nothing to do with morals, and you have the nerve to criticise me!'

'Nothing to do with morals?' said Sebastian with mild mockery. 'Oh, to live such a life of blissful simplicity! You're very proud of your job, aren't you? So far as you're concerned, so long as what you do is part of your job, then you're totally relieved of moral responsibility. Thank goodness that I don't have a godforsaken job, and am thus spared the temptation of such dodgy reasoning!'

'You're unemployed?' asked Julian. He scoffed, almost in relief. 'I might have guessed it – you're one of those people who sponge off the State, living on benefits, and then you have the nerve to take the moral high ground with me?' he added with thinly-disguised disgust.

Sebastian laughed. He tossed his long hair away from his face. He said, 'Obviously, if I'm unemployed, then any opinion I might have on any matter whatsoever is completely worthless – in fact, I'm a worthless waste of space altogether, me with my unconventional appearance and my weird, unconventional ideas about mental clarity, personal responsibility, and the need to generally stay alert to what's going on. I see you're even more – ah ... even more closed-minded and conformist than I feared. I don't work, Mr Crucefix – never have, never needed to, never intend to. I have what they call – ah ... private means. So I'm privileged, and I'm aware that that often makes it easier for me to avoid situations in which I prefer not to engage, but even if I were employed, I hope I should – ah ... I hope I should have the moral fibre to avoid getting myself implicated in the kind of antics with which you find yourself currently involved at Heydn Hall.'

'But I keep telling you – I'm not involved!' Julian protested.

In impatience, Sebastian suddenly stretched out his arm and sharply tapped the side of Julian's head. 'What's going on up here?' he demanded, as Julian backed away in shock. 'I would really like to know, because to me it looks as if the lights are on but nobody's home! I would like to know how a man like you, in your position, with your responsibilities, can be living for three months in that place with the most bizarre goings-on, people disappearing all over the damn shop, and yet it never occurs to you to wonder about it or to ask questions. You say that you had no idea of what was happening, and I'll give you the benefit of the doubt. Whatever else you may be, you don't strike me as a liar. But everything you've been telling me ... ' He sighed, spreading his hands in exasperation. 'You are trying to make me believe,' he said slowly, 'that you are a man with no interests, no relationships, no private identity beyond the job you're paid to do, no curiosity, no values, and no views or opinions, apart from some general rule about doing your job and minding your own business.'

'Well, maybe,' Julian agreed weakly.

'What the hell's that supposed to mean?' asked Sebastian with growing impatience. 'Good grief!'

Julian scowled. 'I'm not going to be interrogated by you,' he said. 'It's all very well for you to talk, but we can't all be like you. Somebody has to get on with the job, or I wouldn't like to think what state the world would be in.'

'If we're going to talk about the world's problems,' said Sebastian, 'it seems to me that they would be a good deal fewer if people like you took responsibility for their own actions rather more than they do at present.'

'Am I supposed to be responsible for what Lord Stephen does?' cried Julian angrily. 'I tell you, I knew nothing about it!'

'Absolutely!' retorted Sebastian. 'Because you chose to know nothing! You turned a blind eye, you switched off your brain, and you went along with what you were told by your employer, whom you regard as morally superior simply on the basis of his being socially superior to you – and as far as I'm concerned, yes, that does make you responsible!'

'Why don't you go and tell the Earl, if you feel so strongly about it,' said Julian. 'Why don't you accuse him and insult him? Why don't you go and talk to him about it, instead of picking on me?'

'To what end?' retorted Sebastian. 'He'd only deny everything. To get to the bottom of what's really going on, I need hard evidence, and I need your help for that. I want to get inside the Prince's Tower and find out what's in there.'

Julian stared at him with incredulity. 'There's no way in – I told you before,' he said briskly. 'And even if there were, I have no intention of helping you to do anything.'

'You'd better think again, Mr Crucefix,' said Sebastian.

'So far, you've coasted along in life by being nice – nice manner, nice appearance, nicely spoken, nicely behaved, nice job, hard-working, polite, agreeable, respectful – you tick every box, don't you – and the sad thing is, if everyone were like you, then the world would be a lovely place, it really would. Believe me, I like you – you're a very nice man, but you have the qualities which are excellent for a charming social situation in a suburban parlour, and not for the front line on a battlefield. If I'm right in my suspicions, all hell is about to break loose at Heydn Hall, and in the face of that, your behaviour so far has been ludicrously pathetic. Now's your chance to redeem yourself.'

'You're taking a damn liberty!' said Julian, with all the ferocity that his timid nature could muster. Then he turned his back and strode off across the beach in the direction from which he had come.

It was growing dark now and only the pale beach and the sea reflected light. Sebastian walked behind Julian, back along the shadowy road. Outside the Black Dog, he apprehended him again and showed him the Earl's keys, dangling them for him to see.

'The first obstacle has already been overcome – I have the keys to Heydn Hall,' Sebastian said, replacing them quickly in his pocket to avoid any attempt by Julian to retrieve them.

'You stole them?' Julian looked shocked. 'Well, it seems you can get into Heydn Hall without my co-operation then, doesn't it? So go ahead and try, and don't involve me.'

'But you're there all the time.' Sebastian said. 'It would – ah ... would be far more simple for you to find out what's happening. You could keep me informed – let me know the best time for attempting to break into the Tower – one

day when Lord Steve's out, perhaps? I could – ah ... you
know – pretend to be a workman, or something – mending
the wall, what? Of course, I'd actually be knocking it
down, but no one's to know that. You're supposed to be
having some repairs done at the moment, aren't you? Well.
So it wouldn't look too odd – and with you as the estate
manager to vouch for me ... '

'This is ridiculous!' said Julian scornfully. 'You're really
serious about breaking into the Tower? What d'you think
you're going to find in there? Hidden treasure? What's
going to stop me from going straight back to Lord Stephen
now and repeating everything you've just said?'

'A more pressing problem for me,' replied Sebastian,
smiling slowly, 'is what I should say to poor old Professor
Aaronberg when he next declares his intention of going to
the police. So far, I've persuaded him to hold off until I've
had a chance to follow up my own investigations into this
– ah ... mystery, as one might call it, if one were to put
aside the – ah ... you know what. Kidnapping and imprisonment,' he added in a mischievous whisper.

The expression of alarm returned to Julian's face.

'But actually,' Sebastian continued smoothly, 'I don't
think we need to worry about all that unpleasantness, because above all, Mr Crucefix, I'm sure that a nice man like
you will be anxious to avoid even the slightest hint of unpleasantness. So, with regard to spilling the beans to Lord
Steve, let's just say I'm – ah ... trusting that you're not the
sort of chap to go sneaking to Sir, being, as you are, so terribly nice and all that.'

Julian stared at him for a moment, then he said defiantly, 'I might as well tell you, it doesn't matter what you
say to me, because I can't help you even if I wanted to. I
shan't be here after tomorrow. I'm going on holiday for a

month. The Hall's going to be shut up – no one'll be there except for the people doing the restoration work.'

Sebastian frowned. 'What d'you mean? What about Lord Steve? Is he going away too?'

'I don't know,' said Julian. 'It's not really any of my business, and it's certainly none of yours, Mr Dorrell.'

With that, he turned and walked away along the road into darkness; and this time, though Sebastian stood and watched Julian until he vanished from view among the deepening shadows, he did not follow.

CHAPTER 17

Dr Kotlowski has a Holy Visitation

In one of the guest bedrooms at Heydn Hall, Johnny Terrier was sitting alone and miserable on the bed. He looked up with a start as he heard a footstep.

Dr Kotlowski stood at the doorway, leering in. 'Sulking by yourself again, Terrier?' he said. 'This will not do. The Devil finds work for idle hands, as people say, and for idle minds, I might add. I was going down to the Chapel to perform my devotions to God. Will you care to join me there? Miss Black, I think, will not be persuaded, and Lord Stephen and Dr Vanderpump, I fear, are occupied with grave matters in hand, down in the cellar.'

'I was thinking of Lady Caroline,' declared Johnny morosely.

'Your mind is troubled,' replied Kotlowski, rubbing his thin hands together. 'You must pray to the Lord – he will give you consolation. Remember, Terrier – whatever happens, it is all God's holy will. Everything is in the hands of the Lord.'

'No, it's in the hands of Dr Vanderpump and Big Steve,' muttered Johnny with a scowl. 'Lady Caroline – it oughtn't to have happened to her.'

'Sacrifices must be made,' Kotlowski murmured with a thin smile that turned his lips downwards at the corners. 'Many shall perish and great shall be the destruction in this terrible purging. The Lord brings all sinners to justice, and those who do not repent shall be consumed in the fires of Hell.'

'Lady Caroline wasn't a sinner!' protested Johnny. 'She didn't ought to be consumed! You got no cause to talk like that when you never even met her. She was a good lady.'

'Let us hope, for the sake of her soul,' said Kotlowski, 'that she was able to confess before she died.'

'She didn't need to confess,' declared Johnny. 'She never done no sin. And anyhow, she ain't dead, Dr Kotlowski – they pushed her through, but she'll get back again somehow. She has to!'

'The Lord will do it, if that is his divine will,' said Kotlowski, his stern eyes glinting menacingly. 'Come now with me to pray for her, Terrier. Our great task is a terrible and holy one, to purge the world of chaos and darkness. How is it for this to be done, unless our souls are guided by the Lord? Come now with me to the Chapel.'

'Oh, all right!' grumbled Johnny, lurching to his feet and shambling after Kotlowski.

Along the shadowy corridors they walked, down the stairs to the first floor, through the Billiard Room and the Study of the eighteenth Earl, into the Library that was quiet and solemn in the deepening twilight. Johnny gazed up timidly at the portraits of the Horsley-Mitchell family that hung on the walls between the tall, book-filled shelving cabinets and over the massive marble mantelpiece. In the red glow of the dying daylight, their faces seemed eerie, like ghostly masks, their eyes dark empty sockets, and Johnny could see in each one of those faces a disconcerting resemblance to Lord Stephen.

Kotlowski strode over to a door on the right and opened it. 'In here,' he said. 'Come along, Terrier.'

Johnny was standing before the fireplace, staring up at the portrait of the fifteenth Earl and his wife. 'Do you think they're cursed, the Horsley-Mitchells, Dr Kotlowski?' he asked. 'They did bad things – terrible bad things, some of them. I heard Steve talking about it. That's why he won't take the title for himself. That's why he's a socialist.'

'I do not like this talk of curses,' replied Kotlowski. 'Only the Lord has the power to judge and punish our sins. Those who do evil shall suffer evil. But Lord Stephen has nothing to fear if he has not himself sinned. In any event, the evil that abides in this house will soon be cast out and destroyed. That is Dr Vanderpump's plan, and that is what we must strive towards, Terrier.' He turned and walked through the doorway, into the small family chapel.

Johnny went in after him.

To the left, stood the altar, covered in a dark red velvet cloth, between two high, narrow, arched stained glass windows. To the right, Johnny could just discern in the gloom the rows of pews extending to the far wall, in which were set more stained glass windows and a door which led out onto the narrow first floor gallery that ran around the walls of the Clock Court. Johnny peered up into the gloom between the far windows, and he could just make out the pale shape of the inner face of the ornamental clock; on the other side of the wall, he knew, the clock had another face that looked down upon the courtyard.

Kotlowski had walked up to the altar and he was lighting the candles in tall golden candlesticks set upon it.

'Unfortunately, I find only black candles,' he said, 'but they must serve. Join me in a prayer, Terrier,' he invited, falling to his knees on the stone floor.

Reluctantly, Johnny squatted beside him, trying to take the matter seriously, but it was hard to concentrate as Kotlowski began to intone his prayers in Polish, his native language, which Johnny did not understand.

Presently, Kotlowski got up and lit some foul-smelling incense in a brass burner. Again he apologised. 'It is all I could find, but it must suffice.'

Johnny coughed, trying to conceal his unease as politely as he could, though he was feeling increasingly nervous. In the gloom of the dusty old chapel, which had plainly not been used in years, with the black candles and putrid-smelling incense, and Kotlowski speaking in a language that Johnny did not know, it began to seem more like a black magic ritual than Christian worship.

When Kotlowski fell to his knees again and began another prayer, Johnny took the opportunity to escape, creeping down to the end of the Chapel and out through the door onto the gallery of the Clock Court.

In the darkness and the cool evening air, he breathed deeply.

*

Downstairs in the Drawing-Room, Karen Black was playing the piano when Lord Stephen blustered in.

'We've done it!' he announced triumphantly. 'There's a way round this power problem, Karen! At last, with a portable power supply we're going to be able to get the bloody Machine going!'

'Oh, really?' said Karen, withdrawing her hands from the keyboard. 'That's good,' she added doubtfully.

'Well, you don't sound very pleased about it!' said the
Earl, a note of resentment in his voice. 'I'm telling you,
Karen – we've made a breakthrough! Dr Vanderpump
thinks we could manage it on a couple of car batteries.
Don't you realise, Karen? This time tomorrow we could be
ready to make the test run!'

Karen turned round on the stool and stared up into the
Earl's red and excited face; her eyes were wide and nervous. 'Oh, Steve – you will be careful, won't you?'

'Careful!' exclaimed the Earl. 'Careful!' He laughed; he
slapped his thighs. 'That's a bloody joke, that is! I've
waited thirty years for this, Karen, and I've been too damn
careful all along, if you want the honest truth. Well, I've
had enough of it – I'm going to take action at last!' He
punched the air with his fist. 'I'm getting right in there and
I'm going to do something about it. Dr Vanderpump can
say what she bloody well likes, but where there's a will –
and now there's a power supply – there's a way, that's
what I say. Tomorrow, Karen, when all the staff have
cleared off, I'll be busting in there!'

Karen covered her lower face with her hands, her dark
eyes very wide and frightened above her closed fingers.
'Oh, Steve!' she whispered. 'But think of your granddad –
that was just where he went wrong, with his power supply
getting cut off just 'cos he didn't plan properly what he
was doing.'

'Oh, stop fussing, woman!' said the Earl with a dismis-
sive wave of his hand. 'You don't know a thing about it.
Grandfather was a silly old fool who should've known
better. I've been working on this thing for thirty years, I
tell you – since before you were born! I should know what
this game's about by now.'

He began to stride up and down with determination, pummelling one fist into his other hand.

'But surely, even if you test the Machine tomorrow,' said Karen anxiously, 'you won't ... you know ... try to get inside the Bubble, will you?'

'Why not?' said the Earl. 'Why not? If the Machine works on the test run, what's the bloody use in hanging about, eh? We might as well get the whole damn business over and done! We'll never know what the dangers might be, unless we bloody well just bust in there and risk them!'

Karen looked down miserably at her knees in their pink stockings. She said, 'But things've got worse these last couple of months – and now this morning, what with Tiffany seeing Mr Duffy like that ... Just think of what's happening!'

'We don't know what's happening, that's why we've got to sort it out!' retorted the Earl.

'But how can you if you don't understand it?' cried Karen.

The Earl stopped his pacing and stood before her. He laid his big hands comfortingly upon her shoulders. 'You're upset, Karen,' he said.

'Of course I'm bloody upset!' retorted Karen bitterly. 'Who wouldn't be, knowing what happened to your dad and your granddad? I'm afraid you're going to end up like them.'

Lord Stephen patted her shoulders gently. 'That's rather a silly thing to say now, isn't it?' he said. 'Look at it this way, Karen – if the Machine works, we'll be able to get them all back again. That includes old Duffy and Lady Caroline, and your cousin Johnny too.'

'Johnny? What d'you mean?' cried Karen, jerking back

from him in alarm. 'What's happened to Johnny? Don't tell me he's gone too!'

'Oh my God!' said the Earl wearily. 'I forgot you didn't know ... '

'What?' wailed Karen.

'Well, you see ... ' began the Earl awkwardly, rubbing his hand over the back of his head as he struggled to find the words to explain what had happened. 'Dr Vanderpump's got this idea, you see, that he's not the same man.'

'What're you bloody talking about, Steve?' demanded Karen.

'It's hard to explain ... ' Lord Stephen began to pace up and down again, running his fingers through his blond hair. 'Dr Vanderpump thinks he may be your cousin's counterpart, as it were, from another Stratum. It fits the facts, you see – the fact that he can pilot a helicopter, and that he claims to have been in the Air Corps.'

'You're saying he's not Johnny?' asked Karen incredulously. 'That's daft – of course he's Johnny. What about his memory and everything? He remembers things that Johnny's done.'

'If he slipped in from another part of the Chronostrata,' said Lord Stephen, 'from a Stratum close to this one, a lot of what he remembers of his life in the other Stratum could well be consistent with your cousin's life in this Stratum. But in other ways, of course, he's not the same. Good God, you've noticed it yourself! This fellow's half-witted – it's becoming more and more obvious. Your cousin was always a bit crazy, but he wasn't a complete idiot. This chap, on the other hand – Dr Vanderpump thinks he's had some sort of brain damage.'

Karen frowned. 'The accident ... ' she mused. 'He keeps talking about them not letting him stay in the Airs Corps after he had his accident. I didn't think anything of it before, seeing as he was never in the Air Corps anyhow. But if he really isn't Johnny ... ' She glanced up in dismay. 'Oh, Steve! It's worse than ever! You're saying that the real Johnny has disappeared, like Mr Duffy and Lady Caroline – that this bloke has taken his place, and we never even knew it!'

'Come on now, Karen – it's not so bad,' said the Earl. 'You can see it as a good sign, if you want. If this chap's come out of some other Stratum, I dare say your cousin's slipped through to another Stratum too.' He gave a desperate laugh. 'Good God, Karen – I dare say, in another part of the Chronostrata, not so far away either, the counterparts of you and me are in the drawing-room of another Heydn Hall, not so different from this one, talking about your cousin Johnny and wondering why the hell they didn't notice before now that he's not the Johnny Terrier they used to know!'

'Oh, don't!' cried Karen fiercely, clutching her hands to her head. 'I can't bear it – all them people – I mean, people who're us! It's like seeing reflections of reflections of reflections of yourself, all round, everywhere you look – like a load of mirrors. Johnny could be anywhere – he might as well be dead, as far as we're concerned. We'll never see him again. But maybe he's not in another Stratum. Maybe he's ... like Mr Duffy.'

'How's that?' asked the Earl.

'Well, Tiffany saw him today, didn't she?' said Karen. 'She said he walked right through the wall, so it's like he wasn't really in the world at all, even though she could see him.'

'He'll be in Interstratal Space,' said Lord Stephen. 'If we get the Machine working, we can bring him back easily.'

'Oh yeah?' Karen said scornfully. 'Everything's been very easy so far, hasn't it? And what would you say if you did get him back? I thought we'd agreed to tell people he was on holiday, so that's what me and Dr Vanderpump have been saying. But now Julian tells me that you told him that Mr Duffy was dead.'

'I know,' the Earl admitted ruefully, 'but I forgot. I've got so many bloody things on my mind. When Crucefix asked me about old Duffy, I just said the first damn thing that came into my head.'

'And now he's guessed there's something funny going on,' said Karen. 'Everybody knows there's something not right around here.'

'And tomorrow, they'll all be gone!' The Earl slammed his fist into the palm of his other hand. 'Free of interference for a whole – '

He was interrupted by a knock at the door; it opened and Electra Vanderpump came in.

'I don't want to bother you, Lord Stephen,' she said shortly, 'but there's some trouble with Kotlowski.'

The Earl towered over her angrily. 'What kind of trouble?' He looked as if he were expecting the worst.

'When I went upstairs just now,' Electra explained, 'he came running out of the Study, ranting and raving like a madman. He's up in the Library at the moment with Terrier. If you want to come and have a word with him, you'd better come straight away, because if he doesn't calm down I shall have to sedate him.'

'What's the matter with him?' said the Earl. 'You brought the confounded fellow here – can't you deal with him yourself? I don't want to talk to him.'

'I merely thought you may want to question him yourself,' replied Electra, 'since this is the second such incident we've had today. I think he's seen something, and it may be important.'

The Earl heaved a sigh of exasperation and strode out of the room, leading the way upstairs to the Library.

'Now what's all this about?' demanded Lord Stephen as he bounded in.

Kotlowski was sitting on one of the high-backed leather-upholstered chairs beside the fireplace. He leapt to his feet excitedly as the Earl, Electra and Karen came in. 'A revelation!' he cried. 'A holy revelation! A visitation! Oh, blessed indeed is your house, Lord Stephen! The holy spot shall be marked and revered as a place of miracle forever!'

'What're you blabbering about, you damned idiot?' demanded the Earl. He glared at Johnny Terrier, who was standing helplessly by the window. 'D'you know what this is about, Terrier?' he asked.

Johnny shook his head, and his black hair flopped over his eyes. 'I was out in the Clock Court when it happened,' he said.

Kotlowski was in ecstasy, his hands clasped together, as if in prayer: he was almost laughing with joy, if such a feat were possible for him. 'The Blessed Virgin!' he cried. 'She has appeared to me – to me! How can I bear such bliss? In the Chapel, as I was praying, there she appears beside the altar – radiant, her gown of shining white!'

'The Virgin Mary?' exclaimed the Earl in scorn. 'Are you telling me you've had a vision of the Virgin Mary? What a load of balderdash!'

'It was the Blessed Virgin!' declared Kotlowski fervently. 'There she stood, more beautiful than any mortal woman, her face shining with mercy and goodness, her hair flaming red and gold like the sun, flowing all around her like a silken cape ... '

'Cor, it sounds like Lady Caroline!' said Karen with a gasp. 'Oh, Steve, d'you think it could've been?'

'I fell to my knees before her!' cried Kotlowski. 'I declared myself her humble servant. I begs her to speak or for she show me some sign!'

The Earl was scowling darkly. 'And did she speak?' he demanded.

'Yes,' replied Kotlowski. 'She lifted up her white arm as if to bless me, and I humbly bowed my head to receive her blessing. And then, from very far off, her voice is coming to me. *Can you hear me?* she says. *Is it possible? Help, please help!* she says. *How can I help thee, Holy Virgin?* I cry. *Tell me what I should do, and whatever it is, I do it. I am in thy blessed service forever!* And then ... ' Kotlowski shuddered, clutching his arms to his body as he turned his eyes up towards the ornamental ceiling. 'She gave me a secret sign!' he breathed. 'It was a sign that only I would understand, but I knew at once what it means, for the very thought had come into my mind at that moment – the idea that I had for many years weighed in my mind and yet never carried out the deed! Now she shows me what I must do.'

'I think Karen's right, don't you, Lord Stephen?' said Electra to the Earl. 'Kotlowski's seen the Countess, just as the maid saw your old estate manager. The Bubble is generating severe disturbances in the Chronostrata, which appear to be growing worse.'

'The whole bloody lot could break down at any time!' the Earl blustered.

'That is what I fear,' said Electra, 'but you must be patient, Lord Stephen. We could throw away our only chance by acting with too much haste.'

'Bloody hell!' stormed the Earl. 'You can say what you like, Dr Vanderpump, but your namby-pamby women's

methods aren't good enough for me! Something has damn well got to be done, and done quickly!' He punched the air with his fist. 'Swift action! Bold action! Tough action, Dr Vanderpump! Better to die trying – better to blow the whole bloody lot sky high – than never to have tried at all!' His brilliant steel blue eyes were alight with a fierce gleam. He struck the palm of his hand with his fist as he strode back and forth with a look of fervent determination. 'As far as I'm concerned, Dr Vanderpump,' he declared, 'it's now or never – I'm busting in there!'

CHAPTER 18

Dr Kotlowski's Preparations:
Mr Crucefix's Resignation

When he went upstairs in the Black Dog in search of Professor Aaronberg, Sebastian found him on the landing, about to go into his room.

'Ah, there you are, dear boy,' said the Professor. 'I'm afraid I feel quite tired and ready for bed. I had hoped to spend another hour or two in conversation with you, but I feel I must go and lie down.'

'Hardly surprising, after all you've been through,' Sebastian said sympathetically. He kissed the Professor lightly on the top of the head. 'I'll see you tomorrow,' he said. 'Have a good night. I'm just going to – ah ... telephone Richard before I go to bed, otherwise he'll be imagining I'm dead, or something awful. And of course he'll – ah ... want to know that you're safe too. He's been very worried.'

'Dearie me,' said the Professor, 'but give him my love, won't you, dear boy? Tell him I'm quite safe and well, and he isn't to worry about me anymore. I shall telephone him myself tomorrow. One more thing ... ' He smiled timidly. 'I wonder if it might be arranged for a cup of warm milk to be sent up to my room? I have a feeling that it may soothe me to sleep.'

'Of course,' said Sebastian. 'Anything you want, Professor. I'll arrange it.'

By the time he had telephoned Richard Mojave to tell him all the news, and had arranged for the Professor's milk, it was growing late and very dark. Sebastian thought about following Professor Aaronberg's example and going to bed, but then he thought about Heydn Hall and changed his mind. He remembered what Julian Crucefix had told him about the staff being sent away for a month's holiday, and he wondered about it: it seemed as if Electra Vanderpump and the Earl might be planning to take their operations onto a further, perhaps more dangerous stage, and that they wanted the staff out of the way first.

Sebastian could not rest: he imagined that Electra might be down in the cellar even now, operating the Time Machine, and he did not like the idea at all. Eventually, he put on his leather jacket, for it was cool outside, and went out to the car. He had decided to drive to the Hall tonight and let himself in with the Earl's keys, as he hoped that another, more careful, investigation of the equipment in the cellar might reveal the precise nature of the project that the Earl and Dr Vanderpump were engaged upon.

*

Electra Vanderpump, dressed in a black velvet catsuit, her black hair loose over her shoulders, was lying on the chintz-covered sofa in the guests' sitting-room, reading a book on psychotic disorders, when the Earl of Newhaven burst in through the door, his fierce blue eyes wide with anger and alarm.

'He's gone!' yelled the Earl. 'He's gone – escaped!'

'For heaven's sake, what's the matter now?' demanded Electra, flinging down her book.

Lord Stephen stood shaking in the doorway, his hair in a frantic tuft, his jacket rucked up awkwardly under his braces. 'The Professor – he's gone!' he said desperately. 'I went down just now to take a look at him and give him something to eat, and he's not there!'

'Oh, for heaven's sake, you couldn't have looked properly!' retorted Electra, swinging her legs round off the sofa and sitting up. 'How could he have escaped?'

'Don't bloody well ask me how!' cried the Earl. 'When I tried to find my keys to unlock the bloody door, the keys were missing from my pocket and the door was already unlocked. Now tell me how that happened, Dr Vanderpump!'

A deep angry scowl came over Electra's face. 'Somebody let him out, and I have a good idea who that somebody was.'

'It wasn't me!' declared the Earl.

'Don't forget Sebastian Dorrell,' said Electra darkly. 'I told you how it would be, didn't I now? I guessed that something like this would happen.'

'That's mad!' Lord Stephen blustered. 'He hasn't been here since this morning, and even then he couldn't have got hold of the keys – they were in my pocket all the time. In fact, when I came up to talk to him, I hadn't even got my jacket on, if I remember – I left it down in the cellar.'

'Then he must have been down in the cellar, found your keys when you weren't there, and let Professor Aaronberg out,' said Electra. 'Really, you should be more careful! Do you realise that, now that he has the keys, it will be impossible for us to keep him out of the house unless we maintain a constant guard. It's absolutely infuriating, Lord Stephen! This is the one thing that should have been prevented at all costs.'

'If the Professor goes to the police, which he surely will,' said the Earl, 'we're finished.'

'Don't be absurd!' said Electra curtly. She stood up, her eyes blazing. 'Is that all you're worried about? For heaven's sake, don't you realise that Sebastian Dorrell has been down in that cellar?' She pointed furiously at the floor with one sharp scarlet finger-nail; she almost stamped her foot in rage.

'He's a bloody poofter! He's one of those cissy fellows!' scoffed the Earl. 'Even if I hadn't already sent him packing, he'd never have the guts to go down there, anyway! A fellow like that wouldn't even have the brains to think of looking. It must've been one of the staff who let the Professor out.'

'If it was someone else,' said Electra, 'it's doubtful that they would understand what they saw down there. But ask yourself, what is more likely? According to what you first told me, you didn't send Sebastian packing – you obliged him by having Mr Crucefix give him a guided tour, during which he asked a lot of awkward questions, because Terrier had told him something to rouse his curiosity. Sebastian Dorrell is a clever man, Lord Stephen – don't ever underestimate him. If he's seen what we have in the cellar, and if he talks about it with Professor Aaronberg, you may be sure he'll know exactly what we're doing.'

'If this fellow Dorrell knows so much,' said Lord Stephen, 'and is supposed to be so damn clever that he knows what we're trying to do just by looking at those machines down there, why the hell didn't we get him in on this, instead of dragging in old Aaronberg who didn't seem to know a bloody thing about it?'

'Yes, you're right, Lord Stephen,' said Electra, but a cold light burned in her green eyes. 'He could solve all your problems – he could do it now, today. But you didn't ask him for help – you asked me for help, and I say Mr Dorrell stays out of this.' She glared at the Earl angrily. 'You and I have a certain agreement,' she said, 'that when my work here is finished, then the Time Machine will be mine. I'm not going to let Sebastian take that away from me.'

*

Julian Crucefix had returned to the Hall; he was in his bedroom, packing his bags by the light of the electric lamp. The curtains were still undrawn, and his windows looked down upon the Clock Court, now submerged in the black shadow of oncoming night.

Julian went about his task despondently, opening drawers and cupboards, taking out his clothes and other belongings, and tossing them into his suitcases, for all the while he was running over in his mind his conversation with Sebastian Dorrell earlier that evening. The more he thought about it, the less sure he became that he would ever return to Heydn Hall after he had left the following morning. He had come to the Hall with the hope of settling down there in an interesting and secure job in pleasant surroundings; but now he was not at all confident that it would turn out as he had hoped. Sebastian Dorrell had aroused in him all the doubts that had troubled him over the months and which he had tried to shut from his mind.

Now he thought back over the Earl's behaviour and the long hours that he had spent down in the cellars; he thought about the rumours about the Prince's Tower, the air of unease that was around every time Mr Duffy or Lady Caroline Giles or the Earl's father or grandfather were mentioned; and he realised that Sebastian was right: something odd had been going on all along. As for Sebastian's claim that Professor Aaronberg had been kept locked in the cellar, Julian did not quite know whether to believe it or not, but whatever the exact facts of the matter might be, he decided that he knew enough now to recognise that something was happening at Heydn Hall in which he did not want to be involved.

It made him angry, when he thought of all that he had given up to come here. If he resigned now, he would have no job to go to and nowhere to live. It was a position that he had never put himself in before, and he feared it; but now that he had been made aware of what was going on around him, he feared even more the idea of staying.

He threw the last item into his suitcase and closed the lid. All the cupboards were empty: he had packed everything. Nervously, he stared out of the window into the blackness of the courtyard. He could see the lights shining in the second floor windows directly opposite on the other side of the courtyard, in the guests' sitting-room, and as he watched, he could see the silhouetted figure of the burly Earl striding back and forth before the lighted window, gesticulating wildly; then Electra Vanderpump appeared in the window, at the Earl's side.

Julian frowned, running his hand over his lips. He wanted to offer his resignation as soon as possible, and he wondered whether now was as good a time as any. He glanced at his watch: the time was just after ten o'clock. He decided that he must talk to Lord Stephen now, tonight, before he changed his mind. In the morning sunlight,

Julian knew, his resolve may weaken and he may imagine his present suspicions to be unjustified.

Quickly he went out of the room, along the passage, to the door of the sitting-room, which was slightly ajar. He peered in and saw the Earl and Dr Vanderpump standing on the far side of the fireplace, beside the chimney recess in which was set the small window that looked out onto the Clock Court. They were engaged in such a heated discussion that they were quite unaware of Julian's presence. He raised his hand to knock on the door, but then hesitated, drawing back a little into the shadows of the passage outside. His new sense of curiosity, awakened by Sebastian Dorrell, had made him wonder what their conversation was about.

'Then we'll have to bust in tomorrow,' said the Earl.

'We'll do nothing of the sort,' replied Electra. 'Why on earth do you have to make such a song and dance about everything? Obviously there has to be another entrance. Are you telling me that you really haven't looked for it before now?'

'Another entrance – where?' asked Lord Stephen. 'There's just the one on the ground floor that's been bricked up. There's no other way.'

'Oh, don't be absurd,' said Electra. 'How did your grandfather get in and out of the Tower himself, if he had sealed off the only entrance? How did your father know what had happened, if he hadn't been inside at least once, and, more probably, on many occasions?'

The Earl rubbed his head in bewilderment. 'Good God!' he said. 'You're right! Why the hell didn't I think of that before? I thought the only way in was through that door, and I walled it all up again after that one time when I smashed through. But how long have you known this, for God's sake?'

'I realised immediately, when you first called me in and told me as much as you knew. It was obvious,' said Electra serenely, walking away from him across the room and seating herself elegantly on the sofa; she crossed her velvet-clad legs. 'Your grandfather sealed the Tower before he began work, so that he could use the place as his secret laboratory without being disturbed. I didn't mention another entrance before,' she said, 'because I think that we should tamper with the Bubble as little as possible until we're ready to take the big step and attempt penetration, and I suspected, in view of your impulsiveness, Lord Stephen, that you would want to go in straight away, if you knew that it was possible without breaking down the wall. Now, however, the indications are that the Bubble is becoming increasingly unstable, and we need to reassess the situation before we go ahead. To achieve optimum results, I really need to take a reading, so that we can co-ordinate the frequencies.'

'But where is this – this other entrance, then?' asked Lord Stephen in agitation, pacing back and forth across the fire rug.

'Well, there're only three places where it could possibly be,' replied Electra. 'Obviously it has to be in the wall of one of the rooms adjacent to the Tower. We know it's not on the ground floor, because the whole wall was replastered when the cafeteria was fitted, and the only door there is the one we know about, which has been blocked off. On the second floor, there are two rooms on that wall – the bedroom I'm in and the guests' bathroom, and there's certainly no door there either, because I've checked thoroughly. That leaves just the room on the first floor, which has panelled walls which may well conceal a secret entrance into the Tower.'

'The Picture Gallery?' said the Earl, stopping in front of the fireplace and turning to face her. 'Good God – a hidden doorway in there!'

'I assume that there must be,' said Electra. 'Really, I'm surprised that your grandfather made no mention of it in his papers, since he must have used it regularly while he was engaged on his project.'

Julian Crucefix retreated quietly along the passage, and then he walked back again with heavier footsteps and knocked loudly upon the door, so that it would appear that he had just arrived and had overheard nothing.

'Come in!' called Electra curtly.

Julian pushed open the door nervously and stepped in. 'May I have a word with you, sir ... Steve, I mean?' he asked.

'What's it about?' bellowed the Earl. 'I'm busy at the moment. If it's business, can't it wait until morning?'

'Actually, it's, um ... personal,' said Julian.

'Ah, well then – come in, come in!' the Earl invited, abruptly adopting an avuncular manner. 'If there's anything bothering you, let's see if we can sort it out, eh?'

Electra sighed heavily. 'Is this going to be private?' she asked, standing up.

'It's all right,' said Julian. 'I just wanted to inform you ... um ... Steve ... of my resignation. I want to ... I intend to leave here.'

'Leave?' cried Lord Stephen. 'What the devil for? I've just given you a holiday, haven't I?'

'Well, I just feel ... ' said Julian vaguely, 'it's not right for me, this job.'

'Come on now, we can sort this out,' said the Earl, slapping him amiably on the shoulder. 'Something's on your mind, Julian, I can see. Whatever's bothering you, I'm sure we can deal with it. You don't want to leave like this now, do you?'

Julian swallowed nervously and edged away from Lord Stephen.

'I'll tell you what's bothering him,' said Electra coldly. 'He's been listening to Sebastian Dorrell. That's right, isn't it, Mr Crucefix?' she inquired, fixing her icy green eyes upon Julian. 'Mr Dorrell has been putting all sorts of silly ideas and fears into your head, hasn't he? And didn't I tell you, Mr Crucefix, what sort of man he is? Has he been here to the Hall again? If you saw him, why didn't you tell me immediately, as I asked you to do?'

Julian shook his head and stared unhappily at his feet; he did not know what to say.

'Is that true, Julian?' asked the Earl. 'Have you been talking to that fellow Dorrell again?'

'I ... met him in Newhaven this evening,' Julian replied cautiously. 'We passed the time of day. But it's not ... it's got nothing to do with that, sir – Steve, I mean – the fact that I've decided to resign,' he added hastily, as he fumbled in his pocket and brought out his keys. 'I've made up my mind,' he said, handing them to Lord Stephen.

Electra smiled as she stood up and stepped closer. 'How very convenient for you, Lord Stephen,' she said. 'You'll be needing those, I think, since you've been so careless as to lose your own.'

'Look here,' said the Earl desperately, 'this is bloody ridiculous! I can't accept this. I'll be plain with you, Julian – I'm a plain sort of chap. The fact of the matter is, you're the best bloody estate manager I've ever had – you're ten times better than old Duffy. Damn it all, I can't afford to lose you!'

Julian blushed, but said nothing.

'What exactly has Mr Dorrell been telling you?' demanded Electra. 'Come along now, Mr Crucefix – we're not going to play silly games, are we? If you're honest with us, then we'll be honest with you.'

The Earl glanced at her in alarm.

'It's nothing … ' said Julian, backing towards the door. 'We didn't talk about anything, really.'

'You're a very bad liar, Mr Crucefix,' said Electra. 'Plainly you've come to know something that's disturbed you. What is it? Did he tell you about the Tower? Did he tell you about the cellars? Or … did he perhaps mention Professor Aaronberg?'

Julian's gaze moved around nervously as he tried not to look at her, but he said nothing.

'Very well,' said Electra impatiently. 'Since you plainly know something about it, I see no reason to try to hide the truth from you. Better that you should know the whole of the matter than believe Mr Dorrell's version of the story.'

'Dr Vanderpump!' began the Earl in alarm.

'Leave this to me!' Electra silenced him sharply. 'Yes, Mr Crucefix, the Earl and I have been working on a secret project, as Mr Dorrell has no doubt told you. The work was begun by Lord Stephen's grandfather and was continued by his father. For the past thirty years, Lord Stephen has been working single-handedly upon this massive undertaking until, six months ago, he approached me to work on the final stages with him. The precise nature of this work I can't explain briefly, as it's an extremely specialised area that requires advanced scientific knowledge in order to be understood. Suffice it to say that we are on the verge of a breakthrough that will rock the scientific establishment. Now you see why it was essential to maintain absolute secrecy.'

Julian glanced dubiously at her, and then at the Earl, who was looking extremely uncomfortable and apprehensive.

'But I see you're still doubtful,' said Electra. 'Why don't you come down to the cellars with us now, and perhaps we can demonstrate something to you that will serve to convince you.' She smiled.

'Well, all right – I suppose so,' Julian agreed.

The Earl looked alarmed.

'You're privileged, Mr Crucefix,' said Electra, still smiling at him. 'Miss Black is the only other person who knows fully about the project. And I'm sure you'll find it very interesting.'

As the three of them walked down to the cellars, Julian felt awkward and embarrassed, like a foolish schoolboy being shown something unpleasant by a condescending school mistress, supposedly for his own good.

They went through the servants' hall to the door at the end. Since his key had gone missing, the Earl had been obliged to leave it unlocked. He opened it, and they descended the narrow stone steps into the cellar.

Electra switched on the lights, illuminating the great vaulted chamber, and Julian stared around him in astonishment at the vast array of glinting machinery and electronic equipment.

'I see you're impressed already,' said Electra. 'Come – I'll show you round and explain it all to you.' She beckoned to the Earl to follow them and to stay close behind. 'Take a look at this,' she said, flicking some switches; coloured diagrams flashed up onto a display screen. While

Julian was distracted, Electra drew the Earl aside and whispered a brief instruction into his ear.

Lord Stephen began to smile.

'But what exactly are you doing here?' asked Julian. 'This sort of thing means nothing to me. Science was never my strong subject, but this ... this is far above my head.'

'Perhaps this will help to make it clearer,' said Electra, walking away down the cellar to the storeroom at the end. 'In here we keep our most essential item of equipment – the Trans-Stratal Conveyance Stabiliser.'

Julian followed after her. 'In here?' he asked.

'Let's go in, shall we?' said Electra brightly, reaching her arm in through the doorway to switch on the light.

Julian stepped forward to peer cautiously into the storeroom.

'Now!' cried Electra, and the Earl bounded forward; together they gave Julian a violent shove that sent him staggering inside.

Hastily, Electra pulled the door to, and the Earl locked it with the key that he had ready.

'Let me out! Let me out!' yelled Julian, banging on the other side of the door.

The Earl roared triumphantly.

Electra laughed. 'Let that be a lesson to you, Mr Crucefix, not to listen to gossip and tales, and not to talk to strangers about matters that don't concern you!'

'You can't leave me here!' cried Julian. 'I haven't done anything! I would've gone tomorrow and never come back! I won't tell anyone, if you let me out. I give you my word – I'll do anything you want!'

'You're not in a position for bargaining, Mr Crucefix,' replied Electra curtly. 'You'll stay in there until our project is completed, and the less fuss and trouble you make, the sooner that will be.'

*

Meanwhile, Karen Black had discovered Dr Kotlowski in the Library. He was up the step-ladder, looking at some books on one of the upper shelves.

'God, it's you!' said Karen in surprise as she came in. 'You didn't half give me a fright. I saw the light under the door and thought it'd been left on by mistake. I didn't know anyone was in here. I thought you'd gone to bed?'

'Ah, Miss Black,' said Kotlowski nervously. 'Yes, yes – I had gone to bed. But I like to read a little, to help me fall asleep, you see, and I find I have neglected the bringing of a book with me. Never matter, here I have found one.' He began to climb down the ladder, holding one of the books in his hand.

'Does Steve know?' asked Karen. 'Some of them books are very old and valuable.'

'I shall take the greatest care,' Kotlowski assured her. 'In the morning I shall be returning it.'

'Okay, I suppose it's all right,' said Karen. 'But which book is it?' she asked, suspicious to see that Kotlowski held it behind his back and sidled across the room as if he were attempting to conceal it from her.

'Oh, it is a history book – that is all,' said Kotlowski.

He stopped beside the large leather-topped table in the middle of the room, and Karen noticed for the first time that a selection of kitchen knives lay there. With a trembling white hand, Kotlowski was reaching for the knives.

'Here – those're supposed to be in the kitchen!' Karen exclaimed in surprise. 'What're they doing up here?'

'Ah ... I was taking them back,' explained Kotlowski hastily.

'No. I'll do it,' said Karen, stepping over and picking up the knives. 'Dr Vanderpump told you to go and lie down, didn't she? I think you ought to be back in bed. I'm going up myself in a minute.'

'Yes. Good night, Miss Black,' said Kotlowski sedately, moving towards the door and hurrying out.

Karen frowned; she was puzzled, and she wondered what he was about.

She climbed up the step-ladder to look at the books on the shelf from which Kotlowski had selected the one he had borrowed. She was even more surprised to find that the other books on the same shelf were not history books, but books on animal husbandry.

Still puzzled, she left the Library, turning out the light, taking the knives with her, and went upstairs to bed.

CHAPTER 19

The Secret Door

Down in the cellar, Julian Crucefix banged on the door for a while and called for help, but he soon tired of that: it seemed unlikely that anyone was going to hear him, and very likely that they had all gone to bed. In despair, he sat down on an empty crate and stared at the door, cursing himself that he had been credulous enough to let himself be led down into the cellars and locked up so easily. He realised that this must be the very room where Professor Aaronberg had been imprisoned, just as Sebastian Dorrell had told him and which he had at first doubted. On the floor in one corner, he noticed a dirty plate and a knife and fork, which he took as evidence of the Professor's last meal in there.

For an hour or more, Julian sat thinking about all the mistakes that he had made, the situations that should have aroused his suspicion many times but which he had chosen to ignore. It was too late now, and he bitterly regretted it; no longer did he doubt anything that Sebastian had told him.

He was just reflecting gloomily that his only hope of being released would be if he somehow made the staff

hear him when they came down to breakfast in the morning, when there was the sound of footsteps in the cellar
outside.

Julian leapt to the door and hammered on it loudly with
his fist. 'Let me out!' he shouted. 'Let me out!'

He heard the footsteps approaching the door; there was
a pause, and then the sound of keys jingling and the lock
being turned.

The door opened and Sebastian Dorrell looked in.
'Hello, Mr Crucefix,' he said with a grin. 'Bet you never
thought you'd be pleased to see me!'

'What're you doing here?' cried Julian in amazement.

'I was going to ask you that, actually,' said Sebastian.
'One doesn't – ah ... doesn't usually expect to find the estate manger locked up in the storeroom, what? Been a
naughty boy, have you?'

'Electra Vanderpump locked me in,' Julian explained.
'It was after talking to you, I decided I couldn't stay at the
Hall any longer, and I told the Earl I was leaving, and that
made Dr Vanderpump think I'd found out something from
you that she didn't want me to know.'

'So it's my fault?' asked Sebastian with a smile.

'No, of course not,' answered Julian. He sighed. 'Look,
you know you said you wanted to get inside the Prince's
Tower? Well, I overheard the Earl and Dr Vanderpump
talking about a secret entrance on the first floor. Lord
Stephen didn't know there was one, but Dr Vanderpump
seemed to think that there must be. She was saying something about Lord Stephen's grandfather having used it to
get in after he'd bricked up the ground floor entrance.'

Sebastian frowned thoughtfully. 'Of course,' he mused,
'it would make sense. I thought at first that the Earl must
have had some way of getting in, but after a while I – ah ...

I dismissed the idea, as you assured me that there was only one door. But I read something in the guidebook this morning – that the eighteenth Earl bricked up the Tower just before he put the glass prism on the roof, and about two years later he – ah ... disappeared. I was wondering whether there could be any connection. I mean, was he doing something secret in the Tower that began when he sealed it up to – ah ... to keep other people out – something that required the glass prism on the roof – and that ended in 1939 with his disappearance? But of course it hasn't really ended at all, because his son had to carry on where he left off, and now Lord Steve is doing something with that Time Machine.'

'What time machine?' asked Julian. 'There's no such thing.'

Sebastian raised an eyebrow. 'Haven't you seen it? It's out here.' He walked out into the cellar and switched on his torch, shining the light onto the great spool-shaped machine that stood there.

'But it can't really work,' Julian objected.

'You're right, it doesn't,' said Sebastian. 'But that's what Lord Steve has been doing all this time, and Electra's been helping him with it.'

'You know, she said something of the sort when she brought me down here,' remarked Julian. 'But after she locked me up, I didn't know how much of what she said was true. I think it was just a ploy to get me in here.'

'What did she say?' asked Sebastian.

Julian was walking around the battered Time Machine, examining with interest its array of controls. 'Oh, just what you said then,' he replied. 'That some project had been begun by the eighteenth Earl and continued by his son, and that now she and Lord Stephen were working on the final stages. She said they were on the verge of a break-through that would rock the scientific establishment.'

Sebastian laughed grimly. 'I don't know about the sci-entific establishment,' he said, 'but judging by their – ah ... judging by their conversation that I overheard this after-noon, it's certainly going to rock Heydn Hall, if it doesn't – ah ... doesn't destroy the place altogether.'

Julian stared at him in horror. 'But why, for God's sake?' he said. 'I mean, what're they trying to do?'

'I don't know exactly,' said Sebastian. 'but in general terms, and to – ah ... to adopt Lord Steve's graphic turn of phrase, they're – ah ... trying to bust in somewhere.'

'The Bubble,' said Julian. 'That was what Dr Vander-pump said, and it rang a bell ... something funny that the Earl said the day I came for my interview – just ranting and raving about this Bubble, whatever it is, because he misheard some remark of mine. Yes, and then Dr Vander-pump said something about *penetration*.'

'She said something similar this afternoon,' said Sebas-tian. 'I didn't – ah ... didn't know what she was talking about.'

Julian rubbed his hand across his lips; he gazed thoughtfully at the floor. 'And you think it's got something to do with the Tower?'

'Yes,' said Sebastian. 'I'm even more sure of that now, as you say you heard them talking about it. And the only way to find out what it's all about is to get inside the Tower, so – ah ... so let's go and see if we can find that secret entrance, shall we?'

'What – now?' said Julian.

'Seems as good a time as any,' replied Sebastian, 'as-suming that everyone's in bed by now.' He looked at his watch. 'If this is telling the right time for once, it's getting on for midnight,' he observed.

Softly, they crept up the dark stairs, through the silent rooms of the great old house, through the Billiard Room and the Study, through the Library where the statues gleamed like ghosts in the moonlight, through the grim dark Chapel where Dr Kotlowski had had his vision of the Holy Virgin but a few hours earlier, and finally into the Picture Gallery.

It was a large lofty room with windows at the far end and a stone fireplace in the wall on the right-hand side. The opposite wall was plain, without windows or door or any other opening. Sebastian shone his torch beam over it: the dark oak panelling extended to the moulded cornice. The paintings loomed out of the shadows as Sebastian passed the torch beam around: there were works of art from the past five hundred years, including a number of modern works, some of which were so large that they had been screwed to the wall in order to support them.

'The Prince's Tower is on the other side of this – is that right?' Sebastian asked. He tapped the panelling experimentally.

'Yes,' said Julian. 'I say, do you mind if I just go and get my suitcases? I left them upstairs.'

'Well, all right, I suppose so,' Sebastian replied with a mild frown. 'But don't – ah ... don't wake anyone up, will you? I'll carry on looking while you're gone.'

Julian hurried out of the room.

*

'What's the matter now, Steve?' grumbled Karen Black. She was lying in the big four-poster bed, trying to sleep.

In the gloom, the Earl of Newhaven was groping

clumsily about the bedroom in search of his clothes. 'How can I bloody well sleep with all this on my mind?' he muttered morosely. 'It's no use – somebody's got to stay up and keep a look-out. For all we know, he could be in the house right now, messing about in the cellars with Dr Vanderpump's equipment – and if any of that gets damaged, that woman'll hit the bloody roof! Good God, Karen, he could even be making off with the Time Machine while we lie here asleep!'

'Oh, Steve!' said Karen in exasperation. She rolled over in the bed, rubbing her forehead wearily with the back of her arm. 'What're you talking about?'

'I told you before,' said the Earl as he pulled his braces up over his jacket. 'Don't you ever listen to what I say? That fellow Dorrell's got my keys – that's how he rescued old Aaronberg. How the hell are we going to keep him out now? He can let himself in any time he pleases.'

'But there's no saying that he will,' Karen observed optimistically.

'If he can, he will,' declared the Earl. 'He's a meddling bloody nuisance, that's what he is. Dr Vanderpump's been telling me about him.'

'Well, if she doesn't think it's necessary to keep watch all night, I'm sure you needn't worry about it. What can he do, after all? He's been in the cellars, so he already knows what's there. He can't get in the Tower, anyhow. And he can't nick the Time Machine either, 'cos you haven't got it working yet, and there's no other way to get it out of the cellar – it's too big.'

'He can sabotage the whole bloody project, that's what he can do,' said the Earl. 'Well, I'm taking no chances, Karen. I'm going down there, and if I find Dorrell snooping around, he's going to find out what sort of punch I can throw – that's all I can say!'

'Oh, Steve – do be careful!' wailed Karen.

The Earl grunted and strode out.

*

Julian Crucefix, about to emerge from his bedroom, a suit-case in each hand, was suddenly alarmed by the sound of footsteps on the landing. A moment later, he heard some-one bounding down the stairs: by the heavy, energetic tread, he guessed that it was the Earl.

Cautiously, Julian crept out, carrying his cases, but his heart sank when he heard the footsteps stop at the first floor, pass briefly across the landing, and then fall silent; he feared that the Earl had gone into the Billiard Room. If Lord Stephen went through into the Library, Julian knew that he might hear Sebastian in the nearby Picture Gallery and go to investigate.

His heart beating nervously, Julian hurried down after him. He hoped that he would be able to reach Sebastian before the Earl did, by running round the other way, through the rooms on the other side of the Clock Court: the Weapons Gallery, the State Bedroom and the Dressing-Room, which led into the Picture Gallery. Leaving his suit-cases on the landing, he raced off as fast as he could, through the shadowy rooms that were lit eerily by the wan light of the full moon, his hurrying footsteps echoing as he ran.

He burst into the Picture Gallery through the Dressing-Room door. Sebastian was there, against the opposite wall, illuminated in the yellow glow of his torchlight as he tapped the oak panelling. He glanced round in surprise as Julian entered.

'I think I've found something here,' announced Sebastian enthusiastically. 'Listen – it sounds different.' He knocked on the wall, and pressed the panel around the edges. 'There's a kind of – ah ... '

'Sebastian – ' Julian began, interrupting him in haste.

Suddenly there was an ominous grating sound and, all at once, the oak panel sprang back and opened beneath Sebastian's touch, revealing a low narrow doorway.

'I've found it!' Sebastian cried.

'Shh!' hissed Julian urgently. 'Lord Stephen's out there – we've got to hide!'

But it was too late. The Earl, brooding on the words of Dr Vanderpump, had also decided upon some midnight investigation and had made his way to the Picture Gallery with the same intention as Sebastian: to find the secret entrance into the Tower. At the very moment that Julian spoke, the door from the Chapel was hurled open, and the burly Earl exploded into the room like a thunderstorm. 'Sebastian Dorrell!' he roared. 'You bloody well clear off my property, before I give you a thrashing you won't forget in a hurry!'

For a moment, Sebastian was taken aback; he almost dropped his torch, but he recovered himself in an instant. He grinned. 'Ah, Lord Steve,' he said, 'what a surprise! You've arrived at a most interesting moment.'

'And none too soon!' bellowed the Earl, glowering as he approached Sebastian with a menacing posture and gait, his fists clenched.

'I've discovered a little door here, you see ... ' Sebastian explained.

The Earl did not wait to hear more; he suddenly struck Sebastian a terrific blow on the side of the jaw, knocking him down. The torch rolled away across the floor.

Lord Stephen roared in triumph. 'Stand up and fight!' he yelled, excitedly dragging off his braces and jacket and beginning to leap about. 'Come on and show what you're made of, you cissy!'

Sebastian sat up, holding his hand to his injured face. 'You stupid man,' he said. 'You could've broken my jaw.'

Julian hurried over anxiously to help him to his feet, but Sebastian motioned him away with a wave of the hand.

'You stay out of this, Crucefix,' said the Earl. 'This is between Dorrell and me.'

As Sebastian stood up, Lord Stephen advanced towards him again, adopting a fighting stance, his fists raised in readiness.

Sebastian backed away from him, holding up his hands as if to attempt to ward off a blow. 'Don't hit me again, please,' he said. 'Can't we just – ah ... you know – sit down quietly and talk about it? I'm sure that would be much nicer, what?'

'You bloody poof!' said the Earl, and punched him provocatively in the chest.

Sebastian recoiled from the Earl's blow. 'But I don't want to fight,' he protested. 'I want to talk to you. If you're not – ah ... not going to be sensible about this, I'm afraid I shall have to leave.'

'You come here, bloody trespassing and looking for trouble,' retorted the Earl, 'so you'll damn well fight, whether you want to or not! I'll make a man of you yet!'

Sebastian turned and tried to run away, but Lord Stephen bounded after him and grabbed him from behind. Sebastian was obliged to concede to the inevitable; and all at once, they were both down on the floor, punching and kicking at each other like maniacs, while Julian looked on in alarm and incredulity.

'You fight like a girl!' Lord Stephen jeered.

In retaliation, Sebastian struck him in the eye. It was the second such blow that the Earl had received, since, to his surprise, though he was reluctant to admit it even to himself, Sebastian had turned out to be a much better fighter than the Earl had anticipated. After a while they parted, backing away from one another, breathless and sweating.

'Had enough?' asked Sebastian.

The Earl leapt at him, growling, but Sebastian threw him off. They knocked one another back and forth across the room, Lord Stephen yelling abuse, but generally receiving worse punishment that he inflicted, for Sebastian was swift in avoiding many of the Earl's clumsy attacks.

Unexpectedly, the electric lights blazed on, to reveal a furious Electra Vanderpump standing in the doorway from the Chapel, dressed in her red satin fur-trimmed negligee, for evidently she had been in bed but a few minutes earlier, disturbed from her sleep in the guest room immediately above: in her thin hand she gripped a threatening revolver.

'For heaven's sake, what's going on here?' she screamed down the room at them.

Sebastian and the Earl stopped hitting one another and swung round in shock to face the direction from which her shrill voice had come.

In a glance, she had taken account of both Sebastian and Julian, as well as the dark secret entrance to the Tower that gaped open in the panelled wall. For an instant, her ferocious eyes met Sebastian's, and she raised the revolver, pointing it at him. She seemed about to speak, but Sebastian did not wait: he turned and dashed for the other door, shouting to Julian to run, as he bundled him out into the Dressing-Room ahead of him.

'After them!' cried Electra fiercely. 'They mustn't escape!'

Limping now from his injuries in the fight, the Earl lumbered out in pursuit, as fast as he could. 'Fetch Terrier!' was his parting yell as he hurried through the door.

Julian had picked up Sebastian's torch earlier, and now he shone it ahead of them to light their way as they ran back through the gloomy rooms and down the stairs; but as they reached the bottom and were about to run for the front door, a man in a black dressing-gown suddenly appeared in the light of the torch, standing between them and the door, bunches of glinting knives gripped in both hands.

'Dr Kotlowski!' gasped Julian.

For a moment, Kotlowski's haggard, thin face became a mask of guilt and fear, as if he had been caught in the middle of some terrible deed; then the echoing voice of the Earl bellowed down from the top of the stairs, and Kotlowski jumped to attention, as if he had heard the voice of God.

'Don't let them get away!' shouted Lord Stephen.

At once Kotlowski was transformed: an evil glint came into his eye. Like a black spider, prancing backwards on his long legs, brandishing his fearsome knives, he moved to bar their escape through the front entrance.

'This way!' cried Julian, darting to the right, towards the door of the Dining-Room.

Sebastian was quick to follow him as they dashed through the Dining-Room, through the Lounge and into the great marble Ballroom at the back of the house.

'The french doors!' said Julian. 'Quick!'

Sebastian got out the keys and tossed them to him,

turning at once to confront Kotlowski, who had come into the room just behind them.

'Aha!' exclaimed Kotlowski. 'Aha!' His tongue flicked around his thin lips in eager anticipation, and he crouched low, his legs apart, prancing spider-like towards Sebastian, while at the same time making menacing thrusting gestures with the bunches of knives that he held erect in both hands.

The next moment, however, Kotlowski was suddenly disarmed, recoiling with a wailing scream, his knives flying, as he clutched in agony at his groin, for Sebastian had landed a well-aimed kick at the most vulnerable part of his anatomy.

Then, to Sebastian's surprise, Kotlowski staggered forward, his eyes gleaming with a strange delight, his arms extended, his hands raised like claws, though the gesture seemed almost one of supplication.

'Again!' he gasped faintly. 'Do it again!'

Julian called to Sebastian at that moment, however, having succeeded in unlocking the French doors, and together they escaped into the garden, just as the Earl burst into the room. Sebastian leapt down the steps from the stone terrace and ran through the Tudor rose garden towards the large stone fountain and the long rose pergola beyond, that now loomed starkly in the bright moonlight.

'Wait!' cried Julian, panting close behind him. 'We can't get out that way!'

But Sebastian did not stop until he reached the wide steps that led up to the pergola; he climbed up into the shadowy refuge and slipped behind a pillar, out of sight of the house.

'We'll have to go out by the front gates,' said Julian

desperately, as he struggled to regain his breath. 'This is the wrong way – we'll have to go back!'

Sebastian frowned. He was breathing deeply. The scent of the roses hung heavy in the night air. 'Can we climb through the hedge, or – ah ... or over the fence, or something?' he asked.

'No,' said Julian. 'The Earl's had all the fences mended and barbed wire put everywhere to keep out intruders.'

'We couldn't have gone round the front,' said Sebastian. 'Lord Steve could've – ah ... could've run back through the house and got there before us while we were going round the outside.'

'Well, he doesn't seem to have followed us now,' Julian observed. 'What's he up to?'

Cautiously, they looked out from behind the brick pillar, back towards Heydn Hall. The great house stood stark and grim beneath the full moon and the bright stars, and no architectural feature in its dark walls could be discerned in the shadows cast by the moonlight; only the ornamental crenellations stood out, etched blacker against the pale grey gleam of the illuminated surface of the sloping roof that rose above.

Here and there, yellow lights had come on in some of the windows, and the contrast of these bright latticed rectangles against the prevailing darkness made the walls of the house seem even more shadowy, almost as black as coal. The fountain in the rose garden stood as a blue silhouette against the light that issued from the open door of the Ballroom beyond, and by the door, they could make out the figure of the Earl moving about. His voice carried out to them through the still air, but they could not hear what he was saying, and neither could they see to whom he was speaking.

'Come on!' whispered Julian urgently. 'We can run round the front now, while he's standing there talking!'

'No,' said Sebastian. 'We can't risk it. We don't know how many people are awake by now. Someone could've been sent round there to keep a look-out for us. We'll have to – ah ... have to wait until all the hoohah's died down a bit.'

'But now's our chance! We may never get out if we don't take it!' persisted Julian. 'They won't wake up the whole household. All along, Lord Stephen's been trying to play everything down and behave as if it's all perfectly normal. It's not going to look normal if the rest of the staff find he's chasing the estate manager round the grounds in the middle of the night.'

'Our only hope,' said Sebastian, after some thought, 'is to go down – ah ... down to the other end of the arbour and creep out under the shadow of the trees.'

But as he spoke, the garden suddenly became filled with radiant light, as all the floodlighting and ornamental lamps, and coloured fairy lights up in the trees were switched on: this, together with the light of the moon, made the garden nearly as bright as day.

'Oh, good grief,' said Sebastian.

'Now it's too late,' said Julian. 'I told you we should've made a run for it. And here comes the Earl now!'

Still limping slightly, the Earl came crunching with determination down the gravel path; he was carrying a shotgun over his shoulder. Behind him, the ungainly figure of Johnny Terrier came shambling, and bringing up the rear came Kotlowski, who walked with an awkward stoop, clutching at his groin.

'That's Johnny Terrier,' whispered Sebastian in surprise.

'Dr Vanderpump got him to come here, along with Dr Kotlowski,' Julian explained.

Sebastian and Julian drew back into the shadows of the rose pergola as the Earl approached.

'Hurry up, Terrier, for God's sake!' said Lord Stephen as he climbed up the brick steps and turned to the left, away from where Sebastian and Julian were hiding. 'You stay and search the garden!' he called back to Kotlowski. 'As far as we know, they're still in the grounds some-where.'

The Earl and Johnny Terrier hurried off to the far end of the pergola and disappeared along a narrow path that led out across the wide grass expanse of the deer park. Kot-lowski, meanwhile, had turned back and was roaming around the borders of the garden, peering into shadows and behind bushes.

'Right,' said Sebastian. 'Come on, let's go – while he's looking the other way.'

Quietly, they crept off along the shadowy walkway be-neath the canopy of climbing roses, towards the circular ornamental stone summer-house at the end. To the right of them, the garden was brilliantly floodlit, so that if they took the straight path that led to the front of the house they would immediately be seen by Kotlowski. To avoid this, they went on a little further and then moved off across the lawns in the direction of the ruined Victorian conservatory that stood within the cover of trees and shrubbery.

Just as they reached the shadow of the bushes, they heard the sound of a helicopter coming from the park be-hind them and, looking back, they saw the helicopter ris-ing above the trees; all at once, a bright searchlight shone out from it, sweeping across the lawns below, banishing the last vestiges of night that lingered on the edges of the garden where the floodlighting had not penetrated the darkness.

'Well, you were wrong, old sport,' said Sebastian. 'Lord Steve doesn't seem too – ah ... too concerned about whether he disturbs the whole household or not. He's going to have a hell of a job explaining this away as normal, I must say, unless he's in the habit of going on midnight joy-rides. I suppose we'd better make a run for it.'

'They'll see us,' Julian objected.

'They can't do much while they're up in the air and we're down here,' said Sebastian.

Crouching in the deep blue shadows of the rhododendrons beside the rusting iron skeleton of the shattered conservatory, they gazed up at the helicopter as it flew across the grounds, its bright beam gliding like a spotlight over the grass and trees below.

As it moved towards the eastern side of the house, away from them, Sebastian stood up and stepped into the open. 'Come on – now!' he said, and they ran out from behind the conservatory, across the wide lawns, towards the belt of woodland a hundred yards away that bordered the lane at the front of the Hall. As they ran, they heard the helicopter approaching, nearer and nearer, until the air around them was agitated by the down-blast from the machine's whirling rotor, and they were caught in the middle of the bright pool of light from the search beam. Before they could reach cover, the Earl fired his gun at them, but the shot missed, spattering into some bushes on their right, sending up a spray of broken leaves and twigs.

'Oh, God!' gasped Julian, 'I know Lord Stephen can get pretty mad at times, but I never thought he'd go so far as to start taking pot-shots at us!'

They dashed on, crossing the path that led to the gardener's cottage, as more shot rained into the grass around them. Within moments, however, they were safe under the dark concealing canopy of the trees, where the search beam could not reach them.

They walked more slowly now, through the wood, approaching the gates, still hearing the helicopter whirring overhead for a while, until, finally, the sound grew quieter as the machine flew back over the house. In front of them they could see where the trees came to an end, and the rhododendron bushes, growing along the edge of the drive as it curved round to the left to meet the lane, were grey in the moonlight.

While Julian waited under the trees, Sebastian crept forward to peer out between the bushes. He could see the great ornate iron gates at the end of the drive, closed now, although he had left them open after letting himself in earlier; and before the gates stood Electra Vanderpump, dressed in a shiny black PVC trench coat that gleamed wetly under the white light of the moon.

Sebastian crept back to Julian. 'Electra's there,' he said, 'and it's the only way out. Have you still got the keys?'

'Of course,' answered Julian. His face was pale and anxious in the wan light; he stared apprehensively towards the drive.

'Well, I'll – ah ... tell you what we'll do,' said Sebastian quietly. 'I'm going to draw her away from the gate, and while I'm doing that, you unlock it and – ah ... you get out and go and wait by my car that's just down the lane.'

'But what about you?' asked Julian.

'Never mind about that,' said Sebastian. 'Now look ... ' He pointed towards the house. 'I'm going to go along there a short way, and then – ah ... walk back along the drive and make sure she sees me. When I call out to you, what-ever I say, even if I tell you – ah ... even if I tell you not to come out, take it as a sign that the coast is clear, and come out anyway.'

Julian frowned. 'I don't understand,' he said. 'Suppose it's not safe to come out – then what?'

'If it's not safe, then I shan't call you,' Sebastian replied. 'But remember, if you hear me call, whatever I say, just get out as fast as you can.'

Without waiting to listen to Julian's objections, he hur-ried off through the trees to the point where the drive be-gan to bend, then he emerged onto the drive and began to walk back towards the gate. As he rounded the bend and Electra came into view, he halted abruptly, pausing only long enough for her to catch sight of him, before he jumped into the concealing bushes.

'Stop!' cried Electra at once.

As he dashed under the trees, Sebastian could hear her footsteps behind him on the gravel; then suddenly there was the sharp retort of a revolver being fired. Sebastian swung round: he could see Electra standing dark against the moonlit drive.

'Mr Crucefix!' called Sebastian in the direction of the house, so as to mislead Electra about Julian's real location, though he made sure that his voice was sufficiently loud for Julian to hear anyway. 'Stay where you are – she's got a gun!'

'You stay where you are, Sebastian!' ordered Electra curtly. 'Enough of your games! You know I have no scru-ples about using this, should you fail to co-operate.' She raised the revolver and the light shone upon it. 'Now come out,' she instructed. 'Slowly.'

Sebastian began to walk forward. 'Look here, old sport,'

he said, 'you're not going to shoot me, are you? I've had enough aggravation for one evening, what with – ah ... what with Lord Steve beating me up, and that lunatic with the knives.'

'Who?' asked Electra.

Sebastian smiled. 'I think it was your – ah ... colleague, Dr Kotlowski.'

'Very likely,' replied Electra. 'And now, Sebastian dear, you have to make a choice. I assume you know about the project that Lord Stephen and I are currently engaged upon. I'm giving you the choice of either working on it with us or remaining here as my prisoner until the project is completed.'

'Couldn't I just – ah ... couldn't I just leave quietly, and – ah ... we'll say no more about it?' said Sebastian.

'No,' said Electra.

'I don't – ah ... don't seem to have much of a choice then, do I?' Sebastian observed with an awkward laugh.

'No, you don't,' said Electra.

'You're building a time machine,' said Sebastian. 'Perhaps you'd care to explain why.'

'If you agree to help,' said Electra, 'everything will be explained.'

'I'm not sure that I want to help,' said Sebastian, 'until I know what I'm letting myself in for.'

Electra beckoned him closer. 'Where's Mr Crucefix?' she asked.

Sebastian glanced in the direction of the Hall, away from where he had parted with Julian.

'Come out where I can see you, Mr Crucefix!' called Electra. There was silence; nothing stirred. 'He's not there,' she said.

'Well, he's certainly not answering,' Sebastian agreed.

'You call him,' Electra instructed.

'Mr Crucefix – you can come out now!' called Sebastian.

When Julian did not emerge, Electra became suspicious. 'Come here!' she ordered Sebastian sternly, stepping back onto the drive.

Sebastian approached her, and suddenly, he took a desperate chance, lunging towards her, grabbing the wrist of her right hand in which she held the revolver. As he forced her arm away from him, the gun went off with a resounding retort, and Sebastian realised with a shock just how close she had come to really shooting him. For a moment, they struggled, until Sebastian's superior strength prevailed and, still gripping Electra's arm with his right hand, with a sharp blow of his other hand, he succeeded in striking the weapon from her grasp, and it spun away into the bushes.

Electra let out a high-pitched shriek of surprise and rage. She stooped to pick up the revolver, but it was hidden from view, and Sebastian was running away from her, towards the gates that now stood open; for while Electra had been distracted, Julian had unlocked them and had escaped into the lane.

She ran a few steps after Sebastian, but saw at once that there was no chance of catching up with him or holding him back.

In fury, she returned to the shrubbery to search for her lost gun.

CHAPTER 20

Desperate Measures

When Karen Black awoke in the morning, she found Lord Stephen standing by the window, fully dressed, his braces already on.

'Oh, Steve, are you up already? You must hardly have had any sleep,' she said.

'An early start, Karen! An early start!' exclaimed the Earl, slapping his thighs. 'We've got a lot of work to get through today. I've made plans, you see. That fellow Dorrell may have escaped from here last night, but one thing's certain – I'm going to make damn sure he doesn't get back in again!'

'What're you going to do?' asked Karen anxiously, sitting up in bed.

'Aha, you wait and see!' replied Lord Stephen darkly, turning from the window to glance in her direction.

'Oh, Steve!' She snatched her hand to her mouth in dismay as she saw his face. 'Your eye! What've you done?'

'It's nothing – just a bit of a bruise,' said the Earl as carelessly as he could manage. 'I'll tell you one thing – I gave as good as I got! Yes, indeed,' he declared, beginning to limp up and down the room, 'I showed him a thing or two!'

'You didn't have a fight with him?' asked Karen incredulously. 'Not with Sebastian Dorrell? Oh, Steve, how could you?'

'He was asking for it,' declared the Earl obstinately. 'If he comes here trespassing, that's what he can bloody well expect!'

*

Meanwhile, on the other side of the house, in one of the guest bedrooms, Dr Kotlowski was also rising early. Standing in front of the dressing-table and peering into the mirror, he laboriously plucked the hairs from his chin with a pair of pliers; it was a slow and painful process, but at last he was satisfied that it was nearly done.

When he had finished, he covered his face liberally with talcum powder, cleaned the pliers with disinfectant, wrapped them in lavatory paper and concealed them in his suitcase. He then began to search for his mouthwash, but was unable to find it anywhere. For a moment he panicked, frantically rifling through the clothes in his case, then suddenly his eye lighted on an aerosol of antiperspirant. A desperate plight called for desperate measures: swiftly he sprayed the anti-perspirant into his mouth, in his armpits and over other parts of his body. Relieved for the moment, he began to get dressed, though the feeling and taste in his mouth grew increasingly unpleasant.

When he was ready, he lingered a little by the dressing-table, fingering the kitchen knives that lay there and smiling to himself; then he took the knives, wrapped them, like the pliers, in lavatory paper, and hid them in his suitcase.

*

While the Earl and Dr Kotlowski had been getting up, however, Electra Vanderpump had already been at work. Taking some of her portable equipment with her, she had entered the Prince's Tower by the secret door that Sebastian Dorrell had opened the night before. Her task completed, she emerged from the dark entrance just as Lord Stephen came into the Picture Gallery from the Chapel.

They each stared at one another in surprise. In the morning sunlight, Electra's pale thin face looked even paler than usual, as if she had just seen something that had shocked her and left her chilled with horror.

'Good God!' said the Earl in alarm. 'I didn't know you were up. Have you been into the Tower?'

'Yes,' said Electra quickly. 'I've taken the readings, and I'm afraid they indicate that the situation is considerably more unstable than we thought until now.' Setting down the box of equipment that she carried, she reached into the opening in the wall and pulled the wooden panel back into place.

'Don't close it!' said the Earl. leaping forward.

'It will open again,' Electra told him. 'There's no need for us to go in there again unless we're ready to attempt the penetration.'

'You should've waited for me,' said Lord Stephen fiercely. 'You shouldn't have gone in there alone, Dr Vanderpump. You had no idea what to expect. I could've warned you.'

'Well, I've seen it now,' Electra replied rather shortly. She pointed to the box of equipment. 'Would you mind bringing this for me,' she said.

As they went downstairs, the Earl carrying the box, Electra said, 'I wonder, Lord Stephen ... have you ever considered ... abandoning the project?'

'What?' cried the Earl. 'What the hell do you mean?'

'Of course,' conceded Electra, 'you have a great deal to lose, but you're gambling still more in the hope of winning back what is already lost.'

'How can you talk like that?' cried the Earl in rage. 'My father gave his life for this!'

'So he did,' Electra agreed, 'and perhaps too much has been sacrificed already. You knew it might come to this, Lord Stephen. We've discussed it before.'

'You're talking about giving in!' exclaimed the Earl incredulously. 'You're talking about throwing it all up and admitting defeat!'

'I'm simply being practical,' said Electra, as she strode through the Dining-Room. 'What is the use, for heaven's sake, in risking the destruction of everything, when something at least can be salvaged from this mess before it's too late?'

She strode through the Lounge and through the Ballroom, where her stiletto-heeled sandals clattered viciously on the marble floor.

'Salvage what, for God's sake?' yelled the Earl.

'You know quite well what I mean,' replied Electra. Before the door to the kitchens, she halted and turned to face him. Very tall and imposing she looked in her red and black cotton print sheath dress; she eyed him coldly. 'I've done everything you required of me,' she said. 'You asked for my assistance and my expert advice, and in return for this you agreed to give me the Time Machine. Well, I've fulfilled my side of the agreement, have I not? Perhaps it hasn't turned out as well as you hoped, but it could have been a great deal worse, I'm sure you realise. So now it's for you to honour your part of the bargain, I think.'

The Earl was almost speechless with rage and disbelief.

'I need ... I need that Machine!' he blustered at last. 'What the hell d'you think I've been building the damn thing for? Not to have you go careering off with it at the last minute, that's for sure!'

'Now, for heaven's sake,' said Electra, 'don't be childish about this, Lord Stephen. You asked for my expert advice, and I'm giving it to you. I strongly advise you to abandon this project forthwith.'

'You're not bloody well having that Machine!' declared the Earl. 'What the bloody hell d'you expect me to do without it?'

'Well,' replied Electra with a thin smile, 'we discussed the possibility of involving Mr Dorrell, didn't we? And I was against it at the time, because I feared he might try to prevent me from having the Time Machine. When I've gone, however, if you really must persist with this business, you might approach Mr Dorrell for help – that's certainly one course of action left open to you. But as far as I'm concerned, the matter is finished, so let's not have any silly arguments about it, please.'

The Earl deposited the box of equipment on the floor. Squarely he stood before her; his face was purple with rage. 'Now look here, Dr Vanderpump,' he roared, stabbing the air with an angry finger, 'you went in the Tower without my permission and without my knowledge, and you've seen what's in there, and it's scared you – scared you half out of your wits! You're in a bloody blue funk about it, Dr Vanderpump, and you want to run out on it, and to be quite honest with you, I can't blame you for feeling that way. I'll be blunt with you – I'm a blunt sort of chap – it scared the hell out of me when I first saw it! Yes, I was bloody well scared, and I don't mind admitting it! But when you talk about running off with my Time Machine before we've seen the job through, and you start telling me to go crawling to that nancy boy, Dorrell, and asking him for help, I'm not standing for that! I'm not bloody well standing for it! Because no matter how tough the going gets, I'm never going to give in to that fear, I'm never going to let it get the better of me, I'm never going to admit defeat, and I'm going to stand up and fight to the bitter end!'

'Well, that's up to you,' said Electra, 'but I think you should recognise that not every problem can be solved by brute strength alone, and if Heydn Hall and everyone and everything in it is not to be destroyed, it's high time you learnt that lesson, Lord Stephen. I at least intend to escape unscathed, and I intend to take the Time Machine with me.'

With that, she turned and walked out through the kitchen, her stiletto heels tapping across the tiled floor.

'Just like a woman!' yelled the Earl after her. 'Just like a bloody woman – back off at the first sign of trouble! But you won't catch a man acting like that!' He shook his fist defiantly. 'That bloody poof, Dorrell, is never going to set foot inside this house again, I'll see to that! I'm going to sort it all out and put it all to rights! I'm going to bust in there on my own, and I'm damned if anyone's going to stop me!'

At the door into the servants' hall, Electra turned and looked back at him with an icy, withering look of utter scorn.

The Earl shook his fist. 'I don't need your help, Dr Vanderpump!' he yelled. 'I can board it all up and keep you all out! I can bust in! I can brick it up! I can smash it! I don't need your help to bust in and block it off! I don't need help from any bloody poofs and women!'

His furious blustering subsided into a moan of frustration and despair.

'Just bring the equipment, and pull yourself together, for heaven's sake,' said Electra coldly. She turned, and was gone.

The door swung slowly shut behind her and Lord Stephen heard her sharp footsteps retreating in the direction of the cellars.

*

Much later, after breakfast, just as the staff were leaving for their month's enforced holiday, their suitcases packed, their taxis waiting on the gravel forecourt ready to take them to Newhaven, Lord Stephen was to be found hard at work, smashing, sawing and hammering. Many were the puzzled and nervous glances that the departing staff cast in the direction of the Morning Room, from where the noises issued.

'Oh, Steve, whatever are you doing?' wailed Karen Black in dismay, running into the room.

The Earl, stripped to the waist, hammer in hand, turned round from the window, which was already half boarded up, to throw her a shaky smile of acknowledgment.

She looked very young and innocent, almost a child, standing there in her pink cotton shorts, white mesh tee shirt, pink ankle socks and white rubber pumps, a pink scarf around her head tied in a big bow.

'Now, Karen, don't you worry about anything, there's a good girl,' said Lord Stephen with paternal reassurance. 'Everything's under control here.'

'Oh, Christ!' breathed Karen. 'Oh, Christ!' Her eyes were wide; her lip was trembling. She stared at the heap of broken wood in the middle of the floor; splinters of wood were scattered across the lush carpet. 'Where'd you bloody get all this wood from?' she cried.

'We need more,' said the Earl. 'A hell of a lot more. We've got to get all these windows boarded up - all the windows on the ground floor, and all the doors, and the first floor too, if we can manage it. Where's Terrier got to - and Kotlowski as well? I need some more muscle power around here - smash up the coffins and get them in the house!'

'Coffins?' wailed Karen. 'What coffins? What're you bloody talking about, Steve? Does Dr Vanderpump know about this?'

'Dr Vanderpump's out of it!' said the Earl fiercely, hammering another board across the window. 'She's leaving. She's got the wind up, and she's bloody well bunking off and leaving us in the lurch, that's what she's doing!'

'Oh ... ' said Karen doubtfully. 'Is that why she's in the cellar taking everything apart and packing it away?'

'What?' The Earl glanced back over his shoulder. 'What's she up to?'

'She's packing it all away - all the equipment,' Karen explained. 'I heard her talking on the phone, arranging for a removal van. What's going on, Steve? She can't take all the stuff away - you need it.'

'I'll manage without,' the Earl declared defiantly, as he boarded out the daylight.

'But why're you doing all this? Why?' cried Karen above the noise of his hammering.

'To keep out that bloody interfering pest, Dorrell!' shouted the Earl. 'I told you I was going to make damn sure he wouldn't get back in here again, didn't I? Well, I said it and I meant it. He'll need a bloody battering-ram to get into Heydn Hall by the time I've finished! And there's a little job that you can do, Karen – see that the gates are properly locked after all the staff have gone. And when I say properly locked, I mean with a chain and padlock, because he's got the key for the gates too.'

'Oh, Steve – you can't!' wailed Karen.

'Can't?' said the Earl, 'Can't what? There's no such word as *can't*. There's been too much namby-pamby messing about and wasting time around here for too long. Well, it's action that's needed now, and I'm going to take it!'

'But you're spoiling everything!' Karen protested. 'You're making it all horrible – you're spoiling the wall and the paint and everything!'

'Spoiling it?' cried the Earl, hammering furiously. 'I'm not bloody well spoiling it – I'm protecting it – protecting it from bloody interfering pests and intruders! It'll be a damn sight more spoilt, I can tell you, if that fellow Dorrell gets in and sabotages the whole project and blows the place up!'

'But he ain't going to blow it up,' Karen protested in bewilderment. 'Oh, Steve,' she wailed, as the summer sunlight was blocked out by the last board that the Earl nailed into place. 'We can't live in the dark!'

'We'll damn well live in the dark, if that's what it takes!' declared the Earl, climbing down from the window-seat and stepping back to admire his handiwork in the gloom; chinks of sunlight gleamed in between the boards. 'We'll damn well live in the cellars on bread and water, if that's what it takes,' he said, pressing the point home. 'We'll board ourselves in, we'll wall ourselves up if we have to –

but we're bloody well going to fight this thing! I'm not going to let it get the better of me, I can tell you – not now, after all these years!'

'Yeah, but you will be careful, won't you, Steve?' whispered Karen anxiously.

'I'm a survivor,' declared the Earl, 'and I'm going to pull us through somehow. Now for those coffins!' he declared, striding towards the door.

*

Meanwhile, something was happening up in the bedrooms. Johnny Terrier, feeling lonely and neglected, sitting in his room, day-dreaming about Lady Caroline, was suddenly roused by a terrible shriek. Across the landing, through the walls it penetrated: a shrill and horrible cry of agony.

His eyes gleaming with sudden interest, Johnny leapt up and ran out in the direction from which the cry had come. He tried to open the door of Dr Kotlowski's bedroom, but it was locked from the inside, and from within came a low groaning and gasping of someone in pain.

'Hello!' called Johnny excitedly. 'Hello there!' He giggled. 'What're you doing?'

'Help!' groaned the faint and straining voice of Dr Kotlowski from within. 'Help!'

'The door's locked,' explained Johnny feebly.

'Fetch Dr Vanderpump!' cried Kotlowski. 'Hurry, hurry – else I expire!' He let out a low wail of distress.

'Dr Vanderpump – she's down in the cellars,' explained Johnny. 'She's packing it all away – Karen told me. She won't want to be bothered with you, will she? No, she don't want to be bothered with nobody, Dr Vanderpump don't. She's busy down in the cellars, she is.'

'For the love of God, fetch somebody – a doctor!' moaned Kotlowski. 'I'm dying!'

'You're a doctor, Dr Kotlowski,' said Johnny smugly. He sniggered.

'God save me!' cried Kotlowski weakly. 'Call an ambulance, Terrier!'

Enjoying this new and interesting turn of events, Johnny went skipping away in search of Karen. Down the white marble staircase he ran, down two flights into the entrance hall, where the Earl was dragging a great plank of wood through the front door, anxiously watched by Karen.

'Oh, Steve, I'm afraid you'll rupture yourself!' wailed Karen.

'Dr Kotlowski's dying!' Johnny cooed gleefully, as he bounded towards them.

'Don't bother me now,' grumbled the Earl. 'Come and help me with this, if you've nothing better to do.'

Karen, however, stared at Johnny nervously. 'What d'you mean?'

Johnny grinned sheepishly, standing on the stairs, screwing his hands together. 'He's locked in,' he said. 'He wants Dr Vanderpump to go up. He wants an ambulance called.'

'What's the matter with him?' Karen asked in alarm.

The Earl was dragging a plank through into the Marble Hall. 'Give me a hand here, young Johnny,' he said. 'I need your help to smash up the coffins.'

'It'll have to wait, Steve,' Karen told him. 'Something's up. Come along,' she said, taking Johnny by the hand and leading him back up the stairs.

At the door to Dr Kotlowski's room, she knocked loudly. 'Are you all right, Dr Kotlowski?' she called. She tried to open the door, but discovered it to be locked.

From inside, a feeble moaning could be heard.

'Is that you, Dr Kotlowski?' cried Karen. 'Are you ill? Can't you unlock the door?'

'Help!' came the weak groan from within.

'Quick,' said Karen to Johnny urgently. 'Go and get Steve or Dr Vanderpump. Make them come up here, d'you understand, and tell them I said so. Get someone to call an ambulance. I'm going to fetch the keys from the office.'

Within minutes, both Dr Vanderpump and the Earl came hurrying up the stairs behind Johnny, who led the way with growing excitement. Karen was just unlocking the bedroom door as they arrived.

'For heaven's sake!' said Electra.

'What the devil's going on?' demanded the Earl.

'Dr Kotlowski's ill,' said Karen, opening the door. Then she gave a little scream of horror, and her hands flew to her mouth, as she saw the sight within.

Kotlowski was lying face down on the floor, his head resting on one forearm, his other hand clutching at his groin. Though he was wearing a shirt and a pinstripe jacket, the lower part of his body was completely naked, apart from his socks, and across the soft white carpet, a bright wet blood stain was spreading out from where he lay.

'My God!' cried Lord Stephen. 'He's killed himself!'

Johnny Terrier began to giggle hysterically.

An expression of disgust and rage flashed across Electra Vanderpump's stony face. 'This is all we need!' she said fiercely. 'More foolishness and time-wasting – what does he think he's playing at?'

She stepped across to the prone Kotlowski and, stooping down, she rolled him over onto his side; he let out a strangled cry of agony.

'You wretched man!' Electra almost spat the words in contempt. 'How dare you – at a time like this! Don't you think we have quite enough problems already? Mm? Don't you? Don't you? I hope you're feeling thoroughly ashamed of yourself!'

Kotlowski's anguished eyes rolled up towards the ceiling. He mumbled, 'The Blessed Virgin ... I believed ... but perhaps I was mistaken.'

'Mistaken you certainly were!' snapped Electra. She stood up again, and the front of her white lab coat was stained with his blood. 'It was the Countess of Warwick you saw, not the Virgin Mary,' she said. 'I've never heard such utter rubbish in my life.' She turned back towards the door, where Karen and the Earl were watching aghast; only Johnny was sniggering, his grubby fingers held foolishly to his mouth. 'Miss Black,' instructed Electra coolly, 'go and fetch bandages, a bowl of water and some towels. We must get this mess cleared up at once.'

'Did you call an ambulance?' asked Karen.

'For heaven's sake,' retorted Electra, 'that's the last thing we want. You picked a bad time for your little scene, Dr Kotlowski,' she said, looking down at him with a sneer of disgust. 'For now, I'm afraid you'll have to make do with some hasty first aid, until we get back to London. We're leaving this afternoon.'

CHAPTER 21

The Barricading of Heydn Hall

In the warm sunlight, Professor Aaronberg, Sebastian Dorrell and Julian Crucefix were sitting on a bench on the platform of Newhaven railway station.

Sebastian was wearing camouflage trousers, pink suede ankle boots, and a pink leopardskin print tee shirt, and his hair was tied up in a pony-tail with a length of pink wool that matched his eye-shadow and feather ear-ring. Professor Aaronberg, unfortunately, was still wearing his soiled white cotton suit which he had worn during his week of imprisonment.

'Dear oh dear,' he said. 'I do feel a shambles. I have no change of clothing.'

'That's a problem I have, too,' Julian complained. 'I've left everything I possess at Heydn Hall, and I don't intend to go back there again – I don't think they'd ever let me out.'

Sebastian smiled. 'Don't worry, old sport,' he said, patting him consolingly on the shoulder. 'I'll go and get it for you this afternoon.'

'This afternoon?' exclaimed the Professor in dismay. 'But surely – '

THE BARRICADING OF HEYDN HALL   283

'Yes, I'm afraid so,' said Sebastian cheerfully. 'I'll be – ah ... be going back there again to get to the bottom of this damn business. Come on now, Professor – good grief, you don't – ah ... don't expect me to give up and forget all about it, do you? Honestly, I don't think I could.'

'You can't be serious,' said Julian. 'If they catch you, they'll lock you in the cellars.'

'Well,' said Sebastian with a smirk, 'I shall – ah ... I shall let myself out again, you know. I have the keys, remember.'

'Are you being deliberately stupid?' said Julian. 'It just isn't a joke. They could kill you.'

'Good gracious me!' said the Professor in alarm.

Sebastian laughed.

'Look here,' Julian continued earnestly, 'Professor Aaronberg keeps saying it, and I agree with him – the only sensible thing to do is to go to the police.'

'I really don't believe this!' Sebastian exclaimed, throwing up his hands. 'Julian, what can I say? Less than twelve hours ago, you were actually working for these people, and now you – ah ... now you speak as if they were criminals or – ah ... or some sort of murdering maniacs! What the hell is this? What's happened to you? Don't tell me you've finally begun to use your powers of critical reasoning?'

'I know a lot now that I didn't know yesterday,' Julian answered irritably.

Professor Aaronberg raised his fluffy white head and stared with an anxious frown along the railway line. 'I can hear the train coming,' he said. 'I shall have to go now. But, Sebastian, dear boy, you are quite well aware of my opinion. When I arrive back at Portmeirion, there will be questions asked. The police are still looking for me and must be informed of my return. When they question me, I shall certainly conceal nothing from them.' He rose from the bench as the train drew in.

The wheels clattered, rattling over the rails, throwing up sparks; the brakes squealed, the doors opened, and passengers climbed out.

Sebastian stood up, a look of dismay in his dark eyes. 'The police will go to the Hall with a search warrant and discover everything!'

'They certainly will,' replied the Professor, 'and not before time, either.' He paused beside the open door of the carriage and laid his hand gently on Sebastian's bare arm. 'You came here to rescue me,' he said, 'and I'm grateful for that. But I would rather have remained imprisoned and have died in that place than have my dear boy go back there and suffer such a fate at the hands of those mad and evil people. And if you decide to go, I would have you remember that I have lost all my family, and there is no one in the world whom I care about more than you.'

Sebastian bent and kissed the little old Professor on the cheek. 'I'll try and remember that,' he said. 'But please don't worry about me so much. Honestly, I can look after myself.'

Professor Aaronberg gave him a grave look, squeezing his hand in farewell before climbing into the carriage, just before the doors closed.

Sebastian and Julian watched as the train moved out of the station.

When it had gone, Julian said, 'How can you go back to Heydn Hall after he said that to you?'

Sebastian sighed, and he rubbed the back of his neck uneasily, a frown upon his brow. Slowly he turned away from the line and walked away across the platform. Julian

followed him, past the ticket office, out into the sunny street.

'If you're going back to Heydn Hall,' said Julian, 'you're not going there on your own. I'm coming with you.'

*

Johnny Terrier was laughing in triumphant glee as he swung his axe, and splinters of wood flew about him. Close at hand, the Earl of Newhaven was labouring hard, dragging the heavy coffins out across the stone floor.

For long brooding years, the great stone mausoleum of the Horsley-Mitchell family had been a place of silence and darkness, of creeping shadows and clinging cobwebs; but now, the doors were open wide and pale shafts of dusty sunlight beamed in, and the silence was shattered by the thud of axe-strokes and the rending and splintering of oak. Lord Stephen Mitchell, with the aid of Johnny Terrier, was desecrating the last resting place of his ancestors.

At the door, in the midst of the dust and sunlight, Karen Black appeared. For a moment she stood there, gazing into the gloom, watching with horror the scene of destruction within. 'Oh, Steve!' she screamed above the commotion. 'Oh God, Steve – what're you doing?'

A bare white skull hurtled across the chamber and crashed near to her feet with a hollow thud, skidding over the flagstones. Karen leapt back with a shriek. Johnny was pulling bones out of a broken coffin and tossing them gaily aside.

Lord Stephen grabbed another axe and swung a heavy blow down upon a coffin lid.

'What're you doing?' screamed Karen again, almost hysterical now. 'Steve!'

The Earl looked up, wiping the sweat from his gleaming forehead with the back of his hand. His bare chest and arms were streaked with smears of dust and cobwebs. 'We need all this wood,' he roared, 'to barricade the house! Keep that wretched fellow Dorrell out!'

'But all the bodies – the bones!' cried Karen with a shudder. 'You can't do this – you can't!'

'Why not?' retorted the Earl. 'They're dead! Dead! They're all dead! They don't know! They can't feel!' He struck the coffin with another mighty blow of the axe, and the wood split with a groan.

'Stop it!' cried Karen. 'It's wrong – it's wrong! Don't you see – it's your family! How can you do this? It's so horrible!'

The Earl clutched the axe in his strong hand and brandished it with a defiant gesture of awful purpose. He strode across the flagstones towards her, and a wild gleam was in his blue eyes. 'I'm not going to be defeated!' he declared. 'I'm not going to let this thing get the better of me – never! D'you want to see Heydn Hall destroyed? Is that what you want, eh?'

'Of course not.' Karen shook her head in dismay.

'You're giving in to your fear!' the Earl rebuked her fiercely. 'Your fear, Karen – fight it, fight it!' He gestured all about him; he laughed with a hollow laugh that echoed back from the cold windowless walls, a chill accompaniment to the steady thudding of Johnny Terrier's swinging axe. 'This is all it is!' the Earl shouted. 'A place of bones, a place where the past moulders to nothing and is forgotten! This was my fear!' He scoffed. 'This was my fear, Karen!' He shook his head in incredulous amusement. 'Do you know, I haven't been in here since I was a boy of fifteen, creeping in the dead of night, half scared of my own bloody shadow. And this is all it amounts to in the end – bones, dead bones! No ghosts! No vampires! No zombies! This was all there ever was, and it was this that made me tremble!'

'Oh, Steve,' said Karen, tears welling in her brown eyes, 'please, please come away. You don't know what you're doing. It's all been too much for you. You need to rest.'

'Rest!' said the Earl with scorn. He strutted up and down before her. 'I found out the truth, Karen – yes I did! I busted in and found out the truth for myself. And here it is!' He strode back down the chamber to a dark stone niche at the far end. 'Here!' he bellowed, beckoning her to follow him.

Johnny Terrier stopped chopping up a coffin and looked on with interest. 'What's that?' he asked with an eager giggle.

Karen hurried to the Earl's side and rested a restraining hand on his wrist. 'Leave it, Steve,' she implored.

Lord Stephen brushed her easily aside. There was a sturdy oak coffin in the niche, its lid loose and laid askew. 'My father's coffin,' he said solemnly. 'This is it. And today I looked in it again – this morning for the first time in thirty years.'

'Don't!' breathed Karen. 'Oh, don't!'

But it was too late: Lord Stephen, laying down his axe, seized the lid of the coffin and dragged it off, hurling it to the floor with a dramatic gesture of rejection, and Karen, glancing within, screamed at the sight of the dead face of the nineteenth Earl of Newhaven.

'This is all it is!' Lord Stephen was almost jubilant. 'This was what made me shake and shiver!' With both hands, he took hold of the head as it lay in the red satin-lined coffin, and with a sudden twist, he wrenched it free.

Karen screamed and screamed, backing away from him, her hands clasped to her face in a distraction of anguish, her eyes squeezed shut.

'No, no, no, no, no!' she cried. 'No, no, no!'

Johnny was chortling with horrified excitement as he watched.

'Look at it! Look at it!' yelled the Earl. 'Haven't you understood what I've been telling you all these years? For God's sake, Karen, can't you bloody well understand a single thing? It's nothing! It's nothing! Waxworks and images, made to deceive children and stupid women! It's all phoney! It's all lies! And this was all I was scared of!' Lifting up the wax head, he suddenly flung it down upon the floor, where it shattered into a hundred pieces.

Karen, opening her eyes, saw with amazement the fragments of wax scattered across the flagstones between them.

'All broken!' said Johnny, his eyes wide with astonishment.

'And now it's finally gone,' announced the Earl, slowly and deliberately, as if he were pronouncing a curse. 'Gone forever! Nothing more to fear!'

'But that's not true,' Karen protested miserably. 'This ain't the real problem – it never has been. What about the Tower? What about the Time Machine? That's the real danger. That's what we ought to be worried about right now.' She was still trembling, and she clasped her arms nervously across her slender body. 'Dr Vanderpump's packed up all her stuff,' she said, 'and the van'll be here soon to take it all away. Don't you care about that? Don't you care anymore?'

Suddenly, Lord Stephen seemed to wither, as if all the strength had left him, and he groaned, holding his head in his hands. A little way behind the Earl, Johnny was still giggling, his eyes glinting in the gloom.

Karen stared around her in despair at the wreck of coffins and bones that lay strewn among the dust that had gathered for so many years undisturbed. The sunlight cast her grey shadow across the cold grey flagstones of the floor. The Earl had begun to sniff strangely, as if he were struggling to hold back tears. 'Of course I bloody well care,' he said at last, dejectedly. 'I'm losing it all. I'm losing control. I'm losing everything.'

And in the gloom, Johnny Terrier whimpered with stifled laughter.

*

It was nearly midday when Sebastian and Julian drove along the leafy lane in Sebastian's green sports car, towards Heydn Hall. Before the gates came into view, they could hear the persistent sound of a vehicle's horn ahead.

'I think something's up,' said Julian nervously.

They turned a bend, and now the gates were before them on the right of the road, and outside the gates, a large chocolate brown removal van was parked, almost blocking the lane. On the side of the van, in tall yellow letters, were painted the words EMPIRE REMOVALS LTD., and below, in smaller letters, the slogan EFFICIENT, DISCREET, NO QUESTIONS ASKED. Around the van lurked a number of furtive-looking men dressed in dark pinstripe suits, white Homburgs and dark glasses: one was armed with a machine-gun, and another, who wore a red carnation in his lapel, was smoking a fat cheroot.

'Hello – looks like the Mob have arrived,' remarked Sebastian, slowing his car to a halt by the verge. He switched off the engine and opened the door to climb out.

The man smoking the cheroot had turned from the gate and was strolling towards them.

'Morning,' he said with a menacing leer, taking the cheroot from his mouth as he walked up. 'Are you the guy who lives in this place?' he asked, eyeing Sebastian's pink tee shirt and feather ear-ring doubtfully.

Sebastian climbed out of the car and slammed the door. 'Ah, no, actually,' he said. 'I'm – ah ... I'm – ah ... you know, a visiting friend, what?'

'The gates're locked and padlocked,' snarled the man.

'Sorry!' said Sebastian. He shrugged. 'It's not really my fault, of course – well, not at all, actually. What's going on, then? Don't tell me Lord Steve's moving out?'

'Lord Steve?' said the man. 'Does he live here? I got a call from a dame name of Vanderpump – said she wanted some equipment shifting.'

'Ah, well, she's – ah ... staying here at the moment,' Sebastian explained.

The man turned away, drawing on his cheroot impatiently, then he walked back towards the gate. Sebastian and Julian left the car and followed a little way behind him.

'What d'you think's going on?' whispered Julian. 'I don't like the look of this.'

'Oh, don't worry about it, old chap!' Sebastian reassured him. 'Typical of the sort of – ah ... sort of underworld riff-raff that Electra gets to do her dirty work for her. They're probably quite – ah ... quite harmless, really.'

'Okay, boys,' said the man with the carnation and the big cheroot to the men by the gate. 'Get the crowbar!'

'Right, Mr Empire!' they responded in chorus, moving around to the back of the van.

'Gosh, I say – you're not going to ... actually break in, are you?' asked Sebastian. 'Isn't that a trifle drastic, don't you – ah ... don't you think?'

'You stay outa this, mister!' retorted Mr Empire. 'Me and my boys can deal with it.'

'Now, look here,' began Julian, stepping forward indignantly. 'I'm the estate manager, and you can't – '

'Steady on, old sport,' said Sebastian, laying a hand on his shoulder. 'What're you saying? This is a stroke of luck for us. If these gentlemen are so good as to – ah ... to open the gates for us, we shan't be put to the trouble of doing it for ourselves, shall we?'

The men had taken a crowbar from the back of the van and had twisted it in the padlocked chain that Karen Black had wound around the bars of the gate as an extra security measure; very soon they had wrenched the chain free.

'Okay, boys – saw through the lock!' ordered Mr Empire.

'Right, Boss!' said the men in chorus.

'I say, we've got the key here, as a matter of fact,' said Sebastian.

Mr Empire scowled suspiciously. 'What's that?' he demanded. 'Why the hell didn't you say so before?'

'Come along, Julian,' encouraged Sebastian, ushering Julian forward.

'Okay, boys – back in the van!' said Mr Empire, waving his cheroot in agitation. 'At the double!'

'Right, Boss – back in the van!' echoed the men, as they hurried to obey.

While Julian unlocked the gates and opened them, Mr Empire and the Boys tried to start the removal van; something appeared to be wrong with the starter motor.

Sebastian and Julian set off on foot down the drive, while Mr Empire was still trying to start the engine. Behind them, as they turned the bend and the great grey stone mass of Heydn Hall loomed into full view before them, they could hear him shouting orders to his men to get out and push.

But now Julian stopped dead in the drive and stared up at the windows of the house in amazement.

'What's the matter?' asked Sebastian.

'They're all boarded up on the inside,' said Julian. 'Look.' He pointed up to the window on the first floor on the right of the facade. 'There's someone doing it now.'

They could hear the muffled sound of intermittent hammering coming from above and, gazing in the direction to which Julian had pointed, Sebastian could see the boards going up across the inside of the window.

They moved closer and stared up, and now they could see that it was Lord Stephen, nailing planks across the upper part of the window. He glanced down at that moment and caught sight of them.

'Come on!' said Julian nervously. 'He's spotted us.'

The Earl quickly opened the casement, which swung outwards, and leaned out to call down to them. 'You bloody well clear off!' he yelled. 'You're not coming in here, Dorrell – I've made damn sure of that! Those keys will be a lot of use to you now! Ha! And you, Crucefix, you miserable traitor – what're you doing, skulking back here? Get lost, before I take my shotgun to you!'

'He's come back for his luggage,' called Sebastian.

'It's on the landing,' called Julian uneasily. 'I could come up and get it ... '

'Don't think I'm going to fall for any of your tricks!' said the Earl scornfully.

The anxious face of Karen Black appeared at the window beside him. She exchanged with the Earl a few words that they could not hear.

'We'd better go,' suggested Julian to Sebastian. 'It doesn't look as if we're going to get in now.'

After a moment, Karen leaned out of the window and called to them. 'I'll bring your suitcases down to you – okay?' she said. 'I'll be a minute – just wait there.'

She left the window, and Lord Stephen reappeared, grinning triumphantly. 'You thought you could let yourself in at any time with those keys you stole, didn't you?' he jeered. 'Bloody poofs and traitors! We can do without your sort at Heydn Hall!'

Julian looked away in embarrassment and moved off to stand in the portico by the front door.

'Bloody queer!' yelled the Earl at Sebastian.

Sebastian smiled and waved.

'Pink – oh, very nice! Suits you, darling,' jeered the Earl. 'Why don't you get your hair cut?' he shouted in disgust, noticing Sebastian's pony-tail.

Sebastian blew him a kiss, and the Earl retreated hastily, slamming the window shut. After a moment, the furious hammering resumed.

Julian waited by the door, and presently he heard Karen's light footsteps approaching across the floor of the entrance hall within. There was the sound of locks being turned and bolts being drawn back, and then the door opened and Karen's tearful face peered out. 'Johnny's bringing them down,' she said. 'Just two cases – is that all?'

'Yes,' said Julian. 'Er ... Miss Black,' he added with concern, 'what's going on here, if you don't mind my asking?'

'It's nothing,' said Karen. 'You'd better just take your bags and go, all right?'

'There were some funny chaps with a removal van at the gate when we arrived,' said Julian. 'They mentioned Dr Vanderpump's name.'

Karen glanced nervously along the drive. 'Are they there now?'

'I suppose so,' said Julian. 'They couldn't get the van started.'

'They must've come to take away Dr Vanderpump's machines and stuff,' Karen explained. 'She's leaving.'

'Have all the staff gone?' asked Julian.

Karen nodded. She wiped away a tear.

'Look here,' said Julian, 'I don't like to see you like this, Miss Black. You're obviously upset, and you know that everything isn't as it should be. I've come here with Mr Dorrell to help, if we possibly can.'

'There's nothing you can do,' answered Karen. She turned back into the house. 'Here's Johnny with your bags now.'

Johnny Terrier came to the door, grinning sheepishly, and set down the heavy suitcase on the step; he turned and went back for the other one.

'This is ridiculous,' said Julian. 'You know it yourself, Miss Black. Why is Dr Vanderpump leaving?'

'I don't know – had enough, I suppose,' replied Karen with a sniff, shaking her head miserably; her pink bow flopped over one eye.

Johnny Terrier appeared at the door with the other suitcase and put it on the step.

'So that just leaves you with the Earl and your cousin?' asked Julian. 'Miss Black, I don't like to say this,' he went on tentatively, 'but they're both ... Well, I mean the Earl needs a doctor – he's obviously a bit ... well ... '

'I know,' said Karen. 'There's Dr Kotlowski too. He was

going to leave with Dr Vanderpump, but I don't think he'll be able to now.'

'He's no help – he's mad,' said Julian.

'I know,' Karen agreed. 'He tried to cut off his dick this morning. There was blood everywhere. It was awful. I think we're going to have to send him to hospital. He needs stitches.'

Julian looked horrified. 'Miss Black,' he said desperately, 'you've got to let us do something. You can't manage this on your own.'

Karen faced him defiantly, tears pouring down her cheeks. 'Just take your luggage and go – please, Julian, please,' she said. 'You're not going to make me betray Steve after all he's been through. I love him,' she declared. 'I bloody love him, and I'm not going to leave him, whatever happens.'

'It wouldn't be betraying him,' said Julian, lifting his suitcases and setting them down again on the flagstones of the portico. 'Don't you see that he needs help? His mind's snapped – he can't take any more.'

Karen gave him an anguished look. 'I've just got to stick it out – see it through to the end with him, whatever that turns out to be,' she said. She began to close the door, then she paused, peering out at him through the crack. 'Thanks anyway, Julian – thanks for ... for caring,' she said shakily. Tears choked her voice. Quickly, she pushed the door to, and Julian heard the locks being turned and the heavy bolts sliding home.

He picked up his bags and struggled down onto the drive with them, where Sebastian was waiting.

'So what's happening?' Sebastian asked, seeing the worried look on Julian's face.

'I don't know,' said Julian, 'but from the little that Miss

Black told me, I don't like the sound of it. Apparently Dr Kotlowski's tried to ... well – mutilate himself, or something. I didn't like the look of him from the start, and Professor Aaronberg told me one or two things about him as well – he's obviously off his head. Lord Stephen's plainly not his normal self, either, and all the staff have left now.' He sighed. 'I must admit, Sebastian,' he said. 'I'm worried about Miss Black, shut in there with those two. Johnny Terrier's all right, I suppose, but he's a bit simple and inclined to go along with anything he's told to do. If the Earl really does crack up and do something he shouldn't, we certainly can't rely on Terrier to make him see reason.'

Sebastian frowned. 'What about Electra Vanderpump? I can't see her putting up with any nonsense, whatever Lord Steve might have in mind. Actually, I'm surprised that she's let him do all this – ah ... all this barricading and boarding up of the windows. But I think it's her activities that we ought to be more concerned about at present.'

'I'm not so sure,' said Julian. 'Miss Black just told me that Dr Vanderpump's leaving. That's why the removal van's here – to take all her apparatus away.'

'Leaving?' said Sebastian in surprise. 'Good grief, that doesn't sound like Electra. If she gets involved in a project, it would take a lot to make her abandon it. Either they've – ah ... either they've finished what they were trying to do – which doesn't seem too likely, judging by the Earl's behaviour at present – or there's been a turn of events that's made Electra decide to – ah ... decide to get out while the going's good. And if that woman's decided to chuck in the towel, I can tell you, it must be something pretty serious. This just isn't like her.' He took one of the suitcases from Julian and began to walk back quickly across the forecourt towards the drive. 'Come on. We've got to hurry,' he said.

'Where're we going?' asked Julian, hurrying after him awkwardly, encumbered by the heavy suitcase. Sebastian was considerably taller than he, and Julian, with his short legs, found it hard to keep up.

'Back to the car first,' said Sebastian. 'Which is the – ah … quickest way to the beach?'

CHAPTER 22

The Mystery of the Tower

In the great vaulted cellar, beneath the blaze of electric lighting, Dr Electra Vanderpump sealed up the last piece of equipment in its cardboard box and stood back with a sigh of relief. She brushed her dusty hands over the front of her lab coat that was stained with dark brown patches of Kotlowski's dried blood. She took a packet of cigarettes from her pocket, a silver lighter and a long onyx holder; she lit a cigarette and smoked it slowly.

Idly, she strolled across to the Time Machine and stepped up onto its circular platform. She smiled slightly as she laid her hand upon its control console. The touch was almost a caress. The Machine was nearly hers already: all she had to do now was to wait until Mr Empire arrived with his van, check that her equipment was loaded safely on board, and then make her own departure in the Time Machine, while the agitated Earl, still in the grip of his hysterical folly, was preoccupied with boarding up all the windows and doors of Heydn Hall with the broken coffins of his noble ancestors.

It was too simple; it was absurdly simple: she almost laughed at the thought of it. Leaning elegantly against the battered console of the old Time Machine, Electra smoked her cigarette and imagined the fury of the Earl when he discovered that his prized possession and the fruit of so many years' labour had been taken away from under his very nose.

The final adjustments and tests Electra had made earlier that morning; and the irony of it all was that she had made her plans fully known to Lord Stephen, but he, obsessed with barricading the house against Sebastian Dorrell (the only person who now might be able to help him in his desperate plight), had not, apart from his initial reaction of rage and indignation, made any attempt to prevent her from carrying out her intentions, almost as if shock and exhaustion had led him to lose sight of his own.

Suddenly, there was a noise: a scuffle, the sound of footsteps in the adjoining cellar. Electra started from her reverie, and her sharp eyes darted towards the dark arched opening at the far end of the chamber. She frowned, and then she gasped: it was an exclamation of anger as much as one of surprise.

Out of that dark opening, Sebastian Dorrell stepped smirking, self-assured and chic in his safari clothing; his pink leopardskin shirt was brilliant under the electric lighting. Behind him in the shadows, the thin nervous face of Julian Crucefix peered out under a fringe of limp fair hair.

'How on earth did you get in?' demanded Electra sternly.

'Hello, old fruit!' Sebastian greeted her. 'Surprised to see me, what?'

'You didn't answer my question,' said Electra. Extinguishing her cigarette, she stepped off the Time Machine and paced down the cellar towards him, her high heels clicking impatiently across the stone floor. 'Lord Stephen must have nailed up every door and window in the house by now, so even though you have the keys that you stole, you'd need a sledge hammer to break in,' she remarked.

Sebastian smiled. 'Nothing so obvious, old sport. There's one door that's been unlocked all the time. I'm surprised Lord Steve didn't think of it, since it's – ah ... mentioned in the guidebook – but perhaps he imagined that a potential intruder would be scared off by that rusty barbed wire on the beach. No such luck, I'm afraid!'

'You have got a nerve, Sebastian,' said Electra coldly. 'How dare you come walking in here so cocksure of yourself! Just give me one good reason why I shouldn't lock you up, along with your interfering friend, Mr Crucefix, in the storeroom right now.'

Sebastian raised an eyebrow. 'What – are you going to – ah ... going to carry us in, then?' he asked. 'I suppose you might just about manage Mr Crucefix, though I can't imagine he'll go without a bit of a struggle. As for – ah ... as for me, I think I should warn you – I weigh about three stone heavier than you.'

'You speak as foolishly as the Earl,' said Electra with a curl of her scarlet lip. 'Intelligent persuasion triumphs over brute strength any day. Have you really forgotten that I have this?' So saying, she produced her revolver from her pocket and levelled it at him grimly. 'I should have used it yesterday,' she continued, 'as soon as I found you engaged in that ridiculous tussle with Lord Stephen, showing off your manhood, as you like to think. At least you haven't got a black eye like him.'

'It wasn't my idea,' said Sebastian. 'Anyway, I'd rather have a fair fight than be shot in cold blood.'

Electra shook her head. 'Oh, Sebastian,' she said, 'you

tempt me, you really do. Why is it, whenever I see you, I never know whether I want to kill you or to make passionate love to you? You see what a predicament you put me in?'

Sebastian grinned. 'Well, I'm all in favour of the second option, if you don't – ah ... don't mind putting it off for a bit. But I really would like some explanations first. Surely it's not that important to you to keep Lord Steve's secret now, is it, old fruit? After all, according to Miss Black, you're leaving today, so I assume you're abandoning the ah ... well – whatever it is you've been up to.'

Electra's pale face remained stony and expressionless. Julian Crucefix, still holding back in the shadows, afraid to say a word, watched her apprehensively.

'You assumed wrongly, Sebastian,' Electra said icily. 'I never abandon anything, if by that you mean that I give up in despair. I engage upon any project only so long as it serves my purposes. I've got what I came for, and now I'm leaving.'

'What did you come for?' asked Sebastian, but even as he spoke, his gaze moved beyond her, to the towering bulk of the Time Machine, its upper canopy pressed against the vaulted arch of the roof.

'Yes,' said Electra, 'you've guessed.' She held out her left hand. 'Now give me the Earl's keys,' she demanded. 'Have you got them with you?'

Sebastian did not reply. Electra glanced at Julian and saw him contemplating the floor nervously. 'Mr Crucefix!' she said sharply.

Julian looked up in alarm.

'The keys!' demanded Electra.

Julian hesitated, then he reached into his pocket and took them out.

Electra snatched them from him. 'Now, into the store-room, both of you.' She gestured to the door open on their left.

They moved towards it reluctantly.

'Hurry up!' ordered Electra. 'I haven't got all day.'

'I say,' said Sebastian, 'really, you know, this isn't going to do anyone any good. At least you could – ah ... could tell me what's going on, so we know why we're being locked up.'

'I can tell you why,' replied Electra. 'Because you ask too many questions, and meddle in other people's affairs. I've no time to explain anything to you now. At any minute, the van will arrive to take my equipment away. In fact, it's overdue already. I shall have to go and see where it's got to.'

'We saw it at the gate, about half an hour ago,' said Sebastian. 'I think it's – ah ... think it's broken down.'

'Empire Removals?' asked Electra.

Sebastian nodded.

Electra made a sharp noise of impatience, and muttered something under her breath; for a moment, she seemed undecided what to do, then she asked, 'How much about this project do you really know?' She seemed to relax a little, lowering her revolver slightly.

'Not a lot,' said Sebastian. 'I know that it has something to do with the Tower, and for some reason Lord Steve thinks he needs a time machine.'

'And you don't know what's in the Tower?' asked Electra.

'No,' said Sebastian, 'except that it's something danger-ous. Well, it certainly bothers Lord Steve.'

'Very well,' Electra conceded. She made a brief gesture with her revolver towards the stairs at the far end of the cellar. 'Walk ahead of me. You too, Mr Crucefix. I suppose there's no harm in showing you. There's very little that you can do about it – and anyway, I shan't be here, whatever happens.'

Sebastian and Julian walked before her across the cellar, up the stone steps and through the door into the servants' hall. Through the kitchen they went, through the Ballroom, dark and gloomy now that the windows were boarded up, through the Lounge and the Dining-Room, into the entrance hall and up the stairs. When they came through the Billiard Room into the Study, the sounds of hammering that they had heard faintly as they climbed up the stairs grew louder and louder.

Electra walked ahead and opened the door into the Library, and when she opened it, no ray of daylight came from within: all was black and shadowy. 'Oh, there you are, Lord Stephen,' called Electra into the darkness.

The hammering stopped momentarily. 'Nearly finished!' bellowed the Earl's voice out of the gloom, triumphantly. 'This is the last one.'

He resumed his banging.

'Go in,' Electra instructed Sebastian and Julian. She followed close behind them, turning on the electric light as she stepped inside.

Lord Stephen hammered up the last board. 'There!' he declared, stepping back from the window, puffing out his bare chest with the pride of his accomplishment. 'Dorrell will never get in now – just let him try!' He swung round laughing, and then, as his eye fell upon Sebastian, the broad smile was dashed from his face, to be replaced by a look of astonished disbelief and rage. 'Good God!' he roared. 'You!'

'Hello, Lord Steve!' said Sebastian with a grin that displayed the gold in his teeth. 'I say, you have been busy, haven't you? Must've – ah … must've worked like a Trojan to get all this done this morning! Practically a superhuman feat, and all on my account!'

'For heaven's sake,' scolded Electra, 'don't tease him. If you want to see this thing, let's just get it over with, shall we?'

'See what thing?' demanded Lord Stephen suspiciously. 'What the devil's going on? What's your idea, Dr Vanderpump – bringing Dorrell up here, when I've been busting a gut trying to keep the damn fellow out?'

Electra swept past him haughtily, without replying, as she ushered Sebastian and Julian before her into the Chapel; but the Earl came bounding in after them.

'You're not going to get away with this!' he bellowed futilely into the echoing darkness.

'Pay no attention to him,' said Electra quietly but firmly as Sebastian turned and looked back. 'You must promise me one thing, Sebastian,' she said, opening the door out of the Chapel into the Picture Gallery; this room was in darkness too now, the tall mullioned windows at the end boarded up like the others. Electra switched on the light. 'Whatever you think of what you see in the Tower, give me your word that you will not try to prevent me from taking the Time Machine.'

'It's the Earl's Machine,' Sebastian objected. 'I don't – ah … don't see that you have any right to it.'

'Well, I do,' replied Electra. 'Lord Stephen and I had an agreement, and I've fulfilled my side of it. He must give me the Time Machine to honour his part.'

Sebastian looked hard into her cold green eyes. 'Is this true?' he asked.

'Yes,' said Electra shortly.

Lord Stephen, however, had other ideas: he came bursting into the room behind them, his hammer raised threateningly in his hand. 'Whatever she's been telling you, Dorrell,' he roared, 'it's a pack of lies! There's nothing wrong around here that can't be put right with a bit of muscle and guts and tough action!'

He paced, limping, up and down the room, back and forth before the works of art that hung on the panelled walls, and he brandished his hammer defiantly. His sun-bronzed skin gleamed in the lamplight, and his eyes glittered a steely blue.

'We came here to help you, sir,' said Julian nervously. 'We thought perhaps there was something we could do.'

'The only thing that you can do to help me now is to clear off!' blustered Lord Stephen. He halted before Sebastian and looked him up and down with a sneer of contempt. 'And as for you, Dorrell, I wonder that a cissy like you dare come back here after the lesson I taught you last night. You'd better bugger off now, damn quick, before I give you another beating.'

Sebastian said nothing, but smiled knowingly at the swollen purple bruise around Lord Stephen's right eye, and the Earl, suddenly remembering with embarrassment, turned his face to one side and raised a concealing hand, as if to scratch his brow.

'Now, enough of this idle talk,' said Electra sharply. 'Pay attention, please. The environment inside is extremely unstable, so if you're coming in, you would be well advised to keep as quiet and still as possible. No sudden noises, mind!' She eyed the Earl sternly. 'No shouting or arguing. We'll just go in there, see what there is to see, and then come out again. Is that understood?'

'No!' bellowed the Earl. His burly frame shook with passion, and his blue eyes glittered, as if tears had welled, about to flow. He brandished his hammer. 'If you think you're taking them into that Tower, Dr Vanderpump, you've got another think coming! No one's going in there without my permission, and I say you're not to go in there!'

Sebastian looked into the Earl's face, and for a moment he was surprised by what he saw there. Lord Stephen's expression was contorted by rage, but behind the rage another emotion showed through: it was a terrible fear – unreasoning, primitive, absolute.

'Why're you so afraid, Lord Steve?' asked Sebastian.

'I'm not afraid!' yelled the Earl. Then he shook his head fiercely, and yet with an expression of despair, and he seemed to crumple; he rubbed his eyes and he groaned. 'Go on, then!' he said. 'You go in, if you dare. See it for yourself, and see what I've had to live with all these years. What do I care if you come out screaming, mad with the horror of it?' He waved his arms in a gesture of angry dismissal. 'Go on, then – if that's what you want!'

Julian looked at Sebastian and Electra in dismay.

'It really isn't that terrible,' said Electra. 'It's quite safe, so long as you don't do anything foolish.' She slipped her revolver back into her pocket and took out a battery torch. She stepped serenely over to the wall where the secret entrance was concealed, and pressed a wooden moulding. One of the panels swung open. 'Sebastian, you go first,' she said, shining her torch into the opening.

When Sebastian stepped forward and looked inside, he saw that there was a narrow passage to the right, behind the wall. He stepped in, followed by Julian, and Electra came after them with the light. The Earl lingered for a

while by the entrance, until they had all disappeared inside, and then, more slowly, unknown to them, he crept
after them.

The passage was very narrow: it smelled musty and
stale, and cobwebs clung to the rough stonework of the
walls on either side. A short distance along, Sebastian
came upon an opening in the wall on his left; his hand
slipped through into emptiness as he groped his way, and
he could feel a draught of cool air against his face. Ahead
of him, the passage came to an abrupt end.

'Be careful of the stairs,' warned Electra. Her icy voice
sounded hollow in the stone-enclosed space.

As they moved through the opening and the shadows
flickered back before the yellow beam of Electra's torch,
Sebastian could see that the movement of air which he had
felt came up from a steep stone staircase that descended on
their left; immediately next to it was another flight of stairs
that went up. They stood on a small square landing, off
which led one door, set in the wall facing them: Electra's
torch beam slid across it.

'Through here?' asked Sebastian. He spoke in a whisper, but his voice echoed strangely. He laid his hand upon
the ancient oak of the door.

'No,' replied Electra. 'It's upstairs, on the top floor.'

They began to climb up, their footsteps ringing on the
stairs. They passed another door on the second floor
landing, and at the top of the last flight of stairs, they came
to a final door, like the others, arched, built of age-dark-
ened oak, bound with iron and set in a stone frame.

Julian shivered. 'I feel ... funny,' he whispered apprehensively. As they climbed the stairs, he had experienced a
curious sensation, as if all the hairs on his body were stirring and rising up, and the feeling had grown stronger and

stronger until, now, as they stood outside the door, it was almost unbearable.

'I feel it too,' said Sebastian. 'What the hell's in there?'

'You'll see, dear,' replied Electra. 'Just go in.'

Cautiously, Sebastian turned the iron ring that raised the latch of the door; he pushed the heavy door slowly open, and it swung inwards on sullenly grating hinges. At that moment, there was a flicker of blue light in the darkness within, so bright and sudden and altogether unexpected that Sebastian leapt back from the entrance and almost stumbled down the stairs, while Julian let out a stifled cry of alarm. Then all was dark once more, though they felt more strongly than ever the eerie sensation of their flesh creeping.

Electra shone her torch into the room, but the yellow light seemed dim and pale, too feeble to penetrate the utterly enveloping blackness within. Sebastian stepped forward, and the air around him seemed to tingle and come alive, and there was another flicker of light, as if blue and green sparks had ignited in the darkness of the lofty stone chamber.

They entered, Julian creeping in reluctantly, and Electra shone her light into the centre of the room, where the gloom seemed deepest.

There was something there: something vast and dark that occupied most of the floor space of the room. They could sense it, experiencing the strange forces that moved about it, but they could not quite focus their eyes upon it, for it seemed insubstantial and shifting. As far as they could make out, it was in the form of a great dome, a half sphere, shadowy and indistinct, its greatest height at the centre, just above the level of their heads; and over it, the void of darkness reached up to the roof, every so often that darkness being split momentarily by jagged fingers of light emitted from the surface of the dome, sparking out in the gloom like needles of lightning striking upwards.

Sebastian and Julian stared at it in bewilderment, and Sebastian remembered the strange lights that he had seen around the Tower on the first night that he had come to the Hall: in here, it appeared, was the source of those mysterious lights. He gazed up at the roof, imagining the massive glass prism that was mounted up there, outside, where the sunlight still shone: but in here, the sun had never shone for decades, for all the windows had been boarded up long ago, before the present Earl was born.

He stared at the shadowy grey dome, and he stepped closer, reaching out his hand tentatively, as if to touch the surface; but he felt a kind of resistance, as if a force emanated from the dome, making it hard for him to move, so that he struggled against it before he was able to lower his hand and touch the surface. To his surprise, the grey substance that covered it came off on his fingers: it was a thick veil of dust that had settled over whatever lay beneath, and had clung to it, even on the sides of the dome that stood almost vertical to the floor. As the tips of Sebastian's fingers penetrated the soft dust, he experienced an icy tingling sensation, like an electric shock, so that he withdrew his hand abruptly, at the same time as feeling it repelled by the invisible forces.

'What the devil is it?' he asked, his voice louder than he had intended in his surprise, echoing around the stone chamber; the dome seemed to quiver with the vibration of the sound.

'Quiet!' hissed Electra in a stern whisper. 'Can't you see how unstable it is?'

'But what's it made of?' asked Julian nervously, seeing Sebastian wipe his hand on his trouser leg in disgust.

'Dust, mainly,' said Sebastian. 'Whatever it is, it needs a good clean, if you ask me. It must've – ah … must've been here for simply years.'

'Since 1939, to be precise,' Electra informed him.

Sebastian frowned, and he looked at her inquiringly, seeing her face pale and grim in the torchlight, and noticing the cold ironic smile about her lips. 'The same year,' he began, 'that the Earl's … '

'Yes,' said Electra. She nodded. 'What d'you make of it?'

'If I knew what it was,' said Sebastian, 'I shouldn't be asking you, old sport.' Another flicker of blue and green light ran across the side of the dome, and he stepped back, startled.

'Don't you know?' said Electra with a smile. 'It's a time bubble.'

'What?' asked Sebastian.

'Look,' said Julian, pointing with a trembling finger to where Sebastian's hand had touched the dome: a faint blue radiance emanated from within, discernible now through the clearing that had been made in the enshrouding dust. 'There's a light inside,' Julian observed.

'So there is,' said Sebastian with growing interest, moving closer again, bending towards the dome to peer through the clearing that he had made in the dust.

For a moment, he stared within, holding his hands either side of his face to shade his eyes from the gleam of the torch, and then, suddenly, he started back with a shock.

'Good Lord,' he said under his breath, 'it can't be … '

'What is it?' asked Julian in alarm. 'What did you see?'

'Eyes,' answered Sebastian in a soft voice that trembled, but whether with fear or excitement, Julian could not tell. 'Eyes – staring back at me! Good grief, Electra,' he said slowly, as he turned to her with a look of incredulity, 'there's a man in there! What the devil is it? Some ... some kind of force field – and he's trapped inside. Who is the poor chap – do you know?'

It was not Electra who replied, however, but the voice of Lord Stephen, booming unexpectedly out of the darkness by the open door.

'He's my grandfather,' said Lord Stephen in a tone of awful dread, as if by his words he pronounced a terrible doom. 'He's Lord Mountjoy Mitchell, the eighteenth Earl of Newhaven.'

CHAPTER 23

The Strange Fate of Lord Mountjoy

At once, Sebastian, Electra and Julian all turned, startled by the sound of the Earl's voice, for they had not realised that he had followed them into the Tower. But Julian was stunned also by Lord Stephen's words, for it seemed that what he had just said made no sense: how could the eighteenth Earl, missing since 1939, be here now, inside this mysterious dust-shrouded dome?

Then Julian's curiosity mastered his fear, and he pressed forward, past Sebastian and, moving his eyes close up to the clearing in the dust, peered within, into the softly illuminated interior of the dome. He could see nothing at first, for the light was dim, faintly blue. Then, all at once, he discerned the glimmer of eyes in the gloom, just as Sebastian had said: eyes that stared out, straight into his own, unblinking, less than a foot away from him. He recoiled with the shock of seeing them, and then, in horror, he was drawn back by the fascination of those staring, watchful eyes, and he moved his face nearer and stared back.

'My God,' he whispered, as his sight adjusted to the strange lighting. 'It is ... it *is* the eighteenth Earl – just like his portrait down in the Lounge! But surely he's not ... he can't be real – not alive? He's not moving – not moving at all. His eyes ... '

'It's some sort of suspended animation,' suggested Sebastian quietly. He glanced at Electra. 'You call it a time bubble ... '

Lord Stephen laughed a strange, desperate laugh, and he walked across the room into the torchlight. 'Yes!' he said. 'A time bubble – that's exactly what it is. And he's been here all these years – stuck in here, trapped like a fly in blue amber – trapped since that day in the summer of 1939 when he tried to travel in time! And he did it, didn't he? Yes, he bloody well time travelled all right, because he's still here! Inside there, it's still July the tenth, 1939, and always will be, while outside here, the years pass by and he knows nothing of it.' Though he laughed, the Earl's face was set, his fists were clenched, his eyes were gleaming by the light of Electra's torch.

'And the glass prism on the roof?' asked Sebastian.

'Solar power supply,' said Lord Stephen. 'Bloody solar power! With that power, he thought he could master the secrets of the universe, bust right out of time and space and be free forever – absolute, immortal freedom! And instead of that, he got stuck – no way out – trapped in there till he dies or the world ends, whichever comes first. And all because his bloody solar power let him down!'

'He certainly went wrong,' Sebastian agreed, looking again into the Time Bubble: it seemed very dim in the gloom now, and the light within it was fluctuating, glowing brighter, then faint; across its surface, the blue and green sparks flickered. 'But tell me, Lord Steve,' said Sebastian quietly, 'what – ah ... what has this to do with your Time Machine? What's it for? I mean, why – ah ...

why on earth finish building your father's machine after you'd seen your grandfather's experiments with time go so disastrously wrong? Presumably you don't – ah ... don't want to end up like either of them?'

'What's it for?' mimicked the Earl derisively. 'What's it for!'

'Not so loud, Lord Stephen,' Electra cautioned him at once, for the Earl had begun to shout. But he paid no attention to Electra's warning. 'What kind of an idiotic question is that, Dorrell?' he yelled. 'I'll show you what I want a bloody time machine for!' he declared. Then he raised his fist and slammed it down again and again upon the dome; but his movement was strangely slow, as if he struggled through water or strove against invisible forces that resisted his mighty blows.

A billowing cloud of dust rose into the air around him, and there came a low, ominous booming, like the echo of a great drum resounding far off. A blaze of blue lightning shot up into the dark void above them, and beneath their feet they felt the stone floor begin to vibrate.

'Solid as a rock!' bellowed the Earl. 'Nothing on earth could bust in here except a time machine.'

But Electra Vanderpump had run towards the door the moment that Lord Stephen had struck the dome. 'Get out of here at once!' she screamed in fury and alarm. 'Leave it, leave it!' With that, she fled from the room, taking the torch with her, plunging them into a darkness shot with blue and green sparks.

Sebastian and Julian, perceiving that the Earl, by his hasty action, had caused some dangerous disturbance, dashed out after her.

'Come back you cissies! Afraid of the dark?' jeered the

Earl; but a moment later, they heard his footsteps running down the stairs after them.

When they emerged from the dark passage into the Picture Gallery, they found that Karen Black was there. She looked shocked to see them all, and she stared in consternation at Sebastian and Julian.

'Oh, Dr Vanderpump,' she began.

'No time!' snapped Electra, striding towards the door. 'Is the removal van here yet? I want all my equipment loaded onto it immediately.'

'I was just going to tell you,' said Karen. 'It's on the forecourt now. Johnny's gone out to try and help them mend it.'

Electra cast her a furious look before striding towards the door. 'It had better be mended by the time I get there,' she declared, 'or somebody is going to have a piece of my mind.' She swept from the room.

Sebastian, now that he was in the relative brightness of the artificially lit room, was beginning to feel slightly ashamed of himself for having retreated in such panic from the dark Tower. He turned back towards the secret entrance, where Lord Stephen had just appeared, glowering.

'What's the danger, Lord Steve?' Sebastian asked him.

The Earl stepped out through the open panel and approached Sebastian with a menacing gait and a strange glint in his fierce blue eyes.

'You're not welcome here, Dorrell,' he said. 'You've seen what you came to see, and I bloody well hope it's satisfied your curiosity, because that's all you're going to get! I'm not going to answer any more of your damn questions, so you can clear off and don't come back!'

'But, Steve, they came to help,' Karen tried to explain, as her gaze met Julian's. 'Dr Vanderpump's leaving now, and she'll take the Time Machine, and without that, it's hopeless!'

The Earl laughed a hollow laugh, and he slapped his thighs. 'It's always been hopeless!' he declared. 'Even Dr Vanderpump can see that, which is why she's getting out. Just now, she thought the whole damn thing was going to blow up on us, and do you know ... ' He nodded slowly, and a strange mirthless smile curled the corners of his lips. 'For a moment back there,' he said, 'I wished to God that it would blow up and put an end to the whole bloody show! Yes, for a moment there, I really thought I'd finally done it, and I was almost glad.'

'Oh, Steve!' whispered Karen, biting her nails nervously.

'And now you come here,' said Lord Stephen, fixing his eye on Sebastian, 'thinking you can sort it all out in five minutes and succeed in doing what it's taken me more than twenty years of trying and failing to do. I'm not going to stand for that, Dorrell – not from a bloody pansy like you! I'm not going to stand for it!'

'But how d'you know what he can do, sir,' said Julian unexpectedly, 'if you don't even tell him what the problem is and let him try to help?'

Lord Stephen stared at him in surprise, and then he laughed again, but it was a laugh without humour. 'Well, why not?' he said, and there was a note of sarcasm in his voice. 'All right, why not?' There was a wildness in his manner, like someone who has thrown reason to the wind. 'What do past disputes matter anymore?' he cried recklessly. 'What're values and principles, anyhow, when we're all going to die! And it's the final absurdity – isn't it, eh – the final indignity, for the last Earl of Newhaven to die hand in hand with his sworn enemy!' With these words, he grabbed Sebastian by the hand to shake it, and pumped his arm up and down frantically. 'Side by side!' he shouted, laughing. 'And when they find our bodies, stripped down to the bone, who could tell us apart then? You and I, who were two such different men in life – but in the end it's all one, isn't it? It's all the same.'

'But, Steve, we're not going to die!' wailed Karen.

'Of course,' explained the Earl confidentially to Sebastian, but casting a sidelong glance at Karen, 'they could still tell that she was a woman, you know. They could still tell, even from the bones. I've heard that there're subtle differences, around the pelvis – or maybe it's the teeth ... '

'But what makes you so sure we're going to die?' asked Sebastian.

The Earl's bright blue eyes gleamed knowingly, and he smiled a patronising smile. 'Good God, you've seen what it's like in there!' He tossed his head towards the secret door into the Tower. 'It's all breaking down – breaking through – and sooner or later, there'll be a bloody great bust-up. Sometimes, even now, the cracks are big enough for people to slip through – like old Duffy, and Lady Caroline. But before long, there's going to be a crack too big to close up, and then, Saint John's Apocalypse will look like a bloody picnic compared to what we'll be up against!'

'So the temporal disturbances, and the strange – ah ... strange lights, UFOs and what have you – they were all caused by that ... ' mused Sebastian.

'But I still don't understand,' said Julian uneasily. 'All I saw was a great blue domed thing covered in dust, with a man inside. You call it a time bubble, but what is it really – what exactly is it?'

'Ordinarily,' said Sebastian with a frown, 'there should be no such thing in the universe. A phenomenon like that could be caused by a time machine in operation, but the self-contained temporal field – or time bubble, as you call it – should be generated only – ah ... only after the machine has left the universe and has entered the inter-temporal layer, where its own environment becomes a self-enclosed universe. It's quite wrong for any such phenomenon to appear actually within time and space.'

Karen clutched at Lord Stephen's arm excitedly. 'You see – he knows about these things!' she said. 'Maybe he could help, if only you'd let him. It's a worth a try, Steve, isn't it? Anything's worth a try.'

The Earl nodded slowly in resignation, as he looked at Sebastian. 'So what's your solution then?' he asked. 'Somehow we've got to get inside the bloody thing and fix the fault and get my grandfather out of there. We don't stand a cat's chance in hell, as far as I can see. Get in and out of there alive, without blowing the whole lot sky high – it's not possible. And without a time machine, it's hopeless.'

Sebastian rubbed a hand across his jaw pensively. 'Hm ... well, if we need the Time Machine,' he said, 'the first thing to do is to get straight down to the cellars and stop – ah ... stop Electra making off with it, what? Come on!'

*

In the cellars, Mr Empire's Boys were beginning to carry away Electra Vanderpump's packed equipment. Electra was making a final check over the Time Machine. She turned and looked up, hearing the commotion on the stairs, as Lord Stephen, Sebastian, Julian and Karen came down, just as two of Empire's Boys were struggling up with a heavy item of equipment.

'Out of the way, you chaps!' ordered the Earl, shoving the men aside, as he squeezed past them on the narrow stairs.

'Don't you dare damage my equipment!' called Electra sternly from below. 'I'll have you pay for it, Lord Stephen, if anything's broken.'

'To blazes with your equipment!' yelled the Earl, bounding down into the cellar. 'What about my Time Machine?' He leapt onto the Machine's circular platform and laid his hand on the control console.

'My Time Machine, I think,' Electra corrected him coolly. She was dressed ready to leave, a short white cotton jacket over her red and black sheath dress, a small, white, net-veiled hat perched on her head. 'I've got it fully operational now.'

'It's mine!' declared the Earl, slamming his big fist down on the console. 'Mine! Mine! You're not having it, Dr Vanderpump!'

For a moment, they confronted one another, fierce eyes blazing; and it seemed that the burly Earl, tall and muscular though he was, quailed beneath the furious, green icy stare of this slim elegant woman who stood before him.

'Get off my Time Machine,' said Electra in a low, terrible whisper. 'Get off it now.'

Standing at the bottom of the stairs, Karen, Sebastian and Julian watched the Earl shuffling his feet in nervous agitation, clenching and unclenching his fists in angry impotence.

'Get off my Time Machine, Lord Stephen,' ordered Electra again, more slowly, a little louder.

The Earl stood there, swinging his arms helplessly; his mouth twisted oddly, as if he were about to burst into tears, and at that moment, he looked like nothing so much

as a child being scolded by his nanny for throwing a tan-
trum. At last, he said feebly, 'But Dr Vanderpump, I want
it ... '

'Well, you're not having it!' snapped Electra.

'Come on now, old girl,' said Sebastian, stepping up
onto the Time Machine, 'don't – ah ... don't be unreason-
able, what?'

Electra fixed her piercing gaze upon him. 'Now look,'
she said, 'I told you not to try to do anything to prevent me
from taking the Time Machine. It's my right!'

'But what – ah ... what harm would it do, you know,'
said Sebastian, 'if we were just to – ah ... borrow it for a
while?'

'And destroy it!' exclaimed Electra. She flung up her
arm, pointing furiously upstairs. 'Do you really think that
you can materialise in the Tower without risking a massive
explosion of alien matter into this universe? We'd all be
killed – the whole Hall destroyed!'

'Perhaps there's some other solution to the problem,'
Sebastian suggested amiably.

'Well, possibly there is,' Electra agreed, 'and if there is,
Sebastian, I have no doubt that you'll find it. But I'm afraid
you'll have to manage without my Time Machine.'

Sebastian smiled as Electra glared at him in rage. He
said, 'That thing in the Tower is dangerous, and we all
know that. Is it really worth risking people's lives for the
sake of saving this – ah ... this old Machine, which is,
frankly, a pretty decrepit wreck?'

'You'd be risking lives whatever you do about it now,'
said Electra. 'But I've waited years for a chance like this,
and all those years, Sebastian, whenever I asked you for
advice about time travel, you were as obstructive as you
could be.'

Sebastian nodded. He stared at the floor, wondering what to say, for he strongly suspected that he did not have the knowledge that Electra sought. As he had admitted to Professor Aaronberg, his experience of time travel had been of an entirely psychological phenomenon, and he knew very little about the mechanical workings of time machines, other than information that he had gleaned from a few books, much of which was speculative. 'I admit that I was somewhat obstructive,' he said carefully. He tugged at his hair uneasily. 'But from now on, I might – ah ... I might be rather more co-operative. On the other hand, if you run off with the Machine now, and it packs in after the first couple of trips, I can tell you for certain that you'll get no help whatsoever from me then.' He smiled. 'Think about it, old sport,' he said. 'One good turn deserves another. Just how long do you – ah ... d'you think this pathetic heap of junk is going to hold out before you need some advice on it from an expert?' He grinned, and the gold in his teeth flashed.

Electra frowned, then she looked with annoyance at Empire's Boys, who had returned from carrying out a box of equipment, and were now dragging another heavy crate towards the stairs. 'For heaven's sake!' she called to them. 'I hope you're being careful with that!'

They grunted a reply. Electra, scowling, turned back to Sebastian. 'So you're offering your assistance as an expert now, are you?' she inquired sarcastically. 'Well, it's a pity it didn't come a lot sooner, that's all I can say!'

'Damn it all!' yelled the Earl suddenly, losing his patience. 'It's my bloody Machine, Dr Vanderpump, and you're not having it! Get off it before I throw you off!'

He took one threatening step towards her but, in an

instant, Electra's revolver was in her hand and Lord Stephen backed away in apprehension.

'Very well, Sebastian,' said Electra, fixing her cold eyes upon him. 'You may borrow my Time Machine, but in return you'll tell me everything – and I mean everything – that there is to know about your Chair. What d'you say to that?'

'My Chair?' Sebastian said. 'But I've -- ah ... I've told you before, it's not a machine. There's no – ah ... no other artefact like it. I requires a special technique ... '

'Then you'll teach me that technique,' Electra told him firmly.

Sebastian shook his head. 'I can't promise what may not be possible.'

'If the Time Machine were to be damaged,' said Electra, 'by what you are going to do with it, could you rebuild it?'

Sebastian shrugged. 'With your help, perhaps ... Well, yes,' he added hastily, as he saw the expression on Electra's face. 'If it comes to that – but honestly, it won't ... I don't – ah ... don't intend to do anything dangerous, you know – I might damage myself!'

Electra put her revolver away in her handbag. 'Then that will have to suffice,' she said. 'Now what's your great plan? Not to materialise inside the Time Bubble, I hope? Because I can tell you now, it won't work.'

Lord Stephen looked perplexed. 'But that was the original idea!' he protested. 'That was what my father had in mind.'

'Lord Geoffrey was a very rash and foolish man,' Electra remarked. 'If not for that, he'd still be here now.'

'What happened to him?' asked Julian, who had been listening to their arguments until now.

'As far as we know,' said the Earl, 'he fell off the Time

Machine on its test run, or something of the sort. In the last entry in his notebook, dated the day of his disappearance, he says he was going to try to dematerialise the Machine for the first time, but whatever happened – well ... well, my father was never seen again.'

'And has – ah ... has the Machine been operated since then?' Sebastian asked, stroking his ear-lobe doubtfully.

'No,' said Electra, 'but we've checked and double checked everything.'

'Hm ... well,' said Sebastian, 'there could – ah ... could be some basic fault with the design.'

'There was,' Electra told him, 'but we've dealt with that. Lord Geoffrey's original design used vast amounts of energy – quite impractical.'

'We would've needed a bloody great nuclear reactor!' explained the Earl.

'But the computer came up with an alternative,' said Electra, 'and we were able to modify the Machine to run on a car battery.'

'Certainly sounds like an improvement,' Sebastian observed wryly. 'I suppose for the time being, then, we have to assume that the damn thing actually works.'

'I can find no fault with it,' said Electra.

'So about your – ah ... grandfather then, Lord Steve,' said Sebastian, beginning to walk slowly around the Time Machine, examining its controls. 'Presumably he's got some kind of time travelling apparatus inside the Time Bubble with him?'

'Ah no, you see, there was the innovation of it,' Lord Stephen explained. 'He didn't have a time machine as such, which was of, course, his great mistake. The idea was to harness the energy of the sun through the glass prism on the roof of the Tower, and use it to power what he called his Time-Field Generator. The time-field itself would be like a bubble in time, you see, travelling through time like an air-bubble through water, carrying with it my grandfather and everything else inside.'

'Extremely foolish, obviously,' Electra remarked, 'since he didn't have a portable power supply, and once he started to travel through time – at a rate of approximately a year a minute, according to the readings that I took this morning – he was unable to stop.'

'Good grief,' said Sebastian. He tugged at his left ear-lobe thoughtfully. 'But it's an elementary consideration, surely? I mean, he must've realised that he'd get himself stuck like that if he didn't have a proper power supply.'

Julian Crucefix frowned. 'Maybe I'm being stupid, or something,' he said, 'but I don't see why there should be a problem, myself. I mean, if Lord Mountjoy's time machine, or Time-Field Generator, or whatever you call it, ran out of energy, why didn't the Time Bubble just break up and let him out – or is that what's happening now?'

Sebastian raised an eyebrow. 'What makes you say that, old sport?'

'Well, you know,' continued Julian awkwardly, aware that Electra was regarding him with a look of mild scorn, 'if your car runs out of petrol, it stops going.'

'Yes,' agreed Sebastian, 'but a motor car loses energy through friction on the road surface, which is why it requires constant power to keep running. Of course, some – ah ... some energy is also used up when you put on the brakes. But in a frictionless environment – and I suppose one might call time a frictionless environment, if it even makes sense to speak of time in those terms – it requires an amount of energy equal to that required in the first place to put an object into motion, to – ah ... to stop it again. The poor old eighteenth Earl apparently cut himself off from his power supply, so he just – ah ... just keeps going, what?'

'Precisely,' confirmed Electra.

'You mentioned some notebook of your father's a moment ago,' Sebastian reminded the Earl. 'Perhaps it would be – ah ... be useful to have a look at that?'

'My father and my grandfather both kept records of the projects they were working on,' Lord Stephen replied. He turned to Karen. 'Run and fetch the notebooks, there's a good girl,' he said. 'They're in my desk in the office.'

Karen went out to fetch the books, passing on the stairs Mr Empire's Boys, who had came back to carry out some more boxes of Electra's equipment. 'The van still ain't working,' one of them grumbled.

'Oh dear,' said Karen. She called back down into the cellar, 'D'you think you could help them to start the van, Julian? Johnny's out there, but they haven't got it going yet.'

'More your cup of tea than time machines, old fruit,' Sebastian observed with a grin at Julian. 'You'd better – ah ... go and see what you can do. Unfortunately we don't live in a frictionless environment – they probably need a tank of petrol.'

'All right, I'm coming,' said Julian, and left the cellar with Karen.

Empire's Boys followed more slowly, carrying a large crate between them, Electra Vanderpump watching their clumsy progress with anxious eyes.

'Right,' said Sebastian, 'now back to your father, Lord Steve. What – ah ... what exactly did he intend to do with this Machine once he'd built it?'

'Materialise inside the damn Time Bubble, of course,' said the Earl.

'Which is quite out of the question,' Electra added, 'as I've already told you. It would be extremely difficult and dangerous to attempt any such thing. The space inside the Time Bubble is scarcely large enough for the Time Machine.'

'Yes ... quite,' Sebastian mused. 'Which tends to support the idea that I have in mind. Have you – ah ... have you by any chance been – ah ... monitoring the Time Bubble? You say it's growing increasingly unstable.'

'Yes,' said Electra. 'That's obvious from the phenomena that's been observed in the vicinity of the Prince's Tower. In fact, I entered the Tower for the first time this morning, and Lord Stephen hadn't been in there for more than twenty years, until today, had you?' she asked, glancing at the Earl.

'Ah, then you'll be able to tell me, Lord Steve,' said Sebastian. 'Did it – ah ... did it look the same as when you saw it last?'

The Earl glowered. 'Stop beating about the bush, Dorrell, and just tell us what you think can be done about this damn mess, if you think anything can be done, which I doubt. Of course it bloody well looked the same! It's been stuck like that since it was first made – that's the whole bloody problem!' Then an expression of vague doubt troubled his brow; he scratched his chin. 'Well, of course,' he admitted, 'first time I went in there, it may've looked different to me, I suppose – but I was young, and I was bloody scared, I don't mind telling you. I didn't know what it was – some damn great thing – it looked absolutely enormous ... '

'Larger?' suggested Sebastian.

'Well – larger, maybe,' conceded the Earl. 'What of it?'

'You think the Time Bubble's shrinking!' exclaimed Electra.

Sebastian nodded his head slowly.

'It's impossible,' said Electra. 'That would mean that it was losing energy, which, as you pointed out to Mr Crucefix, it couldn't do.'

'We know, though, don't we,' said Sebastian, 'that the boundaries of the Time Bubble extend beyond this universe, into the timeless zone between the universes, possibly into some other universe as well.'

'We know nothing of the sort,' said Electra dubiously. 'What on earth makes you say that?'

Sebastian smiled. 'People have disappeared,' he said. 'They're no longer in this time and space, so – ah ... so where are they?'

'They're in the Interstratum,' said the Earl. 'At least, Duffy and the Countess are, from what we can make out. Then something happened to Terrier – apparently we've got the wrong man here – he came through from another Stratum.'

'What?' queried Sebastian.

'It looks as if Terrier has changed places with his counterpart from another universe,' Electra explained.

Sebastian raised an eyebrow. 'And Captain Dorrell ... ' he mused. He frowned. 'Yes ... perhaps that would explain it. But anyway,' he said, 'you see what I mean? How could – ah ... how could this be possible unless the Time Bubble provides access to another universe?'

'Then it's even worse than we imagined!' cried Lord Stephen in horror. 'Are you saying, Dorrell, that this thing's in more than one Stratum?'

'Yes, he is,' said Electra, 'and he could well be right. I should have thought of it before. It certainly makes sense.'

Sebastian grinned. 'But, fear not, Lord Steve,' he said, slapping the Earl on the shoulder. 'That is the very point that will – ah ... save the day, I think! And here comes Miss Black with the notebooks,' he added, as Karen appeared through the door at the top of the stairs.

He took the pile of old leather-bound notebooks that Karen had brought, and sat down on the edge of the Time Machine, laying the books beside him. For the next five minutes, he perused them, examining the fading pencil sketch diagrams by Lord Mountjoy and labouring to decipher the scrawling handwriting of Lord Geoffrey, while Lord Stephen paced up and down the cellar impatiently, and Electra went to supervise Empire's Boys in the removal of her equipment, and Karen sat down on a crate dejectedly, her chin resting in her cupped hands, watching.

At last, Sebastian looked up with a smile. 'Well, you'll – ah ... you'll be pleased to know my conjecture was correct,' he announced.

The Earl ceased his restless pacing and bounded enthusiastically across the cellar, sitting down beside Sebastian on the base of the Time Machine, looking at the pages of the notebook that Sebastian had open on his knee.

Sebastian pointed out a diagram to him. 'You see, Lord Steve,' he explained, 'your grandfather plainly intended that the prism on the roof of the Tower should – ah ... should protrude through the surface of the Time Bubble, as he makes clear in this drawing. Being – ah ... being embedded, as it were, in a time-field, it should've stayed in continual contact, while still functioning as a channel for solar power. If it had worked, it would have given him a constant source of inexhaustible power, since the sun exists throughout time. But unfortunately, it looks as if the time-field that he generated was never – ah ... never sufficiently stable to allow of such a possibility. The prism remained fixed on the roof, while the perimeter of the Time Bubble fluctuated. He must have lost contact with the prism immediately, if his plan ever succeeded at all.'

Electra Vanderpump walked over to them. 'That still leaves us with the problem of the shrinking Time Bubble,' she said. 'The fact remains that whether or not Lord Stephen's father constructed the Time Machine to fit within the dimensions of the Time Bubble, as things stand at present, the Machine's too large to materialise safely inside. If the Machine were to materialise partially inside and partially outside the Bubble, the consequences would be totally disastrous, as I'm sure I don't need to tell you. That kind of breach in the fabric of the universe would create a catastrophic explosion. You could even have an entire alien Stratum breaking through and merging with this one. It was precisely that contingency that we've sought to avoid all along. But, no doubt,' she said, a tone of sarcasm in her voice, 'you're clever enough to have come up with a solution to that little problem, aren't you, Sebastian, dear?'

Sebastian smiled at her standing haughtily over him, her hands on her hips. 'Well, as a matter of fact,' he said, 'I have. It's simple, old girl. We materialise the Machine outside the Bubble, adjacent to it, so that the Machine's field is touching the surface of the Bubble. The interference between the two time-fields should – ah ... should sufficiently weaken the – ah ... surface tension, as it were, at the interface, for us to be able to get through. So we – ah ... we get the old Earl out, what? And then we – ah ... we connect up the Time Machine to his Time-Field Generator, so that

when we come back here, both the time-fields are dissolved at once, as we re-materialise.'

'Good God, Dorrell,' exclaimed Lord Stephen. 'If I only
understand half of what you're saying, it sounds like a hell
of a bloody risk!'

Electra scoffed. She tossed her head in exasperation.
'For heaven's sake, Sebastian!' she said. 'I thought you'd
come up with something better than that.'

'What d'you mean?' exclaimed Sebastian. 'It's a brilliant
solution – though I say it myself.'

'It's ridiculous,' retorted Electra. 'How can you suggest
such a thing?' She threw up her arm in a gesture of impatience and disgust. 'There's no room inside the Tower,
unless you intend to materialise yourself inside a solid
stone wall.'

'Absolutely not,' said Sebastian decisively. 'Good grief!
But who's talking about doing anything inside the Tower?
I don't – ah ... don't intend to be in the Tower at all. I don't
even intend to be in the universe! That's the whole point –
the Time Bubble extends beyond this world. What I – ah ...
what I plan to do is to set the Machine's co-ordinates to go
to the Tower, but we won't actually – ah ... actually materialise inside the Tower, you see. We'll stay in what you
call the Interstratum, because, if I'm right, then the Time
Bubble must manifest itself there as well as here.'

Electra was silent and made no reply. In alarm, the Earl
looked back and forth from her to Sebastian. 'Well?' he
cried. 'Can it be done? For God's sake, say something!'

'Yes,' said Electra quietly; she sounded as if she almost
begrudged saying it, and she glowered at Sebastian with
her cold green eyes. 'It can be done.'

'And even if it wasn't a total success,' Sebastian pointed
out, 'whatever happened, there'd be very little disturbance

in this universe. If we're – ah ... if we're working in the Interstratum and there does happen to be an explosion, it would probably be contained there and wouldn't break through into this Stratum, or any other.'

Karen Black, perceiving that some kind of decision had been reached, rose up off the crate on which she had been sitting, and walked over to them. 'So what're you going to do?' she inquired nervously. 'Steve?'

The Earl got up from the base of the Time Machine. He took a deep breath, as if he were shrugging off a great mental weight that had long been a heavy burden to him; eagerly he slapped his thighs. 'What're we going to do?' he cried. 'We're going to try it! Dorrell's got a plan, and it's the best bloody plan I've heard in years, so we're damn well going to risk it! We're finally going to get cracking and do something about this whole bloody mess, once and for all! Isn't that right, Dorrell?'

'Well ... ' said Sebastian with a smile as he closed the old notebooks and laid them aside. 'Let's – ah ... let's hope so, Lord Steve.'

CHAPTER 24

Out of this World

Everything was ready: the vast vaulted stone cellar, cleared of Electra Vanderpump's equipment (which had now all been loaded onto Mr Empire's van) looked bare, grey and cold beneath the white glare of the electric lighting. Only the Time Machine remained, standing alone, battered and shabby at the end of the cellar, close to the stairs, and humming faintly now, for it was switched on.

Lord Stephen, now fully dressed with his braces buttoned securely over the outside of his brown tweed jacket, was standing on the Machine with Sebastian Dorrell.

Karen Black was there too, but she stood a little way off, eyeing the big, humming Machine with apprehension. 'Oh, Steve,' she said nervously. 'Are you sure it's safe?'

'As safe as it'll ever be!' declared the Earl.

The door at the top of the stairs opened, and Electra Vanderpump and Julian Crucefix came in, followed by the shambling figure of Johnny Terrier.

'We got the van started at last,' said Julian, as he walked down into the cellar.

'I only hope,' said Electra tartly, 'that they can be trusted with my equipment.'

'Well,' said Sebastian, 'we're – ah ... ready to go now, I think.'

'Everything seems to be in order,' agreed Electra, as she made a brief examination of the Machine's controls. 'I think that I've known you long enough, Sebastian, to observe that, in serious matters like this, you're generally a man of your word, thanks to that ridiculous morality of yours, so I'm trusting you to bring the Machine back. From my point of view, it's worth taking the small risk that you might steal it, in order that I might personally avoid the greater risk of going on an untested time machine myself. As far as I'm concerned, you're taking my Machine on a test run, so, as I shan't be coming with you, we'd better go over the procedure one more time.'

'If I didn't have the impression that you might be regarding me as some sort of – ah ... some sort of expendable guinea-pig, I'd say thanks for trusting me,' remarked Sebastian grimly, 'but, anyway, on with the procedure. We enter the Interstratum, set on course for the Tower, but at the point of materialisation we – ah ... don't materialise, but fuse with the Time Bubble instead, connect the Time Machine to the Time-Field Generator, rescue Lord Mount-joy, then re-set the co-ordinates and – ah ... rematerialise outside the Tower.'

Electra frowned. 'I hope you remember to do it all in the right order,' she said, fixing him with her stern gaze. 'Where d'you intend to materialise?'

'Well ... I hadn't – ah ... given it much thought,' replied Sebastian.

'Then I'll tell you,' said Electra firmly. 'Outside on the lawn, to the west of the Prince's Tower. I shall be waiting for you by the gardener's cottage. I've already taken Dr Kotlowski over there, in case there should be some disturbance that we haven't foreseen. Now, Miss Black,' she said, turning to Karen, 'you'd better come with me – you too, Mr Terrier,' she added to Johnny Terrier, who was gazing at the Time Machine with fascination, and chewing his thumb.

'No!' wailed Karen. 'I'm going with Steve!'

'I want to go on the funny roundabout too!' said Johnny, giggling with excitement.

'Nonsense!' snapped Electra, as she took her white gloves from her handbag and pulled them on. 'It's not a roundabout, Mr Terrier – it's a time machine, and it's not for playing with. No, Miss Black,' she said sternly, as Karen began to cry, clutching at Lord Stephen's arm imploringly. 'This is not a joy-ride. I will not have this operation jeopardised by your whims and hysteria. Now come along with me, this minute. Mr Crucefix is coming too, aren't you, Mr Crucefix?'

Eventually, Karen was persuaded to go outside, but only because Julian Crucefix agreed to go too.

'Dr Vanderpump's right,' said Julian. 'The fewer passengers it has to carry, the better, so far as I can see.'

'Give us five minutes to get out of the house,' Electra instructed, 'before you dematerialise.'

Lord Stephen and Sebastian watched them climb up the narrow stone stairs to the door. At the top, Karen, who was last, paused and looked back, tears running down her face.

'It'll take less than no time, Karen – you'll see!' called the Earl; though his voice conveyed a boldness that, at that moment, he did not feel. Doubtfully, he glanced at Sebastian, but noticed that Sebastian's face betrayed no emotion whatsoever.

Above them, the door slammed shut. Lord Stephen looked up quickly and saw that Karen had gone. He looked back at Sebastian, who was silent.

After a minute, the Earl said, rubbing his hands together with a vague unease that he tried to conceal, 'I can understand – in front of the women, you might want to paint our prospects brighter than they actually are.' He attempted to laugh, but it sounded a little strained. He slapped his thighs nervously. 'I mean,' he continued, 'you know how women are – take Karen, for instance. She caused a bit of a scene, I'm afraid. Sorry about that. To put it bluntly, it was embarrassing.'

'You find love embarrassing, Lord Steve?' asked Sebastian quietly.

Lord Stephen looked away awkwardly, and quickly tried to find something completely different to talk about. 'To tell you the truth,' he said, 'it's been a hell of a stroke of luck, your turning up and happening to know about time machines and all that. I mean, if I'd known that from the beginning, I'd never have sent you packing! But then, come to think of it, there've been a lot of very odd ... coincidences, I suppose you could say.'

'Coincidences?' Sebastian queried calmly.

'Well,' said the Earl, 'there's the fact that you're a friend of old Aaronberg, who wrote about me in his book, and who also wrote another book about time travel, and then there's your knowing Vanderpump, and knowing Karen's cousin, Terrier – it all seems a bit odd, don't you think?'

Sebastian sighed, rubbing his face thoughtfully. 'I've – ah ... come across this sort of thing before,' he said, 'and it seems to me that it has something to do with time travel and with alternative or parallel universes – what you call the Strata. They're called alternative or parallel because they're – ah ... they're very similar to our own universe – too much divergence, and you might as well just call them different universes. So, let's say, in universe A, Mr Smith meets Mr Jones at the place where they both work, and Mr Jones tells Mr Smith about the golf club that he attends, and Mr Smith then joins the club at his recommendation. Later, at a social event involving the two families of these men, Mr Smith's son meets Mr Jones's daughter and they eventually marry. No odd coincidences there. In universe B, let's say that it happens the other way around. The son and daughter meet, and then introduce their fathers to one another, and Mr Smith introduces Mr Jones to the golf club, and Mr Jones then tells Mr Smith about a job vacancy where he works, for which Mr Smith then makes a success- ful application. So, no odd coincidences there either. But – and here's the odd part – suppose there's universe C, in which Mr Smith meets Mr Jones at work, and then meets him again, as if by chance, at the golf club, and then they find out that their son and daughter know one another and have been going out, yet there's no obvious causal connec- tion between any of these facts. That's – ah .. that's when people start talking about chance or coincidence, if there seems to be no significance in it, or fate, if such happenings appear meaningful. Now, it seems to me as if the reason for such happenings is because of the parallelism with the other universes, so that the causes of the connections which appear in one universe are absent in alternative universes, though the events in broad outline remain the same. It's almost as if the causal connections of those so- called lucky, fateful or coincidental happenings are hidden away in the parallel universe, except that to use the con- cept of causality in this context is virtually meaningless. It might be better to – ah ... to say that the universes are similar because that very similarity embodies the nature of their being parallel.'

Lord Stephen looked bewildered. 'You've lost me there, Dorrell,' he said. 'You're starting to talk like old Aaronberg now, and we couldn't make head nor tale of what the hell he was blathering on about!'

'Oh well,' said Sebastian with a shrug, 'it's all part of the philosophy of time, which surprisingly few philosophers have addressed. If you're interested, though, there's a little book by Dr Keith Seddon, called *Time: A Philosophical Treatment.*' He glanced at his watch. 'But enough of this – I see that our five minutes are up, so it's time to go!' His hand moved to the control console, and he took hold of the slider-control that operated the dematerialisation; slowly, he pushed it up.

The Time Machine, which until now had been humming softly, began to whine more loudly and at a higher pitch; a shudder passed through it, and it groaned, the overhead lighting flickering. Sebastian and Lord Stephen held onto the edge of the control console to steady themselves, as the vibrations increased: the whole Machine was shuddering violently, as if in an earthquake, and its whining rose to a thunderous roar.

'It's working!' yelled the Earl in excitement. 'It's bloody well working!'

Even as he cried out, the cellar around them seemed to fade, and then, in an instant, it had vanished, and the Time Machine was surrounded by a black curtain of utter darkness: they had entered the Interstratum.

'Good God!' cried the Earl. 'Who would've believed it!'

But Sebastian did not reply: he was gazing out into the darkness. Presently, he said, 'Look over there. He pointed, and the Earl, following with his eye the line of Sebastian's outstretched arm, saw a glimmer, like a tiny ball of light, faintly blue against the surrounding pall of blackness; yet it was rapidly increasing in size, even as they gazed at it, as if it were flying towards them.

Hastily, Sebastian adjusted the Machine's controls, and now the blue ball of light glided slowly towards them, until it was as large as the Time Machine, as it hovered alongside. They could see now that it was like a great mis-shapen capsule of blue glass, but here and there on its surface there flowed ripples like water; and from time to time, a brilliant blaze, like tongues of green fire, flickered out from it or broke away in glutinous masses that were flung off into the void, like globules of flaming treacle. And in the midst of this, seen dim and shadowy through the blue glassy surface of the capsule, they could make out the fig-ure of a man stooping over a bulky piece of machinery.

'Now we have to adjust our time and speed until they match his,' said Sebastian. Again he adjusted the controls.

Lord Stephen was pacing round and round the small platform in an agitation of excitement. 'And now for it!' he cried. 'We bust in there!'

'Carefully does it, Lord Steve,' Sebastian cautioned him, as the Earl grabbed the controls and began to manoeuvre the Time Machine close up to the Bubble.

There was a sudden blaze of green light, and the Ma-chine jolted back, as sheets of fire swept around it. Sebas-tian lost his balance and tumbled to the floor.

'Sorry about that!' cried the Earl. 'Got a bit carried away there!'

Sebastian scrambled up and came to Lord Stephen's side. 'Slowly,' he said. 'Very slowly ... more to the left ... '

The Earl slid the steering rod more to the left. There

came a loud crackling sound all about them, and green and yellow sparks flew out from the Time Bubble. On the control console of the Time Machine, close to Lord Stephen's hand, a red warning light began to flash. 'What the hell's that?' he said in alarm.

'Interference on the time-field,' said Sebastian, raising his voice above the growing roar of the engines. 'Now hold us right here, Lord Steve! I think we must have made contact.'

On the opposite side of the Time Machine from where they were standing, they could now see that something was happening on the edge of the Machine's time-field, where it touched the Time Bubble: a bright disc of orange fire had appeared, about a foot in diameter, but rapidly increasing in size as they watched; and now the space in the centre of the flaming disc was clear, like a porthole into the Time Bubble.

'Right, we've got to get these machines connected up,' said Sebastian, taking up a bundle of electrical leads that lay on the top of the control console. He crouched down and opened a grille in the Time Machine's central column, beneath the console, plugged in three of the leads, and handed the other ends to Lord Stephen. 'Now,' he said, 'this one's the power supply, that's the multiple equaliser, and the green one's the ISB unit, and they're to be connected to the – ah ... B-Phase circuit, the one marked – ah ... marked D on your grandfather's plans.'

'I say, Dorrell, I hope you know what you're doing,' remarked the Earl, as he took the electrical leads. 'This Machine's making a hell of a racket. One false move at this stage, and we could still blow the whole bloody lot – '

At that moment, the Time Machine suffered such a violent convulsion, that they were both thrown off their feet, and Lord Stephen would have been flung right off into the void – the same fate that had evidently befallen his father in similar circumstances – had Sebastian not grabbed him by the arm as he fell, and pulled him back. The surface of the Machine's time-field was ablaze with blue and green fire, and sections of it were breaking away, even as the surface of the Time Bubble had done.

'My God!' yelled the Earl. 'We're losing contact – the time-field's breaking up!' He scrambled to his feet and leapt to the controls, frantically adjusting dials and levers. The Machine was roaring and shuddering like a beast in agony. 'Do something, Dorrell! For God's sake, bloody well do something!' bellowed Lord Stephen above the thunderous noise of the straining engines.

'No! Not that!' Sebastian shouted; but his cry of warning was drowned in the scream of the Time Machine as it rent through the Interstratum, and Lord Stephen's large fist had already closed over the slider-control that initiated re-entry into the universe: he plunged it down.

'Change the location co-ordinates!' cried Sebastian, thrusting the Earl aside in his desperate haste to readjust the controls.

Then, in an instant of horror, Lord Stephen realised his terrible mistake: the location co-ordinates had not been reset for the Machine to materialise outside Heydn Hall, and now, in spite of all their efforts to avoid it, they were materialising inside the Prince's Tower that was already occupied by the unstable and disintegrating Time Bubble.

Sebastian tried to slide up the control that the Earl had moved, but Lord Stephen, whose touch was never delicate at the best of times, and in his moment of fearful panic had been even more clumsy that usual, had thrust down the slider-control with such force that it had become jammed.

Sebastian desperately flicked switches and turned dials, but the Time Machine only shuddered harder. Blades of forked lightning sliced through the fabric of the time-field, and momentarily they glimpsed the grey stone walls of the inside of the Prince's Tower begin to materialise around them. When Sebastian glanced up, for an instant he saw three figures of Lord Stephen standing opposite him, before they merged together into one.

Then, above the tumult and commotion and the roar of the Time Machine's engines, the great voice of Lord Stephen came booming: 'It's no use!' he bellowed, and his red terror-contorted face loomed towards Sebastian in the flickering gloom under the failing lights. 'It's no bloody use! Jump for your life! Bloody jump!'

And with these desperate words, the twentieth Earl of Newhaven took a flying leap off the fragmenting Time Machine and plunged into the dark unknown.

CHAPTER 25

The Burning

On the veranda outside the gardener's cottage, Dr Kotlowski was sitting in a wicker chair, a red and blue checked rug spread over his knees, when Electra Vanderpump, Karen Black, Johnny Terrier and Julian Crucefix came walking over the lush green lawns towards him. Electra was tottering a little unsteadily as her high heels sank into the soft turf: in her smart black, red and white clothes and veiled hat, she looked strangely awkward, like a wedding guest who has gone astray and turned up at the wrong venue. Johnny Terrier came skipping along behind, pausing every now and again to run around in circles panting, as he investigated things in the grass, though Karen urged him to hurry. He was smirking and giggling to himself still, and seemed quite unaware of the potential danger.

'How're you feeling now, Dr Kotlowski?' inquired Karen with concern, as she stepped onto the veranda.

'The excruciating pain eases somewhat,' replied Kotlowski, the corners of his lips turning downwards in a wan smile. 'I humbly beg your forgiveness, Miss Black, for causing this inconvenience. Dr Vanderpump made me fully acquainted with my error. Now I know that it was this woman you speak of, Lady Caroline, and not the Blessed Virgin, whom I glimpsed in the Chapel, and so I was quite mistaken in what I interpreted as a sign for me to carry out the deed that I so incompetently attempted. What shame I feel in my heart, Miss Black, to think that I saw a mortal woman and mistook her for a holy visitation!'

Karen nodded sympathetically. 'Still,' she said, 'not to worry, eh? It's a mistake anyone could make, I suppose,' she added uncertainly, for want of something to say that might console him.

'Don't you think he ought to be taken to hospital?' Julian Crucefix said to Electra, as they walked up and he saw Kotlowski's thin pale face that looked sickly, even in the bright sunlight.

'Don't waste your pity on him!' retorted Electra scornfully. 'Before this day is out, I fear that there may be one or two more casualties who need to be taken to hospital!' She turned and gazed back towards Heydn Hall, shading her eyes with her white-gloved hand against the dazzling sky.

The whole of the western side of the great house was visible from where they stood, its grey stone walls weathered and mellow in the summer light, the leaded panes glinting in its mullioned windows: but brighter than all the windows blazed the massive glass pyramid on the roof of the Tower, casting reflected sunbeams all about it in a glorious radiance; and though that was not the purpose for which the prism had been erected, now, in the early hours of the afternoon, its light would shine the brightest in the shadowy Clock Court in the midst of the grey stone bulk of the house, where the sun's rays could never directly penetrate.

Karen looked also in that direction, at the great house that stood there so serenely within its placid surroundings of rolling lawns, bright gardens and shady woodlands – that had stood thus, unchanged, for centuries, and seemed as if it always would. As she gazed upon it, she found it hard to conceive of the troubled and insubstantial thing that lurked behind those solid grey stone walls, like a seed of chaos, ready at any moment to manifest its awesome and long-contained potential for terrible destruction.

They waited, and the minutes dragged on, long and anxious. Only Electra Vanderpump managed to conceal any apprehension that she might feel, standing a little aloof from the others, impassive in her cool white jacket, white gloves and white stiletto-heeled shoes, her veil casting a netted shadow across her dark, imperious eyes. Meanwhile, Johnny, playing in the grass, seemed oblivious to all concern. Karen, raising her eyes, marvelled at the clear blue of the cloudless sky, for she felt oddly as if a storm were brewing, despite the calm weather.

Suddenly, Julian, who had been gazing at the Hall for longest, gave a startled cry. 'Something's happening!' he said, pointing in the direction of the Prince's Tower.

Karen came to his side, and in her nervousness, her hand crept to his arm and rested there, clutching at his sleeve in trepidation. 'But what is it?' she cried.

Like a blue flame, a streak of light flickered down the side of the Tower, licking across the grey stone of the walls, and rapidly it ran like a fissure through all the stonework, and the Tower seemed to fragment: it quivered, rippling like a mirage projected upon rising vapours.

Karen screamed and began to run forward, but Julian clasped her by the wrist and firmly held her back. 'Oh,

Steve!' she wailed. 'Something terrible's going to happen, and he's in there!'

Johnny glanced up when he heard her cry, and turned towards the Hall, and Kotlowski rose unsteadily from his chair, the rug falling from his knees.

Wave upon wave, the blue fire spread out from the Tower like the circular ripples formed by a stone cast into a still pool, until the whole house was enveloped, and much of the area around it.

'They've failed,' said Electra Vanderpump in a voice hushed with horror and frustrated rage.

'No!' cried Karen. She sobbed, tugging at her short dark hair with both hands, and her eyes were squeezed tightly shut, as her long shrill scream of anguish shivered out on the calm, warm summer air.

Julian, Johnny and Dr Kotlowski stared at the scene in incredulous wonder. Heydn Hall shimmered, its form wavering as if it were an image painted on fine silk stirred by the breeze: a fizzle of blue radiance sparked in the air about it, and then died. There was a sudden stillness, an awful calm, a moment in which the Hall stood poised upon the brink of disaster.

Then, a dull roar broke the brooding silence, and every window in the house shattered at the same instant, exploding outwards, shards of glass scattering in a sparkle of falling sunlight; and an instant later, the gaping holes of the broken windows were filled with leaping gouts of orange flame.

Karen gasped and turned her face away.

'My God ... ' whispered Julian Crucefix, as, in a matter of moments, he saw Heydn Hall engulfed in fire; and then he stirred himself and turned in haste to the door of the cottage. 'I'm going to phone for the fire brigade,' he said urgently. 'Do whatever you can.'

'But Steve's still inside there!' wailed Karen.

'And so is the Time Machine,' said Electra quietly. She stood utterly still on the edge of the veranda, gazing at the blazing building, her pale face stony and expressionless.

Only Johnny Terrier seemed gleeful, skipping excitedly from one foot to the other, waving his arms above his head as he warbled a foolish song of his own creation.

'Alas! I fear the wrath of the Lord has finally descended!' pronounced Kotlowski in a lugubrious tone of morbid relish.

Then Karen let out a sudden exclamation of joy, for a figure had appeared around the corner, from the front of the house, and was now running across the lawns towards them. He was limping badly, staggering, almost on the point of collapse, and his face and clothing were blackened by soot, but Karen knew him at once, and ran wildly to meet him.

'Oh, Steve!' she cried, flinging her arms about him. 'You're safe! You're safe!'

But the Earl groaned and seemed scarcely aware of her presence, even as she struggled to help him to the cottage. Before they reached the shade of the veranda, with a long despairing moan, he stumbled forward without a care and fell onto his hands and knees on the grassy bank close to where Johnny Terrier danced.

Electra Vanderpump, her face sternly rigid, her green eyes blazing accusations, stepped down from the veranda and strode towards the fallen Earl. She halted before him. 'Where's Mr Dorrell?' she demanded. 'Is he responsible for this – this fiasco – or is it you, Lord Stephen? Who's to blame?'

The Earl made no reply, but only a whimpering rose from his throat, like the cry of a dog that has been beaten, and he did not raise his head, but shook it dejectedly from side to side and concealed his eyes with one trembling hand.

'Answer me!' ordered Electra, her voice rising harsh and shrill. 'Where is Mr Dorrell?'

The Earl only moaned, but Karen Black's mild temper was moved to sudden passion, seeing him kneeling there so helpless and miserable, and she turned upon Electra in rage.

'You bloody bitch! Don't talk to him like that!' she screamed. 'How can you talk to him like that? He's the Earl of Newhaven! He's the Earl – he's the man I love, the man I love!' She sobbed, and the colour rose to her cheeks; tears ran from her eyes. 'Can't you see what he's been through?' she cried. She covered her face and turned away, shaken by violent sobbing. 'Bloody leave us alone!'

Electra tossed her head haughtily. 'You're hysterical, Miss Black,' she said coldly, 'so I'll excuse your rudeness. And now, Lord Stephen – pay attention, please! Look at me when I'm speaking to you! I repeat my question. What has become of Mr Dorrell? Where is he, mm?'

Then Lord Stephen looked up at her, a broiling anger in his steel blue eyes, and he struggled to his feet, brutally pushing Karen aside as she tried to help him. He stepped up to Electra and glared into her white face. 'Where is he?' he yelled. 'Where? He's in there, Dr Vanderpump – that's where Dorrell is!' And he thrust out his arm, pointing to the blazing ruins of Heydn Hall, a holocaust of flame. 'And as to what's become of him, Dr Vanderpump,' he yelled, 'I'll leave it to your imagination as to whether a human being could survive inside that hellish inferno –

but if you want my opinion of it, he's dead – bloody dead! He's finished!'

The Earl stormed away, his face thunderous with passion, and Karen hurried nervously after him.

'Control yourself, Lord Stephen!' called Electra Vanderpump in her iciest voice. 'This senseless rage will do no good at all. For heaven's sake, do you really think you're the only one to have suffered a loss?'

The Earl swung round. 'What's that?' he yelled. 'Control myself? Are you telling me to control myself, Dr Vanderpump? I've been bloody well controlling myself for the past thirty years, and I'm damn well sick of it!' He strode back towards her, shaking his fists and stamping his feet. 'There was a lot that should've been out in the open years ago! And if you felt one iota of what I'm feeling at this moment, Dr Vanderpump, you wouldn't be standing there, so cool and precise, talking about bloody losses, as if the worst loss you could suffer was the loss of your precious bloody self-control! Well this is what I think of your damn self-control, Dr Vanderpump!' he declared, and he tore off his braces, in spite of Karen's wails of dismay, and flung them down on the grass. 'There!' he yelled. 'There!' And he stamped on them furiously. He pointed his finger, thrusting, at Electra in angry challenge. 'Now answer that!' he cried.

At that moment, however, Julian reappeared at the door of the cottage, and he hurried across to them. 'Thank God you're safe, sir,' he said at once to Lord Stephen. 'I've called the fire brigade and they'll be here any minute. But what about Sebastian – where is he?'

Julian glanced round anxiously. 'He's not with you ... '

'Mr Dorrell didn't come out,' Electra informed him. 'We

must assume that he perished in the explosion, or in the fire.'

Julian stared towards the burning house with a look of horror. 'What happened?' he asked sharply, turning back towards the Earl, who was beginning to slouch off. 'Do you know for certain that he's dead, sir? He could still be in there, lying injured or unconscious.'

'He's dead,' answered Lord Stephen in a sulky tone, without even looking round. Karen tried to lay a hand comfortingly on his arm, but he pushed her aside.

'We've been through all this before, Mr Crucefix,' Electra explained. She sighed in exasperation, and she gazed towards Heydn Hall that now stood, consumed in fire, under a great billowing cloud of acrid black smoke that was spreading out all around, through the clear summer air. 'There's nothing we can do now,' she said bitterly, 'to save either Mr Dorrell or the Time Machine.'

*

It was growing late in the afternoon when the fire was finally extinguished, and Heydn Hall stood black and cold in the pale sunlight, rivulets of water running down its grim stone walls. Most of the western wing of the house, including the Prince's Tower, had been gutted, its upper floors damaged, the roof fallen in. Only the east wing survived intact, the small fires that had spread to the upper rooms having been quickly extinguished.

Karen Black came up to Julian Crucefix on the forecourt, where two fire engines and an ambulance were parked, and firemen were rolling up their hoses and preparing to leave. Water running out from the house had collected in muddy pools on the gravel; the pungent smell of soot hung in the warm, still air.

'Where's the Earl?' asked Julian.

'I left him in the gardener's cottage,' said Karen miserably. She was rubbing her hands together nervously, and Julian could see that she was distressed, though she did not look up and she kept her eyes diverted from the stark blackened ruin of the old house. 'He blames Dorrell and he blames himself – it's terrible. But it was just a dreadful mistake.'

She glanced along the forecourt towards the drive, where a police car was parked. A policeman and one of the ambulance men stood close by it, talking together, and, a little way off, Karen could see Electra Vanderpump in her pink sports car with Dr Kotlowski in the passenger seat. Electra was talking to a man dressed in a fawn jacket and brown trousers, who was standing beside the car, his hand resting on the bonnet.

'Johnny told me the police were here.' Karen bit her lip uneasily. 'What's going on?'

'Oh, yes ... the police – yes,' said Julian. 'That's the Inspector talking to Dr Vanderpump now. It's nothing to worry about – just routine. The firemen found two – um ... bodies, you see.' Julian hesitated, staring down at his feet, fingering his limp hair unhappily, at a loss for words.

'Sebastian Dorrell ... ' breathed Karen, glancing at him, her eyes wide.

'Well, we don't know,' said Julian. 'Apparently they were found upstairs in the east wing. Sebastian was in the Tower with Lord Stephen. At the moment, it doesn't make sense, but the police want someone to go and identify them. The Inspector suggested that Lord Stephen should go, but I wasn't sure that he'd – well ... be up to it, you know. I said I'd go along – if that's all right with you, of course. I mean, I don't want to be seen to be interfering.'

'Of course you're not interfering,' said Karen, and she looked earnestly into his eyes. 'Steve's not himself, and hasn't been for a long time. You understand that, don't you, Julian? When I knew you suspected that something was wrong around here, there was lots of times when I wanted to tell you about it, but I felt I couldn't, without betraying Steve. Now I just wonder ... ' She stared up at the dripping, dark ruins of Heydn Hall, the shattered windows, and the broken roof of the west wing, through which the blue sky shone. 'Maybe if I'd told you, we could've done something. Maybe it wouldn't have come to this. Now it's all so horrible, and Steve hasn't been spared anything through me not speaking out. I just keep thinking about poor Mr Duffy and Lady Caroline, and thinking maybe they'd still be here now if only we'd done something sooner.'

Julian shook his head. 'I don't see what we could've done.' He stared down at his feet, shuffling them in the muddy gravel in which he stood; he noticed, scattered there, shards of broken glass, glittering in the sunlight. 'I don't think I would've done anything at all,' he added quietly, 'if it hadn't been for Sebastian Dorrell.'

Karen glanced round at the sound of the fire engine, close by, starting up. Electra Vanderpump's car, she noticed, had now disappeared from view, down the drive, followed by the ambulance. The police car was left waiting at the top of the drive where it joined the forecourt, and the plain clothes Inspector was walking towards them.

'Where's Dr Vanderpump?' asked Karen.

'She said that she was going back to Hertfordshire,' answered Julian. 'She's taking Dr Kotlowski with her.' He turned to leave, as the Inspector walked up. 'The Inspector's taking me to – um ... do the identification now,' he said awkwardly.

'I don't like to think of you having to do it on your own,' said Karen. 'I wish I could come with you, but I have to stay here with Steve, the way he is at the moment.'

'I'll be back as soon as I can,' said Julian.

Karen stood on the muddy forecourt, watching him as he walked away with the police Inspector. When he reached the police car, he looked back over his shoulder for a brief moment to see her standing there, before he climbed in.

When the car had driven off, Karen turned sadly, and walked back slowly over the littered forecourt, her arms folded closely around her slight body. She felt small and helpless beneath the looming black spectre of the great ruined house. A cool breeze began to blow, whispering mournfully in the leaves of the tall ancient trees that stood all around, casting their lengthening shadows across the grass. Overhead, high clouds glided across the deepening blue sky of approaching evening. Karen shivered, and walked on, over the darkening lawns.

CHAPTER 26

Lord Stephen's Little Hut

It was some time later, growing dusk, when Julian Crucefix returned. A pall of gloom hung around the black shell of Heydn Hall, and there was a smell of damp soot in the air.

When he knocked on the door of the gardener's cottage, Karen answered it and showed him into the small front room. She was alone.

'Steve's in the Hall,' she said anxiously. 'I told him not to go. I was afraid it'd be dangerous, but I couldn't stop him. Johnny's with him.'

Julian sighed; he sat down on one of the floral chintz-covered armchairs beside the ingle-nook fireplace. Karen switched on an electric lamp in the corner, and a yellow glow filled the room.

'Would you like me to go and look for them?' Julian asked.

'Wait a bit and we'll go together,' said Karen, as she sat down facing him. 'Tell me first what happened. The bodies – was it ... Lord Mountjoy and Sebastian Dorrell?' She stared at him apprehensively, pressing her bare arms together in her lap.

Julian took a deep breath. 'One of them,' he said slowly, 'was Mr Duffy, your old estate manager. Of course, I never met him, so I wasn't able to identify him, but then they showed me the things they'd found in his pockets that had his name on. I knew then who it was. But the other man ... ' He shook his head, bewildered.

'Wasn't it Dorrell?' asked Karen.

'Well ... ' Julian coughed awkwardly. 'That's what I don't understand. I mean, he looked like Sebastian – horribly like him – it gave me a strange feeling to see him lying there on the table. But apart from his face, everything else was wrong. This man had a glass eye, short hair and a false arm, and he was wearing a strange uniform, unlike anything I'd ever seen before. They showed me an identity disc that they found round his neck ... ' Julian hesitated; he fingered his limp hair nervously. 'It said that his name was Captain Sebastian Virgil Dorrell,' he said quietly. 'It was so weird, as if Sebastian had had an identical twin brother – but I couldn't believe that was really the explanation.'

'It's like Johnny ... like a different version of the same person. Steve told me that it's because of these ... Strata,' whispered Karen in awe. 'But Steve's grandfather – what could've happened to him?'

'Well, we don't know,' said Julian. 'Perhaps he's still alive somewhere. Perhaps Sebastian is, too – that's what I hope. We've no evidence that either of them died in the fire.'

*

Later, as night came on and the Earl and Johnny Terrier had still not returned, Karen and Julian went into Heydn Hall to look for them.

The interior of the great house after the fire seemed like an alien world, a place quite unfamiliar. The pungent odour of soot and smoke filled the air. Karen was awed by the black empty vastness of the spectral rooms, now shrouded in the deepening shadows of encroaching night. They walked through the sodden debris of charred furnishings, broken wood and shattered glass.

Karen was too nervous to call out in the eerie blackness. But Julian shouted the names of Lord Stephen and Johnny, his voice echoing gloomily around the hollow rooms.

They climbed the marble staircase, and now they could hear the sounds of hammering booming out through the cavernous empty halls.

'It's Steve!' cried Karen in dismay. 'Oh, what's he doing now?' She began to run towards the noise, round the stone gallery that surrounded the stair-well, along the passage that turned off to the left, towards the part of the house that had been least damaged by the fire.

'Be careful, Miss Black!' called Julian, as he hurried after her. 'The floors may not be sound.'

He followed close after her into the State Bedroom, and there, a strange sight met their eyes, dimly illuminated by the gleam of two hurricane lamps that were set on the floor.

Amid the ruins of burned and sodden furnishings was the great solid oak frame of the seventeenth century German carved four poster bed where, in the past, visiting members of Royalty had once slept. Its charred hangings had been ripped away, and so it stood, stark and bare, blackened by age and soot. Its pillars that supported the frame of the canopy were fashioned in the likeness of strangely posturing corpulent cherubim, their arms uplifted, raising mighty horns above their shoulders, like heralds of the Apocalypse.

Lord Stephen was up on top of the bed, nailing long boards across to form a rough roof, while Johnny Terrier heaped up the broken remains of furniture on one side, binding chairs and tables together with lengths of rope.

Karen clutched her hands to her ears against the noise of the hammering. 'Steve!' she yelled. 'Steve! What're you doing? Bloody stop it and come down here!'

The Earl ceased his hammering, and grinned down at her out of the gloom. 'Ah, there you are, Karen!' he called. 'I wondered when you'd show up! While you've been sulking in the cottage, Terrier and I have been busy. No idling for us – we've got to work to put things straight around here.'

'Come down from there, Steve!' wailed Karen, staring up in alarm at the precarious make-shift structure upon which he was crouching. 'It's bleedin' dangerous!' she cried.

'Stop fussing!' said the Earl. 'Just like a woman, always making a bloody fuss about everything!'

'I think perhaps you should come down, all the same, sir,' Julian Crucefix suggested firmly. 'It's late – you must be tired.'

'There's work to be done!' Lord Stephen declared. 'I should've started sooner. No time to be lost!'

'I'm sure it can wait till the morning, sir,' Julian said, but he added in a whisper to Karen, 'Don't worry, Miss Black – we'll get a doctor to see him before then.'

Johnny Terrier had overheard, however, and he pranced around the bed, chortling derisively, 'Get a doctor to see him? Get a doctor to see him, eh?'

'What's that?' bellowed the Earl. 'I don't need a bloody doctor, if that's what you're thinking!' In his annoyance, he clambered down from the top of the bed to confront them. 'Good God, Crucefix,' he said, 'do I look as if I need a bloody doctor?' He flexed his muscles; he puffed out his bare chest. 'Fit as a fiddle I am!' he declared. 'There's nothing wrong around here that can't be put to rights with a bit of guts and muscle and tough action!'

'Tough action!' growled Johnny, waving his fists in an attempt to imitate the Earl's bold posturing.

'But what're you trying to do, Steve?' asked Karen, chewing her thumb apprehensively, as she looked at the fortified bed.

Lord Stephen gestured at the bed proudly. 'Shelter, Karen! Shelter! That's the first thing that a survivor needs. A few tarpaulins over the top, and there you have it – ideal! Next – ' He waved his arm airily towards the fireplace. 'Heat!' said the Earl. 'We've collected quite a bit of firewood, as you can see. Then we need some provisions. I'm hoping that there may be some tinned stuff down in the kitchens. Anyhow, we'll have to go foraging tomorrow – see what we can come up with.'

'But, Steve,' protested Karen in dismay, 'I don't know why you're doing all this.'

'Don't know why I'm doing it!' retorted Lord Stephen scornfully. 'Good God, woman – what's got into you?' He gave a brief laugh. 'A fine fix you'd be in if I wasn't around to sort things out! Don't you understand, Karen? It's a matter of survival! Survival!' He slammed his fist into the palm of his other hand. 'And let me tell you, I'm a survivor first and foremost! I'm not about to give up the fight now – I'm not ready to lie down and die! If we're to survive this, we've all got to pull together, and somehow we'll pull through.' He shook his fists. 'It's a matter of having the fighting instinct!'

'Bang, bang!' added Johnny, gleefully firing an imaginary pistol.

'Yeah, but there's nobody to fight,' protested Karen.

Lord Stephen gave her a withering look. He shook his head sadly. 'Just like a woman,' he said. 'You're living in a fantasy world, Karen. You've got to wake up and face facts – hard facts! Things are going to be a lot different from now on. Who knows what we're up against? Bands of armed marauders, for a start – we've got to defend ourselves against them. They'll be out to steal our food, you know.'

'No they won't,' said Karen, 'since they can go down the supermarket and get their own bleedin' food.'

The Earl nodded gravely. 'Yes, and that's another point. We'll have to do some raiding ourselves – get some more supplies in before they all run out.'

Karen turned to Julian in dismay.

'I'm afraid you misunderstand the situation, sir,' said Julian respectfully. 'It's only Heydn Hall that's been destroyed – not the whole world.'

'I've made up the beds in the gardener's cottage,' Karen explained. 'We can sleep there.'

Then the Earl's mood changed abruptly, and he moved away from them and began to prowl around the room, between the charred furniture, in the deepening gloom, and desperately he rubbed his head with his hands, while now and again, a low moan escaped from him; and all the time, Johnny Terrier followed close behind him, grotesquely mimicking his every move.

'Come on, Steve,' implored Karen.

Lord Stephen halted beside the bed. 'This is my little hut, you see,' he said weakly. 'I made it myself. I don't ask for much, do I now? Only this, and young Terrier here to keep me company.' Affectionately he put his arm around Johnny's shoulders. 'He'll never desert me, will you, boy?'

Johnny shook his head obligingly.

'That's all I ask,' moaned the Earl. 'Just a tarpaulin over my head and young Terrier to keep me company. I don't want to be a trouble to anyone – only I would ... I would ... ' His voice broke to a quavering whisper. 'I would like you to come here and see me sometimes, if you think you can spare the time.'

CHAPTER 27

Back in the Twilight Home

It was a grey rainy day in autumn, and Electra Vanderpump was working in her laboratory at the Twilight Home. With a sigh of exasperation, she looked up from the console at which she had been working, and pushed her long black hair away from her face.

In the middle of the room, on the other side of the banks of electronic equipment and attached to it by a series of wires, was Sebastian Dorrell's curious carved Chair, squatting there like some malevolent beast, its evil face leering. Even under the glare of the fluorescent lighting, its grotesque misshapen form appeared insubstantial: it seemed to exude a miasma of obscene malignancy that filled the whole room.

Electra turned away from it in disgust. This was ridiculous, she told herself: she was beginning to imagine things. But even so, she was forced to admit that after nearly a month of constant work upon it, the mysterious secret of the Chair still eluded her.

She walked over to the window and stared down into the forecourt and the lawn at the front of the building. It was raining, and dark puddles in the gravel reflected the grey sky. For a moment, Electra gazed out distractedly, hardly seeing the dismal scene below. Then, suddenly, a car that was parked there caught her eye: it was a green sports car. Electra started: her heart pounded. She stepped back from the window in consternation.

But, of course, she said to herself, it could not be Sebastian's car, for Sebastian was dead, and whatever had become of his car, it was hardly likely to turn up here at the Twilight Home. Electra stepped over to the Chair and laid her hand on its back, gripping the dark wood fiercely with her thin pale fingers. The Chair was hers now: he would never return to take it from her.

At that moment, there was a knock at the door. Electra almost jumped, but she composed herself at once. Primly she smoothed down her white laboratory coat over her black skirt. 'Come in!' she called.

The door opened, and Helen, the blonde nurse, appeared. She was wearing a surgical mask, her hands protected by heavy duty rubber gloves. 'Someone to see you, Dr Vanderpump,' she said nervously, as she stepped aside to allow the tall visitor to enter.

Electra froze, her face grew ashen pale, her scarlet lip curled in trembling rage and indignation. Despite the fact that, like Helen, the man was wearing a surgical mask, Electra recognised him the instant that her cold gaze fell upon him. He was wearing a gold lurex jacket, a pink shirt and black satin trousers, and his dark hair was pinned in a chic French pleat adorned at the sides with diamante combs that matched the long pendant ear-ring that hung from his left ear-lobe.

'Ah – hello, old sport,' said Sebastian Dorrell. 'Having fun?'

Electra walked over and stood before him, staring at him in silent passion. Suddenly she reached up and fiercely tugged the mask from his smirking face. 'You're supposed to be dead!' she said. 'You were killed in the fire. How could you restore yourself after that, when I have your Chair, the secret of your power?'

'Ah, yes, my Chair,' said Sebastian, as his eye came to rest upon it. 'You've certainly wasted no time in – ah ... getting your meddling hands on it, have you?'

Electra glanced at the nurse, who was still lingering by the door.

'That will be all, Helen,' she told her sharply. 'Please leave us.'

Helen left the room, closing the door behind her.

'Now,' said Electra bitterly, turning back to Sebastian. 'Explain yourself!'

'I think it's for you to do the explaining,' said Sebastian. 'Good grief! Telling my friend Richard that I was dead – worming your way into his confidence, just so that you could steal my Chair, not to mention breaking the lock on the bedroom door so that you could get at it!'

'Oh, for heaven's sake!' cried Electra. She took out her cigarette holder and her lighter; she lit a cigarette. 'Mr Mojave would have heard of it sooner or later,' she protested. 'Everyone thought that you were dead. What on earth should we think? You've been gone for weeks.'

'Well, that confounded contraption wasn't exactly reliable,' said Sebastian. 'It was as much as I could do to materialise the damn thing at all.'

Electra glanced at him inquiringly. 'Contraption?' she said sharply. 'Do you mean the Time Machine?'

'Of course,' replied Sebastian. 'How else would I get back? It was – ah ... it was touch and go, I can tell you.' He grinned. 'But here I am, as you see! I must confess, old sport, I'm disappointed. I expected you to be a bit more enthusiastic than this. I thought – ah ... thought I'd come back a hero, you know – instead of which, you don't even seem pleased to see me! I mean, it makes a chap feel pretty unwanted, what?'

Electra tossed her head; she laughed contemptuously. 'You can scarcely call yourself a hero! For heaven's sake, Sebastian – Heydn Hall has been destroyed, and Lord Stephen's had a breakdown! You haven't exactly saved the day, have you? And what's become of my Time Machine, I'd like to know?'

Sebastian sighed. 'This is really – ah ... really most disappointing,' he said. 'Even Lady Caroline was more excited to see me than this – and she didn't even know me!'

'What on earth has Lady Caroline got to do with it?' cried Electra impatiently.

Sebastian sat down on his Chair and crossed his legs slowly; he tugged thoughtfully at his left ear-lobe. He said, 'Well, it was after – ah ... after Lord Steve jumped off ... He'd tried to materialise inside – ah ... inside the Tower, you see, which was dangerous, of course. Admittedly it was an error on his part, but he was just in a sheer funk, and he jumped off before I could stop him. I thought he was probably done for, and I certainly wasn't going to risk it myself. So there I was on the Machine alone, and I finally got the control lever to move, and I reset the co-ordinates, but by then, the time-field was disintegrating around me and I didn't think I was going to make it. The Time Bubble had vanished, and old Lord Mountjoy was nowhere to be seen, but there was a damn great fracture in the Machine's time-field where we'd – ah ... we'd tried to make the connections. All I could do was attempt to rematerialise somehow, and I didn't have much choice about where or how or when I managed it. The next thing I knew, there was – ah ... there was this woman – she just appeared from nowhere. Well, she seemed to fly right through the damaged time-field – I don't know where she came from.'

'And it was Lady Caroline Giles?' asked Electra incredulously. 'But, good heavens, we thought we'd never see her again!'

'She was absolutely – ah ... absolutely convinced that I'd intentionally saved her.' Sebastian smirked. 'Of course, I didn't like to disillusion her on that point! I must say, she was certainly ready enough to show her appreciation for all my efforts, unlike – ah ... unlike some people I could mention. Good grief, I could hardly get her to take her hands off me – she was perfectly infatuated!'

'Don't flatter yourself,' retorted Electra haughtily, flicking ash from her cigarette. 'She's besotted with the male sex in general – it's positively pathological. But you still haven't told me what became of the Time Machine. Don't think you're going to get away with it, dear,' she scolded. 'That Machine's mine, and I'm having it!'

'Oh, you're welcome to it, old fruit – no problem,' said Sebastian. He grinned. 'It's a write-off, of course!' he added smugly.

Electra scowled. 'And now, I suppose,' she said, 'you think you're going to walk out of here with your Chair as well, and leave me with nothing!'

'Hit the nail right on the head there, old fruit!' said Sebastian. 'But to make that a tiny bit more bearable, let me assure you, this Chair wouldn't be any damn good for you, anyway. Only I can use it.'

'We had our agreement, of course,' said Electra coldly, 'or have you conveniently forgotten that? You said that you would rebuild the Time Machine if it was damaged. It sounds as if you've got your work cut out.'

Sebastian frowned. 'I think – ah … think I said that I might be able to, not that I definitely would – a slight difference.'

'You meant that you would,' Electra persisted. She pointed her cigarette at him sternly. 'And I'm going to hold you to that.'

Sebastian passed his hand over his eyes; he said wearily, 'Good Lord, I should've stayed lost in the Interstratum! I wouldn't have come back, if I'd known what was in store.'

'Have you seen Lord Stephen?' Electra inquired.

'Yes,' said Sebastian. 'Poor chap – he's in a bad way.'

'I was going to go down there myself,' remarked Electra, 'but I'm afraid I've been so busy that I simply haven't got around to it.' She drew out a business card from her pocket and handed it to Sebastian. 'If you see him again,' she said, 'here's a good psychoanalyst in Harley Street that I can recommend.'

Sebastian read the name printed on the card. He grimaced. 'Kotlowski? A private practice in Harley Street? Good grief!'

Electra smiled. 'I helped him to set himself up,' she explained.

'Oh yes?' Sebastian grinned knowingly. 'And what do you get out of it?'

'Fifty per cent,' said Electra. 'It's a nice little earner on the side – more profitable than if he were still working here full time. I had to get him out of the way somehow – the wretched man was getting on my nerves.'

Sebastian nodded; he smiled wryly. 'And you're seriously suggesting that Lord Steve should go to him for therapy? The fellow's as mad as a hatter himself! Johnny Terrier would make as good a psychoanalyst as Kotlowski.'

'Not quite,' observed Electra. 'There's one small but important advantage Kotlowski has over Terrier.'

'What's that?' asked Sebastian. 'Wealth? Social privilege? Friends in – ah ... friends in high places?'

'Well, of course, he has all that too,' Electra agreed. 'But no, I was referring to his Polish accent. Clients simply love a foreign accent in a psychoanalyst! More than anything else, I think, it convinces them that one is properly qualified. It's practically de rigueur!'

'Oh, I'm sure,' said Sebastian.

Electra smiled. She extinguished her cigarette in an ashtray and walked over to him, laying her hand on his shoulder. She laughed. 'I sense your disapproval. Your moral scruples! How funny you are, you infuriating, fascinating man! I don't know whether I love you or hate you, but I don't think I could live without you.' Then she fell serious, and looked at him earnestly. 'You know that I care about you, Sebastian, don't you?' she said. 'You know that, really – of course you do!' She stroked his neck with her cool finger.

'Only for what you can get out of me,' said Sebastian quietly.

Electra drew back from him. 'Is that what you think?' she said bitterly.

'That's what I think,' said Sebastian.

Furiously, Electra lit another cigarette, while Sebastian, seated in the Chair, his legs crossed nonchalantly, his arms resting on its carved arms, eyed her darkly.

'You're wrong,' snapped Electra. She walked away from him, towards the window, and stared outside at the falling rain; she wiped the window pane with her hand. 'If I ever really cared about anyone, Sebastian,' she said, 'it was you. A relationship can be more than sentimental feelings, and what people call love can take many forms. How many say that they're in love, when their attraction to one another is merely sexual, or financial, or based on a craving for power? I've seen it all in my clients over the years, when they come to me weeping and disillusioned after the breakdown of their wretched, petty little marriages, and increasingly it fills me with cynicism. Far better to admit to the truth and say that I care enough about you to want to have you as a friend and as a lover – but sentimental love of the sort that people seem to expect nowadays is not something that I can ever offer. That's the truth, Sebastian dear, so take it or leave it.'

He did not reply.

'Sebastian?' asked Electra sharply. She turned in surprise from the window, to find herself alone in the room. Disconnected wires trailed from her equipment across the grey tiled floor, where the Chair had stood only a moment before; but now, silently, mysteriously, exasperatingly, it had gone – and Sebastian Dorrell, that infuriating, fascinating man, had vanished along with it.

APPENDIX

Map and Plans

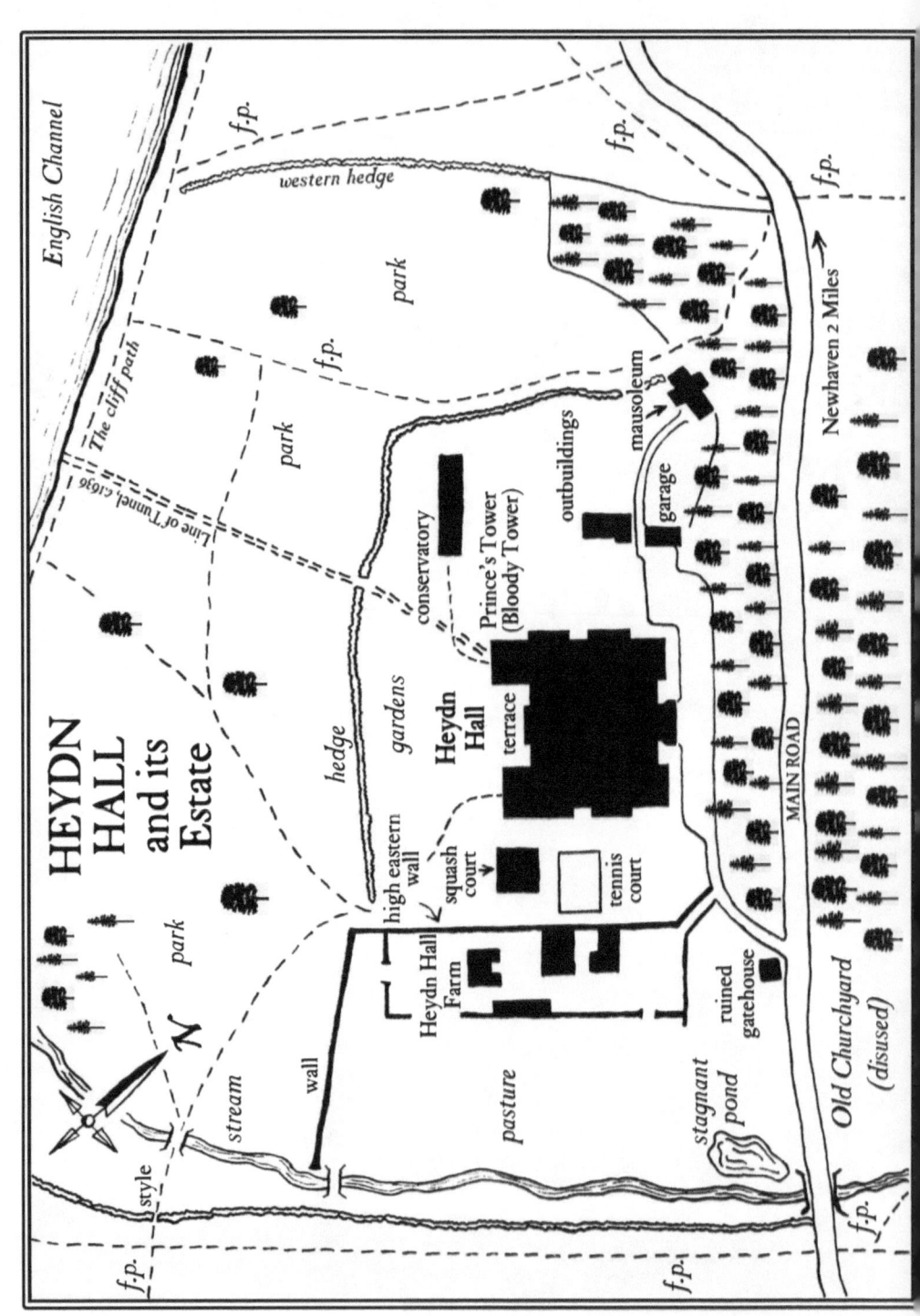

HEYDN HALL and its Estate

English Channel

f.p.

western hedge

park

park

The cliff path

Line of Tunnel, c1636

f.p.

Newhaven 2 Miles

f.p.

mausoleum

outbuildings

garage

conservatory

Prince's Tower (Bloody Tower)

hedge

gardens

Heydn Hall

terrace

high eastern wall

squash court

tennis court

Heydn Hall Farm

pasture

wall

ruined gatehouse

MAIN ROAD

Old Churchyard (disused)

stagnant pond

stream

style

park

N

f.p.

f.p.

f.p.

PLAN OF HEYDN HALL
GROUND FLOOR

KEY

LAR. Larder
KIT. Kitchen
S.C. Stairway to Cellar
SCUL. Scullery
SERV. Servants' Hall
T.R. Tapestry Room

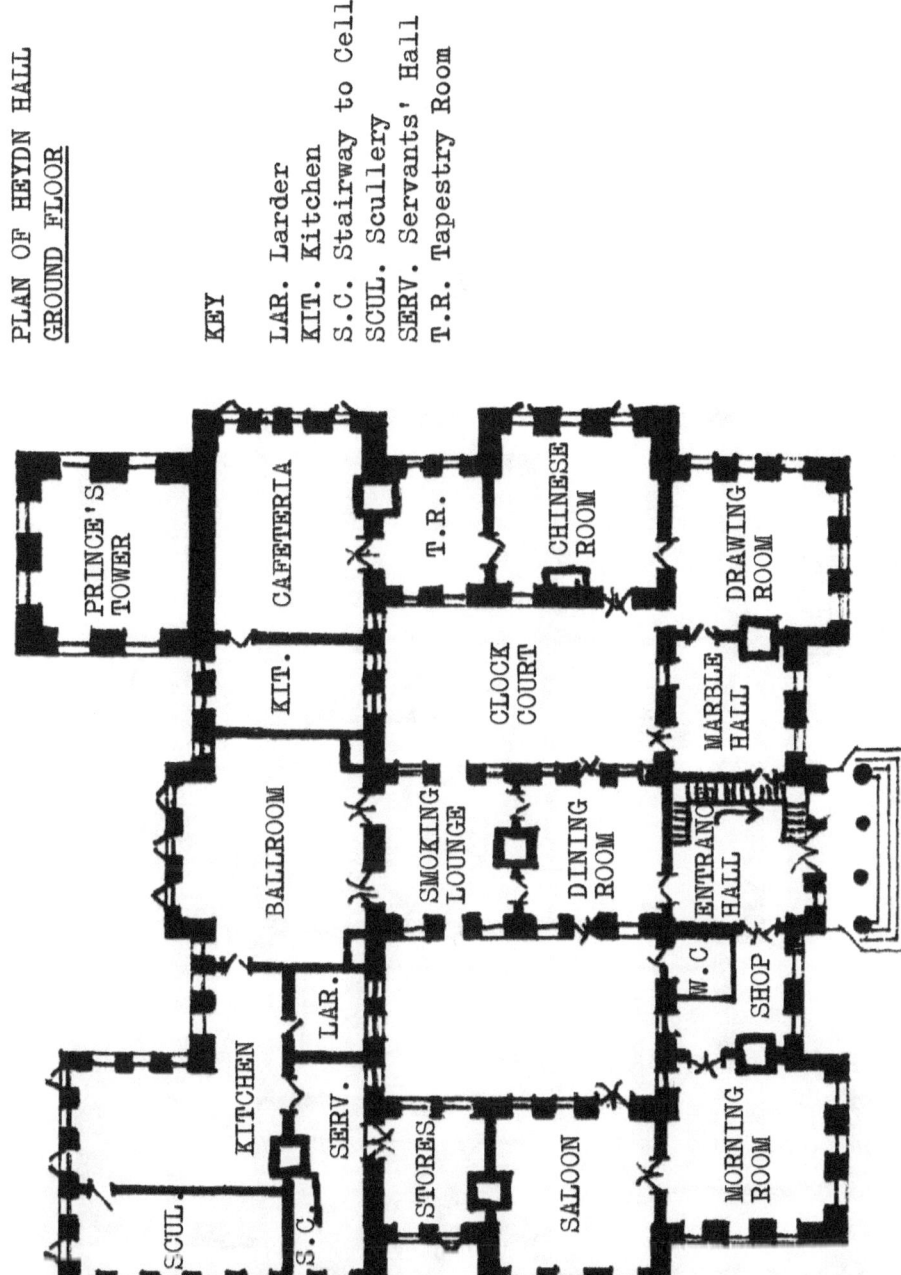

PLAN OF HEYDN HALL
FIRST FLOOR

KEY

18 18th Earl's Bedroom
B.R. Bedroom
CH. Chapel
D.R. Dressing Room
GAL. Gallery overlooking court
    below
L.BED Long Bedroom

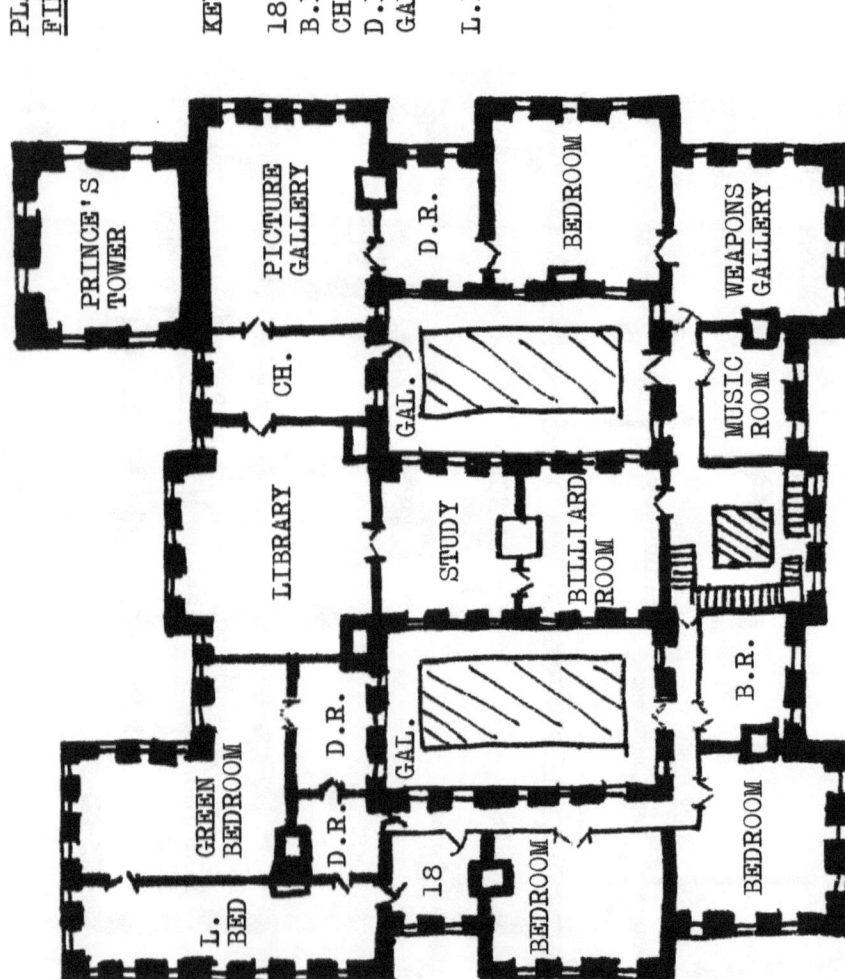

PRINCE'S TOWER

PICTURE GALLERY

D.R.

BEDROOM

WEAPONS GALLERY

CH.

GAL.

MUSIC ROOM

LIBRARY

STUDY

BILLIARD ROOM

L. BED

GREEN BEDROOM

D.R.

D.R.

GAL.

18

BEDROOM

B.R.

BEDROOM

PLAN OF HEYDN HALL
SECOND FLOOR

KEY

Ba Bathroom
B.R. Bedroom
D.R. Dressing Room
EARL'S SEC. Earl's
      Secretary's Room
OC Office Cupboard
OFF. Office
ST. Storeroom for Bar
W W.C.
W. Wardrobe

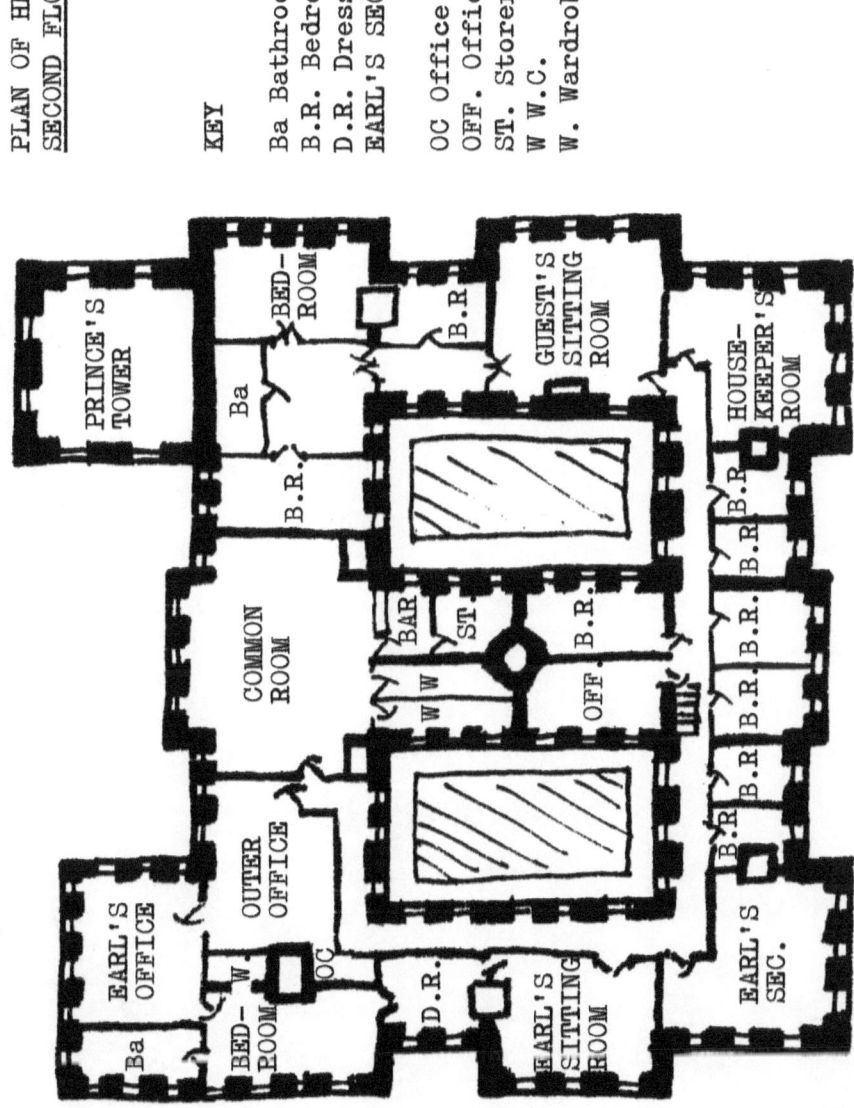

PRINCE'S TOWER

BED-ROOM

Ba

B.R.

B.R.

COMMON ROOM

BAR

W W

ST.

B.R.

GUEST'S SITTING ROOM

OFF. B.R.

HOUSE-KEEPER'S ROOM

B.R. B.R. B.R. B.R.

B.R.

EARL'S OFFICE

Ba

OUTER OFFICE

BED-ROOM

W

OC

D.R.

EARL'S SITTING ROOM

EARL'S SEC.